THE
ICE KING

TWILIGHT OF THE CELTS

BOOK III

M.K. HUME

THE ICE KING

TWILIGHT OF THE CELTS

BOOK III

headline
review

First published in 2015 by HEADLINE REVIEW
An imprint of HEADLINE PUBLISHING GROUP

1

Cataloguing in Publication Data is available from the British Library

Hardback ISBN 978 1 4722 1574 1
Trade paperback ISBN 978 1 4722 1575 8

Typeset in Golden Cockerel by Avon DataSet Ltd, Bidford-on-Avon, Warwickshire

Printed and bound in Great Britain by Clays Ltd, St Ives plc

Headline's policy is to use papers that are natural, renewable and recyclable
products and made from wood grown in well-managed forests and other controlled
sources. The logging and manufacturing processes are expected to conform
to the environmental regulations of the country of origin.

HEADLINE PUBLISHING GROUP
An Hachette UK Company
338 Euston Road
London NW1 3BH

www.headline.co.uk
www.hachette.co.uk

This book is dedicated to my friend and fellow book-lover, Peter Campbell, OAM.

Many years ago, I moved into a semi-rural community on the outskirts of Brisbane in Australia. My husband had purchased land from a local real estate agent who was representing the owners of land development in the area.

Later, I was to discover that Peter Campbell was a member of a long-established family who had settled in our area when most of it was still little more than wilderness. His family is proud of their district and they have been notable for their civic contributions to the inhabitants of Albany Creek. Over the years, I have had the pleasure of seeing Peter at first hand as he grew from being a very competent young businessman into the patriarch of his family. I have been amazed at the variety of his interests and his devotion to those who live around him. As an active member of a number of service organisations, his contribution towards the everyday loves of our villagers is of great value to all of us.

As a knowledgeable and critical reader of good literature, he has often put a smile on my face when he has spoken of my novels. His promotion of my work over the past six years has touched me and given me hope, for it is good for the soul when admirable people give sincere support, not just for the sake of friendship, but because they believe in you more than you believe in yourself. A dedication is all I can give in return, other than to offer my sincere gratitude and admiration.

I thank you, Peter, for all you have done for so many people.

M. K. Hume

2015

ACKNOWLEDGEMENTS

A novel requires a group effort in order to reach the booksellers and, ultimately, the public. The editor and publisher are vital to this process, so I am very grateful for the support and encouragement of Clare Foss at Headline, who never fails to put together a quality product. She asks and, because of her publishing expertise, I do my very best to give.

Similarly, the copy editor who delves into the sometimes turgid depths of my work to turn it into a seamless and attractive publication is of particular importance to me. My thanks go to Alice Wood, and my admiration is genuine and unalloyed.

The artists, designers and cartographers who create the book covers and the look and feel of my novels are also vital. Deftly, they take my maps and charts and drawings, and turn them into a common-sense presentation that encourages the reader to buy my books. My thanks go to Larry Rostant, Siobhan Hooper and Tim Peters. Finally, there are the publicists, the assistants and the many clever folk who keep the wheels greased. My thanks go to Katie Bradburn and Beth Eynon, whose input into my novels is appreciated and will always be invaluable to any success I might achieve.

In my quiet study, far from London and the centre of the action,

I frequently feel divorced from the production of my books. And so, my thanks go to every worker at Headline who turns this writer's dreams into reality – a book that can be held in one's hands.

Equally far away, my agent, Dorie Simmonds, bears with my long silences and eccentricities with equanimity. She is a gem, a clever and talented gem with a generous heart.

On the home front, Michael, my husband and slave-driver, is my rock. I cannot thank him enough. And my sons, Damian and Brendan, gift me with hope in an uncertain world. Brendan never permits me the luxury of doubt, so I am lifted by his enthusiasm. Thank you both.

Another big thank you must go to my little terrier, Rusty, who constantly warms my heart.

A small number of good friends are also vital, because they provide those most valuable of gifts, those of love and belief. You know who you are, so my thanks go to each of you.

Finally, my thanks go to my mother who taught me the old tales and gave me an insight into the minds and ways of the Danish people. While she has long gone into the shades, I know she still watches over me.

We live in ugly times, perhaps, but all eras have their horrors. I prefer to think that great and small people will always rise out of adversity to advance the cause of humanity.

Thank you to all people of goodwill who make life richer for having passed through it.

M. K. Hume
2015

DRAMATIS PERSONAE

Aednetta Fridasdottar	The Witch-Woman. She is the paramour of King Hrolf Kraki.
Alfridda	The sister of Stormbringer. She lives at The Holding with her husband, Raudi.
Arthur	The illegitimate son of King Artor and Lady Elayne. The foster son of Bedwyr, Master of Arden Forest. After his capture by a Dene raiding party, he is taken to the Dene kingdom as a slave.
Artor	High King of the Britons. The son of Uther Pendragon and Ygerne (the widow of King Gorlois of Cornwall).
Atric Poulssen	A landowner who is a neighbour of Stormbringer.
Barr	The young son of Master Bedwyr and Lady Elayne.
Bedwyr	Known as the Arden Knife, Bedwyr is the Master of Arden Forest.
Beowulf	Epic poem of a Geat warrior who helps King Hrogar, King of the Danes, against Grendel, a monster.
Beowulf Minor	Grandson of Beowulf. Captured by Arthur at the Battle of Rugen Island.
Bjornsen, Valdar	(see Stormbringer).
Blaise	The youngest daughter of King Bors Minor

of the Dumnonii Tribe. Captured by Dene raiders, she is taken to the Dene kingdom as a slave.

Bors Minor	King of Cornwall. Father of Eamonn and Blaise.
Bran	King of the Ordovice Tribe.
Breoca	Father of General Mearchealf, who is the commander of the Hundings army.
Diarmaid	One of Arthur's captains.
Eamonn pen Bors	Son of King Bors Minor and Queen Valda of Cornwall. Arthur's friend. He is killed at the Battle of Wener River.
Ector	The king of the Ordovice. He is the son of King Bran.
Elayne	Wife of Bedwyr, Master of Arden. Mother of Arthur.
Elidar	One of Thorketil's bowmen. He suffers from a lung disease.
Eomar (Father)	The abbot of a religious community near Calmar.
Ernil (Master)	The captain of a trading ship serving the Dene islands.
Erikk Halversen	Son of Halver, Jarl of Halland.
Frodhi	The influential cousin of King Hrolf Kraki in Heorot and Stormbringer. He becomes king after the death of Hrolf Kraki.
Gareth Minor	Son of Gareth Major. Raised at Aquae Sulis. He travels through Europe with Lorcan and Germanus in search of his master, Arthur.
Germanus	A Frankish mercenary who acts as Arthur's

	weapons master. He travels through Europe with Gareth and Lorcan in search of Arthur.
Harald Leifsen	A Dene warrior who accompanies Arthur on a patrol that searches for the Roman fortifications at Segedunum.
Heardred	King of the Geats.
Henning Gunnarsen	A young Dene courier.
Heoden	A warrior in Hrolf Kraki's service. He acts as an envoy in discussions with Stormbringer and Arthur.
Hrolf Kraki	Also called Storm Crow. He is the King of the Dene.
Ida	The name given to (and adopted by) Arthur on entry to the northeast of England after leaving the Dene lands with a large contingent of warriors and settlers seeking a new homeland.
Ingmar	Baby son of Ingrid. Brother of Sigrid.
Ingrid	Widow of the Geat camp commander at Lake Wener. She is the mother of Sigrid and Ingmar. Slave of Arthur.
Ivar (Hnaefssen)	A Dene jarl whose lands lie close to the borders with Jutland.
Ivar (Svenson)	A Geat fisherman from Calmar who acts as a guide for Arthur.
Karl (The Owl)	A young warrior who serves at the court of King Hrolf Kraki.
Knud Thorvaldsen	A Dene volunteer who accompanies Arthur on a patrol that searches for the Roman fortifications at Segedunum.
Knut Hard-hand	A smith in King Hrolf Kraki's service.

Lars	One of Arthur's captains.
Llyr Marini Gul	One of the sons of Meirchion Gul, King of Rheged.
Loki	The trickster god.
Lorcan ap Lugald	A Hibernian priest who acts as Arthur's tutor.
Maeve	Sister of Arthur. She marries Stormbringer and bears his children.
Mearchealf	The son of Breoca. A Hunding general who is captured by Arthur's forces.
Meirchion Gul	Celtic King of Rheged.
Mithras	The Roman God of Soldiers.
Myrddion Merlinus	Also known as Myrddion Emrys, he is named after the Sun.
Olaus Healfdene	Commander of the Geat army at Lake Wener.
Ragnar Sigurdson	A warrior who accompanies a Dene patrol under Arthur's command in search of the Roman fortifications at Segedunum.
Roganvaldr	One of Arthur's captains.
Rufus Olaffsen	Hrolf Kraki's champion who fought Eamonn.
Sea-dragon	An under-sea dragon who visits Arthur in dreams.
Sigrid	Daughter of Ingrid. Captured at Lake Wener, she is Prince Arthur's slave. She eventually marries Arthur.
Snorri Nilsson	The helmsman on *Sea Wife*, Arthur's ship. He becomes Arthur's second in command.
Stormbringer	His full name is Valdar Bjornsen. The Sae Dene king, second highest member of the

	Dene King. A member of the Danish (Dene) aristocracy.
Sven	A fisherman who acts as a courier for Aednetta Fridasdottar in Heorot.
Sven pen Bedwyr	The Forest Child. The son of Stormbringer and Maeve. Grandson of Bedwyr.
Talorc	One of Arthur's captains.
Thorketil	The Hammer of Thor. He was Hrolf Kraki's champion who fought Arthur. He also answers to the Troll King.
Thorquil	One of Arthur's captains.

STORMBRINGER'S WORLD

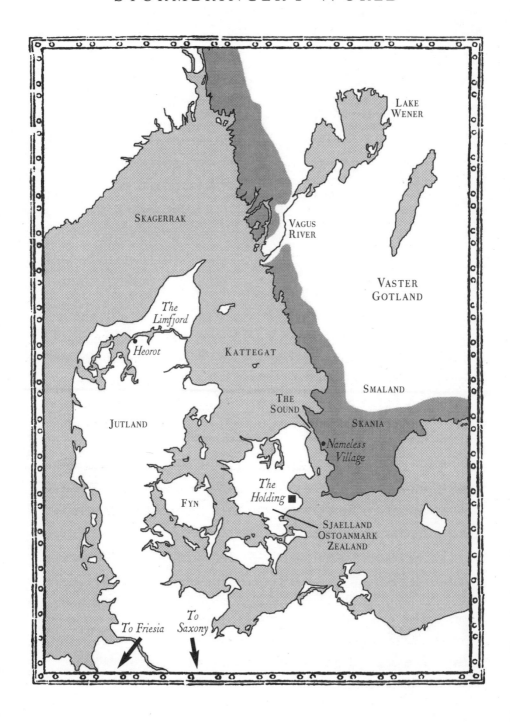

LAKE
WENER

SKAGERRAK

VAGUS
RIVER

VASTER
GOTLAND

The
Limfjord

•Heorot

KATTEGAT

SMALAND

THE
SOUND

SKANIA

JUTLAND

•Nameless
Village

The
Holding ■

FYN

SJAELLAND
OSTOANMARK
ZEALAND

To Friesia

To
Saxony

PROLOGUE

'Let us speak honestly, kinsman. Just you and I!'

The water boiled as the she-dragon giggled in a flirtatious manner. Arthur tried not to shudder because, while she was a figment of his own vivid imagination, she had come to him so often that he frequently thought of her as real. She pursed her carnelian lips, while her forked tongue flickered in and out across the pearly lustre of her teeth and then touched and explored his face.

'Your skin is rough, man-child. I imagined it would have the slick smoothness of your skull-bones. How very disappointing!'

'I'm sorry if I don't reach your high expectations, Majesty! I haven't removed my beard.'

Somehow, suspended over her maw by the familiar thick black weed, he was suddenly oblivious to the terror that had afflicted him in the past. Over the last year and a half, he had often dreamed of the she-dragon as she reclined on her ossuary, and every meeting was a different attack on his emotions. What had once seemed grotesque had now become commonplace within the landscape of his regular night horrors.

Coral-red flushed around her throat as she considered something that seemed to be annoying her. Arthur had learned from their first meeting that she detested anyone and anything that came between his contemplation of her and her terrible beauty.

When she finally spoke, her voice had the petulant whine of a jealous wife.

'Who is the ice-haired bitch who hates you so much? Does she yearn for your hard man-flesh in ways that I will not? She is poison, you know, and she'll sting you with her fangs if you turn your back on her. Or you'll bed her and then the gods will enjoy what you both make of the world.'

'Make up your mind, Queen of the Sea. How can she yearn for me, yet wish me dead?' He bent forward in the inexplicable way of dreams, so that the weed released his hands.

His fingers stirred the muddy ocean bottom, and then dragged up a handful of it. The she-dragon hissed and her breath sent a shiver of hot water towards him, even as the detritus of the sea leached through his fingers.

'This is what these imaginings are worth, my very own dream horror. You'll never add a single bone from my body to your chapel of dead men.'

Arthur laughed then, even though a part of him quailed at the thought of wilfully testing the she-dragon's temper. She might be woven of insubstantial dreams, but he knew that her fires had the power to hurt his sleeping self. It was as if they were oddly matched lovers involved in a complex, depraved game of unnatural lusts. He tried to hide from her unblinking, gem-hard eyes.

Those same eyes narrowed.

'You are growing brave, little dragonlet. Especially when I

consider that you're in my kingdom and the uncertainty of my temper is taken into account.' She belched out gouts of flame that directed a steam shower over his right thigh.

Arthur screamed with a sudden flash of agony, even though his internal voice recited a continuing mantra: 'It's not real! It's not real!'

'Are you quite sure?' the she-dragon hissed, while Arthur shrieked again as her heated breath played over the scald. How any of these monstrous imaginings could make his flesh swell and burn seemed impossible yet, in this fantastic world, it was so.

'We'll not see each other often. But you'll never be free of me, man-child.'

The she-dragon changed tack and traced the golden hair on his chest with a claw. The erotic caress made Arthur's flesh crawl.

'Nor will you return to Mithras in his temple on the hill. Did you think that chapel was real? Did you believe the little priest who lives on sunshine rather than food or drink? You were wide awake in Mirk Wood.'

Arthur shivered. He remembered the chapel in the dolmen, buried in the ancient forest of Mirk Wood. After the Battle of Lake Wener, Arthur had been lost in guilt at the death of Eamonn, his friend. Mirk Wood had taken the chapel into itself, melting it like summer hail, and no one had been able to find that strange place since.

'I believe in nothing that soothsayers of any kind tell me. I certainly don't believe your promises!'

'Liar!' she hissed. 'I'm the only one who really wants you, Arthur. Unfortunately, it's a fine line between madness and the messages that come to us from the gods. Do you want to tip too far and become a gibbering idiot?'

The beautiful she-dragon sighed luxuriantly, but with regret.

'No! You don't desire that fate, my beloved dragonlet. You're well named, Ruin of Kings, because you'll go on and on, with your sister or without, and with your slaves or without. You are fated to become the King of Winter. You will remember me, dragonlet, when you sit in your halls and look out over your broad acres. I am the only creature who truly *loves* you . . . and who truly *knows* you.'

'You do? I live for the day when I can sleep without your intervention.'

She stirred petulantly and her movement sent an ancient skull rolling away from her complex couch of bones. The jaw had been attached to the cheekbones with fine gold wires so that the teeth chattered obscenely as it sank into the ooze. She scarcely noticed as her tail twisted and twitched irritably. The fitful light from far above lit her scales with a soft glow that belied her rising temper.

'You'll be off to war soon enough, dear heart. The Dragon's Brood are spread through your world and their cries affront the ears of the most heartless of men. I wonder that you don't hear them when they weep in the night because of you.'

'But—'

'Be silent, dragonlet! You cannot believe that you can save anyone or anything, simply by issuing orders. Change must be paid for, with blood, heart and spirit. You're not a Dene! And you're no jarl! Nor are you anything of importance to anyone, except to me and the Geat bitch who loathes and loves you in equal measure. But she is changing. Beware whom you trust, Arthur.'

The she-dragon brought her beautifully carved face within inches of his. She hadn't quite finished tormenting him.

'So many wars are yet to come, and you will fight in them, my heart. You will provide bones aplenty for my house when you take revenge for the ruined children. But, as you negotiate the tangled halls of kings, remember what I tell you.'

She paused.

'What is real, is not!

'What is love, can be hate!

'What is kingly, can be cruelty!

'And, finally, my beloved,

'What is loyalty, can be treason.'

Eyes glowing with urgency, she delivered her warning of incipient danger.

'When you can understand what I have said, then, and only then, will you find your way back to your home.'

Suddenly Arthur felt the weed set him free and the pressure of water in his lungs began to choke him. Then he awoke to find himself rubbing at his thigh where the flesh was shiny, red and swollen.

THE SEA BATTLE

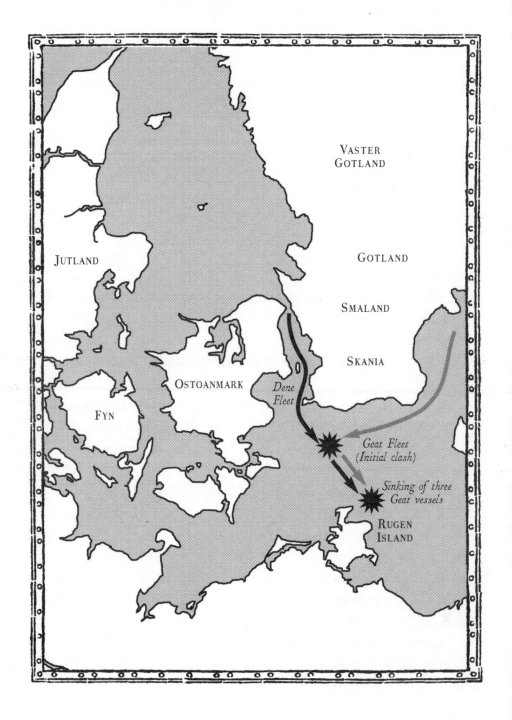

VASTER
GOTLAND

JUTLAND

GOTLAND

SMALAND

SKANIA

OSTOANMARK

Dene
Fleet

FYN

Geat Fleet
(Initial clash)

Sinking of three
Geat vessels

RUGEN
ISLAND

CHAPTER I

THE MASTER OF SKANIA

To be turned from one's course by men's opinions, by blame, and by misrepresentation, shows a man unfit to hold an office.

Quintus Fabius Maximus, Plutarch, *Parallel Lives*

The sea was boiling with struggling men and smashed timbers as Arthur directed his men to edge *Sea Wife* as close as possible to the heaving mass. Weighted down by thick armour and weapons, even the strongest had to struggle to keep their heads above water. A hundred men fought mindlessly to live, climbing over each other in a desperate battle to stave off the inevitable.

'Ship the oars, helmsman,' Arthur ordered Snorri. This Dene helmsman was vastly different from his predecessor, being a hard-bitten pragmatist who had won Arthur's respect during the pell-mell chase from the Vagus River to their present position just off Rugen Island. Stormbringer's fleet had pursued the Geat ships that had tried to ambush them off the southernmost tip of Skania, after Stormbringer had defeated Heardred's land forces in Halland and central Skania.

These land battles had been hard-won, with both sides sustaining serious losses, but the Denes had prevailed. Now the Dene fleet had increased to more than fifty ships of massed warriors, while the Dene populace provided more and more reinforcements that swelled the size of the expeditionary force. The Dene elders were aware that uprisings in the east opened the way for border attacks in the south so, given Hrolf Kraki's inaction, the more prudent of the jarls sent any warriors who could be spared to Stormbringer as a hedge against treason or bad luck.

Meanwhile, Heardred had made a serious tactical error by sending fire-ships in the hope of catching Stormbringer unawares. Unfortunately, they were discovered and destroyed.

It soon became obvious that the re-purposed trading vessels used by the Geats could never hope to compete with the fighting longboats used by the Dene. The Sae Dene ships were manned by seafarers, first and foremost, although their fleet now also included some slower transport vessels and smaller, faster boats used as couriers.

The outcome of the sea battles had never been in doubt.

Then, like coursing hounds pursuing a stampeding herd of bulls, the Dene fleet had swept down on the slower Geat vessels, with *Sea Wife* in the vanguard.

The three travellers rode into Lubeck, relieved to have finally reached the northern sea. Conscious that discretion and diplomacy were necessary for their continued health, the three tried to be unobtrusive but, as Lorcan explained to his friends, they were as obvious as a boil on the forehead.

'This place considers a good day's fishing to be a time when the herring run in gargantuan shoals. For these people, a flock of crows attacking a village cat in a time of drought is a matter of cataclysmic, heavenly intervention. And a babe who is born with an extra finger? Well, that's a message from Loki or the Devil, or the trolls have come to earth to claim one of their own. Such disasters would be far, far less noticeable to these people than three armed men who have come here from the south on a social visit.'

'Please, Lorcan! Can't you just hope for the best for once?'

The man who spoke was probably in his fifties, but showed none of the overt physical decay of his ripe years. He was still very tall and straight, and he wore a pair of ferocious whitish-blond moustaches that overhung his clean-shaven jaw. Only a distinct yellowing around the mouth revealed something of his age. However, his hands were well cared for and muscular, while his shaved head revealed he had spent many years in the sun and was comfortable with strong physical exercise. His vigour in the saddle resembled the energy of a far younger man.

'I'll gladly pray for the rest of the night if necessary, my friend, but no amount of prayer will change your appearance. You are obviously a Frank who is miles from your sodding home and your king. And this sprog,' the priest flipped an expressive hand towards a young man mounted on a superb stallion. 'This paragon of virtue is so fucking good-looking that every female under sixty tries to get him between her legs. Try being observant for once, Germanus. What would have happened at Molzen, in the marches of Thuringia, if I hadn't recognised those fucking Saxons at the inn? You were deeply in lust with that blond-haired pair of tits and wouldn't have recognised Arthur if he'd bitten you on the nose.'

'Shut your nagging, Lorcan! I'm thoroughly tired of how you go on and on and fucking on!'

'Will both of you be silent?' the quiet young man hissed. Around them, on a muddy road near the outskirts of the city walls, a number of plump citizens rode fat donkeys to market; phlegmatic ruddy-faced farmers walked beside wagons laden with baskets of fresh produce; and gape-mouthed women with muddy skirts pulled snotty-nosed children out of the reach of the stallion's hooves. The local population was entranced and frightened by these three men with their angry eyes and dangerous weapons.

Having gained their attention, the young man edged his stallion close to the two older men. Only several children sitting in the crown of a half-grown tree above them heard the hissed conversation that ensued.

'You old bastards have squabbled during the entire journey from Reims, Metz, Speyer, Fulda . . . now that was a prize shit-hole . . . and then through Molzen, Halle, Brandenburg and Schwerin. And now that we are close to our destination, you're still arguing. What has it achieved? As you kindly noted, Lorcan, your arguments came to the attention of a troop of Saxons near Molzen. They noticed us because, after a jug of the roughest red wine I've ever tasted, you took the opportunity to scream out at Germanus that Saxon dogs were watching us. As Germanus was occupied with Blondie Big Tits – my apologies to the lady – you saw fit to repeat your news, only now you suggested that our Saxon friends held strong feelings of lust for their sheep.

'Then, in Brandenburg, Germanus caught a cutpurse who was stealing his silver coin, so he decided to beat the man sense-less. Normally, this wouldn't be a problem, but this thief was the son of a local councillor and the lad's father usually reimbursed the young man's victims but, being ignorant of the arrangements, you decided to trounce the young fellow.

You'd still be in prison if I hadn't paid a gold coin to get you out.

'Then you, Lorcan, met another woman in Schwerin. Married, of course! And you seemed to forget that you're supposed to be a priest. Please! I'd like to reach the land of the Dene alive, especially since we're so damned close now. Can't you smell the sea around us?'

'Is that what that stink is? I suppose we should be grateful that we seem to have outrun the plague and we won't see its return until spring and summer.' Lorcan tried to deflect Gareth from the long list of sins committed by the two old reprobates. One dirty foot in an open sandal made nervous circles against the hide of his mule, so the beast shied fretfully.

Against all the odds, the trio had travelled safely into the north from the land of the Britons and had almost reached the northern seas in their quest to find Prince Arthur, the adopted son of Bedwyr, Master of Arden Forest, and the natural son of Artor, the High King of the Britons. The prince was their master and their friend, so it was inconceivable that they should be so close and yet fail to rescue him. For his part, Gareth had decided that nothing, not even these two old men whom he loved and respected, would be permitted to stop him from completing his self-imposed quest.

With their greater speed and flexibility, the Dene longboats had managed to cut off the erstwhile merchant ships filled with Geat warriors who were seeking sanctuary with the Saxons at Rugen Island.

Arthur knew very little about the niceties of long-distance navigation, but he was fast becoming expert in the killing of men. When the first of the Geat stragglers came within sight as it waddled through the slow swells, Arthur had demanded that the ship surrender to prevent unnecessary loss of life.

'Try to board us and see what you get, you fuckers,' a bearded man roared from the stern of his boat. Those on board who weren't fully occupied with pulling on the oars set up a chant that accused the Dene warriors, their mothers, and their unknown fathers of various unsavoury sexual practices.

Snorri flushed a dull, beetroot red before he snarled a retort back at the Geat crew. 'Our ship sails under the Last Dragon banner. Do you intend to surrender – or will you suffer the consequences? Our captain asks but once!'

Arthur felt the sting of salt water in his eyes from the freshening wind. The dragon sail above him snapped viciously as it filled.

'We don't care who you are, Last Dragon!' A loud voice drifted from the up-wind ship as it began a slow tack to starboard. 'Your captain's just a man – so he can kiss my hairy arse.'

This response was accompanied by further crudities and Snorri gripped the rudder with whitened knuckles. When he looked towards his captain, he shuddered. Arthur's eyes were wintry, but his face was bare of any expression. Snorri knew that the Last Dragon was at his most dangerous when he was quiet and cold.

'We will ram them when they go onto their next tack to port,' Arthur yelled to his crew so they could prepare themselves for the collision. 'We'll run the bastards down midships!'

A ragged cheer greeted Arthur's words, although many of the warriors felt their hearts flutter. Could they hole their own ship in such a risky manoeuvre?'

'Snorri?' Arthur chose not to look at his helmsman, confident in Snorri's seamanship and skill. 'Give the order for full speed at the very moment that the Geat ship commences her next tack. Make sure our bow strikes these bastards about a metre or so behind their midships.'

'Aye, Master Arthur,' Snorri responded and barked out his orders for the crew to lie on their oars. For a moment, *Sea Wife* sat almost still in the water.

Then, at a single command, the Dene warriors drove their oars into the sea and *Sea Wife* leaped forward like a hunting hound to strike the Geat transport midships. As he put his weight on the rudder to turn *Sea Wife* into a killing position, Snorri remembered the madness of Arthur when, as a newly appointed captain at the mouth of the Vagus River, he had ordered *Sea Wife* to be beached and her prow and the front section of the keel to be reinforced with plates of iron. Arthur had issued orders that a one-metre length of tree trunk studded with iron spikes should be attached to the bow of the ship just below the waterline to provide a ramming device that would penetrate the hull of any enemy ship. At the time, Snorri had thought the Briton was crazed. Longboats were built for speed rather than as fighting platforms. Now, however, he understood his master's intentions.

Sea Wife struck the Geat ship directly at the intended point and the ram penetrated the timbers. Normally, such a ramming on the port side would have caused *Sea Wife* to ride over the deck of the Geat ship. The Geat hull would tip to the left and fill with water, while throwing the crew into the sea. Instead, the iron spoke impaled the hull with a screech of wood and iron as it sprang planks and punched a large hole into the vessel below the waterline. *Sea Wife* turned a little and ripped a huge wound in the trading vessel's belly.

'Now! Reverse the oars and row on Snorri's command! Put your backs into it. Row, you bastards! Row!' Arthur roared.

The ram on *Sea Wife*'s bows was pulled out of its obscene embrace with the Geat ship and sea water began to flood into the vessel's lower deck. Terrified, the Geat crewmen began to scream. Unfortunately, many of them had no idea how to swim.

'I knew it!' Arthur whispered in a voice so soft that only Snorri heard. 'God bless Father Lorcan and his passion for the Greeks. I just knew that the Greek ram would eventually do its best work for us.'

Again and again, *Sea Wife* sped in pursuit of stragglers. In each case, the Geat ships were offered the opportunity to surrender, but the first three vessels were rammed and sunk, despite Arthur's offers of clemency. Then, when a trail of thrashing bodies lay in *Sea Wife*'s wake, the fleet of ten remaining ships finally surrendered to Stormbringer, who ordered their sailors to be bound while Dene skeleton crews were put in place to sail the ships back to Skania.

But Arthur felt his usual guilt after the heat of battle had cooled, so *Sea Wife* was ordered to return to pick up whatever survivors might still remain. The other Dene ships had offered no aid to the drowning Geats, for they were eager to claim their share of the captured ships as spoils.

As *Sea Wife* slowed to a full stop, the drowning men struggled towards the Dene vessel, ensuring that the crew was forced to repel their desperate attempts to board which were causing her to list alarmingly. The Dene sailors felt revulsion at having to strike crazed men who'd managed to survive for nearly an hour in very cold waters, but Arthur knew that the Geats could only be permitted to clamber aboard in a safe and orderly manner. The Geat warriors were now at the point of collapse at the very time when they thought they would be saved. Arthur, who had seen similar tragedies at the mouth of the

Vagus River, silently mourned the exhaustion that killed without mercy.

With one hand gripping a handful of greasy hair liberally smeared with bear-fat, Arthur attempted to keep one older warrior above the surface of the slapping waves. Eventually he seized the man's long forked beard, rousing him out of his torpor.

'Help me with this one, Snorri!' he called. 'His beard's full of grease and it's likely to tear out of my hand.'

The Geat warrior tried to thrash about with limp, weakening arms rendered almost useless by a bone-deep weariness, but for some reason Arthur determined that his she-dragon wouldn't take this warrior as one of her victims. She would have many fine new skulls and ribcages, so why should he allow her more? He had an odd feeling about this captive, as if he was somehow going to be important in the future.

Without any thought for the man's pain, Arthur and Snorri plucked him bodily over the rail of the ship. The warrior lay in the scuppers in a few inches of salty water retching up water and vomit.

The captain and helmsman returned to their rescue efforts. Once every living man had been dragged onto *Sea Wife*'s deck, the crew returned to their oars to retrace their course back to the site of the two other sunken vessels. The man atop the mast and the lookout on the ship's bow searched in vain for any trace of life among the slow swells arriving from the open ocean, but other than a few seagulls squabbling and fighting on the wind, the sea was bare.

'They've all gone, master,' Snorri remarked. 'The weight of their armour and exhaustion must have tipped the balance against them. If we'd passed up the survivors from the third ship to return to the first, we might have saved some from drowning, but who could have known what was likely to happen when we were fighting an engagement?'

Arthur knew that Snorri was correct. 'Aye, you're right enough, Snorri. It's Loki's luck for the Geat warriors, I'm afraid!' Arthur's lips twisted. 'In any dealings with the sea, rules of logic don't always apply. Some of the Geats were lucky, so the she-dragon spared them because she was busy with dozens of their brothers.'

Snorri, used to the strange poetic streak in his master, refrained from asking who the she-dragon was. As a good Christian, Snorri was scathing about the old superstitions, but he would have to be crazed to admonish Arthur in any way. He knew his master's mercurial temper, although Arthur had never displayed a cruel or capricious streak.

Snorri kept his eyes fixed on their projected course as the ship negotiated the swells. Arthur was aware that his crew mightn't be entitled to a share in the surrendered ships, but *Sea Wife* had been slowed by the extra weight of sixty men and the young man still hoped that Stormbringer would give the crew some trifling share of his plunder for the punishment that *Sea Wife* had meted out. The Sae Dene knew that the main reason for the surrender of the ten Geat ships was the use of *Sea Wife*'s deadly ram. Stormbringer would be grateful too for the minimal casualties suffered by the Dene.

Three days later, Stormbringer said as much when they made camp inside a sheltered bay on the tip of Skania, while the Dene force enjoyed the largesse provided by the local population. No sooner had the longboats been beached and the crew and captives unloaded than villagers had arrived at the makeshift camp, laden down with a whole deer, skinned and prepared for a roasting pit, a score or more of chickens, at least as many rabbits, a whole butchered oxen, and basket after basket of fresh fish laid out in bundles of sweet grass. This bounty was further embellished with late apples, berries, nuts and whole heads of cabbages stacked up like little pyramids of skulls. The crews crowed and sang with pleasure at the thought of the gorging to come.

'I don't think your idea will catch on, Arthur, because your ram definitely slows *Sea Wife* through the water and her response to the rudder isn't quite as flexible when the swells are heavy.' Stormbringer was devouring the succulent white flesh of a whole fish that had been cooked in a small iron cage lowered over an open fire. His mouth glistened slightly from the butter spread over the fish skin.

'True enough! But when we are next in home waters, I'll redesign the rams so they can be fitted quickly and easily as we need them. We saved many lives during these skirmishes off Rugen Island because of the ram. At least, that's what I tell myself when I think of the Geat sailors who went to the bottom of the sea with their vessels.'

Stormbringer saw no point in repeating himself about yet another decision that Arthur had made in the heat of the moment, so decided to change the subject.

'With Frodhi's assistance, the captives will be sold in Skania and, failing that, in Ribe.' Stormbringer grinned engagingly. 'Frod will get a big cut out of it as well, so he'll enjoy the challenge.'

'What of the Geat jarls? It'd be a bad precedent to sell them into slavery when they can be ransomed by their families for far more than they are worth in any meat market. Personally, I loathe slavery! I know that my people practise it, as well as the Dene and most of the civilised world, but it seems unpalatable to own another person. My foster-father had been enslaved by the Saxons when he was a young man. He was abused and sexually assaulted so frequently that he grew to be little more than a crazed animal. Hatred drove him insane when he eventually broke free and began to take his revenge. For the rest of his life, Bedwyr refused to own any man, woman or child, so he ensured that every servant in the fortress in Arden was paid for their labours, no matter how little, and given free lodgings for their service. The people of Arden would follow my Bedwyr into Hades if he asked it of them.'

'That's all very well, Arthur, but slavery is just another form of coinage in countries such as ours. I've very few slaves and they're mainly enemies taken in battle, often warriors whom I've been loath to kill. You've lived at The Holding. Do my workers seem unhappy to you?'

Arthur could see by his friend's expression that Stormbringer was troubled, perhaps because slavery repulsed him somewhat too. Arthur relented, because he owed much to the Sae Dene captain.

'You can't really consider your workers at The Holding as slaves, Stormbringer, because you treat them as valued servants who are permitted to marry and have children, offspring who are born free. Even the son of a slave can rise to great heights in your society, as long as they have the skill and determination. For myself, I have acquitted you of being a harsh and uncaring master.'

Stormbringer looked much happier as Arthur spoke. While Valdar Bjornsen was a man of extraordinary vision, courage and honour, for all that he had been banished by Hrolf Kraki, he often looked to Arthur for validation. The Briton had a keen sense of justice and a chilling talent for warfare. His cold and rational mind always supplied practical answers to Stormbringer's questions. Eventually, Stormbringer would have considered ransom, but Arthur's suggestion ensured that the process would begin far more swiftly.

'I'm grateful, Arthur. It'll solve my problems of space and supplies that might be wasted on our . . . guests. I'll receive silver rings, or gold, for them! By-the-by, are you prepared to accept your ship's share of the plunder?'

'It's your ship, Stormbringer. I'm a Briton, remember? I have no access to any wealth in the land of the Dene.'

Stormbringer frowned with annoyance. 'For the sake of all the saints in heaven, when will you have done with this talk? I gifted *Sea Wife* to you after your contribution to our victory at Lake Wener, when your skill and bravery robbed the Geats of their leader. You always say that you didn't know he was the Healfdene at the time, but it doesn't matter. We won easily because of your efforts. Did you know that your ship's crew could have chosen to leave you and offer their allegiance to another jarl? No? How many chose to change vessels? None! They wanted to serve with a courageous Briton. Who'd have believed it?'

Stormbringer's sarcasm, delivered with an impassive face, forced Arthur to laugh at his own foibles. Put like that, his scruples sounded ridiculous.

'As any share of the plunder concerns my men, I'll accept your generosity with thanks, my lord. They'll sing your praises at the cooking fires for the next week.'

'So easily bought!' Stormbringer joked. 'Incidentally, I have another matter of importance that I must broach with you.'

Arthur selected a crisp golden chicken that had been roasted over hot coals, then used his delicate eating knife to split the bird down the middle. He appeared to give this his full attention, but Stormbringer knew those keen eyes were missing nothing.

'Speak freely, brother. Whatever you ask is yours for the taking.'

'Strictly speaking, what I desire requires only your tacit approval. The final decision for what I'm about to ask won't be yours to make.'

'Oh?' Arthur's brows lowered with suspicion, but his gaze was still open and friendly, so Stormbringer took heart and plunged back into an awkward, obviously prepared speech.

'As your sister's oldest male kinsman, I want permission to ask for your sister's agreement to a contract of marriage. I know there's a great disparity in our ages – she's fourteen now, and I'm near enough to thirty years old.'

Arthur opened his mouth to speak, but Stormbringer cut him off.

'I know any such betrothal means that she is unlikely to return to her home, but she would become the mistress of a large estate at The Holding, and would be free to order her life as she chooses. I know she chafes under the rules that govern the roles of women in your homeland, so I can offer her greater freedom than she would enjoy elsewhere.'

Stormbringer paused for breath and, once again, Arthur tried to interrupt. But Stormbringer was adamant that he had more to say.

'I realise that Maeve is of high birth and the wisewoman at World's End promised her a throne; a prospect I cannot imagine beyond the Sae Dene throne which I already hold. But I would protect her and cherish her as no other man would. I understand her rarity and her courage, so I'm prepared to gift her with forty acres of prime pasture land, twenty rings of silver and ten of gold, fifty sheep and the same in milk cows, chickens, goats and ducks. These gifts are intended to make her independent of any man until her eventual death. Further, she may bequeath her acres in any way and to any person whom she chooses.'

Arthur was surprised at the size of the dowry that Stormbringer was offering. Suddenly, the succulent chicken was tasteless in his mouth as he evaluated the enormity of his sister's potential wealth. Alone, friendless and without any dowry at all, she was being offered freedom and an economic independence that was the equal of any queen's. He gaped at the prospect.

'Brother . . . I can hardly argue with your proposal, and I'm certain that my sister will be honoured by such a generous offer. If she has to marry anyone, I'd be perfectly happy if the lucky man was you, for you understand how difficult she can be. You may approach her, by all means, but Maeve will make this decision for herself.'

'You're surprised, Arthur. Is the match so bizarre? Speak honestly, my friend, for I love her dearly.'

'Your offer isn't bizarre. I know that Maeve needs an older man who can understand her complexities. She was reared to understand that she would eventually marry to further her family's interests, such are the practicalities of marriage in our society, so the bonus of love and your offer of independence should prove almost irresistible. For what it's worth, I would be proud if we became kinsmen.'

Then the two men toasted the future and attacked the meal with a renewed appetite and a sense that something new and special was coming at last.

The courier arrived three days later. Stormbringer was closeted with him for an hour before the man departed, presumably in the direction from which he had come. Stormbringer, for his part, said very little about the courier's message, an omission which Arthur found vaguely disturbing.

Over three-quarters of the prisoners had been moved to the slave pits, but the ransom negotiations for the jarls had only just begun. Messages must be sent with reliable traders who could move freely between Skania and Gotland.

Arthur was surprised to discover that the man he had forcibly rescued by the beard was a cousin of Heardred and had been given the grandiose name of Beowulf after his maternal grand-father. During his years roaming through the Dene lands Arthur had heard the saga of Beowulf and, with his limited experience of Heorot, had marvelled at what the gifted singers had made of the legends. He had also heard the saga of Hrolf Kraki and found nothing realistic in the hero of this long and courageous tale. Perhaps Beowulf Minor was just as flawed.

Now, talking with the grandson of a legendary hero, Arthur admitted that the situation had all the quality of a surreal dream. The aging warrior with the famed name was good company, and was likely to provide wealth to Arthur and bring him a little closer to his goal of a return to Britain. Besides, he liked Beowulf.

The hide tents where the jarls and Geat aristocrats were housed were far from palatial, but the homely clutter of boots and tunics dropped or draped on every surface reminded Arthur of the tent he had shared with Eamonn and several other British lordlings when they were boys. No matter what age, men almost always created chaos in their living spaces. As one of the rare exceptions to this rule, Arthur understood how freeing it would be to drop his possessions on the floor. He said as much to Beowulf Minor.

'This place smells like a giant's armpit, Beowulf. How can you stand it?' Arthur was nothing if not blunt.

'What do you mean, Arthur? I can't smell anything,' the Geat replied, a little put out at the implication that he might be dirty in his personal habits. 'I wash regularly and my clothes are scrubbed by Hermann's woman at least once a week.'

Arthur's nose wrinkled, but he allowed the subject to drop.

Beowulf was bluff, rather short for his race at a little less than six foot tall, and darker than most of his kin. His nut-brown hair was streaked with white-blond and grey strands and his eyes were a very pale blue. His hands were uncommonly beautiful. Long-fingered, blemish-free and well kept, Beowulf used them to express his feelings, so Arthur watched those fingers to gauge the Geat's opinions at times when the man would be loath to speak freely.

'I expect you to be ransomed within the week, Beowulf. Believe me, my crew will be pleased to receive their share of your asking price, but I'll miss our evening conversations. You're an interesting man, my friend.'

'Aye, lad! In some ways I'll be sorry to leave, for it'll be hard to return to my king as a failure. He'll not be happy with me either. I've learned much from you, young man. You Britons have absorbed the knowledge of people from many lands and cultures. Rome, Constantinople, Gaul and Spain are wondrous places with much to teach us.'

Beowulf's longing made Arthur snort.

'Give you lot a little civilising, and we'd have your fighters knocking at the doors of the south for entry . . . and none too politely either!'

Both men laughed for different reasons, but Arthur continued to watch Beowulf's hands. 'The new ways will come though, of that I'm certain,' Arthur added wistfully. 'The Dene, Goth and Noroway warriors will migrate to the softer lands of the south for living space and plunder, sooner or later. If I manage to return to Britain, I can only hope that I'm long dead before that day comes. I have no desire to go to war against my friends from the northern climes.'

Then he broke the sombre mood with a grin.

'I'd hate to kill any of you, and I know it might come to warfare. Even you, Beowulf of the Hairy Feet, could one day become an enemy of my people if they mistakenly considered you to be the same sort of man as your king and some of your kinsmen.'

It was Beowulf's turn to snort with what sounded like contempt. 'Heardred is consumed with thoughts of you, Arthur, while he's got no idea what sort of man you really are. All he hears are terms such as The Last Dragon or The Ruin of Kings and he froths with rage. I'm sorry for the massacre at Lund in the border lands. The whole matter was unnecessary. Heardred didn't even stick to his word, for Lund isn't in Blekinge.'

Arthur knew he should try to hide any surprise at this new information, but his face revealed his concern. 'What or where is Lund?' he asked bluntly.

'You've not heard of the massacre at Lund then, have you? That damned man! I was sure you would have been informed when the courier came – you being the cause and all! Shite and piss! May that stupid Heardred discover one day just how cold Udgaad will be for him.'

A cold feeling began to form a lump of ice in Arthur's throat. The situation at Lund must have been very severe for Stormbringer to keep all mention of the subject away from him.

'Tell me, Beowulf. Put aside any shame at what your kinsman

has done and tell me what you know. I won't blame you because I can tell that you had no part in it.'

Beowulf nodded. 'I'll tell you, because you can easily learn the fate of the people of Lund from any of the prisoners in the camp if they dare to speak openly of the events that took place there. Heardred boasts of it as a victory over you and blames you for the separate fates of the Dragon's Brood. I had no idea what type of man you'd be until you yanked me back to life by my beard.'

Both men laughed, but cautiously. Perhaps their burgeoning friendship could be killed off by King Heardred's sins.

'I'll not blame you for anything that's occurred, Beowulf, but I need to know if an atrocity has taken place because of me.'

'Aye!' Beowulf sighed. 'There's no nice way of describing the rape and murder of everyone in the villages and hamlets around Lund and the systematic execution of those people who were caught in the town. The ravens grow fat on bodies that were left unburned. Through his enmity, Heardred has sought to humble you and turn your name to a word of dread.'

'How many were killed?' Arthur asked, his voice suddenly very hoarse.

'The estimates vary, but I suppose at least one and a half thousand people of all ages and sexes were killed. I've been told that Heardred demanded that the victims shout curses at you in the hope of being left alive. Such promises were lies, of course! I'm sorry, my friend.'

Arthur rose to his feet and poured a mug of beer. When offered, Beowulf refused the ale with a shake of his head.

'But that's not everything, is it?' Arthur demanded. Beowulf's body language suggested that more had yet to be told – probably the worst part by far.

'Do you remember the threats that Heardred made against

the children of Blekinge aged between five and ten? In that time of their young lives when they are most desirable to certain perverted tastes?'

'Aye, I remember! But I never supposed that any king would stoop so low as to sell little children into such despicable slavery.'

Beowulf turned away so he wouldn't have to see the rage and shame in the young Briton's eyes.

'My king did what he promised! The children have been sold into the vastness of the East and every loyal Geat is now shamed by the blood that has been poured over our hands. I cannot bear such dishonour, Arthur. So, tell me, what can a man do to atone for these crimes?'

Arthur went very white, his eyes icy slits in his skull. Suddenly, Beowulf saw the face of retribution staring blindly past him, as if Arthur could pierce the many miles between him and Heardred and tear the man's throat out with his bare hands.

Beowulf was very glad that this cold stranger had no arguments with him.

THE SMALAND WARS

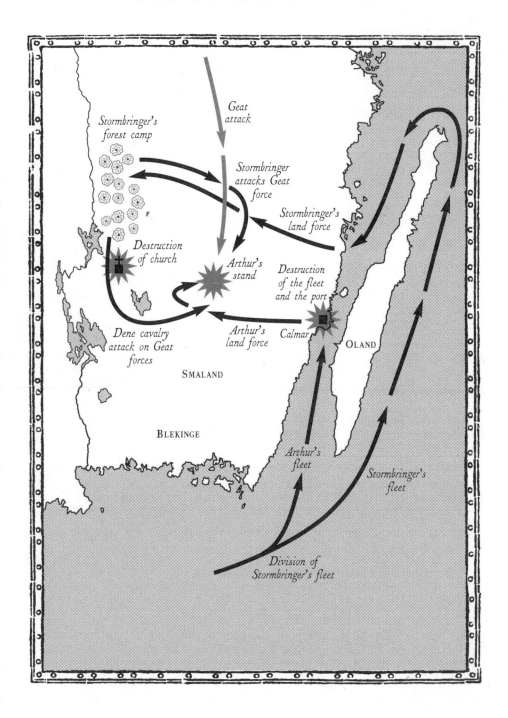

CHAPTER II

COLD COMFORT

He knew that the *essence* of war is violence, and that moderation is imbecility.

Thomas Babington Macaulay, *John Hampden*

The sound of smashing pottery shattered the quiet inside the tent. A jug full to the brim with foaming beer had been thrown into the fire pit. The captive jumped guiltily and flinched.

As Beowulf's sickening information sank in, it ate at Arthur until his rage overwhelmed him. Fortunately, the beer jug was the only object broken. Beowulf Minor could see that the Briton wanted immediate reparation from the Geats for the hundreds of children who had passed into slavery on Heardred's orders. Later, after the captive's ransom had been paid and the Geat jarl had been returned to his home, Beowulf admitted to his wife Mina that he had felt quite nervous in Arthur's presence when he saw the fury in those implacable eyes, and that he feared Heardred's rash decisions would herald more deaths.

But such reflections were in a kinder future. For now, Beowulf shuddered as he visualised the fate of his people when they inevitably burned in their villages.

Slow-burning, inexorable wrath drove Arthur towards Stormbringer's tent. Stormbringer had chosen to keep the grim message of murder and rape at Lund in retaliation for the Geat defeat at Lake Wener from Arthur to spare the Briton from any further feelings of guilt. Yet some secrets are so terrible that the earth that hides the bodies of murdered innocents refuses to conceal them. The suddenness of Arthur's discovery and the link with his night horrors had exacerbated his feelings of impotence.

Arthur burst into Stormbringer's tent without preamble. Stormbringer was studying a series of incomprehensible rolls of hide on which were drawn lists of data on water depths in the channels around the Sound. Usually, Arthur would have been fascinated by the method used to measure the depth of water and the manner in which these records were kept. But not today.

'You should have told me about Lund, Stormbringer. Did you think to spare me?' As Arthur's voice rose, Stormbringer examined his hands with more attention than the situation warranted. 'Heardred promised us that little children would suffer for the insults I directed towards him. The man would be ridiculous if his actions weren't so heinous.'

Stormbringer recognised the depth of pent-up anger and sadness in Arthur's expression. He cursed inwardly that Lund's fate had become common knowledge, for Arthur would no longer be alone in the animosity directed at the cowardly actions of the Geat king. The Skanians were crying out for justice, while his own men would be incensed that Heardred could believe Dene warriors were men of straw who would tolerate such a direct insult after the victories gained in Halland and Skania. As well, the kings in the surrounding states of Noroway, Saxony and Friesia would judge Stormbringer's mettle as they heard how he dealt with Heardred's revenge on harmless traders and farmers.

But time was Stormbringer's enemy. His supply lines were extended and, while he had a sizeable force of men at his command, their numbers could scarcely compare with the horde of warriors available to Heardred. The situation in Jutland grew worse by the day and Hrolf Kraki would have let King Heardred know that he'd not lift a finger to assist Stormbringer. As far as Heardred was concerned, Stormbringer was a traitor who had been banished by his own king. To make a bad situation worse, autumn had arrived. All too soon, snow would turn the sky and the earth into a monastic world of monochrome and the Dene army would be forced to seek shelter for the long, freezing winter. Despite the prestige of his family name, Stormbringer was aware that he couldn't mire himself down in a long campaign in Skania – and Heardred knew it too.

Arthur had considered all these complications. The two friends had on many occasions mulled over the difficulties they could expect while they were developing their plans to crush Heardred's ambitions. Like many leaders, the Sae Dene needed a colleague who could offer his opinions honestly, without worthless fawning or a search for advancement. Arthur always made suggestions that were realistic and pragmatic, making him the perfect sounding-board. But this situation had changed now, for their relationship had developed a crack when the Geat king had employed such dirty strategies. In his bid to shake Stormbringer's resolve and win a reputation for toughness and invincibility, Heardred had tried to steal back the advantage lost at Lake

Wener, Halland and Skania, using the children of Lund as expendable pawns in order to shatter Dene confidence. Whatever Stormbringer attempted now, the weather prevented a concerted campaign against the Geats despite Arthur's determination to pursue the Geat king himself.

But Arthur was still prepared to go alone if necessary, as he bluntly informed the Sae Dene. 'I don't care if I'm captured, killed, tortured or held up to public ridicule. I'll not allow the fate of those children to stain my honour, and I'll ensure that the real culprit will be awash with blood for his crimes. As of this moment, my Britons are at war with Gotland, regardless of the number of warriors that will be aligned against me.'

'Don't be ridiculous, Arthur. You'll be killed before you reach Heardred's palace, let alone gain an entry to his throne room.'

The Sae Dene knew that Arthur's honour had been besmirched, and this young man would mount a personal attack if necessary, but that he was really searching for a sensible and achievable way of gaining revenge.

'Can you provide me with a plan that could defeat Heardred's forces in a short campaign of less than two months in the field?' Stormbringer demanded.

Arthur grinned malevolently. 'Yes! I've devised a plan that would give us time to carry out a destructive raid and then sail back to The Holding before the onset of winter – just!'

Stormbringer's question was a major concession from the Sae Dene king, and one the young Briton had hoped to win.

'I believe that Heardred is a vain man by nature, which suggests he might be a bag of wind as well. He has taken exception to me for imagined insults to him after our successes at Lake Wener. He doesn't plan ahead, so he can be beaten by superior strategies. Like Hrolf Kraki, he's a perfect example of an arrogant ruler with limited competence.'

'True, Arthur. In his position I'd have called for a truce and a parley to gauge the mettle of my adversaries – and then I'd have brokered a face-saving treaty.'

'But that's because you're a man of sense, rather than a fool who thinks that the good luck of being born an aristocrat is a sign of superiority. According to my old teacher, the Greek gods warned them against hubris because such boundless arrogance will always lead to destruction. Heardred reacts to circumstances and would never face us on the field of combat, unless he is certain that he will win. If this were not so, he would already have taken direct action against us.'

Stormbringer, confident that his friend's agile brain had devised an effective way to bring Heardred to ruin, listened intently.

'Heardred went to war against us in Halland and Skania and was defeated. Though these battles were skirmishes rather than full-scale engagements, the fighting was vicious and involved a heavy loss of life for the Geats. But Heardred continues to lose! Such a man could never contemplate thoughts of failure, and he yearns to crush us!'

Although his eyes gleamed with passion, Arthur was aware that only reasoned argument and calm, plausible planning could influence Stormbringer's logical mind.

'Not only does Heardred use ineffective battle strategies, but he wastes his forces by attacking places such as Lund that have no strategic value. His only purpose in that raid was to send a warning to us that he intends to revisit the scene of any skirmishes that are fought and won by us. The Geat king is a coward and a bully at heart. He is trying to demoralise us, but such threats make me angry, because I know he will make ordinary people suffer, again and again, if we don't stop him permanently. As soon as our ships have sailed over the horizon, Heardred will return to revenge himself on our people.'

'You make him sound like an incompetent, a paper king who isn't fit to rule,' Stormbringer observed.

'Aye! He continues to underestimate us because the Goths, the Dene, the Swedes and even the Jutes and Saxons are farmers first and fighting men second. Don't bristle, Valdar, because I mean no insult. War isn't a profession for you and your people, despite your competence in its prosecution. The Romans who trained my people were professional soldiers, so they taught the arts of war to all their subject races, including the Britons.'

Stormbringer looked a little bemused.

'I was raised for war, Valdar! Imagine! From five years of age, every aspect of organised conflict was part of my education, including the legalities of treaties, speaking other languages, weaponry, strategy and the history of great battles. Unlike Heardred, I am a professional warrior and I would never leave a live enemy behind me to be a constant thorn in my side. On the other hand, you take pride in The Holding and its agriculture, because you have been raised to grow crops, as well as learning how to become a gifted warrior, especially in personal combat. Do you understand the fundamental differences in our education?'

Stormbringer nodded as he saw the wisdom of Arthur's deductions about Heardred's nature and his probable courses of action.

'What would you suggest then?'

'We should hit him on his own soil, in those places where he is most vulnerable. That's what really upset him about the battle at Lake Wener. We were fighting on his precious land! We must hurt him so hard that we'll draw him out of his protective shell. Then, when we lure him into our grasp, we must crush him like the insect he is. Eventually I expect us to become the owners of the Geat lands. He won't enjoy that!'

Arthur used the hilt of his eating knife to sketch a rudimentary map of his battle plan in the dust, while Stormbringer scratched his head and looked at the shapes on the earth in search of landmarks. Then, once he absorbed the sense of what Arthur was presenting to him, the Sae Dene's enthusiasm began to grow. Arthur knew that Stormbringer would understand, because any seafarer who possessed the wherewithal to keep track of the depths of water in ports and coves would have little difficulty with the concept of maps and control of territory.

'We are here, Valdar.' Arthur drew a cross at the southern point of Skania. 'And this is the port of Calmar in Smaland, according to the information that Beowulf Minor has revealed to me. The port is protected by that long island, so it has become the main trading centre for the area. Colberg of the Pomeranians, Narva, Memel, Riga and the overland trade routes to the south are all serviced by the trading fleets that winter in Calmar. I know if we burn his fleet and his port, Heardred will be forced to come there to extract his revenge on the Dene traitor and the outlander from Britain. He'll never consider you to be a major threat, because you're a sea raider who's unfamiliar with land warfare.'

Stormbringer's face was blank with his lack of understanding.

'You've come by ship in all your previous raids on his warriors – and you'll do so again if we attack his fleet on the coast as a diversion. He believes your strategy consists of short, fast raids

29

where you retreat on your longboats as soon as you've taken your plunder. He'll never expect us to move inland where we can ambush his forces, or that we would use concealed cavalry as part of our armoury.'

'Why in Loki's name would we commit suicide by attempting either of those strategies?' Stormbringer asked. His face was thunderous, for he suspected that his friend was somehow insulting the courage of Dene warriors.

'Heardred won't imagine that we'll leave the coast to carry out an inland attack, just as he'd never expect us to bring horses with us on our little inland jaunt. I'm not talking about hundreds of horses, Valdar. All I'll need is twenty good mounts and a similar number of competent horsemen, and I'll show you how we can destroy the heart and plans of the Geat king.'

'Explain your strategy then!' Stormbringer ordered. He trusted Arthur enough to be prepared to listen, but the young man would need to be at his persuasive best.

'First of all, I plan to use archers again,' Arthur began. Although the Sae Dene had consented to the use of fire arrows at Lake Wener, only two or three men were involved, all wounded warriors, so he had accepted what he believed to be a cowardly strategy as necessary to achieve their aims.

'There's no honour in killing at long distance, where the archer can't be touched. It's disgraceful for my warriors to even contemplate it,' Stormbringer stated angrily. 'It was only with the greatest reluctance that I accepted your advice to set the stables alight at Lake Wener.'

'I admire your tactical and strategic knowledge, Valdar, but the use of bowmen in warfare is common throughout the civilised world. I can assure you that it won't be too long before it becomes accepted throughout your lands.'

Arthur gave a conciliatory smile to show the Sae Dene that he understood the quandary in which he had placed his friend. Wisely, he then allowed the matter to drop and moved on to safer areas of discussion.

'Our first point of attack will be Calmar, a port that can be taken with relative ease. We'll burn the Geat fleet and leave a lasting memory of our visit. We'll also destroy the warehouses so that Calmar's trade will be in ruins for several years. Heardred will be apoplectic; he'll blame you for the invasion and he'll receive the news of Calmar's fall very quickly. But you won't be a part of Calmar's destruction, because that will be my task. You'll be elsewhere!'

Stormbringer looked distinctly put out, because this was the very type of warfare that the Dene understood.

'I estimate that I'll only need twelve ships to complete my task, but we'll have about twenty other ships, including a force of at least twenty horses, secreted in a suitable cove further up the coast. You'll be in command of this force. I'd suggest that a total of about one thousand men would defeat any army that Heardred will recruit to relieve the defenders of Calmar. I'd caution against using a larger force than this in case our warriors are needed in Jutland. We all know that trouble will eventually come from the Jutes and the Saxons.

'You'll need to reach the wooded country near the smaller lake of the two that lie to the north of Calmar. According to Beowulf, there's a small village there which has a large religious community. He says it has the makings of an important town one day in the future. Initially, I will be marching towards it as if to destroy this community.'

Stormbringer nodded. So far, Arthur's plan seemed sound.

'Beowulf unintentionally revealed far more to me about his

homeland than was sensible. He lives to the north of Calmar and spoke of that part of the Geat kingdom with the affection of a man who is far from home. Were you aware that Beowulf is actually Heardred's heir? Heardred's only son was killed on Rugen Island in a boating accident about a year ago, and Beowulf holds the honour of being next in the bloodline leading to the Geat throne. In fact, the possibility of rule scares my friend because he knows that his cousin neither likes nor trusts him. But then, Heardred doesn't trust anyone. Beowulf assures me his cousin never listens to counsel from any of the wiser heads among his jarls.'

Stormbringer was absorbing Arthur's information with deep concentration.

'There is certain to be good plunder in the district to the north of Calmar, if the opportunity arose to attack the lakes of Smaland as well. Beowulf described the lands there as being suitable for horses, mantraps and a fighting square during our military operations, although he has no knowledge of such tactical manoeuvres. Our task would be to march some six hundred men with as much noise as possible into the north and to camp just outside the town with the religious community, to give the impression that this is our prime objective. I don't know its name, but that hardly matters.

'When Heardred learns that Calmar has fallen, he'll come running to intercept my warriors. At that time, he'll learn that the religious community has been destroyed as well. I'm sorry about this, but it's necessary and I'll let the monks live if I can. Because he's overconfident, Heardred won't stop to think that he might need reinforcements or consider changes to his attack plans. He'll have received intelligence about the number of ships used in the initial attack on Calmar but we'll make damned sure he doesn't hear about you and your secret reinforcements that will be held in reserve at inland locations. This strategy was quite successful at Lake Wener, but *this* time we'll be reversing the positions when Heardred and the Geat army make their appearance. I'll be holding an entrenched position in a fighting square with only a barely viable defensive force, so he'll think we're ripe for the plucking. I'll be easy meat, his favourite kind!'

Stormbringer remained silent, but his eyes were now very bright.

'I'll build concealed mantraps, and my warriors will dig ditches soaked with pitch around our positions where I can light fires in the trenches. I'll also have a group of archers among the defenders who will make life difficult for the attackers once they are committed to the fray. Meanwhile, with Heardred fully extended and believing I am at his mercy, your small cavalry force will explode out of the ruins of the religious community and cut his force in half. Our erstwhile masters, the Romans, used horsemen because a force of twenty cavalry was worth more than a hundred foot soldiers during those stages of a battle where speed and surprise are paramount. At the same time as the cavalry charge at the Geat force, you and your warriors will attack on the opposite flank. I predict that the Geats will collapse under this multi-pronged strategy, once my force goes on the offensive.'

'From your lips to God's ear,' Stormbringer murmured abstractedly; Arthur shuddered as if a shadow had passed over his grave.

'What's wrong, my friend?' Stormbringer asked, all solicitous now that he could see that Arthur's battle plan was both simple and effective.

'My old tutor, Father Lorcan, often used that phrase when I was a young boy. For a moment there, I felt the ghosts of my childhood gather together as if to warn me. My task, the last part of the gamble, is to loosen my troops in all four directions as part of a co-ordinated whole. Caught between our cavalry, your force and my two prongs of warriors, Heardred's army should collapse like walls of sand.'

'Shite, Arthur!' Stormbringer exclaimed. 'It sounds workable!'

'I'm not really so gifted, Valdar. I've just been fortunate enough to serve under some brilliant commanders in major battles and I've observed their tactical expertise while in the front line. The Dene have few opportunities to fight as a unified, cohesive force under a centralised command. Every saga I've heard has praised individual prowess and strength of arms by heroes, but modern battles are won by men who fight together as a single whole. My father defeated the Saxons for many years in this way.'

Stormbringer was still not completely convinced.

'Valdar, much of your future combat, both on sea and on land, will continue to be governed by individual thinking and personal talent. But not against this king – and not at this time! Because this type of warfare is foreign to you, it's essential that I must command the fighting square.'

Stormbringer had suspected that Arthur could have been trying to steal the lion's share of the glory and was happier when Arthur demonstrated that his strategies had nothing to do with a personal search for power.

'If we do as you propose, how do you plan to convince six hundred men to fight in ways that are contrary to all their martial instincts? For that matter, how do you plan to train your cavalry in such a brief period of time? Your ideas are good, my friend, but I'm concerned about their implementation. And where are you going to find your archers?'

'Thorketil, the Hammer of Thor, will find archers among the peasantry. He served with distinction at Lake Wener and, since then, he has discovered that the bow can make a difference to the outcome of a battle. I have no doubts that he'll have a small troop of archers ready within two weeks.'

'Very well, but what of my other concerns?' Stormbringer would be risking a great deal on a plan that held only a limited chance of success.

'What do your warriors say before they go into battle, Stormbringer? Today is a good day to die! If we do nothing, Skania will burn in the spring and you may not be able to return when the weather is warm. In truth, my friend, you have little choice if you wish to preserve any form of Dene presence in the west of Gotland.'

Arthur briefly regretted the need to speak the unvarnished truth. But Valdar Bjornsen was nobody's fool. He understood war and loss of life, so knew he had little choice.

'I will have no difficulty in convincing twenty young bloods to volunteer for cavalry duty. In fact, I'll have to beat them off with sticks. If they are competent horsemen, I can teach them tactical requirements within two weeks. Not much fighting skill is needed, after all, since the horses will do most of the work.'

Arthur was rifling through every Roman battle strategy that Germanus had ever taught him. 'Before you ask, I plan to teach all six hundred of our men a series of strategies that can be used to lure an enemy into an enclosed area where they can be contained and forced to fight on our terms. In so doing, I intend to minimise the casualties suffered by our own forces. If these tactics can be mastered by ignorant Roman peasants, so can they by your Dene warriors.'

The Sae Dene king could hardly argue that his warriors were inferior to Roman foot soldiers. He knew he was being manipulated, but Stormbringer respected Arthur's intellect, so he reasoned that the younger man must take a calculated gamble if he was to defeat the Geat king. At all events, the Geat king must be stopped, crushed *now*, while the Dene force was strong enough to drive the invaders back to their own lands.

As so often, Arthur, the Last Dragon, held the key. All he needed now was a brace of blacksmiths.

The weeks moved quickly as from among the hundreds of volunteers Arthur selected thirty men who owned good horses, were superior horsemen and young enough to learn new methods.

As well, he searched out a dozen blacksmiths who were set to work making large rectangular shields in the Roman style. The Sae Dene supplied sufficient iron for solid metal shields for the front two rows of Arthur's fighting square and the rest must make do with hardwood shields covered with bull-hide and reinforced with iron. The usual rounded Dene shields would be of no use in the coming conflict, so Arthur planned to present the new ones as a fait accompli.

He began basic training for his cavalry and then sent them off to endless practice sessions under the jaundiced eyes of Rufus Olaffsen, the warrior whom Eamonn had beaten in single combat over a year earlier and who now served Stormbringer with a dour and determined obsession. Since Hrolf Kraki had humiliated Rufus for failing in combat against his British enemy, Rufus had hungered to bring down the Crow King. Arthur knew that his budding cavalrymen would be drilled to within an inch of their lives.

Thorketil had been touchingly grateful to Arthur for his trust. The young Briton approached the Hammer of Thor with a proposal that he form a special group of archers whose role would be to supplement the land forces by softening up the enemy with heavy arrow-fire before the other warriors went onto the attack. Arthur explained that many warriors would deem his force to be cowardly, because they attacked from a distance, but Thorketil immediately assured Arthur that he would find youths, older men, the partially incapacitated and those young aristocrats who lacked the required physical prowess to become warriors in their own right. Normally, such young men would die in combat before they had reached their majority, but as archers they would now become valuable members of Stormbringer's force.

As a fighting man wounded in combat, Thorketil well knew the feelings of uselessness when an injured warrior could no longer practise his calling – one for which he had trained throughout his entire life. In the brutal world of the north, most wounded men died, so it followed that starvation, humiliation or shame were the rewards for those hardy souls who survived. Most warriors prayed for a clean, quick death.

Any disabled warrior who could draw a bow and become an integral part of a battle group would be given a sense of purpose. He would feel like a man again in a society where the disabled were expected to sacrifice their lives during the freezing winters, when food was in short supply.

'I'm certain I'll be able to provide you with enough archers, Master Arthur. More than you expect, in fact. And you'll have to search far to find men more committed to a Dene victory, for we all understand what it is to be considered a useless burden.'

Arthur could see the gratitude and respect that glowed in Thorketil's close-set eyes and dismissed any prejudice that the Troll King might be as foolish as his features suggested. Thorketil had suffered from ridicule throughout his life because by chance his features resembled those of a retarded child.

'I have complete faith in you, Thorketil, but you must bring your men to readiness as soon as possible. People are dying while we train our men to take part in the final battle and we have little time to complete our preparations. The weather is against us!'

The Briton looked skywards. Flocks of large northern geese were heading south in their arrowhead formations and he could hear the distant honking of their cries of farewell to the summer homelands. The leaden skies seemed pregnant with the prospect of rain, sleet and snow. Winter had almost arrived.

Thorketil bowed to Arthur. 'I will have our men ready for combat within a month, my lord. I'll stake my life on it!'

'Please, Thorketil, no grand gestures.' Arthur turned away, then remembered another salient point.

'I like you, Thorketil, and I believe our fates are intertwined, so you need to plan for an orderly and safe retreat from the battlefield if the time comes to make your escape. Otherwise, some of your wounded ducks will have to fight in the centre of the square with the other warriors. You'd have to take your chances with them.' Arthur grinned engagingly. 'You're none too fast yourself, my friend, and I need you alive and ready to do my bidding at very short notice. I'm a selfish bastard, Thorketil, so find wagons for your transport.'

As for the six hundred warriors provided by Stormbringer

to become the nucleus of his fighting force, Arthur almost surrendered to their stubborn refusal to accept the Roman Tortoise Movement as a manly defence. He explained the manoeuvre and the use of interlocking shields over and over again until his head began to spin, but the warriors remained obdurate.

Finally, Arthur and Stormbringer called their entire force onto a parade square where the tactics to be used could be explained in detail. Totally frustrated, Stormbringer insisted that the warriors should carry out their instructions without demur or further discussion.

Arthur looked at the six hundred mulish men sitting on the sod in various comfortable positions and saw no promise in the sea of pale eyes that they were prepared to obey their master. The whole enterprise could fail if these men weren't prepared to change their approach.

Stormbringer raised himself to his full height and addressed the Dene warriors.

'Listen closely, men, for I only intend to issue these orders on one occasion. The Last Dragon and I don't want your glorious deaths, and we don't want to grieve for any of our number if that warrior should become a casualty through his own stupidity. We are here to win this war against the Geat army and, as your Sae Dene king, I want you to win for the glory of the Dene people. The whole point of planning this battle long before we're even on the enemy's home ground allows us to implement our battle plans with surety. I want to win, and I intend to live so that we can enjoy the spoils. Is that understood? If there is any man here who puts his own dreams of glory above the needs of the jarls and his comrades, then you must speak out now and leave immediately with your honour intact. This is one time when our warriors must fight as part of a whole, if we are to defeat a unified enemy.'

Stormbringer stood to one side to permit Arthur to take his place. The demeanours of the men had softened a little, but the Briton was sure that the warriors had yet to be persuaded. His heart sank. How could he, an Outlander, succeed when their beloved master had failed?

Arthur began to relate tales of terrible, infamous battles where Romans had defeated superior forces because they had hunkered down and used strategic devices such as the Tortoise Movement to repel attack. They had driven back numerically stronger forces by sheer, bloody-minded attrition. Many heads were shaking at first but then, as he described the ways in which undisciplined warriors threw themselves against the shields of the Romans, hot breath to hot breath, more and more heads began to nod in agreement with his depiction of the Romans' grim and steadfast methods of defence. Arthur was pleased he had remembered the Dene love of sagas and tales of valour. How much easier it was to use the stories of past Roman victories to convince this force of reluctant heroes to adopt new tactics.

'The Romans ruled the world for many centuries, so we must all ask each other why they were so successful.' Arthur's voice was mellifluous now. The warriors who listened so intently began to imagine the small, dark Romans as they sweated in their leather and iron armour within the Fighting Square.

More importantly, they began to understand and accept the points that Arthur was making. He compared Roman battlefield discipline to the combined efforts of Dene sailors as they fought with their oars against nature's fearsome storms.

'What would happen if you all rowed to your own beat and ignored the men around you? The oars would break and the longboat would begin to founder. And then the sea would feast on the marrow in Dene bones. Do I speak the truth?' Arthur's voice roared out.

'Aye!' Snorri called out from the press of warriors. 'All men must row as one, or the boat goes nowhere.'

'Thank you, brother.' Arthur's voice was gentle now as he realised he had six hundred men fixated on his every word.

Firelight lit the men's eager faces now, as the sparks blew upwards towards an ebony sky.

'Can you do what the small, dark men from Italia did? Can you hold the square as your enemy batters at you from all sides until such time as you can be released from your post, and then go on to fight and to kill? Can you obey your orders like a Roman? And can you do better than a Roman, as a warrior who knows when he should fight and when he should think?'

The Dene warriors screamed and beat at their shields with the pommels of their swords to show that no Romans could be more disciplined than they. They swore to stand firm against their enemy and vowed by all the gods that they would not break for any reason.

Nor would the Geats feel their swords until they were ordered to do so by their commanders, but they would eventually drink Geat blood to their satiation.

The night trembled with the force of their excitement and determination.

Tomorrow, Arthur could begin.

In the tent city perched above the bay where the fleet waited, Arthur had acquired a large leather structure and had scrounged various useful items of furniture. These had appeared at regular intervals, and were always a surprise for him. He suspected that Ingrid was responsible for these home comforts. As a practical and sensible woman, Ingrid had decided to make the most of her changed circumstances, and was determined that her master would become wealthy and would always be comfortable.

Many Geat women would have killed themselves rather than surrender to the avowed enemy of her people. Ingrid understood her duty to her tribe and her husband's status, but she also gazed at her infant son and her difficult daughter and decided that she would never sacrifice her children for an abstract concept of honour. A pragmatist and a widow, she knew that once a person passed into the shades, they had no power to protect those kindred left behind.

This new young master was more easy-going and offered her more freedom than she had experienced in the houses of her father or her husband.

Here, she was owned by a man of distinction and her son would rise in his service. Ingrid set about acquiring anything not nailed down that would add to Arthur's consequence and prestige.

As he entered his leather tent, Arthur discovered that he was now the proud owner of a folding campaign chair. Inlaid with an exotic black wood, the design suggested that it was of Roman construction. Arthur lifted the simple chair and discovered that it was surprisingly light.

He was immediately impressed by the simple motif of inlaid woods that ran in a border pattern along the arms, back-rest and seat. This humble household item was a masterpiece, perfectly designed to provide civilised living in the field.

'Do you like your new chair, Master Arthur?'

Arthur observed Ingrid watching him from the shadows as

she wielded a greasy spoon inside a blackened cooking pot. She rose to her feet gracefully and lugged the heavy iron pot to the tripod that straddled the fire pit, where she set it on a hook above the hot coals. Her infant son was sleeping inside a cloth sling that freed her arms to carry out her daily chores.

'It's a beautiful piece of furniture, Ingrid, but I'm not sure I really need it. It looks Roman to me!' Yet his eyes were warm with admiration and his hands stroked the inlaid back-rest with unconscious respect for the chair's beauty.

Ingrid smiled. 'A man of your importance should sit to eat, not hunker on his heels or squat cross-legged on the cold earth like a peasant.'

'But where will all these new possessions fit in *Sea Wife*? Apart from the longboat, I have no other home and she's a fighting ship, unsuitable for transporting furniture.'

Ingrid had gradually grown comfortable as she began to realise the essential decency that lay under her master's mask of cold reserve. She treated him respectfully, but with a sense of familiarity, as if she was a well-born older sister. Arthur was unsure if he approved of their burgeoning friendship, but it never occurred to him to force himself on the two women in his household. Nor did he chain them or make them sleep outside under the stars. Ingrid thanked God every day that He had placed her in the hands of this peculiar young Briton.

'I promise to find a place to put everything, master. A leader of distinction should live with a certain style.'

'Hmmmph!' Arthur grunted noncommittally and seated himself in his new chair. Surprisingly, it felt solid, satisfying and, somehow, powerful, so he took an immediate liking to it. Now he could enjoy the warmth of the fire pit without suffering the cold that bled up through the sod floor. Much as he hated to admit she was right, Ingrid was correct about her new acquisition.

As Arthur warmed within and without under Ingrid's personal touch, a small whirlwind entered the tent through the back flap, burdened by several huge packages wrapped in cabbage leaves. Sigrid's whole presence radiated waves of chill disapproval and dislike towards her master and her mother.

Ingrid's fractious daughter was bearing several slabs of beef for Arthur's table which she had collected from a central tent where meat was distributed to the warriors. The girl's arms and her crude shift were stained with watery blood, while her hair was uncombed and her expression was sullen. Despite his irritation at her arrival, Arthur noticed how well she looked as the first chills of autumn flushed her pale cheeks.

'You'd best see to your girl, Ingrid. She's allowed the beef to bleed all over my pallet,' Arthur snapped. By accident or design, a parcel had begun to leak blood over the coverlet of fur and wool that he used to keep the growing cold at bay.

Sigrid grinned wickedly to express her contempt for anything her mother could say to her. Arthur sighed, aware of the friction between mother and daughter.

'Be careful, you stupid child,' her mother complained. 'You'd best take care of your brother if you're incapable of doing anything else. I'll prepare the master's meat in your place and clean up the mess you've made. By the gods, Sigrid, you never used to be this cloth-witted and clumsy.'

As if Arthur wasn't present, Sigrid attacked her mother with relish.

'But I wasn't a slave then, was I, Mother? Nor was I expected to serve the man who murdered my father. If he wants his meat, he should cook it himself.'

'Hush, you stupid girl!' Ingrid hissed, darting a nervous glance in Arthur's direction. 'We'd be dead now if the master hadn't taken us under his protections.'

'I'd rather be dead than remain alive in his service.'

'That's easy to say, girl! Would you have preferred to have your brother's brains dashed out? You're a selfish little cow, daughter.'

'And you'd like to be a whore for the British bastard, Mother,' she sneered. 'I believe you've already forgotten my father.'

Arthur heard the sharp sound of a slap, followed by an indrawn breath and a half-sob. Then the girl charged out of the tent through the back flap.

Ingrid bowed low in front of Arthur, her shaking hands clutching at the offending packages of meat.

'I apologise for my daughter's behaviour, my lord. I don't know what to do with her, but I pray that you don't punish her for her intemperate words. Her father adored her and I'm afraid that he may have spoiled her when he treated her more like a boy than a girl. Now she refuses to understand the way that our world works for women. Please, my lord, I'll do my best to convince her to behave.'

Ingrid wept freely while her hands absently unwrapped the cabbage leaves, her large blue eyes drenched with tears of misery and fear.

'The girl's a damned nuisance, Ingrid. Can't you control her? Look, I don't have time to think about Sigrid at the moment. We'll be moving into the south soon, and that might be a good time to tell your daughter I could be killed in battle. That should cheer her up.'

Ingrid's eyes registered her horror at his joke. All women understood the painful reality of life in the northern climes, regardless of whether they were queens or slaves. Regardless of

Sigrid's execrable behaviour, Arthur had refrained from beating her or punishing her in any other way. Ingrid had seen the gloating, salacious expressions on the faces of the Dene warriors who came to their tent. Rape would be the automatic fate of most women and the punishment for any young woman who constantly put herself at risk of angering their master. Yet he had not attempted to even touch them. Even his requirements of them were minimal. If there was food on his table, he ate. If there was none, he seemed totally unconcerned.

As for his attentions to women, her master seemed to favour fleeting relationships. She had spoken with many of the young slave women and girls who had warmed his bed. They all seemed to worship the earth under his feet, for he endowed them with the self-respect lacking in their daily lives.

So why did he ignore her? And, more importantly, why did he show such patience with Sigrid? As a beautiful woman who had been courted all her life, Ingrid didn't know whether to be insulted or grateful for his restraint.

'I'd rather you don't talk of Sigrid, woman, but you needn't be too upset about it – at least for the moment. I'm not in the habit of hurting children.'

He smiled across at her, which lightened her gloomy fears.

'Now, what's to eat? I've been trying to talk sense into Dene skulls all afternoon, so I could eat a horse.'

'I only need to stir more meat into the stew and it will be ready. I've added real onions to give more taste to the broth and there are carrots in it as well.'

Ingrid's son shifted in her sling and she felt warm urine soak through his loincloth. With a small sigh for the washing this accident would cause, her hand sought out the old knife her master had given her for household duties and protection. The meat was sliced thinly under her careful fingers and she added the off-cuts to the pot.

'How is your son?' Arthur asked quietly, although her eyes noted the tiny twitch of his nostrils.

He can smell the child's piss, damn it! she cursed inwardly.

'The child's growing quickly, master.' Ingrid made an odd decision that comforted her. 'He will grow strong so that he can serve you and guard your back from harm when he is big enough. I believe that little Ingmar is destined to become a true man who will learn at your knee.'

Arthur blushed – just as Ingrid had intended. He knew what his slave woman was about: saving her infant son, ensuring that the boy's future was linked to the success of his master.

But the honour conferred on him by this proud Geat aristocrat was very flattering for an unhappy refugee from a foreign land. In this northern world, where a woman and her word had more weight and strength than in the British nations, she had allied her family to his interests for the remainder of her life. Arthur felt a strange combination of embarrassment, pleasure and irritation.

'Don't talk nonsense, Ingrid, although I thank you for the compliments. Now, change the boy ... And you needn't worry about our supper, for I'll ensure that the stew doesn't boil over. There's no need to look so shocked, woman, for my mother and sisters would give me a thick ear if I didn't watch the pot.'

His eyes were suddenly dark with sadness, so Ingrid knew that he was beset by memories of home and the mother who waited beyond the grey waters for news of him. Sensitive to his moods, she turned away.

'I'll think of something to do with Sigrid after we've eaten,' Arthur promised her. 'I'll not punish her unnecessarily.'

Or at least no more than the little bitch deserves, he told himself. Warmth spread in the pit of his belly as he considered a churlish revenge.

'I've been far too patient with her,' he told himself, as Ingrid left him alone with the cooking pot and his thoughts. The fire spat wickedly as a globule of fat sizzled in the hot coals, but no heat could match the fire of dissatisfaction that grew ever hotter inside him.

THE BATTLE OF SMALAND

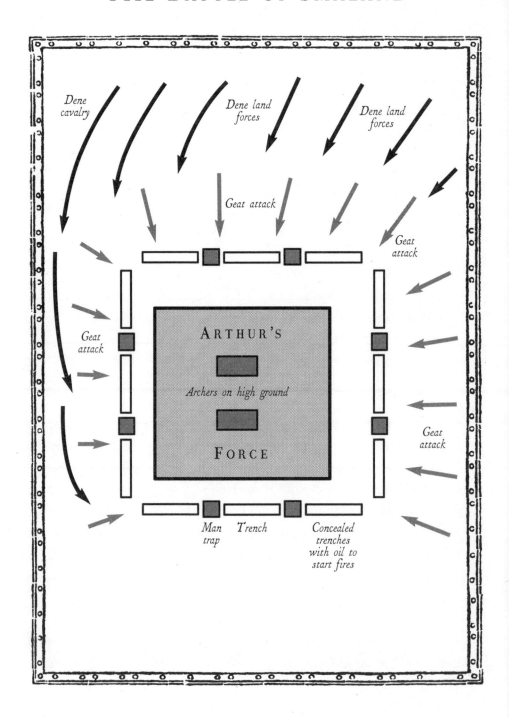

CHAPTER III

MEN OF GRASS

The days of man are but as grass:
for he flourisheth as a flower of a field.
For as soon as the wind goeth over it, it is gone:
and the place thereof shall know it no more.

The Book of Common Prayer, Psalm 103

A horse charged at Arthur suddenly with maddened eyes and sharp, upraised hooves. Riderless, it attacked the line in a frenzy of terror, with blood staining its flanks while more pumped sluggishly from an axe wound in the shoulder. Before he could deflect the beast with his sword, a hoof struck his thigh a glancing blow that almost felled him. Arthur reeled in agony but on one side the adjacent warrior's arm reached out to steady him and, on the other, a shield was rammed in front of his face. Cursing as he massaged his injured thigh, Arthur caught a quick glimpse of the battlefield before Snorri's shield blocked his view.

Chaos swirled around the fighting square. The cavalry charge had hit the massed Geat army on Arthur's left with the force of a thunderclap, and every Dene had felt the dislocating aftershock run through them from the soles of their boots to the press of bodies thrust desperately against the wall of shields.

Along the right flank, the reserves under Stormbringer that Arthur had sent to the battle site by stealth in the days before his own arrival struck out on the opposite side of the Geat army. Once again, the Dene warriors in the centre of this melee of desperate men felt the shock of an attack from the rear. All that Arthur could see in front of him, during that split second before Snorri's shield had snapped back into place, was the bloody detritus of wounded men and the closely packed warriors under attack from two sides. Dead men were held upright by the close thrust of their companions and the retreat of both sides of Heardred's army from the two attacks. Pressed against the shields of their enemies, they were impaled on spears, hamstrung by axes or stabbed by swords, yet even the wounded were unable to turn away from the weapons that were killing them. Terrorised horses flailed out with sharp, iron-clad hoofs as warriors turned on each other, desperate to find some open space in which to retreat, or attack, as the opportunity permitted.

The defining moment in the conflict had arrived. Now, Arthur's decisions would decide the outcome of the battle. Although his thigh ached, his brain was filled with a ruthless surge of power – and he knew exactly where his duty lay. If he kept his nerve, Heardred would be smashed permanently, so now was the time for an all-out, relentless attack.

Around him Arthur could feel the mood of the six hundred men who had endured so much and displayed such discipline and resolve. The warriors were like ravenous fighting hounds as every muscle in their bodies quivered to use their swords in a sustained attack. But could they turn as a single unit and push outwards to strike into the heart of the enemy who were now caught on two sides between two fresh Dene forces?

Arthur could feel their pent-up eagerness. These men would obey him to the death, but their consuming desire was to charge outwards in four directions, so they smashed into the disorganised enemy with axes and swords. His warriors cried out silently with their eyes to release their frustration and rage at the blows and insults of Geat taunts throughout the long morning. Arthur made the final, irrevocable decision: the time to attack had come.

'Pass the message down the line,' Arthur roared. 'When you see the red flag has been raised, each side will attack at their front and push outward! No quarter and no surrender! For Stormbringer!'

Arthur pulled a long strip of narrow cloth from under his cuirass. He handed it to Snorri, who attached it to the head of a long spear. 'Raise it high, Snorri,' Arthur ordered. Then he began to shout his orders to his troops and the refrain was repeated, again and again, as the Dene warriors began to push outward, with their breasts heaving against those of their foes.

'For the Dragon's Brood! For Stormbringer! For the children!'

The Dene warriors began to kill in earnest now – and the afternoon was ruddy with their raised swords and axes. The air reverberated with their war-cries. A waning sun blazed onto the bloody fray as the Dene continued to kill in an ecstasy of rage. All the frustrations were eased now by the fresh blood that soaked the thirsty earth.

Arthur remained at their head in the centre of the line, drenched with fresh and dried blood over his gleaming armour as a red pennon streamed over his head. The Geat warriors recognised him as the Last Dragon and their hearts quailed. Their jarls saw the fresh troops harrying their flanks and driving them into the maw of the fighting square, and recognised the cavalry charge as a Dene tactic designed to demoralise them.

At the last, they were aware that their king had been leading them towards ruin, and the Stormbringer and the Last Dragon had capitalised on his stupidity.

The jarls died and cursed Heardred with eyes of stone turned towards the ridge where their king was watching the carnage he had begun with such casual hubris. In contrast the Last Dragon and Stormbringer stood four square, prepared to bleed with their warriors, as they took the self-same risks as the lowliest warrior in the line.

What the king was thinking as he watched the flower of Geat youth die below him was moot, for any orders that came from his lips were blown away on the breeze.

Three weeks earlier, the Dene fleet had sailed north towards the small, but very important, port of Calmar. Two-thirds of the fleet sailed beyond the inland island of Oland, which protected Calmar from the wild winter storms of the inner sea.

Stormbringer commanded this section of the Dene forces and he would control the cavalry and those warriors responsible for trapping the Geat army at the religious colony, far to the north, if all went well in the initial battle.

Meanwhile, Arthur was in command of the remainder of the fleet as it entered the calm waters of the channel between the island and the mainland. The glassy waters leading to Calmar were shining like polished silver in the sunlight. The island also served to block the wind, so the great woollen sails of the Dane fleet flapped and sagged as the vessels slowed to a crawl.

Arthur saw a beacon erected on a stone tower as it was set alight by Geat defenders. The day was new and crisp, with autumn nipping at the Dene heels. The waterways would soon wear a crust of ice and winter storms would force all seafarers to settle into makeshift quarters for the winter or retreat to a place of sanctuary such as The Holding. But any retreat would provide Heardred with time to reorganise his Geat forces, so Arthur and Stormbringer were rolling the dice while they still had sufficient warriors and ships at their disposal.

Arthur watched another beacon flare into life on a distant hill and imagined the line of fires that would be burning across Gotland to warn the Geat king that marauders had sailed into Calmar. The first step in his complex plan had now been taken. He prayed that he had thought of every eventuality.

All the buildings of Calmar seemed to Arthur to be the colour of mud from his vantage point alongside Snorri at the rudder. As he ordered the sail to be lowered and the oars to begin their long and regular strokes, he looked at the longboats around him, all of whose crews were clearing their decks in preparation for combat. *Sea Wife* was leading an arrowhead formation that mimicked the flight of the wild geese that had passed above him earlier in their voyage and he marvelled at how men unwittingly copied the works of nature.

'God is the great master, Snorri,' Arthur murmured. 'He is the sailor whose ways we copy in our imperfect fashion. May the Good Lord guard us this day, not just for our sake, but for the lost children of Lund.'

Snorri had caught the depth of feeling in Arthur's whispered prayer. Although Snorri accepted that his master was an out-lander with odd fancies, the helmsman had never seen any evidence that Arthur was particularly religious. Then he shrugged. A little supernatural assistance couldn't hurt, since the small fleet was sailing into harm's way, not once, but twice. And the second time, the Dene force would be using Arthur's strange outlander tactics to ensure their survival.

Snorri snorted when he thought of those heavy rectangular shields. Standing in a line with the cursed things interlocked was hard work, as he had learned during the hours of practice back at the base camp. However Arthur was his master and had earned his respect. In addition, Snorri had come to like Arthur, so he would stand beside this strange Briton when the tortoise movement was required and not falter, even if he thought the whole strategy was crazy.

Along the smooth, silvery beach, some of the Geat ships were leaning to one side with the bottom of their keels buried in the sand, while other deeper-drafted vessels were moored to pilings constructed from whole tree trunks embedded deeply into the mud and sand of the bay.

As the Dene longboats mustered before the attack, Arthur had spoken directly to his captains to ensure their obedience to his orders.

'There will be no mercy for Geat warriors! But I'll not repeat Heardred's sins, so the women and children will be spared. Hear me, my captains! There will be no rape under my command. We are not greedy marauders who seek reparation from the Geat king. We will take what slaves we wish when the campaign is over, but I'll not leave seething hatred behind us to fuel the resentments of future generations. We go into battle for the children of Lund, and that shall be our battle cry!'

And then the race to destroy the Geat fleet began as the rowers took to their oars.

'Are the fire pots ready?' Arthur shouted down to Thorketil who had taken over part of the stern as his preparation area. The big man rose to his feet, his shaggy bear-fur collar making him look even more like a troll king than ever. The strappings on his wounded leg were even more obvious than usual as he struggled to keep his footing on the smooth deck.

'Aye, Master Arthur. The pots are filled with pitch, exactly as you ordered.'

'As we approach each vessel, send a lit fire pot into the widest part of the Geat trading ships. Pitch is difficult to extinguish, so one pot per ship should be sufficient, and the crews won't be expecting it. Row your hearts out now, brothers! The Geats know what we're about, so they're trying to move their ships out of danger.'

Arthur's voice was controlled, almost joyous, as he checked the shoreline and observed a clutch of small rowing boats burdened almost to the waterline by seamen intent on saving their vessels. But they were already too late.

Sea Wife drew close to a large vessel that was obviously designed to carry large cargoes of trade goods. Thorketil let out a wild, tribal call and swung a lit fire pot around his head on the end of its chain. At the furthest point of its swing, the Troll King let loose the pot with its trail of red hot sparks directly into the centre of the wooden ship. Within moments, fire gushed up in a long sheet as the decking caught alight.

'Well done, Thorketil. Now, on to the next!'

Arthur selected his next target from the moored vessels in what could only be described as a light-hearted mood. Negotiating *Sea Wife* through the shallow waters, Snorri marvelled at how boyish his master became whenever battle beckoned.

All in all, six ships were soon burning fiercely down to their waterlines while another twenty were in flames along the beach. Nor did Arthur spare the fishing boats or the one-man coracles.

Nothing that rode on Mother Water was permitted to survive on that day of fire.

Then the Briton turned his attention to the township and the farmlands beyond it.

The Dene longboats were soon lined up along the beach and, the moment the prows drove into the shingle, men leaped into the ankle-deep foam. They were holding their new shields with a little awkwardness, but were more than willing to use the iron as a weapon, as well as a protection. Sharpened, and at close quarters, the shield could be driven up into an enemy's throat or chin.

The Dene warriors charged into the town with their customary tribal cries to which were now added roars of sorrow for the children of Lund. The defenders had heard of the massacre of the children, because Heardred had ordered word of his feats to be spread throughout his kingdom. The townsmen paled as they realised their danger and hurried to find any objects that could be used as weapons.

Arthur had ordered that the town should be left unburned; he wished to secure a supply of food sufficient to last the Dene forces for several weeks. However, the off-shore breeze carried sparks from the burning vessels to adjacent vegetation where it inevitably caught alight. The noontime soon became scarlet from uncontrolled flames below a leaden sky that threatened the release of rain. But the gods turned their faces away from the town of Calmar, for no rain came.

Once the town had been taken, Arthur took possession of the Great Hall, a pretentious title for a mud-daubed structure with only a sod floor and a straw roof to keep out the inclement weather. The long room was dim, cold and cheerless, even when the fire pit was lit. Dust motes danced in the fitful afternoon light, while smoke filled the roof. Arthur's eyes began to sting from the moment he entered this grimy space, but as a head-quarters for a single day it would suffice.

The Dene secured the port and began to plunder those houses that remained intact with ruthless efficiency. The women, children and a small number of ancient grandfathers were herded into the headman's house where they huddled together in a sullen group. The smell of fear added its own distinctive reek to the miasma of woodsmoke, wet infants, sweat and closely packed unwashed bodies. When Arthur spoke to the guards, his nose wrinkled at the stink.

'These people don't seem to wash very often,' the guardsman joked, scanning the miserable sixty or so bodies packed into the small and draughty house.

'They wash and use the sweat-boxes, just like we do,' Arthur replied. 'But they're terrified and they reek from it. They think they're going to suffer for the fate of the children of Lund. They've heard all the details of how the Dene children were sold to brothels.'

The guard shrugged noncommittally. Arthur nodded to him and passed on, checking the town, the growing piles of plunder which were transferred to *Sea Wife* and several other vessels, and the stores of food which were being kept for use when the campaign began in earnest.

He issued his instructions to the skeleton crews who had agreed to man *Sea Wife* and the other plunder ships. Their task was to return to their safe harbour in Skania where the riches of Calmar and the Geat slaves taken in various raids would be held in a secure base camp. The emptied ships would then return to Calmar. As well as the plunder taken during the skirmish, Arthur also sent supplies of grain, cured meat and beer for use by the base camp guards if the campaign should fail. Even now that Calmar had been taken and secured, Stormbringer's people in the base camp could need supplies during the winter months, especially if some disaster should overtake the Dene force during the main battle that would soon begin.

The warriors were elated but, even so, Arthur insisted that sentries should be set in case Heardred had warriors in the vicinity whose presence was unknown to the Dene force. Then, tired, but still buzzing from the ease of his success, he slept on a makeshift bed of mouldy furs and dusty wool.

The long, uneventful night was sliding towards a grey morning when Arthur awoke with a jolt of fear as the voice in his head suddenly began to shriek. He rose out of his bedding with his bare chest shivering from the early morning cold. The town seemed to be still and secure through the shuttered window, although thin threads of smoke still rose from one of the hulks on the shoreline and the rows of ruined houses.

Deep in the shadows, he watched the muddy street outside. Intent and silent, he concentrated his attention on a dark object that passed across the road, skirted the holes of sucking mud and then joined another dark shape beside the entrance to one of the deserted houses. Slick as eels and as formless as smoke, two shapes disappeared into the house and the door was carefully closed behind them.

On hands and knees, Arthur moved silently along the length of the hall with the Dragon Knife held in his right hand. He remained in the shadows until he reached the steps that led upward to the hall doors where two Dene warriors stood on guard, yawning behind their hands.

'Stay still and don't turn around,' Arthur hissed. 'You're being watched by enemies who've breached our defences and are hidden in one of the buildings further up the street. They are in the mud-coloured hut with the stack of firewood next to the door. I don't want these men to be alerted. Act as casually as you can, but stroll back to the guardhouse as if nothing is happening and you're just going to check the perimeter. Do you understand me? Clench your fists behind your back if you do.'

Two sets of hands slowly went behind two strong backs and clenched into fists in response.

'There are at least two warriors hiding in the building, and there may be more of them in the adjoining house, the one with the sagging gate that's leaning against the picket fence. The infiltrators I saw were definitely interested in that building before they disappeared. Can you see the houses I'm talking about?'

The hands of the guards clenched in unison.

'When you leave here in a few minutes, move to your right along the centre of the street but stay away from those two houses. There could be more enemies holed up in other houses inside the perimeter. Your job is to warn the guard commander and alert our warriors. They must return here at speed and surround the house. I'll give the attack order when they are in position. Now go!'

With feigned nonchalance, the two guards moved off at a leisurely pace towards the makeshift barracks, as if they were completing their shift and were irritated by the late arrival of their replacements. Arthur made a mental note to discover how these Geat infiltrators had managed to bypass the Dene scouts and guards.

As he considered the punishments he would mete out to any sentries who had been asleep while on duty, three shadows made their way out of the ruined house across the street. They were followed by half-a-dozen more warriors who sprinted down the roadway towards the barracks, while the first three men headed towards the long hall which was undefended except for Arthur who, fortunately, was awake, unlike the half-dozen warriors who were his unofficial bodyguard. Snorri and his friends had been sound asleep when Arthur passed their pallets near the fire pit. Unless luck was with the Dene garrison, his warriors would be locked inside their own barracks and, by the torches that the infiltrators now carried with them, Arthur guessed that the enemy intended to set fire to the barracks building with the sleeping Dene warriors inside it.

'This is a very clever plan put together by some very brave men,' Arthur told himself as he prepared to confront the three men intent on destroying the hall.

Cautiously, the three men spread out to attack the building from three sides, but only the middle man approached the steps to the door of the hall. Inside the gloom of the doorway, Arthur cursed the stupidity that had made him leave his sword beside his pallet. Somewhere in the darkness in the centre of the building, a man coughed in his sleep and Arthur belatedly remembered Snorri and the other crew members of *Sea Wife* who would be taken unawares if he failed to raise the alarm. Because of his oversight, his men could die if they weren't warned.

'Awake! Awake! Awake!' Arthur roared. 'Enemies in the hall! Arm yourselves.'

Now that the time for pretence was over, the enemy at the main door charged up the steps with his sword drawn and his face disfigured by a rictus of fury. Arthur stepped out of the deep shadows behind the door and thrust out with the Dragon Knife at the dark shape that crossed the threshold. The weapon tasted blood, but the main force of the blow glanced off the Geat warrior's breast-plate with a slither of metal on metal.

Arthur grunted. Otherwise, the encounter was carried out in deadly silence. On bare feet, he edged into open space where he had room to manoeuvre, while the light from the open door, although fitful from a setting moon, outlined the enemy's face and form with a line of argent. All the while, Arthur used the point of the long knife like an extra sense to probe the air and the shrouded figure's defences in order to determine what he could of his enemy's ability.

After several minutes of feint and tentative probing, the attacker realised that Dene reinforcements must already be searching the empty houses between their barracks and the hall, so he knew he must despatch this irritating, half-dressed warrior without delay and press on to clean out the sudden swarm of enemy Dene who had invaded the town. With a screamed battle cry, the shrouded figure charged with his shield raised as a battering ram, while holding his blade ready to impale Arthur when he lost his balance.

But Arthur somersaulted away from the embossed shield. As the young man tumbled over, the Dragon Knife scythed out at thigh level, slicing through muscle until it struck the long leg bones. The force of the blow almost wrenched the knife out of his hands, but the cunningly designed hilt of the knife kept his fist in place.

The Geat grunted in surprise and pain. Arthur narrowly avoided an arc of blood and wondered if he had struck the great vein in his enemy's thigh during his knife stroke, but he had no time to dwell on it as the jet of blood slowed. The Geat lowered his shield to clutch momentarily at the wound, but Arthur's hands continued the attack independent of his conscious thoughts. The Dragon Knife sprang upward with all the force of his kneeling body, so the blade punched into the hollow under the Geat's chin, smashing the frail defences at the roof of the mouth before burying itself deep inside the enemy's brain.

The Geat hung above Arthur, with eyes suddenly blank and sightless. He yanked his blade free and then the body fell loosely, barely missing Arthur and pinning his legs to the ground.

As he struggled to free himself, he heard the sound of a desperate struggle from both the hall and the street outside. Then, in a flurry of woollen cloaks and drawn swords, the guard returned, dragging a single captive in their wake. Arthur pointed towards the sounds of affray and all the reinforcements, except for the two warriors guarding the captive, hurried to clean up the last of the infiltrators.

The captive had all the marks of a physical beating from his captors. His lip was split and one eye had already swollen shut, so he was forced to peer myopically out of the other.

'Who are you?' Arthur asked gently. His voice was conversational, but the Dene guards could sense the iron underlying the calm words.

The captive spat at Arthur's feet.

Arthur examined his boots to ensure that they weren't sullied and then casually slapped the man's face with a stinging blow.

'Let me explain something to you, my friend. You're a dead man, regardless of whether you speak or not. I refuse to act like your king, so I can assure you that I won't torture you, regardless of how offensive you might become. However, a full and frank explanation from you will earn you a good and honourable death.'

The Geat raised his shaggy head, his blue-green eyes sharp and knowing.

'And why should I believe you? I don't even know who you are.'

'I am Arthur pen Artor, the Last Dragon, and I am second in command to Valdar Bjornsen, who is known as the Stormbringer.'

Arthur spoke casually, as if the names he repeated were unexceptional. The Geat infiltrator widened his eyes in surprise, but said nothing as Snorri hurried into the room, followed by other members of the guard.

'You're safe, Arthur. Thanks to the gods! When I woke at your call, I was sure that you were sorely pressed. Unfortunately, we were forced to kill the rest of the intruders. I'd like to have kept at least one alive because it would have been useful to question him. But it's of no real matter, because you've bested us all with the one you've captured.'

Arthur shrugged with embarrassment.

'Not me, Snorri. One of the guards caught this man and I'm very grateful for his efforts.'

The guard who had captured the Geat blushed along his high cheekbones and was clapped on the back by his friends. Arthur sketched him a half-bow.

'You're more talkative than usual, Snorri. Where are the rest of your men?'

'I've ordered them to do a complete search of the village in case we've missed any of the intruders. It seems they were hiding and waiting for darkness so they could attack us when our guards became overconfident. They've discovered now that we're slightly better prepared than the children of Lund.'

'Indeed,' Arthur replied. 'What happened to our sentries? Did they fall asleep?'

'No, they didn't,' the captain of the guard stated bluntly. 'The infiltrators were well hidden and must have entered the village after our attack was completed. They came out of hiding at nightfall, once we were certain that we had secured the village. They attacked our guards in pairs by pretending to be Dene warriors in the darkness. It was a simple matter for them to slit the throats of our guards and hide the bodies. They killed the single guards at the port, the entry to the village and the headman's house. Later, they intended to re-form and attack the barracks and the hall. They thought to destroy us in our sleep, using fire as their weapon of choice. I suppose they considered flame a fitting punishment, since we had set fire to their vessels and the village.'

'It would have worked too, if not for you,' the Geat prisoner snapped in perfect Dene, and spat at Arthur once again. This time, Snorri backhanded the man, despite his bound hands, and a narrow trickle of blood escaped from the warrior's split lip.

Arthur looked directly into the eyes of the prisoner and smiled softly to demonstrate his self-control.

'My master, Stormbringer, plans to strike directly into Heardred's heart and make your king feel just as wretched as the children of Lund whom he took pleasure in humiliating. He has instructed me to commence the campaign against your king, to show him that we shall not sail away and leave Skania open to Geat attack. Stormbringer intends to make your king weep tears of blood in the few weeks until the first of the winter's snowfalls and then, in the spring, we will own your lands. It doesn't matter what I tell you now, my friend, because you will die in the morning. You'll be able to watch our attacks on the Geat lands from the place you occupy in the shades. I hope you derive some pleasure from our victories.'

The man was dragged away by the guards. As the captive was

being taken from the room, he heard Arthur ask Snorri to inform Stormbringer of the fate of the sentries who had been ambushed. Fortunately, the captive had no opportunity to see the confusion on Snorri's face.

'What—' Snorri only had time to get out one word before Arthur clapped a hand over the helmsman's mouth.

'Be quiet, Snorri. You've been an unwitting part of some trickery. I've told that Geat everything that I want him to pass back to Heardred, and all I need to do now is to ensure that he escapes in such a way that he is convinced that he gained this information through our stupidity. I can do without any intelligence we might have gained through his torture, because it isn't all that important to us. I believe he was a part of a small troop of Heardred's warriors who were in our vicinity and saw the smoke from the burning trade ships. They were far too few in number to be an actual raiding party.'

Snorri looked around the mean little hall with its cracked and splitting benches and the grime that coated every surface. The filth was so thick that it could be seen even in the half-light. Calmar might be a rich port, but the wealth hadn't filtered down to many of the common inhabitants.

'But how do you propose to organise the Geat's escape so he doesn't realise he's being tricked?' Snorri asked.

'I'll leave it to you and the captain of the guard to decide on the details, Snorri. I think you're quite capable of letting him escape without causing unnecessary suspicion on his part. Perhaps you should arrange for a short period of inattention on the part of our guards.'

Snorri looked nonplussed, but he and the Dene captain walked away to discuss how best to comply with Arthur's requirements. They were arguing over what quantity of beer would be needed during the coming campaign as they disappeared from view.

Arthur returned to his pallet to resume his sleep, considering how fortunate he was to be surrounded by men who so readily provided for his needs.

A short time later, during a moment of inattention on the part of a seemingly drunken guard supervising the captive's holding cell, the prisoner managed to strike him on the back of the head, a blow which felled the man to the ground. Immediately, the Geat broke into the open to sprint towards the shadows of the deep woods nearby. Within half an hour, he had found and released the dozen tethered horses that his companions had hobbled there before their infiltration of the village. Then, riding one horse and leading another as a change of mount, he galloped off into the pre-dawn light.

He swore to himself that Stormbringer and the arrogant Briton would pay for their destruction of Calmar.

The late morning sun was fitful with promises of the ugly winter to come. The Geat prayed that he'd see the Last Dragon again and have the privilege of watching the arrogant figure crawl on his belly like a broken snake.

Thoughts of revenge sustained him throughout the two days and nights that elapsed until he reached the Geat army – and the great plan began.

CHAPTER IV

THE BEST INTENTIONS

And he gathered them together into a place
called in the Hebrew tongue Armageddon.

The Bible, Revelations 16:16

Another grey day came late to Calmar as the nights lengthened
with the onset of the autumn winds. Arthur huddled in his furs
and wondered why he had come to this pass, a foreign mercenary
fighting for no money in a land that wasn't his own.

He dressed with care on this dismal morning, ensuring that
his armour was comfortable over his woollen shirt, for he
reasoned that he would have no time to change his clothing for
a week or more. His well-fitting leather trews, now showing
signs of wear, would suffice for the time being. His furs and a
heavy, waterproofed cloak completed his dress. With a sigh, he
strapped on his sword belt, picked up his helmet, found his
Roman shield and then squared his shoulders.

A flurry of dead leaves swirled around his feet in a small
whirlwind of rust and red. One red leaf attached itself to his
cuirass like a slash of fresh blood over his heart. As one gloved

hand brushed the leaf away, Arthur shivered in the sudden breeze. He could smell rain in the air which promised to make conditions on the march far nastier than the present chill. Birds were calling from a nearby oak, and ravens were resting on rooftops and cawing resentfully at their lost titbits from the Geat dead, whom Arthur had ensured had been rolled into pits in the town midden, away from the reach of scavengers.

It was time to finish what he had started. Snorri was waiting for instructions, his face eager considering the cold wind that ruffled his hair and blued the tips of his fingers.

'Assemble our captains, Snorri, for I intend to leave this place in two hours. Before then, I want to find one of the older men of Calmar who knows the terrain. I'm prepared to promise freedom to any of the prisoners who'll guide us to the religious community near the lakes that lie to the north of here. Find some potential volunteers and bring them to me, one at a time, so I can assess their suitability.'

'You seem very sure that someone will trade freedom for betraying their people, even after what we've done to their village,' Snorri replied with a wry grin. 'What if they refuse?'

Arthur shook his head. 'You're older than me, Snorri, but I'll wager I've seen more of the darker side of human nature than you have. People will act entirely out of character if they think that will buy them and their kin a little more of life. At the moment, the prisoners in this village don't know what we plan to do with them. Their nerves will be stretched taut, and they'll be fearful of what the future holds for them. Most of Calmar's survivors have lost family members and loved ones during the fighting too. And those women who have children will do anything to save them. I think one of the prisoners will assist us with what we need to know.'

Arthur set his bodyguard to work preparing the cleanest bench seats at the one table that was sound. Using cold water and a handful of sand, the men scrubbed the table top to remove at least some of the layers of grease and accumulated grime, and then sluiced it clean. The warriors finished off the task just as the first of Arthur's captains appeared at the hall entrance. None of the jarls complained that the table was wet, being accustomed to Arthur's strange penchant for cleanliness.

Before Snorri returned, the full complement of officers was present. Arthur called them to order and explained the reason for their presence.

'Calmar has been taken and the plunder from this victory is now ours to distribute among our people. Today, in less than two hours, we begin our march towards the religious community that lies to the north. I know many of you are Christian, so we'll spare their lives provided they choose to surrender. Nor will we destroy the precious books or relics in their scriptoriums if they should possess such things. However, the treasures held by the community will be forfeit to us. According to my captive, Beowulf Minor, the church and the village are wealthy. I have no doubt that his information is correct.'

The captains seemed content with his words, although one tall, red-headed warrior from the Jutland peninsula, who had lived his whole life under Saxon threat, asked what would happen to any Dene warriors who disobeyed Arthur's edict on the rape or murder of inhabitants of the enemy community.

'I will brook no disobedience, Roganvaldr. I'm your commander and I'll personally punish any man who disobeys my orders. Men who cannot discipline themselves are dangerous to us all, so be assured that my punishments will prove severe.'

'You may have some difficulty with rape,' one of Stormbringer's cousins rumbled jokingly and the captains laughed good-naturedly.

But Arthur was not yet done with the issue.

'I appreciate your sense of humour, Diarmaid,' Arthur continued without a trace of a smile. 'To be perfectly frank, my friend, I will certainly consider castration as a punishment, for I have no inclination for the flesh of other men.' Diarmaid laughed politely.

'But the problem is not what any miscreant does! It's the fact that one of our men should feel safe to defy my orders. In exactly the same way, you should expect to be obeyed by your warriors. The concept of self-discipline is difficult to understand for some of them, so stress that they will obey all orders during this campaign – without question!'

One of Roganvaldr's compatriots stood to speak, while the room was filled with the hubbub of raised voices. Arthur called for quiet in a voice that brooked no argument; the young man's face stained a bright red under the cold scrutiny of his commander.

'Speak out, young man. No one will think the worse of you, as long as you state your beliefs openly and honestly.' Arthur gave a quick smile that heartened the young warrior.

'What if a significant number of our men should refuse to obey their orders or, worse still, are slow to comply?' He coughed nervously, but stood his ground.

'It is possible that our whole force would be put at risk. We will be facing a stronger force than we can put into the field, so cowardly behaviour or a lack of resolve could kill all of us. Do you understand that, lad? You must stress to your men that we will survive if we obey our orders. Life or death – the choice lies with every man who marches with us.'

The jarls glanced carefully at each other, and Arthur noted that some of the men weren't quite able to meet his eyes.

'If you don't trust a man to obey your orders immediately and without demur, you must leave him behind. A small contingent of men must remain here to guard Calmar and the longboats anyway. This isn't a safe berth, for the Geat king may choose to clean out Calmar and burn our ships to ensure we have no means of escape. That is precisely what I would do if I were in Heardred's boots. However, he's not me, and that might be our edge.'

Arthur watched his captains begin to waver, so he pressed home his message.

'There are men under your commands who are good and honest warriors, but are unsuited to the demands I'm placing on them. These warriors are the very men who can be trusted to save our longboats if Calmar should come under attack during our absence. Protecting what we have won demands heroes, men who are prepared to die for their brothers in the field.'

Several of the jarls looked a lot happier after this explanation.

'You must understand the task that we are attempting, my brothers. Fewer than six hundred of our men must form a fighting square and defy Heardred as he throws his best troops at us. His warriors will probably outnumber us by two or three to one. He will do everything in his power to break us, while we must repel his assaults as best we can without stepping out of the line to retaliate. Many of our number will be killed, but worse than the fear of the Geat warriors will be the claims that we are cowardly curs who won't come out of our lines to fight the Geats as individuals.'

Arthur paused.

'I fought in a similar impossible line at the siege of Calleva

Atrebatum only five years ago. At the time, I was young and angry, for five hundred British warriors were sacrificed by our kings to lure our Saxon and Jute enemies into a trap. Some of my friends were only boys, and they were cut down like chaff on the hooks of the reapers, because they had no idea how to hold a combat line under pressure. I was so angry that I broke from the line and fought without a shield until two beloved friends risked their own lives to drag me back. I should have perished that day! I nearly killed my servant and my mentor and now I'm telling you the truth when I say there is no place for individual glory, or anger, when you are part of a shield wall.'

The stillness that followed was almost visible as it settled over the seated men.

'I will allocate you and your crews to all four sides of our fighting square and I thank you now for the pains that you will suffer during this battle. I will command the northern perimeter. You, Roganvaldr, will command the western side which will not only face Geat warriors, but will have to bear the shock of the cavalry attack on our enemy. You, Thorquil, have the doubtful honour of holding the western side, from which direction Stormbringer will attack. You, Talorc, will command the southern perimeter, and in case you think I've given you the easiest position, you should remember that Heardred is a dog, a mongrel that always tries to attack from the rear.'

He paused again to ensure his jarls were giving him their full attention. 'Should I die in the front line, you will take your orders from Snorri, who knows my mind. Believe always that I will never ask you and your warriors to do something that I'm not prepared to execute myself.'

The jarls were impressed with this last argument and those who weren't allocated to a particular point in the square began to jostle for positions that attracted them. Arthur set Snorri to work taking notes of those who desired set positions in the lines. He had been surprised and pleased to discover that Snorri was literate, because he was now able to depend on the laconic helmsman to keep notes for him, even though the runes used in the northern climes were gibberish to Arthur.

Eventually the meeting was over, and the jarls scattered to select those men who would be detailed to stay behind to guard the fleet while the remaining warriors must be organised into the marching order that would be followed during the trek to the religious village.

As the last captain departed, Snorri informed his commander that he had found a potential guide. Their turncoat was an old fisherman with no kinfolk, a man who had no intention of placing himself at risk for his peers.

'He's a man with a deep bitterness in his soul against his Geat neighbours. Traitors usually sicken me, but I like him,' Snorri explained laconically.

'Show him in then, Snorri. We can give him the benefit of the doubt until such time as we learn more about him and his motivation.'

The elderly fisherman who was ushered into Arthur's presence was a wrinkled gnome of a man somewhere in his fifties, but still sprightly. His seamed and sunburned skin had the texture of a tortoise's and his eyes were very dark and small. He was quick-moving and limber, even though he lacked height. Arthur realised that the man was unlike any other Geat he had met in these lands, for the short fringe of hair that encircled the freckled brown dome of his hairless skull was almost black.

Snorri was correct in his assessment. Every line on the fisherman's face had been deepened by sadness and bitterness.

As another outsider, Arthur knew that this small man was friendless and had suffered his whole life from the slurs and criticisms of his neighbours.

Now the turncoat's actions made sense. Arthur immediately considered how difficult it must have been for this short dark man to be reared in a country such as Gotland. The young Briton knew that the Dene believed fair colouring was far preferable to raven locks and brown eyes. Even now, Snorri's lips twisted contemptuously as the little fisherman sat, uninvited, on a bench seat.

'What is your name, grandfather? I will need to know something about you if I am to trust you.'

The wizened little man grinned engagingly, revealing several brown teeth that were still embedded in his gums. Arthur had to steel himself to overcome the natural advantage of charm that this Geat fisherman had been given by nature. Perhaps this was the only attribute that had made his younger life bearable.

'I'm Ivar Svensen, your highness,' the old reprobate answered. Arthur's lips twitched in response, although he knew the fisherman's pretence of being a harmless old bucolic was false.

'I'm not a king, Ivar. You'll call me Master Arthur at all times, and nothing else. I'll not wear other men's honours.' Arthur tried to look stern, but this old man had a wicked, comic eye and an adroit tongue. It would be easy to forget that this old man was dangerous – but Arthur was no such fool.

'Whatever pleases you, Master Arthur. I've been a fisherman for nigh on fifty years, like me father before me! I can't even remember me mother – who must've been foreign.' He laughed raucously. 'Look at me! Either me mother or me father had to be an outlander, didn't they? Let's say I'm not the usual type of fisherman around these parts. At any road, I wasn't having any kids to share the benefits of bein' different.'

Arthur thought he detected an edge of anger in the fisherman's voice. For a short moment, something hot and burning had peered from Ivar's pupils.

'In the last few years, I haven't been able to catch heavy loads of fish the ways I used to do when I was a younger man. Aye! And I can't live on charity, even if anyone were offering it – which they aren't! I hate my neighbours in Calmar and most of my fellow Geats who've made me life miserable for nigh on fifty years. I'll tell you what you want to know for my life – and for five gold coins.'

Ivar's effrontery in demanding payment endeared him to the Briton. Ivar licked no man's boots, even though it meant that he went hungry. Arthur decided that he sincerely hoped the old man would prove to be worthy of trust. Snorri's instincts had been accurate.

'You know you won't be able to return to Calmar after our little jaunt. Your companions in the village will know that you've agreed to serve us.'

'Aye! But I've had my fill of Calmar at any road. I think I'll try my luck on Rugen Island. Apparently I've got kinfolk there. The gold will set me up. I won't be rich, but I won't starve. By Loki's balls, I can always survive by catchin' some fish.'

'That's true, Ivar. Now! I want you to begin by telling me all you know about the large religious community that lies to the north. I plan to attack it. I don't intend to destroy it, or to harm the monks. However, I'm going to tweak the tail of your king once again, because I want him to come after me and try to destroy me.'

'Heardred's not my king, Master Arthur, but I can tell you

that the religious community is more decent than most. I was sick with the lung disease, you see. Even though I had to walk for days, I made my way to the gates of their precinct, as they call it, but I was too weak to drag meself any further. The monks took me in, cared for me and then prayed for my soul. I don't think the prayers did much good, but I ain't coughing no more so I don't want you to kill the little fathers.'

'I won't. But I intend to plunder their church to gain Heardred's attention. I want him to attack us in the hope of gaining his revenge on me. I can swear to you that I have no argument with true men of God.'

Arthur crossed his heart like a child and this homely action caused Ivar to smile. Something about this intense young man appealed to the fisherman. Perhaps it was the fact that he, too, was an outsider. Perhaps his intention to kill King Heardred also appealed to Ivar, a man who knew how to hate.

'If you can promise to do your best to protect the little fathers, then I'll be your man.'

The old man's face was transfigured with a wide, gap-toothed grin and Arthur realised he was excited at the prospect of experiencing new things.

At Arthur's request, the fisherman used a stick to scratch out a plan of the route to the religious community on the sod floor. He then described the layout of the buildings that housed the priests and the lay members of the monastery. His advice was already proving invaluable.

Arthur sent Ivar off with one of his crewmen to collect any of the fisherman's personal belongings that hadn't been destroyed in the initial attack on Calmar. They were warned that Arthur intended to leave within the hour.

* * *

Somehow, the jarls created miracles and five hundred and fifty men were made ready to march, each loaded down with their rectangular shields, shared tents, a week's supply of rations and their weapons. Dene warriors were always reluctant to travel on foot, so a general air of discontent settled over the massed group of men who were divided, as previously, into squads based on ship's crews as a basic fighting unit.

Another fifty-three men leaned casually against Calmar's walls on the narrow palisade, offering ribald comments concerning the attack force's anatomy. They had been selected by the jarls to remain behind to guard the longboats, the slaves and protect the town from any more brigands.

Arthur climbed on top of a large, flat rock so he could survey his troops as well as the rear guard. He began to address the men under his command.

'Some of you probably resent having to stay behind to guard this town, but every warrior who marches today will be in your debt, because your presence here ensures we have an escape route from the cesspit where we will fight the next battle. I'm certain that you will keep our longboats safe, regardless of enemy attacks, so you can be assured that you'll earn an equal share of any plunder that is taken by the main body. As for glory, we were attacked only a few hours ago, so there is a strong chance that it could happen again.'

A cheer began to rise from the assembled warriors as they absorbed the details of Arthur's generosity.

'And you won't have to lug those heavy shields over hills and rivers,' Arthur added with a boyish grin.

Men slapped each other's shoulders and a festive air gradually settled over the troops who would remain to guard Calmar.

'As for the men who march with me, we are travelling to our

destination like a tethered goat to draw wild cats and wolves from their winter lairs. They will want to tear us to pieces. Heardred will see the plundering of the religious community as a direct insult to his rule. He will see our number and believe that he can crush us with ease. He'll not check the landscape, which I will have chosen to suit our requirements, rather than his. He'll not consider that we have reinforcements at our disposal. As a commander, Heardred tends to make snap decisions based on his own values, and so he believes we have come north in search of plunder. But we have come for revenge! It is my intention to crush Heardred for the sake of Dene pride, for Dene children sold to whorehouses and for his cowardly attacks on unarmed villagers. We will survive his treachery and we will not surrender or run from his warriors until Stormbringer arrives at the battleground with his thousand men and his cavalry. We will prevail! And we will summon our collective wills until Heardred crumbles – and then we shall send him to his death!'

An involuntary cheer rose from the men spread out around him. Arthur gave his jarls the order to move out and the Dene troops with their single wagon of supplies began the long march into the north.

Thorketil had elected to make a supreme sacrifice and remain in Calmar. Knowing he could never keep up with the column, he vowed to be Arthur's eyes and ears by commanding the small occupying force. But Arthur knew that he would miss his friend in the days to come.

The town of Calmar had possessed some horses owned by the headman and his sons, but the beasts had been badly treated and were far from young. The strongest of them had been selected to pull the wagon, but Arthur refused to use one as a mount, although he offered one to Ivar, because of the fisherman's advanced age. Sensibly, Ivar accepted a spavined old horse, although he knew that he, the traitor, would stand out when the Dene troops were inevitably discovered.

Arthur set a withering pace at the head of the column, which was led by the crew of *Sea Wife*. The Dene warriors were mostly long-legged, so they could cover large tracts of land with relative ease, despite being burdened with their supplies. Arthur's decision to march alongside his men was wise, for it earned him respect at little cost.

The whole column moved as one, while covering nearly as much ground as the legions would have done under Caesar.

Arthur watched the landscape unfold and marvelled at the difference in the soil and the terrain compared with the islands of the Dene.

Once the coast had been left behind, the plains began. Arthur saw their potential for farming and their use as rich granaries for the Geat farmers and landowners. Too many of the Geat warriors considered tilling the earth to be beneath them, but the Dene were living proof that warriors could be farmers, landowners, fishermen and artisans as well. This windswept, sighing land of long grasses, punctuated by the occasional field of stubble, should have been rich, managed and settled. But, half-wild, it brooded under a dying sun while ghostly moons rose to share the sky when night slowly settled over the land.

Undeterred, Arthur kept his men on the move, although their muscles were beginning to howl under the strain of constant movement.

'Ivar! I want you!' Arthur called. Within seconds, the old man had ridden up to him.

'How may I serve, Arthur?' Snorri took immediate offence at the fisherman's sarcastic tone of voice. His hand strayed to the hilt of his sword, a movement that Ivar spotted immediately. 'My apologies if I'm curt, master, but an old man's bones hurt when he's on a beast with a bony spine under his arse.'

'You could always walk,' Snorri suggested silkily.

'Enough!' Arthur's words cut them off. 'You know this terrain, Ivar, so I need you to find a place where we can set up camp for the night. I intend to use some fires tonight so we can let the villagers know our column is on the move.'

Ivar peered off to his right. The hard life of a fisherman had made his observations acute and one gnarled arm immediately pointed towards a distant smudge, a knoll that hardly rose above the plain.

'Over there in that copse of trees. You'll be a little higher than the rest of the plain and there's some shelter there that'll protect you from the rain that's coming. I seem to remember that there's a stream as well that cuts around the base of the rise. If you're a Geat with a mind to notice, your fires should be seen for miles.'

'Well done, Ivar. You've managed to anticipate my needs.' He smiled across at Snorri. 'Pass the word, my friend. We'll eat and sleep on the knoll tonight.'

With renewed enthusiasm, the Dene troop set their sights on the distant slopes and the promise of rest.

With long, loping strides, the column devoured the miles to the knoll, where the crews set up their individual bivouacs with the speed of hungry and tired men. After a full year under the command of the Last Dragon, they knew his ways well and individuals from each crew began the perimeter patrols that would ensure their security. Within fifteen minutes, the balance of the warriors had begun preparing their encampment by raising tents, finding suitable stones for fire pits, collecting clean water and foraging for firewood. Arthur watched with satisfaction as his junior officers carried out their tasks with pride and skill.

'They'll never respond to the beat of their officer's commands like the ancient Romans did, Snorri, but in their individualistic fashion they show the same sense of discipline. I'm confident now that our gamble is actually going to work. Would you tell the jarls to ensure we place some of our sentries in the trees? It's hard to sneak up on a lookout when he's above you. Once the sentries are in position, they must remain there and only come down on the orders of their own jarl. There must be no exceptions to these instructions. Is that clear, Snorri?'

The helmsman nodded, but his expression suggested that he was affronted his commander deemed such precautions necessary.

'If the men should query my orders, tell them I lack all trust in the vagaries of good fortune.'

On a sudden whim, Snorri asked an impertinent question. 'How old are you, master? You always speak like a seasoned warrior, but your face is still unlined.'

Arthur had to think about his answer for a few seconds. He had been eighteen when he had been captured on the road to Onnum, while his dead friend, Eamonn, had only been seventeen. The girls had been twelve. 'By my calculation I'm barely twenty-two! Not that age makes any difference in this world in which we live. I was in my first battle at thirteen and I killed my first Saxon when I was still a young boy of seven.'

Snorri winced and said no more, but he wondered where the joy in Arthur's young life had fled. On odd occasions, the helmsman saw a wicked sense of humour in his commander's eyes. He had also viewed Arthur's generosity to defeated enemies

again and again. Snorri was far more observant than many of
his contemporaries would believe. Arthur's sense of humour, his
acute sense of analysis and his generosity told Snorri that
his captain was a very unusual young man.

A cold, wet night followed their warm evening meal, but
inside their leather tents the Dene warriors mentally thanked
their commander for forcing them to lug their equipment on
their backs in the Roman fashion. As consistent rain fell during
the early morning, the warriors remained snug and dry on pallets
of freshly cut grass.

Even the cries of a hunting owl lacked the menace that would
normally crush their optimism. Although they knew that death
was on the wing, it came for other, less-provident souls, for
they had placed their trust in Arthur as the Last Dragon and
Fortuna's favourite.

Three days of marching improved nobody's mood because the
autumn weather had decided to worsen in a concerted rush.
Light, freezing rain told the Dene column that this whole
enterprise was being conducted far too late in the year. The sun
was scarcely in the sky by mid-morning when it would finally
break through the charcoal cloud cover. The wet wool rubbed
unhappy thighs raw, and the dampness crept under leather
tunics, cuirasses and even penetrated the men's heavy gloves.

Because their presence had probably been noted already,
Arthur permitted his men to draw what comfort they could
from fire. Hot food always gave a warrior a more cheerful view
of a campaign, and every nearby farm was a potential source of
fresh provisions. His jarls would obey him if he forbade pillage,
but that route led to resentment. Better that he should instruct
his warriors to take only enough to meet their immediate

requirements and leave the farmers the bulk of their livestock to ensure that the families survived the coming winter. Arthur had no desire to foment life-long enmity between the Dene and the Geat populace.

The Geat farmers, after an initial period of terror, were pathetically grateful for the Dene forbearance. Heardred had allowed his men to strip the farms bare and left famine in his wake, so the farmers hoped that all future invaders would pursue Arthur's generous policies.

On the third night, the column halted on a low ridge over-looking a long valley. Off to the left in the far distance, Arthur could see a large lake, while to the right a smaller but still substantial finger of water obviously provided a plentiful supply of fresh water to the rich countryside. Narrow trails of smoke rose from a fold in the long plain.

'Does that smoke rise from the homes of your little fathers, Ivar?' Arthur pointed towards the densest concentration of smoke.

The gnarled fisherman had dismounted and was in the process of checking his limbs to ensure his muscles still worked.

'Aye, boyo, that's where the little fathers have their hospice and their apothecary. Only Loki knows where the folks in this place would be without them. They cure as many as die, which is more than can be said for their prayers. Hold to your word now, boy!'

As this was the longest speech that Ivar had made so far, Arthur decided that the old fisherman genuinely cared for the members of the religious community.

The men ate cold rations for the evening meal, for fires would now be clearly visible during the long night. Immediately afterwards, the jarls were instructed to attend Arthur's tent so he could outline the final details of his plans of attack. The commander's accommodation was cramped and reeked of wet fur, wool and sweaty feet but the leaders came willingly, knowing that the tent would be lit by an oil lamp.

'We'll attack the community at dawn. As I have outlined before, this attack is a feint and has only one purpose, although any plunder we find will be nice.' The jarls laughed politely, but Arthur could tell that they were pleased.

'We are using this attack to draw Heardred out from the safety of his northern fortress to fight us on ground of our choosing. We have no reason to kill harmless farmers and priests to achieve our ends, so we'll only take sufficient life to secure the surrounding village and place it under our control. The plunder that is ours for the keeping includes any gold, silver or reliquaries that come into our hands. We will also take enough food to augment our supplies. But I stress that we will leave most of the community intact. For effect, we shall burn two buildings only, namely the barn used for the animals in winter and the priests' refectory. They don't need these buildings for their survival during the winter, but the damage will look far worse than it is. We don't kill any of Ivar's *little fathers*, the women or children. I've given my word to the Geat fisherman – and I'll not knowingly break my oath.'

Rufus Olaffsen raised his dishevelled head with its new threads of white. His tightly curled beard was bristling with indignation.

'None of our warriors will cause you to break your oath, Arthur, for these men know what is required of them. But what of Heardred? Or, more to the point, where is Lord Stormbringer?'

'Stormbringer's column made their landfall before we came ashore, so he reached his base earlier than we did. He plans to beach his longboats to the north of Calmar at a place which is much closer to our destination than our starting point. Stormbringer's out there . . . in the forest to the east of us, so his warriors are dug in, invisible and waiting. They can be here by forced march in half a day – no time at all.'

Several of the jarls grinned like grizzled wolves and licked their lips as if they could taste blood on their muzzles. Others considered how long half a day might seem if they were locked in combat within the confines of a shield wall.

'As for Heardred, he's coming to meet us! His pride won't allow him to overlook an attack so deep within his lands, or the burning of his trade fleet. Judging by his actions at Lund, Heardred expects us to act as he would, if he were in our boots. He thinks we'll make a lightning-fast raid into his lands and then retreat with our spoils. When he discovers that our force is fewer than six hundred in number, he'll be convinced that he has us between his thumbnails, to crack like lice.'

Several of the jarls winced.

'But we won't crack, will we?' Rufus answered dourly.

The other jarls were more animated and raised a tentative cheer.

'No! For Heardred's amusement, I'm prepared to play the part of a foolish barbarian, and lure him to engage with our force. He'll come roaring at us from at least two sides, just like the Geat warriors did at the mouth of the Vagus River. But that won't matter to us, for our warriors are aware of what they have to do.'

'Aye, Arthur,' Snorri agreed. 'Rufus has drilled our warriors mercilessly and each man knows that the success of our defence will depend on individuals acting in concert.'

Arthur felt relief that his complex plan would soon be put

into action, for he was tired of the cold weather. Strangely, he was missing Ingrid and her children, and he longed to see Blaise and Maeve again.

'For now, all we can do is encourage our crews to sleep. After tonight, there will be little chance of rest until Heardred is dead and his army has been destroyed.' As Arthur spoke the dragon's fire glowed in the pupils of his eyes.

Snorri watched quietly while Arthur tossed Ivar a leather pouch that clinked. Ivar checked each gold coin and bit into it, showing a wise man's distrust of glib words when actions spoke obvious truths.

'Snorri will requisition enough food for you to travel to the coast and find a boat that will take you to Rugen Island – or wherever your heart desires. I wish you well, Ivar! You've kept your word and I'll do my best to keep mine.'

Ivar stared out into a darkness lit by a large orange moon. In the far distance, white-topped mountains marked a jagged horizon that formed a prison wall holding back the glaciers and their walls of green ice and black stone. He shuddered involuntarily.

'I wish you luck, Arthur of the Britons. We'll not meet again if I've anything to do with it, because death follows wherever you travel. But you're a good lad for all that you're a born killer. The Geat king would be a fool to stand against the Last Dragon, but I'll bet my left ball that he proves to be an idiot. I'll listen for word of you!'

'And I of you, Ivar. My hand on it, for I'll never raise it against you and yours.'

Ivar was led away by Snorri with an anticipatory spring in his steps that belied his age and the swellings in his joints.

Arthur stared out towards the ominous line of mountains and felt danger scratch at the inner walls of his skull. That night, sleep was elusive.

The Dene attacked the religious community just on dawn, but the monks were already praying in the chapel.

The town had been easy to quell and few bodies were cast into the midden for the scavengers. Most of the Dene warriors remained in the lower part of the town to search out all items of value, while Arthur went to the church precincts with fifty men.

The Geat monks seemed to expect that they would be slaughtered at their devotions, and the air hummed with the combined prayers of thirty men.

But Arthur could still recall the small town of Spinis in Britain with a monastery and nunnery on its outskirts. The cruelty he had seen there was burned indelibly into his mind. He had been little more than a youth and, in company with his foster-father, had placed himself under the command of King Bran, who was attempting to relieve the siege of Calleva Atrebatum from an attacking army of Saxons and Jutes. His foster-father, Bedwyr, had shown him where the holy men and women had been tortured and slaughtered at prayer for the amusement of a war-party of Jutes.

Arthur could still remember the stink of old, corrupted death and see the agonised face of one huge priest who had protected another prelate with his own body, again and again, regardless of the blows that were delivered to cause unbearable agony. Mercifully, when the spectacle of such passive courage had palled with the Jutes, the two men had been slain to put them out of their misery. Men and women of God in many northern lands had good reasons to expect cruelty and depravity from barbarians and pagans alike.

The precincts of the community were large and the fat beasts in the fields, rows of cabbages waiting to be harvested, apple-laden trees and collections of beehives suggested a farm that was productive and wealthy. The chapel itself was small and unpretentious, much like a simple long-hall, but light flooded in from small apertures set into the walls. Men in dark-dyed homespun kneeled and prayed on the cold stone floors, their hands folded in front of them.

Arthur unerringly identified the abbot of the community as the priest stood at the simple wooden altar. The abbot raised his tonsured head to watch as the stranger approached. Abstractedly, Arthur noted the Aryan cut of the priest's hair and realised that he rejected the trappings of Rome. The priest had no fear in his eyes, only a deep well of acceptance.

'I'm of the Christian faith, Father, so I'll permit you and your fellow servants of God to live, subject to you telling me where the church plate and its scrolls are kept. I command a large force of Dene warriors whose attitudes to piety are often different from mine and yours. You must remember, Father, that nothing is worth more than the service you give to the dying and diseased of this land. That is your salvation, so I beg you to obey me in this matter. In return, I will set you all free, along with every patient in your infirmary, once I have what I seek from you and your town.'

The abbot was a young-old man with a plump, cherubic face and a pair of intense blue eyes. These same eyes scrutinised Arthur with disconcerting shrewdness.

'Why?' The single word filled the silence.

'Would you prefer that you and your people should perish

because of your curiosity? I am a Briton, if that means anything to you. Your distant cousins from Jutland and Saxony are burning churches and killing innocent priests and nuns because our clergy won't fight back when attacked. The northerners steal food and precious objects, simply because they don't perceive my people to be either courageous or even human. But I'm not Jute, or Saxon, or Geat. If you wish, you may consider that God has melted my barbarian heart.'

The abbot muttered a short prayer in Latin. Tired of denying the educated part of his nature, Arthur replied in the same tongue, except his accent was far purer than the prelate's provincial one. The man's eyebrows rose as he betrayed his comic surprise. A barbarian warrior who spoke the purest Latin?

'You're an educated man, sir. Will you give me your word on this sacred fragment of the scriptures that was brought to this place from Toulouse near to a century ago? You may be sure that God will know if you lie.'

'I'll know if I lie! I am the Last Dragon and, as you may have heard, the children of Lund were captured, imprisoned and raped on my account on the orders of King Heardred of the Geats. I seek my revenge on *him* alone.'

Arthur's face was flinty with a suppressed fury. Like most persons of power in the kingdom of the Geats, the plump and freckled abbot, Eomar, had heard of the Dene attack on Skania and had been told of Heardred's revenge. The pious churchman had prayed for the souls of the children of Lund out of feelings of communal guilt, feeling a deep sense of shame at what his king had done to the innocents but, for now, he eyed this young Briton with some doubt. How this Last Dragon had become the weapon of the Almighty confused Eomar – and frightened him.

'Gold, silver and precious objects only have the value that the world places on them. These metals are good for little but human adornment or pride, since they are far too soft for practical use. You may take our chalices and plate, our reliquary cases and the boxes that contain our scrolls. Simple polished wood will suffice to replace what you have taken, but I ask that you leave us the finger bones of our saint and the religious books that bear the holy word of God. Do you agree?'

'Happily, Abbot. Like you, I don't lust after gold and precious stones, so the religious scrolls will remain in safe hands.' Arthur's stern countenance concealed his relief that so much had been won with no loss of life.

The abbot showed the Dene jarls how to access the trapdoor in the chapel floor. Below, in darkness lit only by an oil-soaked torch, the bodies of their dead brothers from the priesthood slept for eternity. Here, deep inside the crypt, the abbot had secreted several platters, chasubles and some fine golden chalices. The cavern was full of shadows and superstition, so Arthur's warriors stripped the crypt of whatever wealth they could find in relative silence.

What an appropriate place to hide their valuables, Arthur thought. But that means the priests knew we were coming! He asked Eomar as much; the abbot smiled deprecatingly in response.

'The ordinary people care for us insofar as we minister to their souls and their bodies. We were warned yesterday by a farm boy. He seemed to think you were odd barbarians because you only killed the populace when you were forced into doing so. After I had prayed for God's guidance we decided to stay, but to hide our treasures. For safety's sake, you understand.'

'You're a true man of God,' Arthur replied ambiguously. 'Collect your patients and some food, and then you may depart.

You have one hour. Don't look back when you leave, Eomar, and don't attempt to return for seven days.'

Then he turned to Snorri.

'Begin the search of the community, Snorri. Take a share of all their food, and confiscate any precious objects that in his haste the good abbot has forgotten to mention.'

Outside, Arthur pondered the possibility that he could have made a fatal error. His squeamishness regarding the farmers and their respective fates had allowed a warning to be sent to this small but wealthy community. But, even if Eomar sent word to the Geat king that the Last Dragon was planning a trap, the abbot had no idea that a thousand men were hidden in the woods and were no more than half a day's march away.

And so, two buildings in the compound were quickly set alight, leaving black smoke to stain the cold blueness of the sky where it would tell Heardred that his enemy had foolishly remained within his lands. The smoke rose straight up into a windless sky as it waited to deceive the unwary. And Arthur prayed that he hadn't brought his force to ruin.

All he could do now was wait.

CHAPTER V

THE SHIELD WALL

They have sown the wind, and . . . they shall reap the whirlwind.

The Bible, Proverbs 612:36

Can the Ethiopian change his skin . . . or the leopard his spots?

The Bible, Proverbs 605:16

Arthur had chosen the ground carefully. The landscape was flat and the soft long grasses underfoot were perfect to disguise man-traps; water was nearby, so the warriors could wash themselves and clean their hair; the land sloped upward towards the centre of the encampment, so the warriors slept in apparently random groups, but every man was only a few feet away from his proposed position in the shield wall; and Snorri had set a small pile of white stones at each corner of the planned fighting square, so the sides of the shield wall would be readily visible to each warrior, wherever his position in the formation might be.

Arthur sent out an order that all crews should light fires during the night and enjoy the edible spoils taken from the farms and the religious community. But he let all men know that any warrior who drank wine, mead, beer or cider too deeply would be shamed in the eyes of his fellow Dene forever and would be deemed untrustworthy.

'At least we'll die with full bellies,' Roganvaldr joked with Beren, his much-younger second-in-command. They were lying on their backs staring up at a night sky so full of stars that midnight was almost as bright as day.

'Do you really think we'll die here?' Beren asked with a slight catch in his young voice. An aristocrat, he had been blooded on the Jute borders in small skirmishes, but he was still a boy at heart. Roganvaldr remembered his own formative years, so answered Beren more kindly than was his habit.

'Hell's a sweet furnace, boy! We all have to die sometime, but the important questions are why, when and how. It may well be that we'll die tomorrow for the simple reason that we intend to revenge ourselves for the murders of our brothers in Skania. And as for how it is done? I'm not too keen on allowing those fucking Geats to attack us and insult us. But even so, I won't break the shield wall and shame my ancestors, even if it seems like a fool's game to me.'

The stars seemed like pin-holes of different sizes in a jet-black curtain through which the argent skies of heaven could be glimpsed.

'If we are to meet our fate in this battle, we must die with our faces to the enemy and with our wounds on the front of our bodies. Then your mother and your sweetheart . . .'

Roganvaldr almost crowed with amusement for Beren had blushed a deep red up to his corn-yellow hairline.

'Your beloved women will weep for you and tear at their faces with their nails, but they'll be proud, for the man they loved was honourable until his heart stopped beating in his chest.'

'What good am I to them if I'm dead?' Beren muttered, and Roganvaldr remembered with a pang how agonising life had been when he had been a young man.

'They will be comforted by your courage, Beren, for they will be envied by less fortunate women and you'll become an example to other members of your family as the courageous young man who stood with the Last Dragon at the shield wall, for the honour of the Dene race.'

Roganvaldr almost believed his own words.

'I'll take my chances, as will we all, because the Last Dragon hasn't steered us wrong yet. Watch him, Beren. You will meet many men in your life who will seem to be his equal in skill and fighting prowess, but they'll rarely equal him for cool-headed thinking.'

Roganvaldr examined his nails closely, and started to clean them with his eating knife.

Beren pursued his doubts, but Roganvaldr was weary of discussion.

'He's an extraordinary young man, so he'll not bide in the Dene lands forever. Men such as he are born for greater purposes than to be the captain of a longboat. You would do well to learn everything you can from the Last Dragon while we have the opportunity.'

'He's not much older than I am, Master Roganvaldr. Besides, this ground is too flat. My old father swears that battles are fought best on high ground.'

'Your old father never fought battles in this way, Beren, so go to sleep. I'm tired of your gibble-gabble. We won't get any rest until Master Stormbringer relieves us, so we have to grab as much as we can while we still have the chance.'

Beren began to speak again, but Roganvaldr had already turned away and closed his eyes. His breathing soon came in little rumbles.

Beren lay awake, beset by tangled thoughts and nameless fears.

Morning came late, long after the warriors were alert and stirring. A light rain was falling, so fires were difficult to keep alight; most of the warriors merely dressed themselves in their tents while they waited disconsolately on the water-logged plain for the enemy to arrive and engage them.

But Heardred and the Geat army did not come.

At noon, under a weeping sun, the men snatched portions of cold food while they pretended to be busy, so Arthur put them to work, digging ditches around their position.

Germanus had explained to him as a callow youth how waiting for the start of a battle required a warrior to be ready to fight and kill at a moment's notice. The body became highly sensitive, every muscle quivering and ready to react. This *state of readiness*, as Germanus called it, could be dangerous and destructive if it was permitted to go on for too long, so wise commanders kept their men's minds and bodies alert, but fully occupied.

The exercise gave the nerve-stretched warriors something to do and provided an area where attackers could be contained beyond the shield wall. To Arthur's surprise, Snorri was aghast.

'Have we abandoned any pretence of being simple marauders, master? Surely, if we stay in one place for days on end and continue to dig into the landscape, we are demonstrating that we are waiting for Heardred to come and attack us. Heardred may be stupid, but even he might guess a trap is being sprung here.'

Snorri was familiar now with Arthur's constant mental gymnastics; he was accustomed, too, to Arthur's charm so was less likely to be manoeuvred into acquiescence by his master.

For Arthur's part, he still missed the companionship of Eamonn, his friend, after the young man's untimely death at the Battle of Lake Wener. Now, he yearned to share his thoughts with an equal again; many people were either too intimidated or too charmed by Arthur's size and intellect to contradict him.

Since the loss of Eamonn, Snorri had gradually become more important in Arthur's daily life because of his irony, quick wit and sardonic sense of humour. Best of all, Snorri seemed immune to Arthur's inherited glamour. Snorri could refuse to believe Arthur, and showed his incredulity by a simple raised eyebrow. The only drawback to their friendship was the inequality in their respective standing.

'That's what I like about you, Snorri, you're blunt and you always manage to tell me in advance what other people are likely to be thinking.' Arthur grinned and clapped Snorri hard on the back.

Gently alerted, Snorri grinned in return. He listened carefully as Arthur explained his thoughts.

'When Heardred *does* come, he'll see us dug in and presume that we're daring him. Well! We are, aren't we? He'll be affronted, but he won't be deterred. Besides, if he's not coming immediately, we may as well make life as difficult as we can for our enemy.'

'True!' Snorri replied. 'In any case, we could use some timber and tinder to set fires in the ditches and to make man-traps. If we're going to relinquish the pretence of returning to Calmar, it makes sense to consolidate our defences as best we can. The forest is some distance away, so is it worth sending men on a foray for lumber? They could find themselves caught in the open, especially if Heardred is foxing. In any event, we must be careful, Arthur. You're contemptuous of Heardred, but he's ruled his people successfully for many years, and the Geats make unruly subjects. He's not entirely a fool!'

Arthur frowned, and Snorri watched the mechanisms in his commander's brain click over as the young man considered Snorri's words of warning. Then his face cleared.

'You're right, Snorri! Our men must be kept gainfully occupied, so call for volunteers to take the wagon to that copse of thick trees over to the east. They'll have to take about six other warriors with them to maintain a lookout. Order them to fill the wagon with straight lengths of timber suitable for sharpening into stakes. I'll detail some of our men to work outside the perimeter digging man-traps. Then, once the stakes are inserted in the ground, they can be disguised with dry leaves and vegetation. Some of the long grass can be replaced, allowing any running warriors to fall and impale themselves. We'll use the darkness to mask our activities. Remember that I don't want man-traps on the eastern side where Stormbringer's horses will be manoeuvring, and there must be no stakes in that ditch. Let's give our cavalry a fighting chance.'

With renewed activity, the short afternoon turned into night, but the preparations continued, using the minimal light to cover their labours. The Dene warriors attacked the rich black soil with gusto and cut down and trimmed saplings, embedding the prepared stakes into the sides of the ditches and the bottoms of the smaller man-traps, places where an unwary enemy could be impaled. They sweated and strained in shifts throughout the night. All the workers were stripped to the waist, despite the cold. Men grinned with white, exultant smiles as they pitted their muscles against nature in lieu of a breathing and bleeding Geat enemy.

And so, Arthur occupied the endless, terrifying period of waiting for death to appear on the horizon.

A dim morning followed, and still Heardred's Geats didn't come.

Arthur put on a brave face as he walked through the Dene encampment, cracking jokes about Geat tardiness and commenting on the provident natures and greed of his warriors through their accumulation of food supplies. His jokes left a trail of laughter behind him. Arthur might have difficulty calming his own terrors, but he was expert at hiding them from his warriors.

Then, an hour into the afternoon, the sun began the downward slide towards the evening darkness, and a shape appeared to the north before moving off quickly in the dim yellow light. One of the sentries cried out a warning and Arthur hurried to the northern perimeter with Snorri at his heels.

'I saw two horsemen,' Snorri cried, his helmsman's eyes accurately picking out the shapes. 'One of them has moved out fast and he's out of sight now, but there's something odd about the other horse's gait. It's coming towards us, so we'll soon know what's happening.'

'Send two sentries out to cut the horse off. Don't let it reach the ditch, or the beast and its rider will come to grief,' Arthur ordered. 'Move!'

Two men raced out from the perimeter and halted the lathered beast before it reached the man-traps. Arthur could see that the cowled figure of a man was tethered into the saddle.

He steeled himself, for he recognised the disreputable horse and the threadbare cloak covering the bent body.

'I fear that Ivar will never see Rugen Island.' Snorri flinched at the controlled anger in the eyes of his master.

By the time Arthur and Snorri reached the horse, whose head hung to its knees with exhaustion and fear, the man had been cut down and laid out reverently on the freshly levelled sod of the perimeter. Arthur kneeled beside the shrouded corpse, sensing invisible eyes in the far distance as they imagined his shock and horror at what lay under the stained old cloak. Snorri drew back the flap of the unravelling wool and exposed Ivar's half-naked body.

'So unnecessary,' Arthur murmured. 'And so damned pointless.'

The fisherman must have been taken not long after he had left the Dene encampment, probably before they had entered the town and its central religious community.

Geat scouts must have captured him easily for his horse was neither young nor fit. And the old man could not have offered any resistance.

The cold part of Arthur's brain expressed its relief that he had never mentioned Stormbringer in Ivar's presence, for no man could have suffered the hideous torture inflicted upon the old body without the sufferer telling his tormentors everything they wanted to know.

Ivar's pitiful hand lay stiff and unresponsive on the green sod. Every finger joint had been broken and twisted. His thumb had been wrenched so hard and so repetitively that the bones had broken through the skin while Ivar had still been alive.

Ivar's other hand and his feet had suffered the same treatment. By the time his torturers had finished with his extremities, Ivar would have told them everything that Arthur intended, how he wanted Heardred to attack his pitifully small force from a strong defensive position in an attempt to gain his revenge for the children of Lund.

Whoever had ordered this torment had enjoyed inflicting unendurable pain on this hapless old man. His hand bones had also been snapped, probably with the haft of an axe, and these wounds were followed by damage to his wrists and ankles. Arthur imagined the old lungs straining for air as his vocal cords screamed in agony. The lower arm and leg bones had followed, obviously requiring more effort, and there were pitiful signs that showed how Ivar had fought. A fragment of cloth was caught between the old man's teeth and even a trace of another man's blood on an old canine showed how the fisherman's strong and rebellious spirit had continued to resist even when his arms and legs were rendered useless.

They had toyed with him then, burning the wrinkled flesh over his ribs so that every breath would have been agonising. Another torturer had used a hot iron on the old man's genitals, but all their efforts were eventually fruitless. Arthur had seen the blue lips and fingertips before, when an old retainer in Arden had died after crippling pains in the chest. Ivar's body had defeated his spirit, and a premature death had robbed his torturers of their victim. Arthur smiled.

'Stand the old man upright, and we'll lash his body to the longest piece of timber we can find. We'll set it into the ground so he can watch as we destroy his murderers.'

When Eamonn and Arthur had first come to Skania nearly two years earlier, they had seen the lifelike stuffed hide of a dead horse set on poles at the entrance to one of the smaller Dene settlements; the two Britons had been impressed with the symbolism, for the horse appeared to be flying unaided through the wind in order to protect the village. Now, Ivar's corpse would fill the same role for Arthur's defensive square.

When no suitable timber could be found for the task, Arthur opted to drive the carthorse to the copse of trees, although Snorri raged at him for risking the whole campaign by leaving the perimeter of the encampment.

'I used Ivar for my purposes, Snorri, so any risk should be mine. I became fond of that old reprobate and I know he'd long to have his revenge on the cowards who enjoyed every scream they wrenched from his pain-filled body. No! I'm going to find him a suitable throne from which his spirit can watch the coming battle. The last thing the Geats should see as they die is Ivar, standing over them and damning their souls for his murder. You may come to the copse if you wish – but you won't dissuade me!'

And so, in a darkness lit by a hollow and ghostly moon, Arthur cut down a young oak with the height and strength to raise Ivar's corpse high above the shield wall. Horse and man dragged the twelve-foot length of timber back to the Dene camp where Arthur supervised its elevation.

On a cross piece that was lashed into place to hold Ivar's arms, the old fisherman hung in greater majesty than he had ever possessed in life. Arthur had slipped a red cloak around the old man's shoulders, a piece of rich fabric that he had kept in his pack to remind him of the hellish battle of Calleva Atrebatum. In that battle, his king had tried to draw attention to the young Arthur, hoping that he would be killed and, therefore, save King Bran from the possibility of an heir to his throne making an unwanted claim. Bran could never accept that Arthur wasn't interested in power, for each man judges others by the weight of his own soul. But this cloak had almost brought an early death to Arthur, so when he gave the cloak to Ivar's corpse, he intended to alert Geat eyes to the cruelties inflicted by Heardred on a harmless old man. He knew his symbol would neither be ignored nor misunderstood.

Then, with his preparations complete, Arthur went to sleep. The sentries had been warned. Heardred would almost certainly attack before dawn.

After the skirmishes that had taken place during the last eighteen months, Arthur was convinced that a large group of Geats were already crawling through the darkness to get into attack positions, whereby they could outflank the Dene encampment. He said as much to the jarls during his final briefing, suggesting that they should inform their warriors of likely Geat strategies to reinforce their sense of purpose and sacrifice.

'Remind them of who we are and who we speak for. We are the voices of the dead,' Arthur explained in a hollow voice. 'We are the arms that can no longer lift a sword to protect the innocent; we are the legs that cannot stand four-square to stop the cruel thieves who steal our children but, most importantly, we carry the spirits of the dead, the dying and those lost innocents with us in our righteous cause. Our motives are just.'

The jarls shivered to see that his eyes appeared to be silver in the moonlight.

'Your rallying cry for tomorrow will be: For the dead: For the unsleeping dead. I have placed the peasant, Ivar, above us to warn the enemy that the dead will judge each and every one of them. The Dragon's Brood cries out to avenge his innocent blood.'

One of the jarls snickered, but his friend elbowed him sharply, for no right-thinking man should find any amusement in the prospect of the coming conflict. One by one, they took their final embraces; who could know how many warriors would still be living when the next night came?

Once again, certain that the sentries would keep a sharp watch, Arthur stretched out on his pallet to gain a few hours of sleep. He had tried to anticipate all eventualities, so the outcome of the coming battle was in God's hands.

Volunteers spent the night in hollowed-out advance posts, scanning the darkness with their senses alert for any sign of movement within twenty spear lengths of the man-traps. Finally, breathless, bathed in sweat and swathed in black from head to foot, the first Dene sentry to see the enemy movement raised the alarm with a prearranged password.

Smoothly, after many hours and long days of tiresome practice under Rufus's tutelage, the warriors moved into their fighting positions so they could face the onslaught of the Geat army that was spreading across the plain.

Arthur watched as men moved in near-darkness to smoothly engage their shields together while forming lines that faced outwards towards the four cardinal points. Several cooking fires continued to burn, for he had issued orders during the previous evening that the encampment should appear to be perfectly normal throughout the night. Then, at a nod, Snorri cupped his hands and replicated the distinctive call of a snowy northern owl, the signal that would summon the sentries back to safety. Eager now for the action to start, Arthur's eyes scanned the heavy, shadowy plain to the north as a man materialised out of a pool of shadows and ran fleetly towards the Dene lines.

The time for subterfuge was over.

'Rufus? Order your archers to use fire arrows to give us some light.' Arthur sounded calm, although his stomach had a familiar hollowness and the invisible fingernails had begun to scrape inside his skull, warning that danger was all around him.

Rufus disappeared like dissipating smoke as Arthur stood among his warriors and locked his shield into place. Before the fleet had left for Calmar, only twenty archers had been found and, although they had a huge number of arrows at their disposal, there were too few bowmen to be more than a token irritant to any concerted enemy attack. Now, in the centre of a mass of nearly six hundred men, Rufus's archers were perched atop the wagon which had been moved to the very centre of the square.

Arthur watched as arrows flamed overhead in an arc before falling to the ground some distance from the square. Other arrows were fired to the east and the west to briefly illuminate the pitch-black ground beyond the Dene man-traps.

There, lit by intermittent flares from the fire arrows as they settled point first into the sod, shapes swathed in dark clothing were exposed as they crawled on their bellies to avoid discovery. Behind them, in the darkness too deep for human eyes to penetrate, huge shapes seemed to hover.

Arthur heard the indrawn hiss of breath as the Dene warriors began to appreciate the sheer size of the enemy force. They were outnumbered at least two to one, with the possibility of more warriors held in reserve.

'Your men are on their bellies like snakes! Come and face us like men, Heardred! But come on your feet – so we won't have to bend too far to find your cowardly heart!'

Arthur's shouted insults raised a titter of laughter from the men around him, which grew as his words were passed down the line.

'They're coming from the north and the east, Lord Arthur, just as you predicted,' Snorri observed, as one of the sentries re-entered the square, touched his helmet in respect to his commander and squeezed through the press of warriors to his position near the archer's wagon.

'Ensure your shields are interlocked on both sides, men,' Arthur shouted. 'Archers, fire at anything that moves. Pass the word back, men. You are to kill all enemy warriors who come towards you – but don't break the line!'

Arthur gazed over the bare earth before him and the ditch with its stakes and, invisible, the man-traps beyond them. He saw the first of the Geat warriors as they leaped to their feet, when the fitful light of the descending moon escaped from behind the sable bank of clouds. A distant horn sounded, and the Geats responded to its call.

Here, in the shadowy terrain that had concealed them, was the Geat army. Heardred's force was far larger than the combined companies of the Dene warriors, including Stormbringer's reinforcements and the Dene cavalry. Only raw courage and strategy could hold off such a large and determined attack until Stormbringer arrived. The whole task would have been terrifying had Arthur not sensed the voice in his head ordering him to remain calm and confident.

You can survive, the voice whispered. *The Dene can win, if you stay calm and think.*

As Arthur looked out at the wall of running men advancing over the plain, he thanked the soldier god, Mithras, for the Geats were running pell-mell, without any caution or disciplined strategy except to pound their Dene enemies into the dust.

Several screams rose, as high and as tremulous as the shriek of a coney in the claws of an eagle. 'The Geats appear to have found our man-traps,' Arthur quipped, knowing that a controlled manner gave heart to his men as they readied themselves to fight in this strange battle formation. 'Perhaps the bastards will watch where they put their big feet in future.'

As before, his words were repeated along the length and breadth of the packed warriors. Nervous titters and guffaws rose from behind him, then several more screams were heard, closer and more desperately pain-filled than the last.

'They're slow learners, Snorri!' Arthur's deliberate ploy was working, for he sensed some of the nervous tension slowly leaking from the bodies of the men around him.

'Get ready, men! Brace yourselves! They've reached the ditch and some of them won't impale themselves. Some of them will get through.'

Along the front line, men wedged themselves against the warriors behind them who were using their chests and shields to give a firm purchase to those who would be in direct contact with the enemy. Boots of sheepskin were anchored into the sod along the north and south walls while the warriors near the corner points used their whole bodies to support their brothers who were facing the enemy head on. Arrows whizzed over their heads and, even in this deadly half-light, the barbed points were easily finding their targets. The Geat warriors were so tightly packed that the archers could hardly miss hitting human flesh. Soon, the roared war cries of the Geats were drowned out by the screams of their wounded.

The spears used by the Dene warriors were normally very long with large heads suitable for hunting boar and wolves that encroached onto the farms and villages. When Arthur first suggested using these weapons in conjunction with the shield wall, the Dene warriors were horrified. Where was the honour of fighting an enemy who impaled himself on bristling spears while the bearer was hidden behind a series of large shields?

Arthur had mastered his irritation and showed the men how the long hunting spears could be shortened for greater man-oeuvrability They listened out of respect for their commander, but their eyes told Arthur that his arguments were falling on deaf ears. He planted his spear haft onto a patch of solid earth, then wedged it with his foot to ensure it remained in place to demonstrate how its shorter length made it an even more effective weapon.

'Would you rather have us die as outnumbered and inadequately prepared warriors than utilise a tactical advantage over your enemies? Are you all mad?'

Finally, the Dene jarls had agreed to use the shorter stabbing spears as the weapon of choice.

The four lines of interlocked shields suddenly sprouted a bristling, sharp protection that looked like the wicked spines of a hedgehog. The Geats howled with mirth and threw themselves at the northern wall of Denes like a breathing wave of iron axes and swords.

The force exerted by rows of surging Geats shook Arthur's shield, his knees and his whole body, until he began to fear he would be swept off his feet by the combined weight of five rows of sweating muscular Geats, all obsessed with smashing the shield wall at a dozen points. Using his shield's sharpened upper rim, Arthur rammed the metal upward to cleave open the unpro-tected chin of a Geat who towered over him. A crunch, a rush of blood that drenched the Briton from head to toe and the Geat was gone, to be replaced by another.

The warrior rained axe-blows down on the spot where Arthur's head should have been, but the second and third rows of Dene defenders had raised their shields over the heads of the row directly in front of them. The axe became embedded in a shield as the Geat swore and tried to wrench it free. Arthur used the Dragon Knife to castrate the fool before ramming his spear into the face of the next Geat to enter the fray.

And so the dance of death continued unabated.

But the Denes were also suffering casualties. As a man swayed and began to fall, the warrior directly behind him took his place, while the injured were passed back to the centre of the square where the archers did what they could for men with untreatable wounds. Arthur had issued an order that a defensive wall should be built with the bodies of the Dene dead, two spear lengths from the wagons so, if a final disaster befell the Dene force, the survivors could retreat to a last defensive position from which they could fight in the final, cataclysmic skirmish.

'Götterdämmerung,' Arthur murmured. Snorri looked at him sharply as his spear stabbed, almost of its own accord, into an open Geat mouth until the point smashed Geat brains into porridge.

'The twilight of the gods? What does such a day of terror have to do with us?' Snorri's panting voice was puzzled, and some of the other men had heard his casual comment; grunting with effort and pale with weariness, they still darted the odd nervous glance at their battle chief.

Arthur's spear-point snapped off, so he immediately pulled Oakheart, Bedwyr's gifted sword, from its scabbard. Made by the greatest swordsmith in Britain, the iron in this weapon was reputed to have fallen from the stars. The hard metal in the blade appeared to have a blue tinge in the weak light and, within seconds, seemed both blue and red as Geat blood and teeth marred its pristine surface.

Then, as he extended his body to finish the killing blow, Arthur's boots slipped in greasy mud. Only Snorri's steadying left hand saved him from disaster.

Arthur raised his shield once more to slice down the side of an enemy jaw. Another Geat, smaller than his peers, slid below Arthur's sword and dealt Arthur a long shallow gash from wrist to elbow.

'You'll pay for that,' Arthur said in the Geat tongue and stepped half a pace backwards without relinquishing the firmness of the wall of iron around him. As the small Geat moved forward with a crow of triumph, Arthur lowered his shield for a second and took off the man's head as neatly as if by a surgical incision. The corpse stood upright for a second, pumping blood all over Arthur, although his shield was immediately slammed back into its position in the line.

Then, almost as if the Geat warriors had heard him, the enemy began to pull back from the shield wall. Shaking blood out of curls that had escaped his helmet, Arthur saw that the enemy had withdrawn on all four sides to re-form behind the man-traps. The sun was higher now, so several hours had been lost during the madness of battle fever. Arthur estimated it was still two hours before noon.

'Close the gaps in the line,' Arthur roared. 'Leave the Geat dead as a wall that they'll be forced to scale. This first engagement was a battle of attrition, so the bravest and the most stoic warriors will live and win. We will not fail!'

The young prince realised that he had probably lost a third of his men to wounds or death. But Geat bodies lay nearly four feet high around three sides of the square, although there was now a space of six feet between the Dene warriors and the piles of Geat dead. Inevitably, their own casualties had reduced the size of the lines that made up the square.

The surviving Dene warriors must prepare for the arrival of Stormbringer's relief column. They must trust that the Sae Dene was almost upon them, and this blessed pause in battle would allow his friend to reach them and outflank Heardred's force.

'If we have sufficient time, stack the Geat corpses to one side on the eastern and western lines so Stormbringer's men can attack without becoming entangled. On the northern and southern lines, provide a narrow passageway for entry by the next wave of attackers. Those Geat fuckers will either have to climb over the corpses of their friends or enter through a gap of our choosing. If we arrange it well, our archers will appreciate having some clear targets.'

Arthur could barely be heard now, for the enemy warriors had begun to beat their axes and swords on their shields while chanting contemptuous threats. The vilification spurred the Dene to carry out Arthur's orders with extra enthusiasm.

'You Dene are cowards! When are you coming out to fight like men? Or will you stay like mongrel dogs, and hide behind the door to bite braver men on the heels?' The chants were repeated, again and again, with added refinements comparing Dene women with breeding animals that resulted in the cowardice of their progeny.

'Stand fast, men! Ignore their insults! There will be no surrender!'

Arthur's face split into a pale grin. He was covered with splashes of dried gore, and now wiped more from his eyes. Noticing that the wound he had suffered along his forearm was still weeping, he bound it with a length of white cloth that he had secreted inside his shirt. But otherwise he left the gore in place where it could serve to frighten his enemies before they had struck a blow.

'Rest now, and eat while you can! The archers have butts of fresh water in the wagon and you have beer in your supplies. Remember the enemy will return as soon as they've recovered enough to mount another attack.'

Once more, every word was passed back to all the men, now fewer than four hundred, who were either eating, moving corpses or sitting quietly as they sharpened and repaired their weapons. Completely surrounded as they were, there was no possibility of evacuating Arthur's wounded, so those men who were still able to fight made their way into the inner rings of the shield wall. The sorely wounded lay suffering and awaited death. They knew full well that wounded warriors rarely survived an engagement.

Meanwhile, some of the archers were prowling outside the perimeter of the fighting square, recovering whatever usable arrows could be salvaged from Geat bodies.

Small fires had sprung into life on the plain, so the Geats were resting, something that made Arthur shake his head with amazement. He knew that his force was in serious trouble. Only a madman would call off his troops to rest and eat when a small push now could smash the Dene force once and for all.

'If Heardred is so timid that he lets his men fight without him, then he's capable of only pursuing an attack if he believes he can win. Let's hope his jarls convince him that a force of four hundred men would not be a threat to him.'

Snorri, aware that all their men were beginning to feel thirsty, suggested that he and Arthur should leave their position in the front line to carry water butts to those men whose lips were already beginning to crack as a result of the strengthening breeze and the warming sun.

After this brief hiatus, Arthur realised he had a duty to offer comfort to the dying. He instructed Snorri to summon him if Heardred made a move.

Such a task is never easy; men who know that death is imminent and who are racked with agony are tortured by the prospect that their family could descend into poverty and starvation without a breadwinner to support them. Arthur allayed these fears easily, for he assured the wounded that their families would receive their portion when the spoils of Gotland were distributed among his warriors.

Other men, especially those youths whose chins bore only the thin fluff of early manhood, often pined for a sweetheart or called for their mothers. Arthur had read in Myrddion Merlinus's scrolls that the healer had sometimes taken on the role of such loved ones so that men in delirium could die in a state of peace. As he tried to do this Arthur was ashamed to feel tears slide down his cheeks, but nothing could deter him from his self-appointed task. Dene warriors were dying for him: he would honour them in turn, as best he could.

Warriors who saw their commander moving through the densely packed men to resume his place in the northern wall noted his wet cheeks and looked away. They were touched that a master, a captain of a longboat and a warrior of renown, would bother to speak to dying men. Such behaviour was unnatural to the northerners because leaders needed to appear invulnerable and impervious to criticism.

Back on the line, Arthur settled back into the demands of the shield wall as if it was all he had ever known. The lookout atop the wagon had sent word that the Geats were massing on all four sides. Perhaps four hours of daylight remained, but Arthur realised his entire command would be spent or near to death by the time three hours had elapsed.

Stormbringer must come soon. Tall as he was, Arthur could only just see over the piled bodies stacked to the north and the east where the Dene force had absorbed the bulk of the Geat attack. Further out, small clusters of corpses disturbed the long flat plain into the far distance where the flush of the forest formed a crescent. These warriors had been on the fringe of the Geat attack and had obviously been killed by Dene arrows. If he were Stormbringer, he would have travelled south-west down the curve of the crescent, although the forest would have slowed the larger force down to a crawl, especially if they wanted to avoid discovery. Even now, Stormbringer might be only one mile away. Arthur's heart leaped. Surely they could survive for another hour!

Yes, Stormbringer must arrive in short order. Arthur knew better than to voice his desperate thoughts aloud, so he deliberately cracked a casual joke with Snorri for the sole purpose of calming any nervous warriors for whom the waiting had become a trial.

Stormbringer won't fail me, Arthur reflected. Not unless he had already been discovered and ambushed.

Then, even before the word was passed on to him that the enemy were resuming their attack, he had roused the line and a distinctly smaller row of shields clicked smoothly into place.

The real test was now upon them, for the Geats were aware that the Dene invaders must be tired and their defences thinly stretched. The jarls had obviously estimated the size of the force they faced, so Heardred must have been convinced that he couldn't lose this battle. Although they outnumbered the Dene by at least two to one, the Geats were also tired and dispirited. Heardred had driven them hard, so they had run fifty miles before fighting a pitched battle only hours after their arrival. Their king had ordered his tent to be erected at a makeshift Geat encampment where he could observe the battle from a safe position that was beyond arrow-shot of the perimeter and well removed from the Dene man-traps. On horseback, and with his sycophants around him, Heardred sent orders to his jarls, often contradictory and always unreasonable, while watching the shield wall repel his best warriors, again and again.

The rank and file warriors, many of whom were part-time farmers from Vaster Gotland, resented the screamed orders and the careless insults issuing from their king when the commanders passed down the order to retreat just before noon. A slow-burning feeling of resentment was souring Geat bellies, while many of the men wished fervently that Heardred might receive a barb from a stray arrow or vanish in a puff of smoke before all his warriors dashed themselves to death against the iron wall of shields that confronted them.

Shortly thereafter, the battle recommenced with no side having the advantage, except for a slow attrition that robbed Arthur of his warriors as the men in the front line were replaced, again and again. The mounds of corpses grew higher, and the shield wall contracted.

Then, just as Arthur was beginning to taste defeat, he suddenly heard wild Dene yells over the other noises of the battlefield and felt the vibration of galloping hooves on the hard-packed sod.

Stormbringer had finally arrived.

The Sae Dene's force poured onto the battlefield at a gallop, having covered several miles in an arrowhead formation, led by

Stormbringer's cavalry who had swept far to the north of Arthur's position so they could attack from the west in a brutal pincer movement. Heardred had finally gained his first sight of the army as it advanced towards him. Belatedly, he attempted to organise a retreat, but battles have lives of their own. Fully committed, the front ranks of his troops couldn't disengage from the attack that had been mounted on Arthur's shield wall and, without the direct guidance of the king and his counsellors, the rear troops were left in a state of confusion. The lack of a leader at the head of his troops was to cost Heardred dearly.

The warriors in the Geat rear turned to face the new foe and tried to prepare themselves for a clash against an unknown number of enemy warriors; Stormbringer's relief force had moved so quickly and so compact were its ranks that the jarls in Heardred's command had no idea of its actual size. Confused and outclassed, and with their communications in ruins, the Geats were defeated before Stormbringer had even blooded his sword.

In the blinking of an eye, the battle was won.

After a day of enforced discipline which the Dene warriors in the shield wall had borne with patient fortitude, they were eager to advance now and engage their enemies like men. Arthur loosed his warriors like dogs from the leash and they leaped free of the wall and the hated Roman shields. In the vanguard, Arthur hacked and slashed, forcing his way through more and more victims who died on his knife or his spear.

At last, the shield that had served him so well throughout the day was abandoned to fall into the bloody mud.

Arthur had but one goal now.

Throughout that long and vicious day, he had yearned for some sight or sound of Heardred, but the Geat king had remained at the rear of his command. Now Arthur caught a fleeting glimpse of a regally painted tent far beyond the man-traps, where it had been erected out of harm's way. Arthur fought his way towards it with Snorri hard at his heels.

How Arthur could force his weary limbs to put on a burst of unnatural speed seemed miraculous to his helmsman and the other three crew members who had followed him. Yet Arthur outstripped them easily, as he fixed his stony eyes on the cause of so much pain up and down the western coast of Skandia. Heardred had even lacked the balls to put his own neck on the line during the attack.

He'll be gone on horseback if I don't hurry, Arthur thought. But, God damn his black soul, he'll not survive to kill children and old men again, if I can get to him first.

Then, although his lungs were on fire, Arthur laughed with a rusty, cavernous sound. I'll be lucky if I can raise an arm to strike *anyone* down. So will Snorri and the others, for we're all exhausted!

But Arthur still lusted after the life of one last person on this battlefield of death or, at the very least, an opportunity to chain Heardred to an oar and tow him through the waters until he drowned behind *Sea Wife*.

Then, just as Arthur's eyes were filled with red and black explosions of strain, and each breath rasped, the party came to the king's tent and the few warriors who had remained to protect their lord and master. The sycophants had fled on horseback at the first opportunity, but they had loosed the spare horses to prevent pursuit, leaving Heardred behind, to suffer whatever fate the Dene forces determined.

'Catch your breath first, Arthur,' Snorri panted. 'We'll look after Heardred's dogs. You can find the king and teach him what it's like to feel extremes of terror.'

Sucking air into his burning lungs, Arthur ignored the entrance flap and slipped around to the rear of the structure. With the Dragon Knife he split the heavy hide as if it was delicate silk. As he shouldered his way into the darkened interior, he noticed that an oil lamp provided the only illumination, placed there by the king so that any interloper entering the tent by the entrance flap would have the light shining directly into his eyes. By contrast, Arthur could see everything from his position in the rear of the tent. It was almost as if time had been stilled by Fortuna, as she decided Heardred's fate and stopped her wheel with one lead-white hand.

A middle-aged man dressed in sumptuous cloth was seated on a cushioned chair behind the light. He half-turned towards Arthur with his mouth gaping open to show ruined and browned teeth. His features were attractive, but constant frowning and disapproval had deepened the lines around his eyes into off-grey seams. Even in the half-light, Arthur could tell that the king's nails would probably be black and crusty with grime.

I always considered the Geats as a clean race, Arthur thought, his nose wrinkling at a stench that wafted from the king's clothes, garments that seemed so tidy when compared with Heardred's dirty skin. This man is filthy, Arthur decided. His servants have cared for his possessions, but they've all fled and left him to his own devices. It seems they don't care for him as a person.

Suddenly, a knife materialised in Heardred's right hand.

'Who are you to disturb your king?' Heardred snapped, mistaking Arthur for a Geat warrior in search of plunder. His voice was high-pitched and coarse-grained. 'My guards will cut your throat if you don't take to your heels and leave my tent.'

'Your guards are mostly dead or dying, Heardred, but those who remain are preoccupied with saving their own skins,' Arthur replied, for the sound of desperate, hand-to-hand combat could still be heard beyond the tent walls. A high-pitched scream raised the hair on Arthur's arms, but Heardred's eyes swivelled wildly around the room as he desperately sought a means of escape.

'You're one of the Dene dogs then,' Heardred hissed. 'I'll pay you in good red gold if you allow me to pass.'

'You can keep your gold, Heardred. You've killed and enslaved children in my name, so *our* business is personal. I'm not a Dene! I'm a Briton, and I believe you've heard of me.'

'The Last Dragon!' Heardred snarled and attempted to snatch up a long-hafted axe from beside his sleeping pallet. Unfortunately, he was unexpectedly clumsy. In a blinding panic, he dropped the axe – and almost lost the knife as he tried to pick it up.

Arthur was close enough now to smell the hot stink of urine adding to the cesspit of smells emanating from Heardred's greyish flesh and soul. Arthur was almost gagging, but his iron discipline stood him in good stead. This sad excuse for a king was almost too vile to kill.

'Then I'll make sure you *are* the last of the dragons,' Heardred shouted and threw his knife at Arthur with the speed of an arrow. The act was so sudden that a lesser opponent would have been killed.

Arthur was tired and the dagger had buried itself in his thigh. But, leaving the weapon in place to minimise the loss of blood, he took three quick paces forward to extract his revenge.

Heardred yelped like a frightened hound and his panic only accentuated the sly expression on his face.

'No one will come to help you, Heardred,' the Briton told him. 'I sent a warning to you that I was called the King's Bane, so you should have listened.'

Heardred began to shout for help in a voice that rose higher and higher. Arthur took no notice, but simply padded after his prey with the king's dagger jutting out of his leg like an obscene finger.

Outside, Snorri and the crewmen heard the screaming begin, but they forced their ears to hear nothing. After all, dragons must be paid their measure of blood and pain, if they are to be recompensed for their service.

PLAN OF THE HOLDING

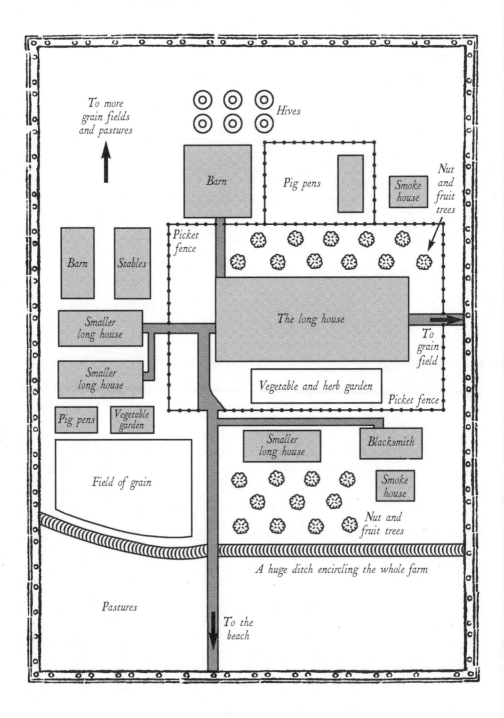

CHAPTER VI

HOMECOMING

Where your treasure is, there will your heart be also.

The Bible, Matthew 6:21

'I want to go home,' Arthur whispered to himself, so softly that the wakeful Snorri barely heard him as the helmsman tried to find a comfortable hollow in the sod to ease the persistent ache in his spine.

The long exhalation that accompanied the words convinced Snorri that Arthur was deeply unhappy with his lot. Not for a moment did the helmsman consider that the young prince was speaking of The Holding, Stormbringer's farm complex, even if his sister and Blaise were awaiting him there.

My master wants to leave behind the man he thinks he has become, Snorri thought with a sad feeling of compassion.

In the end, Arthur had chosen to give Heardred a quick death when the snivelling coward curled into a foetal ball on a soiled carpet. The man had wept noisily until Arthur had turned away from his intended task in disgust and shame. Finally, the Briton had sheathed Oakheart to protect the noble blade from any dishonour that would stain it with the base blood of such a monster.

Arthur's reluctance to execute the pathetic Geat king was so strong that he almost decided to call in his companions to drag Heardred away in chains, but the scream in his brain suddenly became piercing.

Instantly he ducked, dropped down to one knee and half-turned as if felled by a blow. Above his head, the blade of Heardred's axe whined uselessly to cleave empty air rather than the neck that had been exposed only an instant before.

Arthur's howl of rage mingled with the scream in his head so he was unable to tell which sound was real and which was not. Heardred had extended his reach in an attempt to slaughter Arthur without making a sound, but he was completely unbalanced when his weapon failed to come into contact with Arthur's body. The weight of the heavy axe dragged Heardred's whole arm downward, while Arthur reacted out of hard-learned weapons' practice. The Dragon Knife slithered into his hand and the king's eyes blinked at him in the lamplight as the dagger slid between his ribs.

'You've killed me.' Small flecks of blood appeared on Heardred's lips. 'How can this be?' The king's eyes darkened with confusion.

'You took one treacherous step too far, Heardred, and you've offended all good men by your actions. Yes! I've killed you, and I wish I could kill you a hundred times for the sins you've committed. You'll not suffer like the children of Lund who are still living in the brothels of the East. You'll not feel the agonies of burned flesh like the women you've incinerated in their own homes. Yet you will surely die! And once will suffice!'

To punctuate his words, Arthur twisted the knife viciously in the wound and cut through tissue and bone until blood gushed from Heardred's mouth and nose. Then he wrenched the blade free and the blood flow doubled in its wake. Heardred dropped to his knees and tried to hold his chest together. The tide of blood prevented the king from speaking, but Arthur was grateful when he finally fell on his face. The monster's muddy green eyes had accused the young man, almost as if the king was an innocent, murdered senselessly in his own tent.

Snorri appeared through the tent flap into the circle of light in time to hear the Geat's final, shuddering breath. The Dene helmsman grinned drily.

'That was quick! I expected a worm like Heardred might take some time to die.'

'Behead the bastard and put the head in a box. Send it to Beowulf with my compliments, and an explanation that the king attacked me when my back was turned after he had surrendered. You can also express the hope that his kinsman's death will not be an impediment to any treaty between Beowulf and Stormbringer, a pact that would be of great value to both their peoples.'

Arthur's voice was sad under the determination, and Snorri was even more bemused than usual.

Arthur would have left the tent and the grisly remains of its owner, but Snorri restrained him with one careful hand. 'No, Arthur. Allow us to carry out your instructions for Heardred's dismemberment elsewhere and I'll order my men to clean up the tent. It can serve as a perfect headquarters for Master Stormbringer to use once he has sent the last of the Geats packing.'

'As you see fit, my friend.' Arthur turned away so he wouldn't be obliged to watch the removal of Heardred's corpse.

As he waited inside the tent, Snorri observed that Arthur was staring at his bloodstained hands in a daze. What thoughts shocked Arthur so profoundly were a mystery to Snorri, but he sensed that Arthur was carrying guilt. All men were fated to kill their enemies when they became warriors, so their hands would regularly be drenched in lifeblood. Like all pragmatists, Snorri believed such results were a sign of prowess, but Arthur was obviously tortured by the fates of those men who had fallen victim to his sword.

Arthur was remembering himself as he had been in the past, in those days when he was a boy-man with prospects of a happy life before him. He had hoped for a loving wife, children, a fortress of his own and success in carving out a Saxon-free world for his people and his imaginary family.

However Mareddyd, the traitor who had sold him to Stormbringer so long ago, had robbed him of any future that could be resumed in his homeland. Although he loved the Sae Dene sailors for their reckless courage and determination, his role as their war chief and his service as a Dene warrior was searing his heart and shrivelling his soul. He wasn't killing for home, a hearth, or for God. He was a despicable mercenary.

'I can't go on in this way. I must return to my own lands, or I'll be lost forever!'

Stormbringer was elated. The spoils taken from the dead Geats and from Heardred's supply wagons were far larger than he had expected and the most valuable trophies were sufficient to fill three huge wagons to groaning point. Stormbringer decided immediately that the relics from the Christian churches of Skania should be returned to the survivors as proof to the religious community that God would ultimately triumph over wickedness, while the huge stockpiles of food which Heardred had insisted on carrying with him during his campaign would help to keep the farmers of Skania alive during the freezing winter. Since the Geat king had stripped farms bare, Stormbringer would enjoy returning the vital supplies to the impoverished families of Lund and other beleaguered villages.

The Sae Dene was bubbling with good humour when he strode into Heardred's tent sometime after midnight. Those Geat warriors who had escaped the cavalry and his net of warriors were running as if the Last Dragon personally was pursuing them, while Stormbringer had taken enough captives to know that Arthur was now viewed by the Geats as a supernatural demi-god.

Among his own warriors, the consensus of opinion was that Arthur had been gifted with Loki's own luck. Over a six-hour period, the crew members could only guess at how many enemy warriors had met their fates through Arthur's superior skills; they reported his regret at the wounding and deaths of many of his own men, and told Stormbringer that he had comforted the dying in their time of need. He had shown no fear, even when the line was close to failing. Finally, when victory was assured, he pursued the Geat king and killed him without mercy. The Dene warriors prized courage above all things.

'Are you asleep already, Arthur? After a battle? Truly, you must have ice water in your veins rather than blood,' Stormbringer said happily as he dropped a leather bag in a corner of the tent set aside for his possessions. One of the servants appeared out of nowhere and scurried off to find hot wine and food to assuage Stormbringer's gargantuan hunger. Snorri helped the Sae Dene to remove his long sheepskin boots after the bindings were removed.

'Wake up, Arthur!' He smiled down at his friend, spread out on his pallet. 'If I didn't know better, I'd say you're trying to ignore me. You should be awake, carousing and drinking Heardred's beer with the remnants of the shield wall. They'll be singing about the Last Dragon for many years to come. In fact, they'll be singing about you as we speak. Yet, here you lie, fast asleep, after an astonishing victory that will save the lives of many hundreds of our people.'

This was a long speech for the usually phlegmatic Stormbringer, but their special relationship mitigated Stormbringer's natural reticence. From slave, to friend, to confidant and then to future brother-in-law, is an unusual series of developments in any relationship, so Valdar had learned to rely on the quick wit of the Briton, and relished the pleasure of having a truly close friend who wasn't numbered among his blood kin such as his cousin Frodhi.

Looking down at Arthur's thunderous face and arctic eyes gazing back at the Sae Dene with mutinous resentment, Stormbringer knew immediately that Arthur was suffering from one of his regular post-battle fits of depression. Whereas a more venal man would drink deeply and take a woman to drive away the shades of his dead enemies, Arthur examined his errors in judgement and magnified those mistakes out of all proportion. With a resigned sigh, Stormbringer set to work to improve Arthur's mood. From his bag he pulled out a packet that had been folded into a coarse palm-sized wad and unwrapped it.

'Do you think Maeve will like this token of my regard? Will she accept me, or would this trifle be an insult?'

Stormbringer's rapid-fire questions trailed off because Arthur was looking at him as if he was crazed. 'For the Lord's sake, Arthur, get your mind off the battle that's just been fought and won, and help me with my real problems. I need your help to find a suitable gift for your sister.'

Arthur reluctantly looked down at the jewel laid out on his pallet. The heavy silver in the necklace glittered in the light from the burning torch. With one hand he felt the links of the beautifully polished metal and recognised the buttery feel of very high-quality silver. Set within the links of the necklace, which were almost the width of a woman's palm, were strangely hued stones of a type that Arthur had never seen before. Some were a pale purple shade that glowed softly in their nests of silver, while others had an odd green tinge that seemed to mimic the sea. Arthur had once seen an emerald and the glow from its heart was a completely different shade. The stones had been ground into oval shapes and had the smoothed feel of glass, except for chips of clear stone linking the coloured pieces. These smaller stones were sharp and glittered wickedly.

'I'm certain that Maeve will love it,' Arthur answered with a noncommittal glance. 'The stones will complement her hair and the width of the silver band will sit at the base of her throat and make her neck appear to be long and slender. Yes, like all women, she will be entranced by this beautiful object.'

'But will she accept it as a bride gift?'

Arthur managed to reward Stormbringer with a wintry chuckle.

'My limited knowledge of women tells me that she'll give you due consideration, especially with a gift such as this. I believe she will be flattered! For what it's worth, I believe she'll accept you as her husband. You were her favourite from the moment when you were the master and we were the slaves. My felicitations, Valdar! She'll accept you as surely as the sun rises each morning.'

Stormbringer grinned like a beardless boy and reverently

129

rewrapped the neckpiece, stowing it carefully back into his travelling bag.

'I have a gift for you, too, Arthur. Don't look so grumpy, my friend. One of your own men found it on the battlefield and brought it to me, certain that it should be yours.'

Arthur wanted to turn away, but his curiosity was stronger than his pride. He glanced down at the object resting in Stormbringer's outstretched hand.

'It's a dragon brooch! It looks as though it might be precious, but what's so unusual about it? The whole north seems to worship the winged worm or sea dragons.' Arthur sounded petulant, but Stormbringer refused to take offence.

'Look closely at it, brother, and then you can tell me whether its presence on a battlefield in Gotland isn't unusual.'

Grumbling, Arthur took the hand-sized pin, for so it proved to be. The brooch was very heavy and decorated on both sides, implying that it had been made for some other purpose than adornment. The young man knew that the northern dragon had vestigial legs, huge wings, an incredibly long tail and a massive head. Further, the northern dragon was really more serpentine in appearance than Arthur's concept of this mythical beast.

This pin was coated with some red metal or enamel, and the dragon possessed four muscular legs, wings and a tail that were in proportion, much like a large cat. Arthur had seen a similar creature before made in gold and red enamel and depicting the mythical beast in profile. But, despite all his efforts, he was unable to recall where.

'This isn't northern workmanship,' Arthur pronounced emphatically. Then he noticed an odd addition under the belly of the heavy piece. At some time in the past, a large pointed metal fitting had been welded on the back of this object, so the double-sided figure had been designed to be affixed to a long pole as a standard, similar to the Eagles of Rome.

All at once the solution came to him like a revelation.

His foster-father had once told him about the Dracos Legion, the last Roman legion to leave Britain when it finally abandoned its barracks at Isca, near Venta Silurum, nearly two centuries earlier. This dragon had been the legion's standard. The pin, which had been modified to hold barbarian cloaks together, had started its useful life atop a tall pole that led the Roman legion to whatever godforsaken places they were assigned by assorted emperors.

'The Dracos Legion never crossed the Rhenus River, so how did this standard find its way into these northern climes?'

'I can't answer your question, Arthur, but I believe you should accept this gift from your men. They believe it is *your* dragon, for young Eamonn described such a beast as being among the totems of your birth-father. Your crews insist that you should have it. I might add that their gift is offered out of love and respect for their leader, my friend.'

Arthur felt a flush of shame. He had been churlish to his good friend because, as often seemed the case, he'd been in a bad mood. And so this small fragment of Rome reminded him once again of his own home, and the memory caused his stomach to lurch painfully. With his friend, Eamonn, and his sister, Maeve, the original Arthur had set out from Tintagel for the Otadini kingdom as an escort for Eamonn's sister, Blaise, who had been promised in marriage to the Otadini heir. Would the same prospects for happiness ever arise again?

'Thank you, Stormbringer. Please thank the crewmen for me. You can tell them they have found a Roman standard which is very important to me and to my family. I am proud that they deem me worthy of such an outstanding gift. How the object came to be in Gotland will always be a mystery, but perhaps God sent this pin to remind me that we hold the future of our people in our own hands and we carry our homes with us wherever we go.'

'I've decided that we will begin to burn our dead tomorrow, and then we shall set sail for home,' Stormbringer explained with a wide grin. 'Home! I've missed my girls so much! It's part of the disadvantage of parenthood, my friend, as you'll discover one of these days.'

'I doubt that somehow, Stormbringer. My family is cursed with dragon's blood, so we seem to kill everyone we love.'

'Bollocks!' Stormbringer cursed pungently. 'Who told you such fucking nonsense? From all reports, my father's father was a tyrant, a monster and a vicious savage. His curse didn't blight my father's life – or mine! Why should you be any different?'

'You don't understand—' Arthur tried to protest.

'You have one life, Arthur, and the dead can't shape you unless you let them,' Stormbringer interrupted with a finality that brooked no further argument. He had effectively turned the direction of the subject away from hidden shoals.

'Home!' Arthur's voice was full of longing, but the Sae Dene wisely ignored it. They talked until dawn began to stain the sky and the burning of their dead began. Neither man felt any weariness.

The time had come to leave Gotland and allow a new chapter to begin in their lives.

'How many men can there be in this benighted part of the world who are called Arthur? And how many of them are renowned by one and all as the Last Dragon?' Lorcan's voice was edgy with irritation and excitement.

'Arthur has only been here for four years!' objected Germanus. 'The man you're talking about has been made an outlaw after alienating the High King of the Dene, but the same man seems to have won numerous battles for the Sae Dene king, Valdar Bjornsen.'

'You seem to doubt my Arthur's skills?' Gareth responded pugnaciously.

'No, but I have my doubts that he could carve out a huge reputation in such a short period of time,' Germanus shot back.

'So what do we do? Do we accept the rumours of this Last Dragon who is the protégé of this Valdar Bjornsen? Do we travel to his base which is purported to be on one of the larger islands to the north of the Dene lands? I believe it is called The Holding, and the innkeeper assured me it is heavily defended by Dene seafarers totally loyal to the Sae Dene king. If the Arthur mentioned in the rumours I heard is not our man, we could be entering a place of great danger to us. Or do we keep looking, and commence our search in Heorot which is the seat of power for Hrolf Kraki, the High King of the Dene?'

Lorcan drained his mug of beer and wiped his mouth and beard on his grimy sleeve.

'We can't just ignore the information you've gleaned for us,' Germanus countered sullenly. 'I think The Holding seems a reasonable place to start our search. This Stormbringer person sounds like the type of man who'd sail to Britannia in search of spoils so, even if Arthur isn't there, we might discover his likely whereabouts.'

Lorcan gazed around the grubby inn with its straw-covered floor that had obviously not been changed for years. The stench that rose from the filthy mildewed hay caused him to clear his throat constantly and breathe exclusively through his mouth.

The inn was cheap and served most of the strangers who found their way to Lubeck. Lorcan was pleased to note that the local beer was very good, while the girls were rosy-cheeked, flaxen-haired and plump.

He scratched his armpit reflectively. While he might pretend to be untidy and dirty in his habits, he hated catching bedbugs from shared pallets. This inn was no filthier than most, but after three years of wandering, Lorcan and Germanus were tired. They longed for their new families in Arden, and Germanus frequently worried about his wife and their infant son who would now be running and playing on two sturdy legs. Those years with his child could never be replaced.

Now that they were so close to the end, Lorcan was convinced that the information he had received about this Last Dragon referred to Arthur. Their long journey through the wild, northern world could be almost over.

'I propose that we go directly to The Holding. The Sae Dene king should know of this Last Dragon and may be able to give us some word of Arthur.'

'I agree with you, Father,' Gareth replied, his eyes dancing with the old zealotry that Lorcan thought had vanished after the experiences of their long wandering.

'And I,' Germanus grumbled. 'Anything would be better than these flea-pits.'

'Then we are all agreed,' Lorcan summarised. 'We'll take ship to the island, and then find our way overland from the nearest port. Our funds have shrunk during our travels, so I hope that Arthur has acquired some gold during his absence. Otherwise, we might find ourselves marooned in the north and will have to seek gainful employment.'

* * *

The corpses of those warriors who had served on the shield wall were laid on a huge pile of tree logs. Stormbringer ordered the nearby copse to be razed to provide the fuel necessary to send his warriors to their destinations in Heaven or Valhalla. Arthur's only demand was that the Geat fisherman, Ivar, should go to the flames with the Dene dead.

'But he was a traitor to his own people,' Stormbringer complained. 'His corpse will contaminate the pure souls of our dead heroes.'

'Ivar was a brave man, Stormbringer. He abhorred what Heardred had done in Lund and was generous in his demands that we spare the lives of the brothers who inhabited the Abbey. For those virtues, he was tortured to death by Heardred's minions. What was visited upon him was perhaps the most barbaric and wicked thing that these eyes of mine have ever witnessed. He has earned his place on the pyre.'

Stormbringer was persuaded, but was still unhappy that a Geat's ashes should mingle with the remains of the loyal Dene warriors.

'The winds will mingle all our ashes in time,' Arthur replied, and his face seemed to glow in the noon's weak light. 'Enemy and friend, saint and sinner, we will all await the judgement that is certain to come. Ivar's intentions were good. I, for one, wouldn't flinch from lying with Ivar in the shadows.'

Arthur had his way and the pyre of the Dene warriors burned all through the day and into the night. When the glowing fragments of the great logs finally collapsed in a firestorm of sparks, the dead had been totally consumed and their ashes were blown away by the winds that came off the great, lonely plains until, in time, they reached the sea where they became a part of the huge, grey mother ocean. So the battle of the Smaland Plain was done, and the survivors were free to return to their homes and their families.

The three travellers had no difficulty in finding a boat whose master was willing to take them to Ostoanmark, but the captain had no intention of pushing his luck by dropping the strangers off at The Holding. He was acutely aware of his bastard Saxon heritage and was quite certain that the Sae Dene would object to his presence, especially with uninvited strangers on board.

The travellers had been forced to pay an exorbitant price to have their horses transported with them for, as the captain pointed out, their beasts would take up storage space that could be allotted to trade goods. Quick to realise that beggars can't be choosers, Gareth reluctantly accepted the captain's conditions. At the very worst, possession of the horses would allow them to travel to The Holding quickly once they disembarked.

As when crossing the channel between Dubris and Gesoriacum, Gareth spent the days either comatose or vomiting over the side, racked with what Lorcan called the *mal de mer* illness.

The voyage was protracted for both passengers and horses, for the vessel put in at most of the settlements dotted throughout the small islands that made up the Dene homeland. Trade goods of all descriptions changed hands while the horses pined for leg-room and Gareth hungered for solid ground under his boots. Unable to eat or drink, he lost weight and remained pallid for the five days it took to reach Stormbringer's island. Meanwhile, the captain spent most of his time scanning the eastern horizon where Skania was hidden behind thick autumnal cloud banks or glancing over his shoulder into the seas that lay to the west. In truth, the wily trader expected piratical longboats to appear out of the fogs at any moment.

'I'll trade with the buggers who frequent these islands, but I'll never trust them. This ship is still intact because I know when to pay and when to run,' he told Lorcan with a knowing wink. Although he was a staunch pagan, the captain had developed a soft spot for the dishevelled priest, mainly because, unlike most of his fellow prelates, Lorcan was partial to both a drink and a warm woman. He also swore like a farm worker.

'I know you are chary of the Dene people, Master Ernil, but what's the problem with their king? This Hrolf Kraki seems unwilling to stir out of his palace . . . hall . . . or whatever the hell it is that these heathens call their meeting place, while your Saxon and Jute kinsmen pick away at his border villages like cracking fleas off a blanket. And why would he declare that the king of the Sae Dene is a traitor? Wouldn't he need his sailors to hold an island kingdom together?'

Master Ernil shrugged expressively. 'Hrolf Kraki isn't called the Crow King because he's a man of generosity and loving brotherhood. According to everything I've heard of him, he's a vicious and greedy son of a bitch who likes few people and trusts even fewer. It appears he's become a hundred times worse since he took up with his fancy piece, the witch-woman called Aednetta. I've been told that she plays on his fears of treason and reminds him constantly that he has been cursed by the gods. If he engages in any warlike activity, the gods' curses will come crashing down on his head.'

Lorcan's face must have looked blank, so Master Ernil attempted to explain the tangle of superstitions that existed in northern religion.

'Hrolf Kraki decided to invade Vaster Gotland and the sagas describe his theft of the Geats' gold by stealth in the dead of night. As the Crow King and his guard attempted to escape, the alarm was raised. Personally, I'm sure that Loki was to blame, because the Crow King's answer to his dilemma had the stamp of the trickster god on it.'

While Lorcan showed a mute appreciation for the story he had spun, Master Ernil swilled something brown and potent from a leather bottle he had taken from his shirt, swallowing the liquid with an appreciative shudder. After Master Ernil's dirty palm wiped the lip of the container, the priest declined to sample anything when the bottle was offered.

'As the king and his guard made their escape, Hrolf Kraki began to throw handfuls of golden objects behind him, knowing that their pursuers were fallible creatures, even if they had sworn oaths to their gods and the Geat king. The warriors paused to squabble over each of the precious objects, and this allowed the Dene warriors to escape with the bulk of the treasure.'

'So? How does such a victory convince the king not to go to war?'

Despite himself, Lorcan was captivated by the tale.

'The gods aren't overfond of being mocked, even by Loki who is one of their own. Hrolf Kraki was cursed for his greed and guile, so he's been warned that he shall die with ignominy if he stirs himself to attack *anyone* – ever! That's quite a punishment when you consider that the Jutes are hungry for the return of their lands along the Jutland Peninsula. He stays put in his hall while his enemies nibble away at the fringes of the Dene kingdom.'

'Surely the Crow King is being stupid,' Lorcan put in. 'The curse of the gods might or might not happen, but invasions by his enemies will surely occur if he remains afraid to protect his people and his kingdom.'

'That may well be so! Rumour whispers that Valdar Bjornsen,

the Sae Dene king whose bones should rot in hell, crossed swords with Hrolf Kraki in a dispute over some strange captives whom Stormbringer had gifted to his king. Bjornsen was outlawed and banished for his trouble. Now that was stupid, but it was good for us traders who have no ties to the Dene rulers. Stormbringer would never let us sail in these waters if he hadn't been involved with a revolt in Skania.'

'Stormbringer? That's a powerful name!'

'I'll give the Sae Dene his due, for he's one of the truly great sailors and he seems to be blessed by the gods. He has sailed further out over the seas than any man in the north. It's said that he brought back a large hoard of treasure and some valuable captives after his last voyage to the British lands.' Ernil chuckled until his double chins quivered like jellied meat. 'It's worth noting that Hrolf Kraki managed to confiscate that treasure.'

'Naturally!' Lorcan replied drily.

Almost immediately, a shouted warning came from the lookout that land had been sighted off the bow.

'That's Ostoanmark, Stormbringer's island,' Master Ernil said. 'And it's close as I want to go to Stormbringer's lair! I'll be dropping you at the first available cove, but you and the horses will have to swim to shore once we enter the shallows. You must understand that I'll not beach my girl and risk being caught with a bare arse.'

'Yes, I understand! I'll rouse my friends and we'll be ready to depart when we are close enough.' Lorcan grinned suddenly and bared his sharp canines.

'You'd not dump us too far out, Master Ernil, would you? We'd hate to part from you on bad terms.'

Ernil had survived for a long time because he judged men accurately, so he decided to play fair with these three travellers, not least because their swords were long and sharp. Particularly, the captain could sense that the young warrior was a trained killer who would be pitiless in combat. Yes, Ernil decided, it's always better to be prudent in this wicked world.

Arthur was at sea with the Sae Dene's fleet as they slid through the swells with a fresh aft breeze blowing them northwards to their destination at the bivouac in Skania. The other ships in the fleet were close-hauled around him with Stormbringer's longboat, *Valhalla*, in the fore. As they skimmed over the waves like a hunting gull seeking shoals of fish, the crews knew they were heading for land and a well-deserved period of rest. Their hearts were lifted by the promise of soft pallets, sweet and pliant women and the leisure time to drink deeply.

Then, from his favourite position beside the mast, Arthur heard a warning cry from the lookout. Perched precariously high up on the swaying mast, the young sailor pointed towards the west where the setting sun was turning the sea to molten basalt in the ruddy light. Arthur realised that an unknown ship was scudding towards them which bore the dragon emblem of Stormbringer's house.

This strange longboat, obviously lightly crewed, was sliding through the waves like a marine creature until it came within earshot of Stormbringer's vessel.

The shouted conversation between the Sae Dene and the captain of the strange ship was clearly audible to Arthur who had positioned *Sea Wife* at the stern of *Valhalla*.

'Lord Bjornsen, I bear tidings from my lord, Jarl Hnaefssen whose lands lie on the Jute border. He reminds you of your promise to assist him if the Hundings should attack him, and my master is sorely pressed for the Crow King refuses to aid us. If we should fall, the way to the Dene lands lies clear before the invaders.'

'Who speaks to me for Jarl Hnaefssen?' Stormbringer shouted from the prow of *Valhalla*.

'My name is Henning Gunnarsen, master. Our need was so great that I was forced to seek you at your home base for we were unaware of precisely where you had gone. I also bear tidings from your cousin, Frodhi, who implores you to help us. He bade me tell you that Hrolf Kraki has become more and more disturbed and is openly ruling in concert with the witch-woman, Aednetta, and that the Crow King must either be forced into action to help his people or be swept away with an iron hand.'

'Do not speak treason to me, my friend, and not in my cousin's name,' Stormbringer shouted from longboat to longboat. The young courier paled.

'I beg your pardon for my unwise words, lord, but our plight is serious and we don't know what to do. When I arrived at The Holding, I found that your kinfolk had only just escaped murder at the hands of armed assassins. Your sister sends a message to assure you that all is now well after the defenders beat off an attack. The Crow King had sent a band of his warriors to destroy your lands and kill your children, but disaster was averted by the woman, Blaise, and a small group of strangers who have recently arrived at your home. Your children are safe and well, but she instructed me to tell you that Hrolf Kraki will always be a threat to you and yours for as long as he is permitted to live. She insists that you must resolve your disagreement with the king, one way or another.'

The wind had begun to freshen so the boats were driven slightly apart. The lighter foreign craft would have been swept away had its crew not tacked and weaved slightly to keep it travelling at the same speed as the heavily laden *Valhalla*.

'Do you need provisions?' Arthur shouted as the longboat edged closer.

'Aye, master. Our water supply is low for we've had no time to break our journey.'

'Then follow me to our safe harbour,' Stormbringer interrupted. 'Once there, we will all board *Sea Wife* where I can hear all your reports. We will feed you and decide on a concerted plan of action.'

Stormbringer allowed *Valhalla* to increase its speed and sail ahead of the fleet to the large cove where their new slaves, their plunder and provisions were under guard. Her astonishing power soon had her slicing through the waves like a huge dolphin.

Dumped unceremoniously on a shingled shore, the three travellers quickly adjusted to being on horseback, although Gareth still remained an odd shade of grey for the entire morning of their slow trek into the north. The group found themselves forced to move slowly through this unusually flat landscape because their horses took some time to acclimatise themselves to the land after their cramped sea passage.

The island of Ostoanmark was small by Frankish standards, its wide plain scarcely above sea level. Germanus observed to Gareth and Lorcan how the sea could easily break through the dunes to poison the land with salt, a persistent threat in these parts. Long grasses grew to the height of a horse's belly until they reached the small hillocks of sand where the vegetation eventually disappeared. One particularly coarse species of vine with livid yellow flowers grew riotously on the edge of the dunes, binding the sands together and changing guard with the stiff grasses and their waving seed-heads. Germanus gazed at a wide, pale-blue sky alive with thin, scudding clouds and felt the breeze with its nip of cold air on his face.

The Frank decided that he was wondrously happy.

'Well! These are healthy cattle! Very healthy!' Lorcan commented, with one wary eye running over a large horned specimen some distance away. 'Let's hope we don't anger any of the bulls.'

'We're high in the saddle, so other animals consider we're too big to attack,' the country-born Gareth suggested. 'This Stormbringer probably owns the beasts anyway so he must be a very wealthy man.'

'I don't give a shit if he's a Midas! If he's got Arthur, Eamonn and the girls in his care, he can bloody well give them up,' Lorcan growled. 'I'm fair sick of travelling. Let's get the young ones into our care and we'll get the fuck out of here.'

'I'm pleased you're taking such pains with your manners and your language. You'll certainly impress the king of the Sae Dene,' Germanus sniped. 'Get a grip on your temper, Lorcan. I'd like to leave this rather beautiful place in one piece if I can. Look around you, and then consider the cesspits we've seen since we embarked on this journey. This land is a paradise.'

'There'll be something wrong with it,' Lorcan countered grimly. 'There always is!'

And so, with their customary bickering and insults, Germanus and Lorcan passed through the soft landscape as the scenery changed to fields of stubble that were ready for the plough. Gareth blocked out the voices of his companions and enjoyed the views around them. The crops had been harvested; the density of the dying growth spoke of a bumper crop, while the absence of overlooked grain in the stubble spoke eloquently of good husbandry and careful gleaning.

By early afternoon, the three friends had devoured a hurried, horseback meal of stale bread and goat's cheese without pausing to rest. The noontime sun was mild and Lorcan was elaborating on the differences between this pale-lemon sun and the white-hot, moisture-sucking heat that was ever-present in the lands of the Middle Sea.

'Do shut up, Lorcan,' Gareth interrupted and pointed towards a line of thick, black smoke rising above the landscape.

'The colour of that smoke ahead seems to indicate a burning building,' Germanus said crisply and dug his heels into his stallion's ribs. 'The farmers might need help, so I'll ride on ahead.' His horse leaped forward leaving Gareth and Lorcan in its wake.

Using a small whippy branch on his mule's hindquarters to encourage the stubborn animal to speed up, Lorcan grumbled and puffed with exertion.

'Are you sure that sticking our noses in won't get us into more trouble?' he asked Gareth.

'No, but a fire is a good excuse to come calling, wouldn't you say?' Gareth countered. 'The homestead ahead of us might need our help, even if it's not The Holding. They'll be able to give us some directions that will lead us to our destination.'

'I hope so! I'm too old to go gallivanting all over the north.'

Ahead of them, Germanus's horse had raised a small pall of dust from the dry stubble as he cantered towards the smoke. But it was Gareth's sharp eyes that saw the two longboats drawn up on the beach of a small cove to their right.

The ships had been dragged above the high water mark, where they lolled about in the softer sand. Several warriors who were keeping guard over the longboats raised their heads at the sound of galloping hooves and turned to face this new threat with upraised axes. One of the men held a huge round shield decorated with a painting of a great, black crow with outstretched wings.

'Hrolf Kraki must be here,' Lorcan shouted. 'That fire is no accident, so someone needs our help. Ride like hell, Gareth, and catch up with Germanus. The Crow King's obviously decided that attacking a fellow Dene with only two ships isn't actually fighting a war.'

Gareth had already spurred his destrier into a gallop and released the reins controlling the packhorses. Pausing only to hope that the northern gods would curse Hrolf Kraki and his minions, Lorcan tried unsuccessfully to force some extra effort from his shambling mule.

The afternoon was beginning to dim as Gareth and Germanus reached the top of a slight rise on the outskirts of The Holding and realised that a pitched battle was being waged between the farm buildings while a barn was burning fiercely in the background. Gareth could see that the defending force included women and children.

'Let's ride like hell, Germanus,' he yelled, 'even if the horses are killed in the process. Those are our people down there – and they need us now!'

THE BATTLE OF THE HOLDING

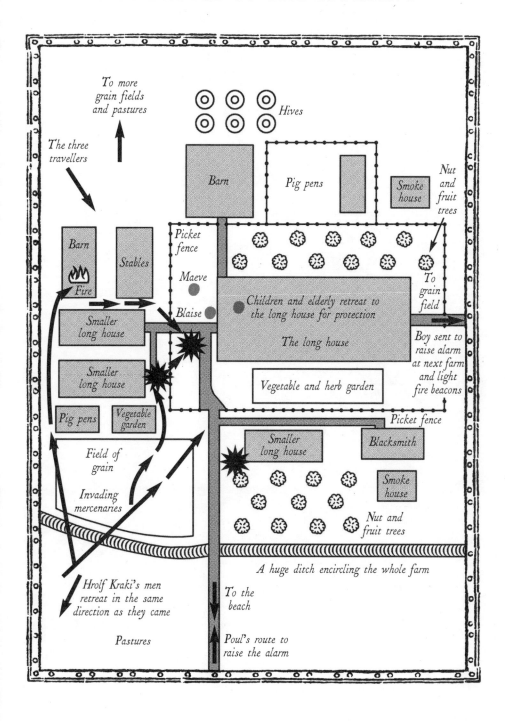

THE ENEMY MOORINGS

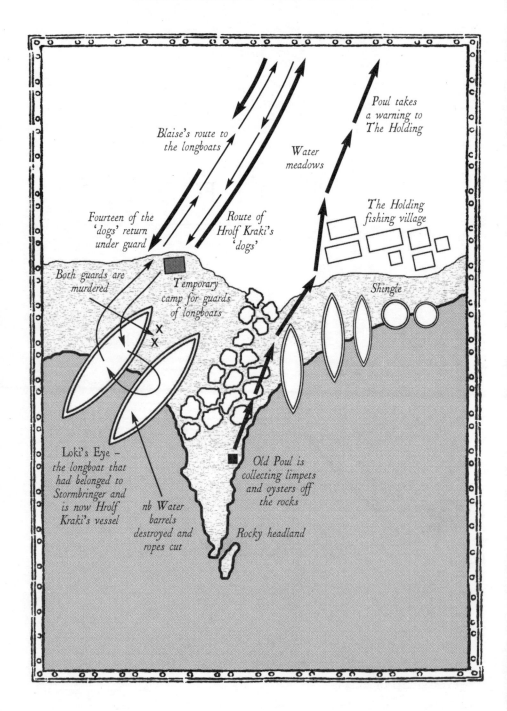

Blaise's route to
the longboats

Poul takes
a warning to
The Holding

Water
meadows

Fourteen of the
'dogs' return
under guard

Route of
Hrolf Kraki's
'dogs'

The Holding
fishing village

Both guards are
murdered

Temporary
camp for guards
of longboats

Shingle

Loki's Eye –
the longboat that
had belonged to
Stormbringer and
is now Hrolf
Kraki's vessel

Old Poul is
collecting limpets
and oysters off
the rocks

nb Water
barrels
destroyed and
ropes cut

Rocky headland

CHAPTER VII

TRAITORS, FOOLS AND LOVERS

Who is she that looketh forth as the morning, fair as the moon, clear as the sun, and terrible as an army with banners?

The Bible, Song of Solomon 6:10.

The Holding had been attacked an hour earlier, but Fortuna sometimes favours women with bold hearts and children who are brave, loyal and obedient. Whatever the reason, an old man was hunting for shellfish on the rocky point when the longboats hove into view.

The arthritic swelling disease had ravaged old Poul's elbows and knees but, so far, his fingers still retained some dexterity so, with his worn knife, he contributed to his family's diet by prising small shellfish off the rocks and hunting for large bivalves where bubbles rose along the sweep of the tide-line. An old woollen bag carried his rotting fish; the bivalves responded to the miasma of decay dragged over the sands to betray their positions to his ever-sharp blue eyes.

Initially, the elderly man assumed that Stormbringer had returned, so his face shone with anticipation. But then he made out the circular shields set in their cradles along the sides of the longboats and the device painted on the two large sails – and he knew.

The symbol of the black crow! The High King was the avowed enemy of Stormbringer, his master, and armed foes rarely approached the homes of their enemies with conversation on their mind. The Holding would soon be under attack.

This attack had come from the sea and all the best warriors in Stormbringer's force were fighting with the master in Skania.

Ignoring the pain from his hip joints, old Poul knew something had to be done – and now! He scrambled over the rocks of the headland, up the dry sand dune and across the water-meadows leading to The Holding with the speed of a much younger man. Within minutes, he reached the fields where the farm labourers were ploughing the fields ready for sowing.

'We are under attack!' the old man yelled. 'The Crow King comes with armed men in two longboats. Return to The Holding at a run! Move your arses, boys, for they'll be right behind me.'

Poul caught the arm of one young boy as the lad ran past him. With his mouth gaping foolishly, the boy stared back uncomprehendingly.

'Run to Atric Poulssen's farm as fast as your legs can carry you, boy. Raise the alarm there and beg them to give us whatever aid they can. Also, ask Master Atric to light the beacons so we can warn the other farms that the wolves have come while our master is away. Now, boy, or we'll all be dead before you get started.'

Finally panicked, the boy ran for his life, his twelve-year-old legs pumping.

'At least the lad is out of harm's way,' the old man muttered to himself with a twinge of guilt, because the boy was one of his grandsons. Then he scuttled off to the small house where he lived with his daughter. With only the briefest of explanations, he pushed her to one side and found the clothes chest in his room. From under his most prized possessions, he lifted out an old sword, a knife and a small circular shield. Cursing vilely, he hunted at the bottom of the chest until he retrieved a battered old helmet that he planted on his head with a growl of pleasure.

All over The Holding, the male workers and slaves were arming themselves while women sought out staves, spears and, in the case of Maeve, a sturdy bow and a good supply of arrows. Alfridda and Blaise had already decided that the invaders must be confronted before they reached the main farm complex, where Blaise intended to protect all the children with her brother's sword and a knife produced by Alfridda. Maeve loped away with her bow and quiver strung over her shoulder, while she braided her mane of scarlet hair so she could thrust it under a knitted cap.

'I'll need a supply of flammable oil, Alfridda, the sort you use when you are burning off the refuse at the end of the sowing season,' Blaise demanded. The young girl's face looked odd and stretched, as if a stranger was trying to break through her skin. 'I'll take as much as you can give me! I don't care about the quality, just the quantity. I want to make sure that Hrolf Kraki's pigs regret coming here – especially if they intend to harm the children.'

Alfridda stared at the British girl with a puzzled expression on her face. Although her initial reaction to Blaise had been to admire the girl's delicate beauty, living with Blaise had failed to bring Alfridda any deeper understanding of the girl's character.

151

She never encouraged anyone at The Holding to know and understand the *real* her.

Conversely, Maeve was easy to like and threw herself into the farm's life. Both girls worked hard, especially with the children, but there was a coldness in Blaise's nature that repulsed Alfridda, who was a warm, open woman with a strong and practical bent.

Yes, Blaise was an enigma. Especially now.

'We have some seal oil. But why do you want it? I can't understand what you propose to do with it, if we are under attack.'

Blaise grinned at Alfridda, her merciless eyes flat. 'I intend to spring a little surprise on our unwelcome visitors before they gain entry to the buildings. If it works, Maeve can pick the bastards off with her bow and arrows while our attackers are cooking slowly in blazing seal oil. I detest creatures that prey on women and children.'

Alfridda knew that she was incapable of inflicting such agonising damage on another human being. Blaise, however, was dewy-eyed with expectation as if she was anticipating a visit from a demon lover. In its pseudo-innocence her beatific smile made Alfridda's blood run cold.

Stormbringer's sister stared at the young girl with wide, astonished eyes.

'I thought you were the gentle one of my pair of Britons, Blaise, so you've surprised me. We Dene have a horror of fire because we depend on it to keep us alive in the depths of winter. Many deaths in our communities have been caused by fire in our houses, and most children suffer small burn scars from accidents. Still, we will always need it for the bounty it gives us.'

'One of my ancestors was the Boar of Cornwall, a king well versed in the deadly arts of war,' Blaise responded. 'Another ancestor was Pridenow, a brilliant ruler whose disposition was as cold as your ice packs. Mercy has no place in the British world where I grew to womanhood. Had I not been stolen from my country by your brother, I would have been wed by now to a young king in the embattled north of Britain. In those tribal lands, my true destiny was to see my husband and my sons die before their time, just as the women of my family have done since the Saxons first arrived on our shores. I've seen fires burn nuns in their nunneries and priests in their churches, and my kin wait every day for raiding parties that come into our lands every spring and kill and maim and burn. You may think me cold and ruthless, but how could I be anything else?'

Blaise squared her shoulders proudly. Alfridda realised that she would break before she would surrender, and there was nothing that she wouldn't do to survive.

'Aye, Alfridda, the blood of heroes runs in Blaise's veins,' Maeve explained. 'Her brother carried this gladius because he knew that the Romans were far shorter than the barbarians who served them as mercenaries and that a short sword kills at short range just as nastily as a longer blade. Blaise will blind them with her softness and beauty, so they will come within the reach of her blade. And then she'll not hesitate.'

'Your children will be safe with us,' Blaise promised with narrowed, savage eyes. 'It's time for you to see to the defence of this place. We'll do our part!'

As Alfridda ran to organise the workers who would defend the farm and its inhabitants, she shuddered with amazement. Little Blaise? With hell in her eyes and murder in her heart, the tiny girl was proving to be a princess in truth – and not just by birth.

According to the ancient who had first seen the strange longboats, they were faced by a force of at least thirty men, excluding the few who had been left to guard the vessels. The Holding boasted over fifty slaves who worked the earth and cared for the livestock and, because Stormbringer was essentially a kindly master, his slaves were treated far better than those at other estates. Over time they were permitted to marry and raise their own Dene families. As a result the slaves were eager to fight for their homes and families on the farm. Underneath their fervour lay the knowledge of what their fate would be if they were taken as prisoners to the halls of Heorot and judged under the despotic rule of Hrolf Kraki and his vicious bitch of a paramour. They would truly become slaves – if they were allowed to live.

As well, fifteen fierce women, all mothers, were armed with spears, axes used for wood-chopping, wicked adzes and hoes. Alfridda knew that a woman defending her hearth and children can often be more dangerous than any man.

She could also count on another twenty young boys under sixteen and a motley group of old men who were still hale enough to lift a sword. These reserves had assembled around the farm buildings with makeshift armour, old shields and swords; both the young and the very old would succumb to the weaponry of the experienced warriors very quickly, but their numbers would help to slow the attackers down and make it possible for the farm labourers to swamp them with their numerical advantage. Nevertheless Alfridda sincerely regretted the need to use them against the might of Hrolf Kraki's thugs.

All told, her force outnumbered Hrolf Kraki's assassins by eighty-five to forty. However, her untrained and inexperienced defenders were no match for combat-ready Dene warriors; only chance and their limited advantage in numbers could save some of her people from total annihilation. Alfridda knew the inhabitants of The Holding were in serious trouble.

Some of Stormbringer's strategic skills and the fire in the blood that drew men to his service were shared by his sister. She immediately understood that they must divide their force to protect each side of the main path leading into the heart of the property. Her motley force of untrained combatants would have slightly more chance of success if they could force their enemies to fight in enclosed and awkward spaces, so she decided to place some of her defenders in the laneways beside the workers' quarters, narrow paths which created ideal ambush positions. She divided her makeshift army pragmatically to use the women, old men and the striplings as bait while the able-bodied slaves were placed where they could strike at the heart of the invading warriors.

When the Dene mercenaries arrived, full of swagger and arrogance, the women bared their buttocks disdainfully and shouted unflattering descriptions of their manhood and Hrolf Kraki's ability to pleasure a normal woman. When these insults didn't work, one tall and buxom woman threw her spear at one of the Dene warriors with an almost masculine arm. With more luck than skill, her weapon spitted the man through the gizzard after a throw that was strong and true, and, mortally wounded, the man fell to the ground.

Then, enraged, the other mercenaries rushed at the woman to kill her out of hand.

Maeve's arrows brought two men down in the initial charge, and she watched as they tore at their chests with ineffective fingers. She had aimed at the base of their throats, determined to strike at unprotected flesh rather than the mailed shirts that covered their chests. They died, gurgling in their own blood.

The warriors came on, splitting into three groups. One group went to the left while another slightly larger group went to the right. The central group was soon carving its way through the few slaves guarding the main entrance to the central farm hall as if the resistance was made of butter. Alfridda could only hope that Blaise was as good as her word. They were all as good as dead if Blaise was unsuccessful.

Gradually and painfully, the inhabitants were being driven back, leaving behind them a litter of broken bodies, sorely wounded defenders and discarded weapons. Stormbringer would return to find their bodies had become scattered bones, gnawed at by scavengers that would find their corpses a tasty titbit before the beginning of the long winter.

Then, with the prospect of bitter failure in Alfridda's mouth, she heard a man scream violently. Many of the wounded had howled their agony that day, but the voice-box creating this terrible sound was almost destroyed in the process. The high-pitched shriek rose and rose, then suddenly stopped, leaving Alfridda's skin crawling with a sick horror.

She continued to stab with her long spear at the line of warriors in front of her, but the concentration of one of the men was so broken by the sickening sound of pain that her spear blade managed to slip past his shield to pierce the side of his body. As his axe lowered, one of the house-slaves hit him squarely on the head with a wooden hammer, smashing the side of his skull with a satisfying, wet thump.

Alfridda turned and saw a figure lying inside a core of white and yellow flame with a burning arrow shrivelling in the centre of the man's charcoaled back. As the smell of burning flesh reached her, Alfridda had to force down a wave of vomit and bile. Then, from out of a darkened corner near the entry to the hall, she saw another man stagger into the open space and she watched in horror as he set the afternoon alight with his death. One of the defenders, probably Blaise, had doused him in seal oil and had set him alight. As the flames rose up in a great explosion of heat, the victim danced for a moment like an animated scarecrow.

And then, mercifully, an arrow struck his chest and dropped the agonised and capering man to the ground.

Other Dene warriors ran from behind the corpse of the burning man, while tearing at their mailed shirts, tunics and cloaks as they tried to remove the oil that coated them and ran in long runnels through their hair and down their faces. Sickened by what they had seen during the death of their comrades, half a dozen warriors were fleeing from the form of a small woman, barely five feet tall, with long black hair bound into braids around her head. She was holding a bloodstained gladius in one of her hands while the other held a flaming torch that she was using with indiscriminate fury to set her victims alight. Men dodged around her, too fearful of her flames to cut her down.

Such a sight should have galvanised the defenders of The Holding, but with the same dramatic impact as the appearance of Blaise breathing fire and brimstone, two strangers had suddenly appeared from out of nowhere and galloped into the rear of the fray with swords drawn and swinging. The older of the two men swept the head off one of the assassins as neatly as a woman would sweep dirt from a doorstep, while the younger man, with white-blond braids flying around his face, impaled another attacker on his sword before withdrawing the blade with a neat twist of his wrist.

As the two strangers leaped off their warhorses to carve into the enemy from the rear, another stranger on a slow-moving mule could be seen plodding into view. If the defenders had had time to observe his approach, they would have seen that the rider was a priest.

He, too, climbed off his mount with less grace than eagerness, while pulling out a very clean and sharp sword. Alfridda barely had time to ward off a red-faced warrior wielding an axe before the priest attacked the warrior from one side to remove the hand holding the weapon that threatened her.

'Didn't your mother tell you to be nice to ladies?' he asked with a beatific smile.

The mercenary howled, clutching at the stump of his wrist to stem the arc of arterial blood spurting out. The priest shook his head ruefully, muttered something about bad manners and removed the wounded man's head with a clean blow to the neck. He bowed gallantly to Alfridda and moved on to his next victim.

The tide of battle seemed to have turned back in favour of the defenders with the arrival of the three strangers, obviously highly skilled warriors with the advantage of being able to attack their enemies from the rear. At the front of the attacking force, the struggling men were suddenly distracted from their individual battles when Blaise screamed with rage like one of Lorcan's banshees. One of the mercenaries had grabbed her hair from behind. As he tried to drag her close enough to cut her throat with his knife, Blaise never hesitated. She twisted sideways and moved slightly closer to his body before burying her gladius deep into his belly. Then, when the man's grip on her hair relaxed as he clutched at his vitals, his scream of unbearable pain mingled with her howl of fury. Without compunction, the fierce-eyed young girl picked up her torch and set the mortally wounded man alight.

'Jesus!' Lorcan muttered in surprise and awe at the cold-bloodedness of the girl's actions. To be burned alive was a terrifying way to die – and a woman had sent this man into the shades.

'Jesus!' he repeated to himself. 'She's one hell of a woman!'

And then he recognised her.

Lorcan's eyes were starry with admiration as he stalked towards a new adversary. Around them, arrows whizzed as Maeve used her bow to pepper any unprotected enemy flesh. The priest could see that the tide of battle had turned once again for Hrolf Kraki's dogs were slowly and surely being forced backwards toward the picket fence that surrounded the inner enclave.

Lorcan and Gareth could tell that the high number of casualties suffered by the defenders had, in the main, been inflicted on the untrained farm workers and slaves. However those who survived seemed to be the fittest and most capable from among Alfridda's small force.

Alfridda estimated that the three strangers were older on average than Hrolf Kraki's mercenaries, and although they were more skilled than the attackers and held the element of surprise, the number of trained men facing the enemy was still fewer than the remnants of the Crow King's minions.

Meanwhile, as Gareth hacked at each warrior who appeared before him, he sensed that the big difference between the two forces was the dramatic violence of Blaise and the toll of victims slain by Maeve's archery. Moreover the invaders lost all confidence when two women forced them to take defensive action, a shame too profound for Dene warriors to bear.

At the fence, the last fifteen men of the Dene force formed themselves into a defensive circle. They were ready to fight and die to the last man, but Alfridda pushed her way through the circle of surviving farm workers.

'You have one, and only one, chance to surrender your arms!

Do you wish to die at our hands? Should I give you to Blaise and Maeve? They may be women but they have no fear of you and they have killed many of your friends during this unwarranted and cowardly attack. We are prepared to encircle you and pick you off until we have you and the last of your men. You have one chance to decide your fate, so what do you choose?'

A tall warrior, with a nasty, long-healed scar across his nose, stepped forward with his shield raised defensively, in expectation of trickery.

'I believe that you will kill us, Lady Alfridda, no matter what decision we make. Yes, I do know your name! My master was thorough when he issued his orders. On the faint chance that you don't kill us out of hand, my master will carry out that task himself. For myself, I would prefer to die with my sword in my hand than be remembered as a coward.'

Blaise materialised out of the crowd. Her face was deathly white at what she had seen and done on this violent and vicious day. Her arms were stained with woodsmoke and soot, as were her clothes. A smear of blood covered the back of her simple shift from shoulders to buttocks and her gladius had been wiped on the hem of her dress, leaving an ugly blot. The Dene warrior shuddered. Her pale, frozen face spoke of amazement at what she had been able to do to other human beings. But now that her blood and her rage had cooled she was sickened by her actions. No matter what she did now, the memory of those blazing and blackening men with their hair and flesh turned to charcoal and their lungs seared into silence by flame would remain with her all her life. She wanted no more lives on her conscience this day, so she intended to force these warriors into surrender by any means at her disposal.

Yet she grinned like a gargoyle when she saw the eyes of the

Dene spokesman. This scarred warrior thought he could hide his true feelings, but men are amateurs at the ancient games of deceit that pass between the sexes. Women learn before they are half-grown how to disguise disagreeable or insulting thoughts.

'I can see you are still soaked with my oil, as are at least four of your men – and probably more!' She raised her voice so that every person present could hear her and, as her message sank in, Blaise raised her torch and held it high for all to see.

'I can ignite my torch and light the oil that soaks you in the flicker of an eyelid. You must wonder whether any of the oil has found its way from your tunics to those of your friends.'

Blaise's hollow black stare dared the eyes of each of her enemies to call her bluff, but Hrolf Kraki's dogs looked away in fear of the dreaded torch. 'Will you burn as furiously as your brothers who have already passed into death? We'll only know if you decide not to surrender your weapons, so make up your mind. I can light my torch while I wait on you.'

She held up a small lamp and the oil-soaked wick burst into flame.

The warriors who had been doused in oil found themselves deserted by their companions who shrank away from them as if they had been infected with Justinian's Disease.

'No! Wait! No!' the warrior in the forefront of the circle called out desperately. 'Don't be hasty about this matter! If you agree, I'm prepared to take my remaining men and leave your island in one of the two longboats that brought us here. If you wish, you may keep the other vessel as the blood-price for your dead. It is owned by Hrolf Kraki so it can rot for all I care. *Loki's Eye*! It's a bad luck vessel!'

Blaise and Maeve gasped with a sudden shock of recognition, and Alfridda swore in a most un-ladylike way.

'What did you say?' Alfridda took a short step towards the scarred man.

'I said the vessel is called *Loki's Eye?*' he replied doubtfully. 'My master was amused by its name, and said he was inflicting the justice of the gods on Stormbringer.'

None of the women saw fit to explain that *Loki's Eye* was Stormbringer's longboat, the same superb vessel that had taken the Sae Dene across the trackless ocean to Britannia. During the voyage, Stormbringer had won valuable plunder and great knowledge and had captured four young aristocrats from that green and fertile land. All of his spoils had been given to Hrolf Kraki as a personal tribute. When Stormbringer eventually refused to kill the captives on the king's orders, Hrolf Kraki had saved face by declaring the Sae Dene king to be an outlaw.

But *Loki's Eye* had finally come home.

'My men and I will run from the Crow King's revenge as far and as fast as we can. We have no right to ask for mercy from you, but fire is a filthy death and no man deserves such a punishment. Can we agree on this matter?'

'Very well,' Alfridda answered for Blaise, who placed the torch on the ground, extinguished it, and melted back into the press of bodies. Unconsciously, the farm workers allowed her to pass between them without allowing her to touch them.

'Before you depart, you will abandon your weaponry!' Alfridda decided. 'I also want to know exactly what Hrolf Kraki desired of you, including any instructions he gave that might affect my people in the future. I can promise you that Stormbringer will hunt you and your men down if you should betray us in this pact.'

The tall, scarred warrior nodded mutely, although his eyes kept turning to watch the smoking torch as it lay on the ground.

'What were your orders from Hrolf Kraki?' she persisted, but his reticence soon filled her with alarm. The scarred man cleared his throat nervously and addressed his dirty boots, rather than meet Alfridda's eyes.

'We were ordered to make an example of every person who lives at The Holding – men, women and children. No survivors! I can swear that many of us thought our king was crazed when he ordered us to take the children from the farmsteads, both high-born and low, and nail them to the front wall of the long-hall while they were still alive.

'Yes . . .' the warrior said softly and paused. 'We were appalled by the order, but you know Hrolf Kraki. What the Crow King wants, the Crow King gets!'

'Was that all that he asked of you?' Alfridda asked in a voice thick with sarcasm.

The warrior looked shame-faced, as if he had been caught out in a lie. 'I was told to ensure that you were killed, my lady, and your corpse was left on display in a prominent place where your brother would be certain to find you. We were to sack The Holding and kill everyone and everything in it, right down to the last hen in the chicken coops. Hrolf Kraki intended his wrath to be complete and terrible.'

'I think you'll find that Stormbringer's revenge and fury will be more than the equal of the king's treachery when my brother is told of what you have done,' Alfridda retorted with no trace of passion, apart from a promise of justice.

'We are fighting men, my lady. We are paid to carry out a task allotted to us by our master. We don't claim to be good men, but such orders are sickening to us. However, we are Hrolf Kraki's dogs. He owns us, so we must obey or our oaths are meaningless. Our family members are held hostage against our compliance with his wishes. I regret to say that we would have killed you all if circumstances had allowed.'

'At least you're honest. I'll give you that,' Lorcan interrupted almost cheerfully , as if that afternoon of blood had been a minor amusement. 'I'm quite sure that these young ladies would have cheerfully seen you and your men dead if they were given a reason to thrust you into the shades. Personally, I'd rather face down a slew of banshees than anger one woman who believes she's been wronged.'

'You don't know Hrolf Kraki,' the warrior retorted glumly.

'Then you have a problem, boyo. In your place, I'd be looking for fairer climes than Jutland and travel to some place where you can live in relative safety. Saxony perhaps – or Thuringia! They both need men who are handy with swords and are looking for gainful employment. For what it's worth, your longboat will be worth a small fortune to the right people. If I were you, I'd be going while I had the chance to run, meaning *now*, before this good lady decides to change her mind.'

The warrior was torn between conflicting emotions. Threats meant little to a man who had lived his whole adult life in the service of ruthless, brutal masters. He preferred to ignore any thoughts about the afterlife, and stated openly when he was in his cups that there were no gods in existence who could punish him for his misdeeds. However, he never courted death openly and, for the most part, enjoyed the pleasures of being alive. Eventually, after weighing up the relative merits of the situation, retreat won out. Besides, he told himself, his men could beach their vessel to the south of The Holding and return overland during the darkness of the long night. A few strategically placed torches thrust onto the reed-covered roofs and the farm buildings would burn like tinder.

And these two bitches from over the sea would blaze brightly with the other defenders. Perhaps he should spend some time with them first, teaching them the wisdom of forgetting his surrender and the fear he had shown when he'd been at a disadvantage. Then, when he saw the terror in their eyes, he'd feel like a man again.

Hrolf Kraki might not approve of all the details of this second attack on the farmsteads, but the message would be passed to the Sae Dene king with brutal force. Hrolf Kraki would be the ultimate winner in a game of power.

Maeve saw the warrior's eyes shift sideways and noted the tiniest flicker of his mouth because he was unable to disguise an anticipatory smile – and she recognised his contempt! He had decided on a way out of his predicament that would still deliver The Holding into his hands, so Maeve quickly scanned the faces of the farm survivors in search of Blaise. Together, they should be able to counter moves made by such a dumb brute. But Blaise had vanished without warning.

'Then we'll surrender to you, and I trust you'll allow us to leave the island in safety,' the spokesman muttered slowly, his crafty eyes darting from Gareth to Alfridda and the rest of the farm workers with an oddly ambivalent brusqueness.

This bastard is far too unrepentant, Maeve decided.

'Be careful, my lady,' Lorcan whispered softly into Alfridda's ear. 'I don't trust these swine as far as I can kick them and, at my advanced age, that's not very fucking . . .' His voice trailed off.

Embarrassed, the priest bowed his head and apologised as Alfridda fixed him with an arrogant blue stare. 'I should have said that I can't kick them very far, my lady.'

Alfridda turned back to face her captives.

'Your weapons,' she demanded. 'You will strip off your

armour, and lay all your arms in a pile alongside the fence. Your valuables will be placed on that boundary stone near the farm gate. Consider them confiscated!'

A look of chagrin flashed through the warrior's sly eyes. Then they became blank again as he mastered his emotions; there was replacement weaponry on board the longboat, so he was the first of the Dene warriors to move to the appointed spot and unbuckle his sword belt. Then he proceeded to remove several concealed knives from his boots and his belt, draw off his mailed shirt and tunic and, finally, place his shield and a beautifully wrought axe onto the pile. While the defenders of The Holding watched blandly, he moved to a whitewashed marker stone and placed a gold ring, a silver coin and an oddly shaped cloak pin on its pristine surface.

The rest of the raiders followed suit. For the best part of an hour, the warriors were thoroughly searched and everything of value was taken from them. Many of the warriors tried to secrete coinage as well as valuable gems taken as trophies while in the employment of Hrolf Kraki; one man was found to have gold coins secreted in his mouth.

Then, accompanied by the full complement of the farm defenders, even the children who had escaped from the store-room where they had been held, the defeated Dene warriors trudged away towards the cove where their two boats had been beached. The children enjoyed their humiliation hugely and tossed tussocks of grass and mud, cow turds, rotten food and human faeces at the invaders with the shrill enthusiasm of scavenging birds.

Part way to the shingled beach Blaise suddenly appeared at Maeve's shoulder.

'Where have you been?' Maeve whispered. 'I don't trust these bastards one bit and I've been looking for you so we could find a way of protecting The Holding from a surprise return.'

'Quiet!' Blaise hissed. 'I've been seeing to things – so hush! My plan might still go awry if they realise what I've been doing.'

And then Blaise noticed that the young man she remembered as Gareth, Arthur's servant and friend, was standing alongside her. She smiled beatifically. 'I remember you! You're Gareth, aren't you? It's remarkable that you've managed to find us after all this time. I must say that you're rather late!'

Gareth noticed several spots of blood on one of Blaise's shoes and a red edging around the sole of the other, as if she had stepped in a puddle of fresh blood. The young man shuttered his eyes and ignored the small oddity. He bowed to acknowledge her greeting, but any talk of their return to Britain was premature, so Blaise took Maeve's arm and they sauntered to the rear of the column making its way towards the beach.

Seemingly, nothing had changed at the cove sighted by Gareth during his gallop to the farm except for the absence of the two warriors who had been left to guard the longboats. Lorcan soon found their corpses lying together, side by side, with their hands devoid of weapons and their clothes soaked with blood from deep frontal slashes to their throats. One of the men had loosened his trews which had almost fallen to his knees, leaving his pale, shrivelled genitals bared pathetically to the grey sky and several persistent gulls that were searching for a special treat. Lorcan winced.

Maeve was thinking rapidly. How could Blaise overcome two fully grown warriors? Maeve never doubted that her friend had killed the sentries but, until this blood-soaked day, she would never have believed that Blaise had such a capacity for carnage.

One of the longboats had been inexpertly ransacked in such

a manner that it was unsuitable for an immediate voyage. Its water barrels had been stove in and sharp knives had slashed a number of ropes attached to the great sail. The other was untouched, as if the persons who had killed the guards had been interrupted before they could vandalise it. An adze with a wickedly sharp blade was lying on the shingle near the disabled longboat.

Maeve looked blankly at Blaise who gave her a limpid smile in return.

'Have faith, sister,' Blaise whispered softly. 'These bastards won't get far.'

Maeve felt a little queasy when she saw a gloating in Blaise's black eyes. Unbidden, her father's voice echoed in her head.

'The children of Cornwall are touched, Maeve, so it wasn't just the Pendragon line that had a strange heritage,' Bedwyr had said. 'I will always remember Morgan and the stories that were told of her. When I knew her, she'd turned herself into a grotesque and ugly object of horror. No man could look at her and not feel his balls shrivel, but Artor swore to me that his sister was once so beautiful that she could call any man she chose into her bed. With both these unnatural bloodlines, Artor should have been a monster, but something good resulted from the dark blood of two families cursed by fate.'

'God help us then!' Maeve breathed. 'What has Blaise done?'

Stormbringer paced frenetically up and down the narrow spaces in his tent as Arthur, the jarls and the courier from the Saxony border, Henning Gunnarsen, awaited his decisions. Tension made the air hum as strong men fidgeted on their folding stools.

'We have three clear problems, friends. Correct me if I've forgotten any details, but our first priority is the attack on our southern borders on the mainland. Ivar Hnaefssen has dealt fairly with us from the earliest days of the Skanian campaign and sent men and ships to us that he could ill afford to lose. I must repay my debts to him, so I propose that we sail to give him relief as soon as we can re-provision our vessels.

'Are we agreed?' Stormbringer demanded of the assembled captains.

'We are agreed, lord. Their aggression should be fought with our combined might and resources,' Erikk Halversen replied gruffly.

'Thank you! Our people must depend upon your honour and devotion to all of our land without reservation,' Stormbringer responded with dignity. But then his face twisted slightly.

'Secondly, I must ask permission from you to make a detour to The Holding while we are travelling to the relief of Ivar Hnaefssen. I must ensure that my family and friends are safe after the attack, and that I provide them with slaves and supplies in case the winter provisions have been destroyed. Something must be done about our king once I have proved the circumstances of his raid. Meanwhile, the fleet will continue under the command of one of your number while I discover what damage has been done to The Holding.'

'There is no need for you to divert to The Holding, my lord,' Arthur interrupted. 'I can perform this service on your behalf and then chase down the fleet once I find out what has occurred there. *Sea Wife* is a very fast longboat and my crew are superbly trained oarsmen. My boat can make the crossing quickly, while taking whatever booty, slaves and goods that you wish to be left in the safety of your broad acres. Truly, the fleet needs your steadying hand in command. I, too, have a stake in what has happened at The Holding so I will ensure that your girls are safe and well and determine the health and condition of your farm labourers and slaves. Then I will rejoin you in the south of Jutland. Please allow me to perform this small task for you, Valdar.'

The jarls were relieved by this proposal. The Sae Dene king should lead a Sae Dene fleet into any war, and each man present knew that personal worries should never deflect a king from serving the greater good, so they overruled Stormbringer's wishes and endorsed Arthur's solution. A ruler would be a fool to disregard his counsellors, and Stormbringer could never be considered a fool.

'By his recent actions, Hrolf Kraki has finally shown that he has been ensorcelled by the witch-woman and has deserted his people during their time of trouble. By attacking The Holding, he has shown that he rejects the ancient agreements that existed between the Land Dene and the Sae Dene. As the High King, Hrolf Kraki has broken our sacred covenants when he attacked my home at a time when he knew I would be absent. He has waged war on peasants, slaves, women and children, while refusing to assist his loyal vassals at a time when his subjects were under direct attack from our outside enemies. His actions are lacking in honour and reek of foolishness.'

'Hrolf Kraki is a fool!' Erikk Halversen punctuated Stormbringer's words gruffly.

'He's worse than that!' Arthur added. 'If the border lands should fall, he won't be able to protect the north from invasion by those who would do harm to our people. He refuses to wage war on legitimate enemies when jarls such as Ivar Hnaefssen have called for his assistance. How can he permit such a decent man to abase himself on his knees and ignore his legitimate pleas for aid? Is our king a pawn in a larger game? Hrolf Kraki must be confronted to remove the poisonous presence of the witch-woman from his court. Then, once he has been separated from his treasonous paramour, the Crow King might see sense and we could withdraw from Heorot in peace.'

'And if he doesn't agree to change his ways?' a hard-bitten, older jarl from the central Cimbric Peninsula asked morosely. This man knew only too well that his broad acres would be the next to succumb to the advances of the Hundings, once the lands of Ivar Hnaefssen had fallen into their hands.

'If he doesn't change his ways, Hrolf Kraki may have to be forcibly removed. If that should happen, my cousin, Frodhi, is next in line to the throne and he has generously provided men, ships and coin to the Skanian campaign. We would not have won without his support. If Frodhi should become the High King, the ancient ties between the two rulers could be re-established,' Stormbringer explained forcefully, and Arthur could think of no reason to contradict his master – although he immediately felt the tiniest warning scrape of a hidden claw along the inner surface of his skull.

'Are we decided then?' Stormbringer asked, and waited as, one by one, the jarls nodded their agreement.

'And so, Henning Gunnarsen, your questions have been answered,' Stormbringer said with some regret. The audience was over.

The longboat given to Hrolf Kraki's dogs by Alfridda ploughed through the deeper waters of the channel. Her woollen sail bellied out over the deck in the stiff breeze. The helmsman, however, continued to complain that the rudder had an unusual shudder and there was a drag on the vessel's forward movement, a sluggishness that this greyhound of a ship had never previously displayed, even in bad weather. The helmsman had sailed on her many times before and was familiar with her peccadillos.

The warrior who had acted as spokesman for the raiding party after the attack on The Holding had assumed the captaincy of this longboat after the death of its original captain. At first he ignored the helmsman's complaints, but as they became more strident the captain ordered the boat to come about into the wind so he could carry out an inspection. He ordered two of his crew members to check below the false decking that elevated the crew's feet above the outer skin of the hull.

The two men recoiled when they discovered that the crawl space below the decking that was normally used for food storage and drinking water was awash with sea water. Ordered to find the source of the leak and to stop the inflow that was causing the longboat to wallow in the waves, the two men searched along the planks of the hull with their feet and made a number of plunges into the freezing water until they found two planks that had been forced apart by an adze or some similar implement. Then, with ropes tightly tied around their waists, they were lowered into the heaving sea in an attempt to force rags and other stuffing into the widening gaps to reseal the hull. But such intervention was far too little – and much too late! Sea water continued to fill the hull.

The captain knew that his lack of care and his inaction had doomed his short command, and the vessel would not survive the tricks of the jokester god. The scarred man recalled that *Loki's Eye* was still resting on the shingle of the beach at The Holding. Loki had decided to save his namesake, but had gifted the captain and his crew to the *Sea Dragon* in its lieu.

As the vessel began to sink lower in the water, despite the efforts of the crew to bale the sea water out with any receptacles to hand, the captain ordered it to be turned towards the nearest land. But he had left this too late. The land was a black smudge in the evening sky when water began to rush over the sides as the longboat became more and more waterlogged. With a sudden rush, the dragon's head at the prow sank beneath the surface and the ship slipped into the depths.

The crewmen began to swim, but the autumn waters were freezing cold. Even ten minutes in these icy waves would bring death to humans and their bodies would sink below the surface to follow their ship into the gelid depths.

As the captain succumbed to the mind-numbing cold that made it impossible for him to swim, he wondered wearily who had killed them with such efficiency. He tried to raise his arms, but his limbs were too heavy to move and he no longer had any feeling in his body. He was so very tired that he hungered for sleep. As he slipped below the waves, he knew how pointless it was to hold his breath and struggle against the inevitable, so like the brave man he had once been, he permitted his own weight to drag him down into the lightless depths.

In dreams that night, the green she-dragon called Arthur to her throne where the bones of her ossuary were transmogrifying into pearl. Arthur heard the she-dragon giggling with splutters of steam that heated the water around his body. With long, emerald claws, she pointed to the bodies that hung on thickly branched seaweed like obscene fruit.

'You must thank your sister's friend for my latest gifts. It is rare that I am sent such a large number of warriors who are so tall and strong, and at the peak of their physical beauty. Their skulls will be smooth and perfect, while their bones will be without flaw after I've flensed away the ugliness of their flesh.'

Then the she-dragon chuckled as she told her story, but Arthur knew it was only a dream because the wilful and tiny Blaise could never act with such murderous intent. In response the dragon's tongue caressed Arthur's biceps in a gross parody of a kiss and lingered on the curve of his jaw, as if she could taste the purity of his bones.

'You delude yourself, Arthur, my dear one. I haven't met the little sow you call Blaise, but she can only tear away your peace at some time in the future. You must avoid becoming enamoured of her pillowy breasts or lusting after the delicate beauty of her mouth. I suggest that you do not ally yourself to her because she is of your people, regardless of the truth that her brother was your dearest friend. Blaise is dangerous for all that she is loyal, because too much of Ygerne's daughters lives in her blood for her to mate safely with you.

'If you do choose to wed her, you will regret your decision when you see the true face that she wears below her undoubted beauty. You must leave her for another man who will love her for who she really is, not what you think she should be. Have a care, Arthur!'

As the she-dragon curled on her terrible couch, small sea creatures flitted away from cleaning her scales to approach the hanging corpses. Once given permission to feed, they scattered over the shrouded bodies in a cloud of delicate, tiny claws and sucking lips.

As the underwater currents shifted, the dead warriors turned in the banks of seaweed. Arthur recoiled because their eyes and lips had already been nibbled away, and only empty holes stared back at him. The corpses were silently screaming that they wanted to live. Then, in a rush, the dragon spread her transparent green wings and blew him away on the ocean currents.

Arthur awoke to find himself in his own bed, completely drenched in sweat. Something heavy had lodged in his belly and he prayed for wisdom in the troubles that lay ahead. Then he vowed he would watch his friend's sister very carefully, although he was almost certain that his suspicions were traitorous.

Yet he was inclined to trust the words of the she-dragon and her hideous, but curiously honest, code of conduct. After all, she was very rarely wrong.

CHAPTER VIII

BLOOD KIN

Enemies' gifts are no gifts and do no good.

Sophocles, *Ajax* 1:665

As the wind filled the sail, the dragon motif came to life so it seemed to be flying in a nest of fire.

Arthur stood beside Snorri as the helmsman threw his whole weight against the great rudder. The stiff breeze caught at Arthur's curls and gave him a delicious feeling of freedom, lifting his spirits and lightening his heart so that he was actually whistling a country tune he had learned in Arden Forest. Unflappable, Snorri looked at his master and marvelled that the lad should be so cheerful. By all reports, The Holding had been attacked and who could know what they would find when they arrived back at those green acres?

Sea Wife was sailing through a narrow strait with a fair wind at their back; below decks, Stormbringer had given instructions that three large chests filled with the confiscated wealth of the Geats should be stored in the bilges, and Arthur was looking forward to good meals and fresh food. Not only was he returning to the pleasant world of Stormbringer's farm, but his three slaves would ensure that every detail of his life would be easy and well structured during a restful, albeit brief, stay at The Holding after a long period of trouble and strife.

The sound of his tuneful whistling caused Sigrid to raise her blond head, the hair chopped around her face inexpertly so she resembled the full and exotic chrysanthemum that Myrddion had drawn in his personal scrolls. Her blue eyes glittered for a moment as she gazed at him. Ingrid sighed inwardly. After weeks of nagging and lectures, the girl had finally accepted her mother's advice that it was stupid to persist in waging a war against the master. Arthur would lose patience eventually, and their lives might be forfeit. Much as Sigrid had loved her father, she was equally aware of what he would have done in Arthur's boots, so she determined to become at least a little more amenable than usual.

Sigrid sat beside her mother and watched the waves draw her away from the world she knew. Perhaps Arthur hadn't killed him, but he had been one of the leaders of the force that had fought in the battle where her father had met his death. As always, there was no right and no wrong. Sigrid was discovering that the world remained as it had always been, regardless of how much she protested.

Before they left Skania, Arthur had noticed that Sigrid was making an effort to be more agreeable, and he was so grateful that he gave Ingrid a small finger-ring decorated with a tiny enamelled flower which he had found among his share of the booty taken in Vaster Gotland. Ingrid had been touched by this gesture and swore to herself that she would keep her daughter so busy with the master's household duties that Arthur would be free of Sigrid's bad temper. Ingrid told Arthur as much, while

Sigrid pretended she couldn't hear their conversation. The girl hoped fervently that her mother would resist the temptation to shape her daughter's opinions.

Ahead, a beach at a secluded cove shone in the moonlight like a white sickle. The sun had already set, although only a few hours had passed since noon. The days were markedly shorter, as autumn wore away towards winter and winter snow hovered and waited for autumn to die. Farm workers stripped the last fruit from the trees and finalised the preparation of their dried meat and fish supplies that would feed them through the long, cold months.

But now, *Sea Wife*'s short journey was almost over.

Snorri turned her prow into the breeze. Then, at a gesture from Arthur, warriors began to strip and roll the great sail. Sigrid sat sullenly upright but, against her will, she was impressed that this living ship moved and breathed at Arthur's smallest command. The warriors seated themselves at the oars and waited for the signal to commence rowing.

'To The Holding now,' Arthur cried out over the wind; the warriors dug their oars deep into the strengthening waves and *Sea Wife* plunged towards the shore like a horse freed from its reins.

Sigrid felt her heart lift with the wonder of the night, the lonely cold wind and the men who bent their backs like beasts to force the slender vessel onwards. She was captured by the strange smell of foreign earth that she had never known under her feet. Could the experience outweigh the humiliation of being a slave?

Sigrid shook her tousled hair and moonlight danced on strands of silver among the pale-blond locks. For just one night, she wanted to experience strange and exciting places that had no link to her long period of hatred. She had carried her father's untimely death around her neck like a yoke far heavier than any slave collar, especially as Arthur had never required any of his captives to wear one.

Ingrid had told Sigrid that Arthur's foster-father had been a slave during his youth, but the girl had never considered how this knowledge might affect Arthur's treatment of his own servants. In Skania, the weight of Sigrid's hatred had rendered her blind to the many kindnesses showered on her family by those Dene strangers who had every right to detest them.

But a glimmer of understanding was beginning to break through.

'Mother?' she whispered, with her back pressed against the mast. 'I've been thinking about the things you said concerning our master and what the future might bring. As often happens, I'm beginning to think that you're probably right. I have had a fortunate life, so I'd probably been spoiled by Father over the years, which might have prevented me from understanding just how generous Arthur and his people have been to us.'

The shadow beside her stirred, and Ingrid bared her face from inside the enveloping cloak that was providing her and her babe with warmth.

'I'm so glad that you're coming to your senses, Sigrid. It's a hard thing to be owned by someone else, after we've enjoyed the advantages that wealth and status have given us. I was a careless mistress in our home and I never cared how our house slaves felt or lived. I remember how we sold off one strong young man who was a gifted horse-master. He begged your father not to send him away because he had gone through a form of marriage with one of the kitchen maids who was with child.'

Ingrid's eyes filled with tears. 'We didn't listen, because we thought slaves had no business marrying or trying to raise a family without the permission of their masters.'

Sigrid hugged her scratched and dirty knees up to her chest. She was unwilling to hear any criticism of her father but, even so, she was prepared to listen. Every detail of his life that her mother revealed was cherished and considered carefully.

'What happened to the girl and the babe?'

'She hanged herself, so the child died with her! Your father was very angry at the time, because the loss of the slaves cost him a ring of silver.'

'I can't believe that Father could have been so callous.' Sigrid frowned. 'I'd never have thought that Father would value silver over the life of one of his servants.' The girl was confused now, so Ingrid cursed her frankness at a time when she was finally beginning to knock some sense into the stubborn skull.

She tried to make amends to her daughter.

'I was just as bad as your father. I was in total agreement with him at the time, for I was incensed that the dead girl had been such an excellent slave. But I was really angry that I had lost her because of my own selfishness. Sadly, I never considered how I would feel if my husband had been ordered to leave us and never return. How would I have managed if I was forced to raise a child alone? Worse still, I knew that many owners sold child slaves when they were old enough to carry out light duties rather than bother with the difficulties and expense of raising them, but Master Arthur has sworn he'll never break my heart by taking my son away from me.'

Sigrid was silenced.

She desperately wanted to defend her father, but she knew that any such assertions would probably be lies. With a pang, she remembered a time when she had hit a small boy who was a slave in the household of one of her friends. The lad had taken too long to fetch a pitcher of milk for the girls to drink, so her friend had knocked him down and kicked him. When the boy scrambled to his feet, weeping and rubbing at his bleeding nose with one grubby fist, Sigrid had added to the boy's humiliation by slapping him.

Across the years, she had come to realise that the boy would probably have been six years old at the time and the pitcher must have been very heavy. She had been three years older than the slave boy and she, too, had experienced difficulty in pouring the milk from the heavy container.

Now Sigrid flushed with remembered shame.

'I don't want to argue with you, Mother. I just thought you'd like to know that I understand we may have been fortunate when we became the vassals of a master such as Lord Arthur. At the very least, he let us live when we were captured. He didn't have to be so generous. I'm also pleased that our master isn't a Dene!'

Ingrid sighed. This admission from Sigrid was the best the girl was able to manage, so her mother was grateful for the small concession. Besides, Ingrid herself took conscious pride in the fact that her master was more civilised than those Dene who were his allies.

Sigrid stared over the side and gasped as she realised that the water was so clear that she could make out the vague outline of stones and weeds in the shallows, even by moonlight. In front of her, the banks of rowers raised their oars in response to an unseen order and *Sea Wife* ploughed its way onto the shingle beach. Then she heard the crunch of timber on stones and shells as the bow of the hull sliced its way into the sand.

The crew leaped from the deck and pulled her further up the

beach to a point where the tide couldn't snatch her back into deep water.

Then, as he looked about his mooring, Arthur discovered that his longboat had been beached alongside a large familiar-looking raptor-shape. When he saw the dragon on the vessel's leaning prow, Arthur immediately recalled the journey on *Loki's Eye*, which had carried the four captives to a land far removed from everything they knew and loved.

Eamonn, one of the four, had already met his death.

Arthur put aside his sad memories and jumped down from his ship as his men scurried to square her away and store her sail. Then the crew moved the three treasure chests onto the shingle, gathered their possessions and collected their shares of the spoils. Finally, the captives bound for service at The Holding were led up the sand dunes. As his men carried out their duties, Arthur watched their disciplined behaviour with pride. As part of his training regime, Arthur utilised the tried and true methods used by the Roman commanders over the centuries. He knew that men of action will risk everything for commanders who lead from the front.

So far, none of his warriors had let him down.

Most of these men had been young and inexperienced when he had first selected them a year earlier. Since then they had seen much in the way of warfare and learned the value of iron discipline. His men took pride in the knowledge that every man was equally important in Arthur's crew; they gave their commander their unquestioning loyalty and they expected, and got, his in return.

Scarcely had they negotiated the low sand dunes with their heavy loads in tow than a dozen men in sturdy leather cloaks emerged out of the darkness from the direction of The Holding.

Bowing their heads respectfully in Arthur's direction, the farm workers soon had the heavy loads redistributed so that the crew members were relatively unencumbered. Then, the whole group headed up the path.

The servants and the other Geat slaves followed with wide, amazed eyes, for they had been taught from childhood that the Dene people were barbaric and brutal masters. As the farm buildings came into view, Sigrid's eyes grew saucer-shaped. The land stretched out as far as the night lights permitted them to see and, as they passed by a number of well-built barns, the sounds of domestic animals spoke of a wealthy farmstead. The sheer number of workers on hand demonstrated that The Holding was in the same class as the Geat king's country estates. For the first time, Sigrid was forced to accept that Stormbringer was a powerful king, having long clutched at the prejudiced belief that all Dene warriors were boastful liars. By her reasoning it followed that Arthur had inflated his ancestry and importance as well. Now, to her chagrin, Sigrid was finally forced to accept that the Briton was probably better born than she was.

Upset and disconcerted, she began to feel quite foolish.

The cavalcade was greeted by the entire population of The Holding, including the slaves.

A very tall blond woman met Arthur at the gates near the centre of the farm precincts where the long-hall was built. Her cool courtesy, coupled with Arthur's solicitous greeting, marked her as a woman of note. Then Arthur was embraced by two very different and very beautiful girls, one of whom was a tiny, raven-haired beauty who was far smaller than the fourteen-year-old Sigrid. The other girl had hair that was so remarkably red in contrast to her pale skin that Sigrid was unable to tear her eyes away from her consummate beauty.

She was visibly put out by Arthur's popularity, so much so that Ingrid was concerned that the girl might embarrass herself. Sigrid was perfectly capable of carrying a grudge for the silliest of justifications. Ingrid also wondered if Sigrid's problem might stem from jealousy; she could be nursing a hidden affection for Arthur.

But no sooner had the idea occurred to her than she rejected it. Her daughter had been so single-minded in her hatred of Arthur that Ingrid was unable to believe she could harbour any feeling for their master, other than loathing.

No! Ingrid thought, as she moved Ingmar from one hip to the other. Sigrid has no tender feelings for the master. She's about to burst into flames out of fury – not at the girls, but at him.

Arthur explained to Alfridda how he came to be in possession of three slaves and Stormbringer's sister examined mother and daughter with clear, critical eyes. She nodded to the women and stroked Ingmar's fuzz-covered skull before sending the slaves off with the red-haired British girl.

Frightened and weary, mother and daughter were led to a large house that was the exclusive sleeping area for those farm women who had no men to care for them. The communal fire pit was generously provided with large wooden mixing bowls for bread-making, while iron hooks, tripods and pots were in evidence for cooking stews. Then, when Ingrid looked up into the rafters, she saw bags of grain strung up on ropes to prevent vermin from devouring their winter food supply. There were even containers of smoked fish, dried pork and smoked mutton hanging from the rafters for the same purpose.

Ingrid discovered that the small cubicles allotted to them were palatial by Geat standards. A half wall, whitewashed for cleanliness, delineated an area of some ten feet square for the three servants. Two wool-stuffed pallets had been laid on the rough wooden floors; Ingrid stooped to lay Ingmar down on a loose pillow and discovered that the wool smelled sweet and clean, while Sigrid found that assorted dried herbs had been tied into little flaxen packets to discourage bedbugs, lice and other vermin, thereby sweetening the air. Although there was minimal light, a seal oil lamp could be lit if light was needed in the darkest hours of the night. Some thoughtful person had even laid out a small flint-stone, tinder and some flat slate to strike a spark, and a supply of twigs for cleaning teeth with charcoal and chalk.

'Alfridda and Stormbringer like their servants to smell sweet and clean,' the red-haired girl explained bluntly. 'You will be expected to keep your hair, nails and teeth clean at all times. You will also ensure your breath is sweet to the smell by chewing on the herbs provided. In the winter months when baths are difficult to arrange, you are required to use the sweat box to cleanse your skin. It works surprisingly well!'

Sigrid tried to keep her temper under control, for she was aware that she hadn't washed for several days, so her clothes and skin smelled bad. How dare this superior bitch suggest that she stank! To come to the realisation, as she stared sullenly at her toes, that this . . . this creature, was Arthur's sister enraged Sigrid beyond reason, although the girl was unable to explain why.

With an adult woman's sensitivity, Ingrid understood that her daughter was feeling completely inadequate when confronted by such a magnificent creature who was little more than a year older than she was. Somehow, from Sigrid's point of view, Maeve's pleasantries, her courtesy, were designed to insult the Geat girl and make her present herself as a spoiled, ungrateful brat. The fact that this assessment was true barely improved the girl's temper.

Maeve approached the sullen girl and laid one hand on Sigrid's forearm.

'I know you think I dislike you, or that I consider you contemptible because of your slavery, but you're wrong. When we first arrived in these lands, we were also enslaved. Fortunately, my master was Lord Valdar, a man we came to know as the Stormbringer. I can assure you that no one will harm you or mistreat your family in *this* household. My brother, Arthur, is held in great respect here and no insult will ever be offered to his people.'

'His possessions, you mean!' Sigrid spat. Maeve was forced to step aside or be soiled with the girl's spittle. However, she continued with her introductions to mother and daughter with gentle dignity.

Maeve managed to avoid any further contretemps by helping the family move their few possessions into place while searching for useful objects such as a large bowl that could store water from the well. Ingrid was touched at the gesture because it would enable her to avoid night journeys to the farmyard for water at those times when Ingmar's loincloths needed changing. As a youngest child herself, Maeve had spent many hours with her mother as the older woman helped the families of Arden, so understood what happened to the tender flesh of an infant if the child wasn't washed regularly.

So, sullen and happy by turn, the family settled into the servants' quarters.

Immediately after his arrival, Alfridda drew Arthur into the privacy of the fire pit where they could speak without being overheard.

She was eager to garner all the details of Stormbringer's campaigns in Gotland.

With laudable tact, Alfridda began their discussion by explaining the unfolding drama of the attack that had occurred five days earlier. She paid particular attention to the surprising transformation of Blaise into a murderous harpy.

Arthur could scarcely believe the half of what Alfridda described. Yet her widowed status as Stormbringer's sister meant her word was sacrosanct within this community.

But how could Blaise, of all people, be capable of burning men to death with such cold indifference to their agonies?

'Blaise was always difficult as a child, but she demonstrated her courage at World's End, and she never complained during the long voyage to Skandia and Jutland. She experienced a terrible loss with the death of her brother, Eamonn, and her fall in prestige after her intended, Gilchrist, was murdered at the hands of one of my kinsmen. Her life hasn't turned out according to her expectations, but she's never complained or cried out for revenge on those responsible for his death.'

'I can understand her feelings in this regard,' Alfridda agreed. 'But, although I've noticed that she never really shows emotion, I believe that Blaise is resentful of my brother's feelings toward Maeve. If I am right, in your land Blaise would normally have more status than Maeve. Blaise is a princess, while Maeve is the youngest daughter of a man who could best be described as a jarl or a thane.'

Arthur nodded reflectively.

'The knowledge that Maeve will outrank her in this new land must leave a bitter taste in her mouth. Yet, she doesn't show her any rancour – if she feels any.'

'I've never considered Blaise's position before, Alfridda, but you are correct. I'm a blind fool when it comes to women, so I'm unable to take their full measure.'

'You seem to get the measure of my maids without any difficulty,' Alfridda said drily, with a twinkle in her eyes. There were few available young women at The Holding that Arthur had failed to bed.

His eyes lowered as he examined his booted feet while Alfridda continued with her description of the battle with Hrolf Kraki's warriors for control of the farm.

'By my accounting, Blaise killed seven men, not including the warriors who were permitted to sail away under a truce. The principles of honour seem to mean nothing to Blaise. She explained to me that the warriors intended to return within a day or two and would have killed us all, so she had no hesitation in ensuring their deaths by her sabotage of their ship.'

'How many did she kill, all told?' Arthur asked, looking pale.

Alfridda carried out a studied count which was checked against her fingers and toes until she eventually came to a conclusion.

'She was responsible for the deaths of twenty-two warriors, Arthur. I'm not afraid of Blaise, but I'll not be sorry when she eventually moves on to a new life.'

Arthur had already concluded that Blaise's actions had saved the entire settlement. It was also evident to him that no one, other than Maeve, was comfortable that a woman should have shown such martial prowess.

Suddenly, Arthur recalled overhearing a discussion between the two young girls when they were travelling along the roads leading to the north of Britain to meet with Blaise's betrothed. The girls had spoken of the chains that bound the female sex, and he finally understood their concerns.

With the coming of dawn, the farm still showed evidence of the desperate struggle as the house slaves and the carpenter from Stormbringer's ship-building crew were already at work in a bid to repair the barn before the arrival of winter. Blood had stained the crazy paving laid in front of the long-house and the women were busy scrubbing it. But the rust-brown splashes and pools had left shadows on the pale stone, almost as if the spectre of sudden death refused to be washed away entirely.

The areas of soot and burning were even more grisly, for they were man-shaped and grotesque. They marked the white-washed walls with a capering grey intensity and the stone paths became epitaphs to men who had curled up like infants in the intimacy of the flames. Arthur recognised the oily shadows immediately and shuddered inwardly at the sight of Blaise's victims. Alfridda knew she would have to order her workers to heavily whitewash the walls to remove the last traces of violence.

'I feel guilty when I see the shades of men who perished in fire. I wish I'd prevented such horrible deaths.'

Arthur's face registered his surprise. 'How would you have achieved a victory without the use of fire? Hrolf Kraki's dogs would have slaughtered you without any thought for you and your children. Any commander worth his salt will *always* use whatever weapons are at hand.'

Alfridda's face remained drawn and undecided.

'I suppose I must live with any decisions I made that saved the lives of innocents.'

Arthur felt torn and perplexed. On the one hand, he was proud of how the girls had worked together to save the lives of the defenders, but mention of the pleasure exhibited by Blaise during the skirmish sickened him.

'You must discuss this matter with Maeve, Arthur. Your sister was kept busy killing Blaise's wounded victims so they didn't suffer as much as Blaise intended. Blaise was quite pleased that the mercenaries fell for her ruse with the two ships. The sailors wouldn't have stood a chance once their ship started to sink in open waters. I had no argument with her treatment of the Geat survivors, but I cannot help thinking that she derived unnatural enjoyment from their deaths.'

Arthur remembered the dream he'd previously experienced and his face was ashen in the light of the fire pit. As his hands closed around the cup of spiced mead that Alfridda pressed upon him, his thoughts returned to his previous experience of Blaise.

'Since the battle, I've wanted to scream at her to stay away from my sons whenever she approaches them,' Alfridda added. 'I feel like a traitor now, because I had admired her before. Strangely enough, she reverted to her normal self at the exact moment the danger had passed us by, but I can't forget her setting those men afire without the slightest hesitation, for I could feel the coldness in her spirit for the very first time.'

'Can you still bear to have her remain here?' Arthur dreaded the thought of trying to find somewhere for both girls to live throughout the winter. One thing was certain. Maeve would not remain at the farm if Blaise was forced to leave.

'Yes, Arthur, it's best that she stays – at least for the immediate future! I'd be an ungrateful wretch if I forgot the gratitude that is owed to her. At the very end, it was only the terrifying prospect of cooking in hot oil that frightened Hrolf Kraki's dogs into agreeing to surrender. Blaise convinced them that an honourable truce was better than a horrible death.'

Arthur heaved a sigh of relief, and smiled. 'I had a strange dream a few nights ago, where a she-dragon told me my future.

She specifically warned me not to wed Blaise because she would bring me great suffering and I'd be involved in murder because of her. It alarmed me, so this whole conversation has been unsettling.'

Alfridda had liked Arthur from the first time she had met him, although she wasn't really sure about the three travellers who had arrived so opportunely during the attack by Hrolf Kraki's mercenaries. The priest had promised Alfridda that he would curb his colourful language when he was in the company of the children and, as a mark of respect to her dead, he had presided over the burials with heartfelt prayers that reduced Alfridda to tears. She really liked Germanus, but Gareth was such an intense young man that he frightened her a little.

'Do you like surprises, Arthur? No? Then you must brace yourself! Three men came to The Holding, claiming they'd come to rescue you. They've been searching for you for some years. They seemed to believe you needed saving from the Dene, so they were pleasantly surprised when I described your new circumstances in the lands of our people. They arrived here at a very opportune time, because they took part in our battle against Hrolf Kraki's dogs.'

Arthur was caught completely off guard and his mouth gaped foolishly at Alfridda's triumphant announcement. 'Who are they? Tell me, Alfridda, before I burst with curiosity.'

With a girlish giggle, Alfridda told Arthur all she knew of her three guests.

'My tutors are here? And Gareth? How is this possible? How could they have penetrated so far into the north and still arrive with whole skins? And you say they helped with the defence? By the gods, Gareth is almost impossible to harm.'

Alfridda looked blankly at Arthur. 'I realise that Gareth is a very competent warrior and Father Lorcan makes me laugh every time I speak with him. But are you saying that Germanus was your tutor in weapons and swordcraft?'

Arthur could see her considering the advantages of having an arms master to supervise the training of her own sons and the young men who performed her guard duty. Then at that moment the man in question came barrelling into her private apartments uninvited.

'My boy! My boy!' Germanus was moist-eyed and his huge arms reached out to lift Arthur bodily off his feet. 'Look at you – you're all hair and muscles, and you've grown into a wild man! And you've gone native on me! Oh, it's so damned good to see you – especially as you're healthy and in one piece!'

I'll never get Germanus to remain here if this is an indication of their relationship, Alfridda thought. Then she shrugged and smiled.

Suddenly, the door was roughly pushed open to reveal Lorcan and Gareth standing on the threshold. No one had even considered that it would have been good manners to knock.

'I knew you were up to something, you old bastard, so I asked the servant where you'd gone off to in such haste.' Lorcan sounded amused and angry at the same time. 'You thought to find him first, you ass. Why? Did you think he'd have changed and we'd be disappointed?'

Lorcan slapped his friend with a stinging blow across the ear, and Germanus reluctantly released his charge.

'As you can see, he's a man now – and he's obviously this Last Dragon we've been hearing about for weeks. I never thought that our Arthur would become such a famed warrior.'

'You ought to have known he can survive anywhere,' Lorcan replied. 'I knew the boy must have done well, as soon as I saw

Blaise and Maeve. They've grown into beautiful young women, although Blaise's demeanour seems to have changed since she left her homeland.'

At this juncture, Germanus kicked Lorcan on the calf muscle to silence him and the priest squawked from the unexpected pain.

'I'll speak to you about Blaise at some later hour, after you've described your travels to me,' Arthur responded with damp eyes.

Gareth walked into Arthur's arms, embraced his friend, and then fell to one knee and kissed his master's hands. 'I have finally completed my quest, my lord,' he said brokenly. Arthur, embarrassed, lacked the heart to push his friend away.

'I knew that you would do your best to rejoin me, if it was possible to travel so many weary miles. I'd not have held you to such an oath, except that I felt the girls needed to be provided for. However, I now have a feeling that Maeve is happy in this place. It's likely that she'll marry here.'

Alfridda had a smug look on her face and Arthur realised that she had noticed her brother's partiality for his Maeve. 'Yes, Stormbringer has formally asked if he can wed my sister, but I advised him that she must be allowed to make her own decisions, for such a marriage would maroon her in the north for the rest of her days.'

Germanus looked puzzled when Arthur caught his eye.

'What troubles you, Germanus? Come on! Out with it! No matter what it is, I won't be angry with you after the travails you have suffered to come to my aid.'

'What happened to Prince Eamonn? We know he's dead but we've had no opportunity to speak to the young ladies since we arrived here. Everybody is working double time to return The Holding to its normal state, and, for a time, I simply assumed that Eamonn was with you on your campaigns in the north.'

Arthur felt his eyes prickle with tears but brushed his emotions aside and tried to speak in a neutral tone of voice.

'Eamonn is dead! He was killed at Lake Wener in Skania, when we faced a Geat army that had invaded our allies in the north. His ashes lie in a far-off, watery grave, but I returned his sword to Blaise and Stormbringer sent her a fine black stallion and Eamonn's share of the booty, for our friend fought and died with distinction.'

Arthur paused, his eyes very sad. 'I will miss him every day of my life. And I blame myself for his loss.'

'You're taking too much on yourself, Arthur,' Alfridda contradicted him. 'I have been told that Eamonn chose to fight the Geats in the vanguard where the danger was the most immediate. That young man never shirked in his duty during a battle and he revelled in facing danger. You could never have stopped him,' she added.

'But I didn't even try,' he muttered, brushing away a single tear. 'Where are your girls, Alfridda?' Arthur attempted to change the subject before he disgraced himself.

'They're asleep in the women's quarters. They've already greeted you, so you can become reacquainted with them in the morning once the formalities of your return are finalised,' Alfridda explained a little brusquely. 'They will be delighted when they awaken and discover that your arrival hasn't been a dream.'

Alfridda spoke with a general's confidence and Father Lorcan was impressed by her natural mien of command. He picked up her smooth, work-callused hands and kissed her knuckles.

'Your brother is a very fortunate man to have such a kinswoman as you, Lady Alfridda,' the priest said. 'He could well have returned to his home to find burned earth and the corpses of murdered children if it weren't for your leadership and courage.'

Alfridda flushed a deep pink, and then pulled her hands away quickly while assuring the priest that she was merely a prudent housewife who had been fortunate enough to have competent fighters to assist her. It was an understatement that no person present was prepared to believe.

'Unfortunately, I must leave in the next day or two and rejoin Stormbringer's fleet in the south of the peninsula,' Arthur announced. 'The Hundings have invaded our lands in the south and you can guess what they plan to do if they can gain a foothold on our soil.'

'They would insist on the total subjection of our people and the annihilation of the Dene jarls,' Alfridda answered slowly, her eyes darkening with anxiety. 'And we'd be decimated, one island at a time, if Heorot should fall. Even the Sae Dene would fail if the land settlements were overrun – even the best and fastest ships must find safe harbour sometimes to replenish their supplies. Has Hrolf Kraki made any plans to repulse the invaders?'

Arthur grinned in the manner that Germanus remembered in the boy he had known before his departure into the northern lands.

'Of course, his forces should be in the field, but he hunkers down in his great hall of Heorot with his witch-woman whispering in his ear that he'll die if he takes part in a war, even an honourable one! I believe she's in someone's pay, probably the Hundings', but the Crow King won't listen to anyone else. Even Frodhi is ignored, and he's the only jarl who has Hrolf Kraki's ear. No, my lady! The Dene jarls will look in vain if they expect aid from their king.'

'So when do you expect to leave for the south?' Lorcan asked seriously. 'I trust there's time for sleep and breakfast before we depart.'

'Oh, no! Not another damned ship,' Gareth added in a woebegone voice.

Germanus almost laughed, until Lorcan stood on his foot to save their young friend any further embarrassment.

'It's all very well for you lot to tease me, but I'm the one who has to put up with the misery of getting seasick,' Gareth pointed out. But he couldn't help but smile at his own discomfort, for he was happy; three long years of danger and death had been wiped away by their arrival here. 'Still, things could be worse, for Justinian's Disease seems to be disappearing from the northern climes.'

'What's Justinian's Disease?' Arthur asked. Alfridda looked puzzled as well.

Quickly, Lorcan and Germanus explained the disease that had racked the south as soon as winter was over. Alfridda gaped when she heard how whole villages were reduced to burned husks after the plague had killed every soul within its walls.

'The only defence against the plague seems to be fire, and then it only seems to be effective for a short time,' Gareth explained. 'Then, when it begins to rage through the survivors once again, the people seem to go a little mad. We saw villagers, so-called human beings and members of the Christian faith, who reacted in ways that seemed crueller and more evil than anything that Satan could hope to devise. Cannibalism, crucifixion and prowling gangs of young children – the plague is surely one of the dark angel's true horrors.'

For once, Father Lorcan was very serious when he gave his explanation. His large hands twisted together in a manner that described his fears more vividly than the words he selected with such care.

'If the plague should come into your lands during the coming spring, you must forbid any trading ship to put ashore on your island. We know that ships carry the disease, even if we don't know how the illness moves from one person to another. If you hear of any such disease on your island, you must refuse permission for any person to come to the farm or for anyone to leave. I can swear to you that only a total quarantine will defeat this illness. You must speak to your visitors from a distance and you must be brutally strong, otherwise more than half of the souls on this farm will suffer the most horrible of deaths.'

Alfridda's eyes grew wide at the graphic descriptions given by her guests.

'I'll leave instructions with Maeve on how victims of the disease must be treated if I'm absent, although I hope we won't be fighting all through the coming winter. Maeve has had experience with healing that she learned from her mother, the wise Elayne. You must pray your precautions keep the plague from your door.'

Arthur felt odd, almost dislocated, as if something was looming in the darkness of the future. What would he do if anything happened to Maeve? Or to his servants, especially the infant, Ingmar, who was totally dependent on Ingrid and himself? Even the difficult and ever-argumentative Sigrid? Arthur was surprised to discover that he cared for the Geat girl. As Germanus showed his audience the scars under each armpit, the young man thought of Sigrid's perfect, golden flesh being marred so grossly, and shuddered.

I'm obviously in need of a woman, he thought. But Sigrid is only fourteen and she's far too young for me.

Then he realised that she was the same age as Maeve and he had already agreed to Stormbringer's proposal of marriage to his sister. And the Sae Dene king was considerably older than he was.

'But that's completely different,' Arthur protested aloud to a suddenly-silent room.

'What's different, Arthur?' Alfridda asked warily and watched in surprise as the Briton flushed with a deep strawberry-red hue.

'Nothing! I must have been thinking of trifles and forgot for a moment where I was. But I'm obviously too tired for any more decisions right now. Just point me towards a deep pallet and I'll sleep away the wonders I've seen tonight. I want to be freshened before I speak with the girls in the morning.'

'Of course, Arthur,' Alfridda said. 'I've been very remiss as your hostess. I'll ensure you wake early so we can have a long discussion with the girls in the morning.'

Arthur pressed her hand and rose to his feet to follow a servant from the room. Gareth padded away behind his master. If he had his way, he would never permit himself to let Arthur out of his sight again.

Once they had left, Germanus spoke for them all when he rose, thanked Lady Alfridda and shuffled off to his own rooms, yawning hugely as he went. Lorcan followed soon after, while the servants began to clear this section of the hall with quiet efficiency.

In their wake, Alfridda heaved a sigh of relief. For tonight, she could sleep in peace.

As she slid under the warm covers, Alfridda thanked all the gods that ever were that The Holding had been protected and her brother was safe. If Arthur was correct, the fate of the Dene people rested on Stormbringer's large shoulders, coupled with the military acumen of this young and alien warrior.

'The gods have been kind so far! Perhaps they'll protect us from this horrible disease *and* the threats from the Hundings,' she mused.

But the wind continued to blow harshly around the walls of the wooden building and whistled through the narrow upper windows with a moaning that boded no good. Somewhere beyond the hall, an owl shrieked, and as she sank into slumber Alfridda wondered briefly who was going to die. She tried to pray but sleep seduced her.

THE CIMBRIC PENINSULAR

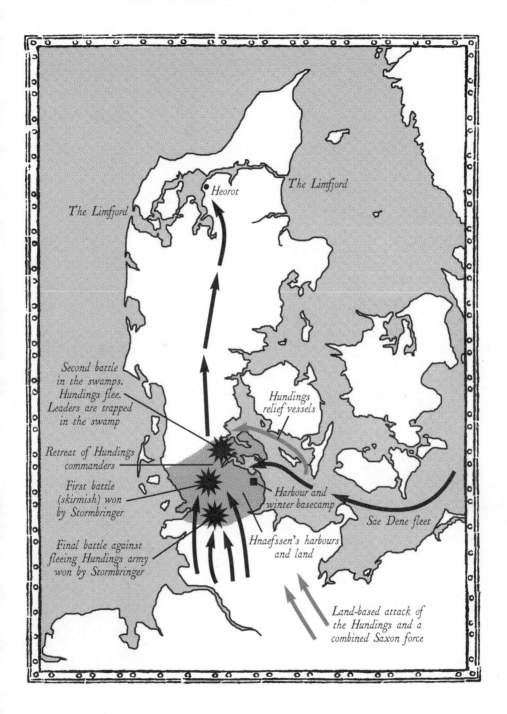

The Limfjord

Heorot

The Limfjord

Second battle
in the swamps.
Hundings flee.
Leaders are trapped
in the swamp

Hundings
relief vessels

Retreat of Hundings
commanders

First battle
(skirmish) won
by Stormbringer

Harbour and
winter basecamp

Sae Dene fleet

Final battle against
fleeing Hundings army
won by Stormbringer

Hnaefssen's harbours
and land

Land-based attack of
the Hundings and a
combined Saxon force

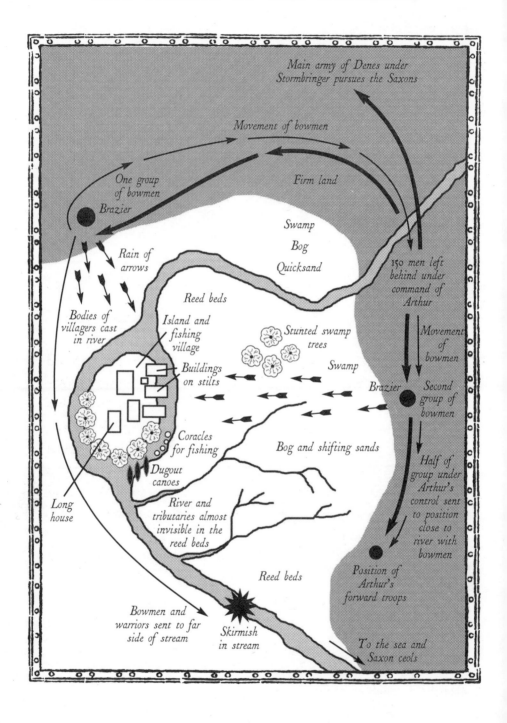

Main army of Denes under Stormbringer pursues the Saxons

Movement of bowmen

One group of bowmen

Brazier

Firm land

Swamp

Bog

Quicksand

150 men left behind under command of Arthur

Rain of arrows

Reed beds

Movement of bowmen

Bodies of villagers cast in river

Island and fishing village

Stunted swamp trees

Buildings on stilts

Swamp

Brazier

Second group of bowmen

Coracles for fishing

Bog and shifting sands

Half of group under Arthur's control sent to position close to river with bowmen

Dugout canoes

Long house

River and tributaries almost invisible in the reed beds

Position of Arthur's forward troops

Reed beds

Bowmen and warriors sent to far side of stream

Skirmish in stream

To the sea and Saxon ceols

CHAPTER IX

WHEN LOKI LAUGHED

Be sure your sins will find you out.

The Bible, Numbers 32:23

The old jarl, Ivar Hnaefssen, stared out over the swampy ground with morose concentration. The furrows on his old-man's face criss-crossed his weathered skin like the waterways separating the bogs from the few pathways through the inhospitable land.

'Shite, boys! After chasing these buggers all over the landscape, they decide to hole up in a freezing, fucking swamp where we'll lose scores of our warriors if we try to get to them. We could just sit here and pick them off as they come out starving, but that could take months.'

Arthur looked at the jarl with a cold grin, until Ivar shuddered at its chill humour.

'The temperature is down to freezing, so I propose to use our archers to harass our friends into some sort of action. The Troll King'll be thrilled to set fire to whatever cover the Hundings are cowering under. Then, if we succeed, the fires will leave them without shelter when the cold sets in. Shite, why should we waste the lives of our friends when we can use old Father Winter to kill the Hundings for us?'

The cold was a living thing. Arthur could smell the first snow in the air as winter came to life. A thin coating of leaves obscured the margins of the swamps where the shallow water was already beginning to freeze over. The reeds were brown and sere, ready to crumble at a touch. The bitter wind came from the sea with the taste of salt and ice in its maw, causing the warriors in their heavy furs and cold armour to shiver.

'If Thorketil thinks he can set fire to the Hundings' village, I'll be happy to overlook the use of arrows, my boy,' Jarl Hnaefssen muttered magnanimously.

That's very generous of you, Arthur thought. The persistent prejudice against archery in the north irritated Arthur constantly because Saxons, Dene, Jutes and Angles all agreed that the bow was only a weapon for peasants, even though Caesar's Romans had used bowmen to devastating effect in their conquest of Gaul. Arthur refused to believe that the northern warriors had such short memories.

The Hundings had commandeered a small village that stood on a slightly elevated strip of higher ground within the heart of the swamp. The village was obviously poor, to judge by the reed roofs and the poles used to raise the houses above any possible flooding. Arthur had seen similar structures in The Wash in Britain.

There were insufficient houses for the villagers to remain, so when Arthur's force had taken up their attack positions they found that every villager in the settlement had been executed, including the women and children. Arthur had sworn a vicious oath when he saw the bodies piled high in the shallow, freezing waters of a nearby bog. Even now, several hours later, he was still shocked at the stupidity and superstition of his enemies. To leave so many dead bodies in open waters close to living quarters was an open invitation for disease to breed. To make matters worse, the stink would gradually become unbearable until the corpses froze solid.

Arthur could feel nothing but contempt for warriors who could treat their victims with such casual disregard.

'The Hundings must believe that we're not prepared to retaliate for this outrage. If so, they don't know much about me,' Arthur snapped angrily to Stormbringer. 'With your permission, I'll organise Thorketil and Rufus into place with the twelve bowmen who travel with them. Let me unleash my bows, brother, so I can burn them out and force them into fighting us in open battle.'

Stormbringer knew that any such strategic decision on the use of archery could result in a loss of prestige with the mainland jarls. Fortunately, he remembered that both the island and the Skanian jarls had originally held the same reservations until Arthur's men had proved archery's usefulness in earlier battles. Finally Stormbringer nodded his permission.

Thorketil was hovering anxiously outside Stormbringer's campaign tent and once the decision to use archers was made, he was ushered in by Arthur with the complete lack of formality given to a respected and trusted friend.

The passage of years since Thorketil's combat with Arthur in the halls of Heorot had wrought massive changes in the Troll King's physical appearance. His upper body was even more powerful now than it was in his days as Hrolf Kraki's undefeated champion. Since Thorketil's mortal combat with Arthur and his eventual acceptance as one of the young prince's captains, the Troll King had practised obsessively with the bow, increasing his strength to almost supernatural levels. Thorketil's arms now matched the thickness of a normal man's thighs; likewise, his always powerful neck was now a column of pure muscle on which his head seemed unnaturally small and delicate.

At the time of his wounding, Thorketil had begged Arthur to put him out of his misery and kill him, especially when the Crow King had cast him out of his personal guard. But Arthur knew Thorketil was intelligent, sensitive and loyal to a fault. With his new purpose as an archer, the Dene Warrior was restored to manhood.

In many ways, Thorketil's lower body seemed unnatural. One leg was heavily thighed and strong, the other shrunken and seemingly shorter, giving the Troll King an odd and lopsided look. But such was Thorketil's certainty in his own skills that none of the jarls thought of him as a cripple.

Arthur still continued to feel guilty whenever he gazed on his friend's wasted leg. But the Troll King had done his best to forget Hrolf Kraki's treachery. 'I've gained more renown as the Last Dragon's bowman than I ever won as a warrior. Women come to my bed now just to hear my tales of our exploits. The price of my freedom was my knee, but I consider it to have been a cheap price to pay.'

Arthur introduced Thorketil to the assembled jarls, many of whom remembered him well from his days in Heorot. Within five minutes, they were forced to admit that Thorketil was a changed man. He had schooled himself to be gregarious, well spoken and even amusing, and he was able to poke fun at himself as the old Troll King would never have attempted. Further, he was now standing taller than he had ever stood before, despite his ruined leg and the cane he leaned upon, for Arthur had showed him that he had hunched over in the past. Thorketil could now look every man squarely in the eye, regardless of their status.

When Arthur explained the tactical situation to Thorketil, the big man grinned boyishly in response.

'I'll enjoy burning that cesspit to the ground, especially for the sake of the babes who were tossed into the bogs when the Hundings took their homes. I'll try to kill any of the mongrel dogs that comes within bowshot of the corpses, and I'll also fire off some of my barbs on the crows and ravens that try to steal their eyes. We can always burn the corpses once we've taken control of the village. I can only hope that their shades are close enough to our world to know that we'll also be burning their murderers to revenge them.'

Several jarls noted that old Ivar's face held a perplexed look as he gave his unwilling authorisation to an activity that he considered dishonourable. Of course, the Troll King spotted Ivar's ambivalence immediately.

'Don't fret yourself, my lord. All the men in my troop are warriors, trained and tested, who have been wounded in battle during their many years of service to the king. Once, their lives were considered to be over. But no longer! Perhaps you can still tell me that my archers have no place in battle when we fill the night with fire.'

The jarls were embarrassed because so many of the Troll King's observations were true, so Arthur hustled Thorketil out of the tent to let the Dene leaders speak frankly. Outside, Rufus and twelve other men were assembled with a large supply of arrows and two braziers for lighting fire arrows. All still young or in their early middle years, they had the unmistakable bearing of fighting men, except one unfortunate warrior with the con-cave chest and hacking cough of the feared lung disease. The man's pallor and the trace of blood at the corners of his mouth warned Arthur that this particular warrior was deathly ill and he would have sent the man back to the tents, but Thorketil stopped him.

'Yes, Arthur, our boy is dying. But I'll not willingly deprive the boy of a chance to strike a blow for his family and his tribe. He desperately wants to make his mother proud . . . and I've promised that I'll allow him to give service to you. Please, Arthur, for he'll soon be sleeping till the end of time.'

Arthur allowed The Troll King to have his way.

If the jarls thought that their cripples were useless, they would soon be set to rights. Rallying his kinsmen under their new title of Loki's Bastards, Thorketil sent six men under Rufus, with one brazier and a supply of fuel, to the opposite side of the swamp. Arthur gave permission for the seven to use some of their precious horses to get to the firmer ground.

'I'm not waiting for daylight because I smell snow in the wind and it'll dampen the thatch if it starts to fall before we commence our little target practice. No, I want those sons of whores to burn, so find a good position from which to pepper them with flaming arrows. You have one hour!'

'Depend on me, Thorketil,' Rufus replied in his usual dour fashion.

'I am, Rufus! We all are! Tell me you're in position by sending a single fire arrow straight up into the air – and as high as you can power it. Then you can send every arrow you have at the enemy. We'll show them what happens when you kill the children of the Dene, even peasant children.'

The crippled and wounded bowmen respectfully touched their forelocks and turned and hobbled, limped and shuffled towards the picket line and the horses.

Behind them, none of the jarls or the guards laughed, not even when one warrior slipped in the mud.

Darkness fell like a shroud and the jarls were sure that Thorketil's archers couldn't expect to know exactly where the village was relative to their firing point. But the big man was clever, and had memorised where to position his men.

The jarls were impatient as they waited for the bowmen to send up their message arrow, for they were certain that the whole plan was a mare's nest. Arthur sensed their doubts.

'Make sure that the village is well and truly alight, Thorketil,' Arthur told his comrade as the big man left his headquarters. 'Your fellow lords are sure that the darkness will render you as blind as they are.'

'We don't have the time to wait till after the first snowfalls. The weather conditions are so quiet that I can sense the first snowflakes coming, even as we speak.'

As Arthur looked up into the black night sky, a small swirl of snowflakes began to spiral down on them.

Old King Winter would soon hold the land in a grip of freezing iron.

Thorketil ordered the coals in the brazier to be stirred back into life while more fuel was added. The Troll King and his men laid their fat-soaked arrows close to hand and began to string their longbows with efficiency and muscle-cracking force.

The only exception was the young man with the racking cough. Thorketil approached him with an offer of assistance. 'Do me a favour, Elidar. I like to think I can still string a young man's bow, even the longbows that the peasants use to bring down stags, so could I try to string yours?'

Elidar looked at Thorketil with unreadable blue eyes. After a moment's reflection, the lad handed over his bow, then smiled, and Arthur was struck by the sick man's almost supernatural beauty.

'There! See, Arthur? I can still string the strongest of bows. Except for this knee, I'm better than I ever was. Thank you, Elidar, may your aim be straight.'

'It will be, Thorketil. I'll set the village alight for you!'

At this point, a fiery comet of light shot straight up into the sky.

'The signal has come, Arthur,' Thorketil announced with a boyish grin. 'We can now reduce this confounded village to ashes.'

If you can hit it! Arthur thought morosely. This darkness with the slowly falling snowflakes would make any precise attack almost impossible.

'It's time for the fire arrows, Arthur,' Stormbringer called and both men moved back to their positions near the extra brazier.

'They're in position,' Thorketil answered. 'Now, let's create some light to kill by.'

Calmly, Thorketil placed the head of an arrow into the brazier and turned it until the fat-soaked cloth caught alight.

The arrow nocked, Thorketil drew back the bow string while, all around him, his six fellow archers followed suit. His first arrow shot upward into the darkness then fell back to earth and briefly lit a wooden wall when it struck the timbers.

Then other arrows snaked out of the night like a disciplined shower of sparks. At first, Arthur was quite certain that the arrows would fail to set the thatched roofs alight for the snowfall was increasing. But Thorketil's skill prevailed and the thatch of a pole-house caught fire. Visibility was no longer a problem.

'Ayee!' Thorketil keened in a high-pitched scream of primal

victory. 'Now we can watch the Hundings as they dance. I suggest you guard the perimeter of the village and the swamp, because the rats will soon be scattering to find a safer shelter.'

'It's already done, my friend,' Arthur replied. As Stormbringer's second-in-command, he had been given free rein to besiege the village.

Meanwhile, the fires in the village were beginning to spread. This village had originally been built to repel an attack by floodwater; none of the builders had considered fire danger in this watery world.

Arrow after arrow snaked out into the night sky in long, burning curves that found their marks in the roofs, walls or out-buildings. Some guttered before the fire took hold, while others were extinguished by dark figures that ran and capered as they carried bladders of water along the raised walkways between the buildings. But for every arrow that died without setting its target aflame, two others set timber or thatch flickering into a quickly spreading conflagration.

Now, the slight breeze that was beginning to die with the approach of snow started to bring more danger to the Hundings' warriors huddling in the village. It retained sufficient strength to turn frail sparks into a growing firestorm. Years of neglect had made the thatch brittle and dry, the perfect flammable material for feeding an inferno.

Given only the briefest of warnings, the Hundings were forced to dive among the reeds and huddle in freezing water to gain relief. As far as Stormbringer could ascertain from his scouts, the Hundings in this village were mostly men with strong tribal affiliations, or were senior commanders with the Hundings' army who were being taken to places of refuge where they could rebuild their defeated forces. To huddle in the water like beasts would be an especially humbling experience to the arrogant and angry Saxon lordlings.

Hours would pass before the conflagration began to cool. As soon as they were able, the cold and miserable survivors made their way out of the maze of swamp waters and climbed to the higher ground and the few ruins that could still provide some shelter.

Arthur had half expected an attempt by the defenders to fight their way out of this ring of steel with which Stormbringer had encircled the swamp, but the Saxon hounds were too stubborn to present the Sae Dene commander with any semblance of an easy victory. As the fires began to burn out, the survivors returned to the dubious shelter of the village ruins, places where they could dig in.

One hundred and fifty senior Hundings officers were surrounded by a Dene army of more than a thousand men, while their own main force was retreating in some disorder towards the distant Saxon borders. The brains of the Hundings were penned up in this ruined village.

During a brief discussion before finally going to his tent for an hour or two of sleep, Arthur suggested to Stormbringer that it would be a prudent move to take the major part of their force and drive their enemies to a suitable place where the Sae Dene king could attack and destroy the bulk of the Saxon army in one decisive battle.

'Wounding a snake isn't enough! The head must be cut off, and it must be done quickly and cleanly. Otherwise they will rise again in the spring and threaten the border marches all over again. Meanwhile, I'm confident I can eliminate these defenders with a force of one hundred good warriors.'

'That's seems like a reasonable assessment,' Stormbringer said.

He was reluctant to leave his friend to complete the destruction of this village and its defenders with only a handful of warriors and the detested archers at his back, if they were forced to wait out a protracted siege. The hundred-odd men inside the village were the most effective leaders of the Hundings; cold and miserable they might be, but only a fool would underestimate them.

'Very well, Arthur, I will take your advice. But I accept it only because your plan makes good sense. Dividing our forces at this particular juncture is practical. The body of the Hundings army without its leadership will be easier to destroy and, if they are allowed to cross their borders to safety, they'll simply wait until another leader comes to the fore who can initiate a new campaign against us.'

'Stop being so genteel, Valdar! You're my friend, and you're the Sae Dene King, while I have no real status in these lands. If you're going to be my brother when you eventually marry Maeve, then it's my earnest desire that you build a great reputation in the Dene lands, one that will reflect well on me and mine. I'll expect you to be off in the morning, when you can leave me to mop up these fools. I can see no good reason for us all to sit here on our arses and watch the Hunding commanders freeze to death in a disgusting swamp. They've allowed themselves to be trapped here for the most foolish of reasons.'

Then, on a dark morning when the snow lay to the height of a man in every hollow in the landscape, the Dene army dug itself out, the warriors cursing the circumstances that meant they were fighting a war in winter. Shortly thereafter, Stormbringer led his men away from the swamp to plough their way through the snowy landscape. The small army slid through the trees in a meandering route that avoided the deeper snowdrifts with their skins of glittering ice crystals. Arthur watched near to a thousand men slowly depart as they battled the terrible conditions with humour and a certain degree of self-pity.

'Well, boys, we can hunker down now and wait to give these fuckers a goodly view of hell,' Father Lorcan said jovially from behind his friend's right shoulder. 'What do they expect? Do they think we'll go away, just to avoid freezing our balls off?'

In full growl, Father Lorcan's dissatisfaction with his lot was all too apparent. With only the bulbous tip of his nose showing through a collection of wrappings, Lorcan looked like an angry vole awakened from its winter hibernation. But, on closer examination, the priest's eyes were wickedly humorous.

'So! What can we do? Do we attack in the morning when they're good and cold? They'll have seen the bulk of our army leave our bivouac and they're still trying to keep fires alight.'

Germanus's nose was just as red as Lorcan's, and he was bundled up as thickly as his friend.

'At this stage there's no need to attack, for all we have to do is to wait.' Arthur ignored the critical tones and expressions of his erstwhile tutors. He had been making strategic decisions for years now.

Gareth was wise enough to realise that Arthur's demeanour had changed, along with the decisiveness of his manner. Though he appeared to be the same pleasant and quick-thinking boy they had known several years ago, his sense of fun had vanished and been replaced by a coolness of intellect that all three men found a little disconcerting.

'Do you have any idea how many enemies are in the swamps?' Gareth asked mildly.

'Our scouts are warning us there are a good one hundred and fifty men hunkered down in the village. They are mostly older officers, but there are at least fifty very loyal retainers and bodyguards. When their main army was routed, these men escaped into the swamps and have refused to surrender.'

Arthur's dry voice was laced with contempt for leaders who had abandoned their men and then allowed them to retreat, headless, towards the Saxon borders. Meanwhile, the leadership settled into what they believed was relative safety.

But a familiar fingernail was scratching inside Arthur's skull; he had wondered at the tactics of the Hunding commanders for days, while trying to catch some glimpse of their motivation. His previous dealings with the hounds of Saxony had indicated that these leaders were anything but foolish.

Marooning themselves in a no-name swamp made no sense. What advantage could there be in defending this particular village? They could have fled anywhere with their army as protection, but they had chosen to risk their lives in this desolate place. Their whole course of action seemed nonsensical.

He and his two tutors turned and stared through the greyness of the morning towards the ruins of the village, where wisps of smoke from fires rose upwards. All three men were bemused by the enemy leadership's decisions. Why would they persist in remaining within the village's walls? Anything would be better than being trapped in a swamp during the first snows of winter.

To the left, the swamp became denser with reeds and water but, in the far distance, an estuary became the grey sea and the fingernail at the back of Arthur's head began to stir once again. It was almost as if a wight was running its ghostly fingers through his hair.

'Just ... wait ... a ... moment!' Arthur whispered slowly, as his mind raced to follow the thread of an idea.

The estuary was clear of reeds, so Arthur guessed that the

water there was deeper and more saline adjacent to the swamp. His eyes scanned along the glints of distant water to the points where the reed beds began, only a few at first, and then thick swathes of the brittle, brown stems that rattled in the cold wind.

'The village is mostly waterlogged and is surrounded by bog, so there's no real evidence of agriculture – just a few goats, a cow or two and some chickens.'

Germanus was quickly following the direction of his words, used as he was to assessing the landscape and opponents for hidden dangers.

'The villagers have to live on something and, if you look at the buildings carefully, there are a few small lean-to sheds that seem to serve no rational purpose. I think they might be smokehouses for curing fish. We are close to the open sea, so I expect this village would normally survive on fishing for daily sustenance.'

'Aye,' Arthur replied slowly. 'We assumed that from the beginning, but we never saw the implications. Look over there at those coracles hanging on the unburned wall. They are light, one-man vessels that even a child can manage. I think the Hunding generals are waiting for the arrival of prearranged ceols that will whisk them away to safety, while leaving their junior thanes to usher the remnants of their army over their borders. The Hundings must have had this emergency plan in place from the very beginning of the campaign. The generals would have known that Stormbringer has often spoken of his intention to eliminate all threats from the Hundings by crushing them completely. Essentially, the strategic brains of the entire Hundings tribe are in the village in front of us, and they're waiting to be taken to Saxony by water.'

'Isn't it too late for ceols to approach the shore without ice piercing their hulls?' Lorcan asked doubtfully.

'The Saxon ceols are heavy ducks when compared with the Dene longboats,' Arthur explained. 'They're designed to carry all manner of cargo. They lumber along the coast efficiently enough, so the thin rime of ice that's formed on the estuary so far won't cause them any problem. Once they are clear of the village, the Hundings only have to sail a hundred miles into the south and hug the coastline to deliver their leaders to home and safety.'

'If these dogs should get away, the Dene borders will come under attack again next year,' Lorcan pointed out as he worried away at a thumbnail.

Germanus considered Arthur's assessment of their strategic and tactical situation. 'Even if Stormbringer manages to eliminate the combined Saxon, Jute and Angle forces, the north will still have a large number of displaced warriors who will be hungry for a strong leader to follow, especially if he promises to reward them with land,' the Frank decided with grim practicality.

'I can't imagine how these ceols would know that they're needed.' Lorcan had placed his finger squarely on one of the flaws in Arthur's reasoning.

Fortunately, Gareth provided a plausible answer.

'Beacon fires. The generals could have arranged for a particular fire to be lit that would instruct the crews of the ceols to proceed to a specific destination where they would collect any party that needed evacuation. In this case, the collection point would be on the beaches adjacent to the village.'

Whatever the answer to the communications problem, it was of little importance in the current scheme of events.

The sun had barely warmed the cold air and Arthur could smell more snow coming their way. Although conditions in the village must be uncomfortable and freezing cold, the warriors would still be strong and they would be well fed in the immediate future. Arthur knew it took time for famine to weaken strong and vigorous men. 'Yes,' he reminded himself. 'They'll be fucking uncomfortable, but the knowledge that a ship is on the way will sustain them.'

He was finally beginning to understand why the village had been captured and occupied in the first place. Now that he knew what he was searching for, a few minutes of staring into the grey and dreary landscape revealed that charcoal-coloured shapes were clustered around the eastern side of the village. These were obviously primitive wooden boats, dugouts carved from tree trunks. They were capable of carrying two or three men at a time and, by Arthur's count, there seemed to be about twenty of these vessels.

Dugouts could carry more men than coracles, and this made the situation more urgent than previously thought.

'I should have known! Houses on long poles along the coast always have dugout boats or round coracles for use as water transport,' Lorcan said. 'I must apologise, Arthur. Back at my home, where swamps and bogs are a normal part of the landscape, any pole village will have its share.'

'Don't berate yourself, Lorcan. I didn't come to the most logical conclusion myself, and I should have known better after the time I've spent in the north. Not that it matters! I think we still have time to position our warriors in ambush positions on the opposite side of the village.'

Arthur glanced around at his lieutenants.

'Find Snorri for me, Gareth. I need him now!'

Gareth complied, albeit unwillingly, and Arthur briefly felt a delicious sense of freedom. Like a faithful dog Gareth had refused to permit Arthur to leave his sight in recent days in case his master should vanish.

When Snorri arrived, Arthur explained the strategic situation to him and issued orders that his hundred-strong force should be divided into two groups that could move independently into ambush positions along the opposite banks of the main waterway leading to the sea.

'Our view of the village won't be as good as it is from this hillock, but we'll send scouts into positions where they can inform us of any movement by the Hundings as soon as they begin to stir. We'll definitely need our archers again for this skirmish, unless all your warriors feel like swimming in the cold water.' Arthur had seen the men's downcast faces when the main body of the Sae Denes had left to do battle with the remnants of the Hundings' main force. He could understand their frustration and disappointment.

'You can explain how vital it is that we stop the commander of the Hundings from escaping to fight another day. A lizard can lose a leg or cast off a tail and those limbs will re-grow once more. Yet the same lizard will die if the head is crushed! The head of the Hundings lives in that village, so we must crush it.'

'I will obey, master,' Snorri answered impassively. 'Our men are always happy when they understand their mission.'

'Remain at my side, Snorri, for I need to select the most suitable of the jarls to lead our attack groups. Once they are selected, warn them about the need for complete silence when they are positioning themselves for the ambush. Meanwhile, there's another important matter for your consideration. You must select a group of good swimmers in case we have to fight in the waterways. Weed out those warriors who can swim, gather them together and leave them with me.'

And so another grey day came to a close. As the light began

to fail, small groups of Dene warriors moved cautiously around the village to take up their ambush positions where they could cut off any small boats that attempted to escape towards the open sea.

Arthur was woken from a troubled sleep by the screaming of his mental warnings. Seconds later, Snorri appeared out of the mist and swore sharply when Arthur sat up before the helmsman had even touched him.

'I wish you wouldn't do that, Arthur. Shite, it gives a man the queasies when you seem to read my mind. The Hundings are on the move! One of our scouts has returned from his patrol downstream. There are two ceols moored at the mouth of the river. One looks like the main transport vessel, while the other seems ready to assist it if there is an emergency.'

'In that case, we'd best stop our enemies from reaching these boats,' Arthur replied. Then, instead of donning his armour, he pulled on a knitted shirt, and knitted socks to wear under his boots. This whole ensemble was covered by his cloak and, instead of his sword he picked up the Dragon Knife. Finally, he tied the scabbard of the Dragon Knife securely around his neck with a thong.

A feeling of paradoxical happiness welled up in Arthur's chest. The thrill of the chase gave his life texture and meaning; he hoped to save families from the loss of their sons, villagers from being murdered for the sake of their cattle, their sheep or a few jars of grain. At the same time, he hoped to help the many priests and innocents in religious communities who were turned into prey. There were times when a single man could make a difference and, by doing so, influence the turning of Fortuna's Wheel. He prayed that today would be such a day.

'Snorri!' he called, and watched as the helmsman shouldered his way through the group of men.

'I'm giving you the task of putting together a group of twenty-five men to stop those Hundings who are abandoned in the village by their masters if they try to make an escape bid by land. You'll be using that group of our men who are on the other side of the stream. Caught between two pincers, the warriors who can't escape on the dugouts and coracles should be easily crushed. But, before you undertake this task, I want Lars to select twenty men from among our warriors who are good swimmers. He will have first call on these warriors because he will be performing a specific duty for me. The remainder of them are under your command.'

Snorri seemed confused by Arthur's orders, and the Briton's irritation rose accordingly.

'Obey my orders, Snorri! The Hundings don't have enough boats to move all of their one hundred and fifty men in the one voyage. Or do you doubt that fifty Dene warriors can stop seventy-odd Hundings who have been cruelly abandoned and left to their own devices?'

Snorri flushed guiltily. 'I'm sorry if I sounded as if I was questioning your instructions, my lord. We should be able to mop up those who have been separated from their masters.'

'And I'm sorry I snapped at you,' Arthur added, for he genuinely liked his deputy. 'Take Rufus and two archers with your group, preferably ones who have mobility. Now! You must hurry! The Hundings are ready to start running and, like all cornered hounds, they'll be very fast and savage.'

As Snorri began to leave Arthur called out to him, 'If you can, I'd like you to capture at least one man who can be questioned. One of their senior leaders if possible. But if we can't have a leader, I'll take whoever I can get my hands on.'

Unleashed, Snorri ran to the gathered warriors and rapidly separated a group of twenty-five men from the main body of the warriors, leaving behind the twenty swimmers and all but the two bowmen he had been instructed to take.

Like mist, the selected warriors disappeared into the reeds to position themselves close to the outer boundaries of the village. One of the forward scouts wormed his way to the reed beds and crawled across the marshy ground to reach the force that had originally been sent to guard the village. These warriors were briefed on the coming action and instructed to hunker down into the mud to await the attack commands.

'Lars!' Arthur called to a tall young blond warrior with a striking red beard.

'How may I serve you, Master Arthur?'

'As of now, you're in command of the swimmers you selected. You can send the Troll King and his archers to me while you're arranging your warriors. I'll be joining you in the water, but you'll be in command of the attack in case I have some other task to deal with. Don't fuck around, Lars, because the Hundings are on the verge of making a run for it.'

Lars looked towards the village which was still mostly invisible from their ambush position, but several breathless scouts were hastening to strip off their body armour while staying as warmly dressed as possible. Several hundred yards away, lights could be seen bobbing through the reeds as overloaded dugouts and coracles were being alternately dragged or paddled through the choked waterways. As if he had planned their escape for them, Arthur had positioned his men at those points where the water was mostly clear of reeds and the stream had begun to widen.

'Thorketil! Arrange your archers so that you can pepper the Hundings as they pass into the main part of the channel,' Arthur ordered brusquely, and then turned back to face Lars.

'Are all your swimmers here? Come forward, men, because I haven't the time to give you your orders individually. Move!'

The group parted so that Thorketil could marshal his bowmen as close to the banks of the streams as he dared. Braced, and with bows drawn, they waited. Only twenty of his detachment, as well as Arthur, had admitted to being competent swimmers, so Arthur hastily explained what he required of them.

'We must use any means at our disposal to stop them from escaping. If I know these Hundings, they won't have expected us to ambush them. They have some dugout canoes and these boats are surprisingly stable if they are anything like the vessels our peasants use in Britain. If a few of you can get your hands on one of the sides, the boats can be capsized by rocking one side of the vessel until it begins to ship water and it will sink. I doubt that many of the enemy warriors can swim, so they'll be quite vulnerable once they're in the water. But they'll have an advantage over us while they are in the boats because they can skewer us with relative ease.'

'Lovely!' Lars muttered with a jocular grin. He had completed his tasks quickly and efficiently, so Arthur had no objection to his joining the swimmers. The swimming detail would be the most dangerous task in this skirmish and those young men who couldn't swim were sullen because they would be forced to deal with any exhausted Hundings warrior who reached solid ground.

'The coracles will be easy to sink with your knives. Once the hides are breached, the coracles will start shipping water immediately. For our part, the water will freeze our balls off when we get in, but you'll begin to warm up when you start to swim. Keep moving! We must be waiting for them in the middle of the stream.'

The water was so cold that it momentarily robbed Arthur of breath. But he ducked his head under the surface and began to swim slowly towards the middle of the channel while taking pains to minimise the splashing of his arms. As he moved, he prayed that he would be spared numbness in his digits, a side-effect of the intense cold that could kill living tissue. With grim determination, he kept his arms and legs moving vigorously while treading water under the surface.

Once the men were in position, they trod water while keeping their bodies as upright as they could with only their heads above the waterline. In the darkness, they were almost invisible. The faint hubhub of raised and excited voices began to travel to the swimmers over the soughing and clattering of the reeds.

Silent in the water, surrounded by the heads of other swimmers and with the Dragon Knife slung securely around his neck, Arthur listened to the high-pitched laughter and hissed orders coming through the curtain of reeds. Oaths and the sounds of slapping hands removing shattered vegetation from their clothing easily permitted the Briton to plot the movement of the first Hunding craft.

A crude torch barely lit the passage of the escaping Hundings. The faint orange light picked out vaguely defined cheekbones and the curve of shoulders moving oars and poles through the dark water, but their eye sockets and lower faces were invisible in the dim light.

On cue, Arthur and his compatriots sank their heads below the surface. Then, half-a-dozen coracles and two dugout canoes pushed their way through the reeds and entered the open stream. Behind them, even though he was under water, Arthur could hear more small vessels as they struggled to make their way through the reeds. The water was thick with sediment that made visibility difficult while, nearer to the bank, the surface had a visible film of ice forming from the bitter cold. Fortunately only a light breeze brought the freezing chill of winter's breath onto Arthur's blueing skin.

Then, as the first coracle passed abeam of him, so close that he could touch it, Arthur kicked upwards with his legs and his body surged up like an attacking shark in pursuit of a school of fish.

The two men in the coracle scarcely had time to scream before Arthur's hand holding the Dragon Knife leaned on the edge of the vessel, while his free hand grabbed the closest man by a handful of cloak and pulled him over the side. Obviously a non-swimmer, the man immediately began to sink, effectively cutting off his scream of terror.

A quick three-foot slice with the Dragon Knife parted the leather sheath that covered the boat's spars, leaving it to fill up and slip into the turgid waters.

Arthur grabbed at the head of the sinking warrior as the man was going under for what was obviously the last time and used his left hand to firmly grip the man's greasy hair and yank him upwards towards the air.

Then the half-drowned man suddenly came to life again, his eyes wide open and glazed with terror as his armour began to drag him down once more.

Mad with terror, the warrior spluttered, coughed and attempted to climb over Arthur's body in a bid to stay above the waterline. Arthur immediately clouted the man forcefully above the temple with the knife's hilt then, swimming vigorously, he dragged his unconscious victim to the bank and the waiting mercies of Germanus and Gareth.

Meanwhile, the other warrior had somehow made it to shore where Lorcan despatched him efficiently.

And so, as more and more vessels were sunk, Gareth and several of the Dene warriors along the shoreline were kept busy dragging half-drowned Hundings from the water's edge. All of the escapees refused to surrender.

Arthur and the other swimmers were still occupied with the first vessels when the second group of motley boats burst out from the reed beds. Thorketil quickly summed up the situation and realised that these dugouts and coracles were likely to escape or would cut down the men in the water without his direct intervention. With a few terse words, he ordered his archers to fire directly at the Hundings' leadership before they reached the melee taking place in the main channel.

The archers aimed directly at the men holding the torches so, for the most part, the lights were quickly extinguished. The darkness assisted Arthur and the other swimmers, who then had more chances to slice the skins of the coracles or overturn the dugouts. The water soon became a seething mass of struggling men in heavy armour, many of whom were fighting against panic and the debilitating cold while attempting to right their dugouts and make their escape. Unfortunately, any men who did reach the bank were then confronted by armed and dangerous Dene warriors who gave them no mercy.

On Arthur's instructions, some of the Hundings were given a chance to surrender but, despite being half-drowned and freezing cold, they were determined to fight to the bitter end.

To a man, they elected to die.

Even from low in the water, Arthur could hear the sound of

a fierce fight taking place inside the reed beds where Snorri was engaged in a vicious battle for survival with that half of the Hundings force who had expected to be travelling to the safety of the ceols in the second wave of escapees. Instead, the entire group was confronted by cold and determined Dene warriors set on their extermination.

Snorri attempted to obey his master's orders, so he gave the Saxon Hounds an opportunity to surrender, much as Arthur's force had done. However, the Hundings sneered at Snorri's offer, for they deemed surrender to be a sign of cowardice. Snorri was forced to order his men to fight to the death and take no prisoners, an instruction that the Dene warriors enjoyed obeying, although a number of their own warriors were killed in the process.

By the time Snorri returned with thirty-five surviving Dene carrying the bodies of their slain companions, the entire garrison of Hundings had been exterminated. The only exception was Arthur's original opponent who had been rendered unconscious by the hilt of the Dragon Knife at the start of the ambush. The warrior had lain in the mud until he was found and trussed up like a plucked turkey to prevent him from killing himself. When the bound man regained consciousness, he tried to roll into the stream and drown, but Father Lorcan elected to sit on him to ensure his safety. Meanwhile, Arthur and his fellow swimmers were changing into dry clothing while the rest of the Dene warriors were recovering whatever bodies were relinquished by the stream.

When Arthur rejoined the Dene warriors and his British friends, his mood was ebullient.

'Perhaps we'll discover now what, or who, is the traitor in Heorot who's been betraying us behind the scenes. I would be missing a valuable opportunity if I didn't check with at least one of the Hundings to find out the identity of the man who has been suborned. Unfortunately, sir, you are the only survivor, and your continued survival will depend on your attitude to the questions I will be asking. I've a mind to discover everything you know by whatever means I feel are necessary.'

Around Arthur, Snorri and the three British companions, the Dene warriors were completing the many tasks that followed a victory over their enemies. The bodies of the Hundings were stripped of everything of value and their naked corpses were cast into a large hole in the earth. On a small rise to one side of the bank, the dead Dene warriors were laid out, along with their weapons, and their corpses made ready for the cleansing by fire if the weather permitted. At the same time, the Hundings would probably be covered with a thin coating of earth and sufficient stones to discourage scavengers.

Success in battle always determined how the dead warriors made their respective entrances to the shades.

Arthur shivered within his cloak and laughed as he recounted to Lorcan how he had laid his wet tunic and trews over two low bushes as he dried his frozen body and changed into clean clothing.

'My trews will be frozen as stiff as boards of wood by now and the cloth will splinter like pottery or glass if I should hit it too hard.'

'I'm sure you'll manage, Arthur. Now, what do you want to do with our fat friend here?'

Snorri kicked out at the heavy thighs of the trussed Hunding.

The man was richly dressed in clothing that indicated his status, although he was wet, half-frozen and miserable. He should have looked pitiful, but his hard eyes belied that impression.

Father Lorcan soon stripped him of his ornate trappings. The priest was particularly enamoured of a quantity of golden necklaces, cloak pins of gold and ivory, rings on every finger and a gold-edged mailed shirt, all immediately confiscated. The ever-present sigil of the leaping hound on his cloak pin told of the man's senior rank without any need for further explanation.

Afterwards Lorcan had placed his shivering form in an upright position in a simple long shirt; Arthur discovered the Hunding had hidden a little paunch under his previous finery. Distaste for the task ahead filled the Briton's mouth with salt and bile.

'I require very little of you, my friend. Once I have the information I require, you will be given warm clothes, food and drink. I, the Last Dragon, give my word that you will be sold back to your people without any harm to your person.'

The general, for so he proved to be, spat onto the ground at Arthur's feet.

'I am Mearchealf, son of Breoca, and I will not speak to any Dene mongrel. Nor will I speak to a Briton, a race who lies even lower on the list of men than any of the northerners. You can do your worst, but I'll not give you a useful word.'

Arthur sighed regretfully.

'You are boasting needlessly, Mearchealf, son of Breoca, because we both know that everyone eventually speaks under torture. I would happily spare you that, because it will give me no satisfaction. But you need have no doubt that you will provide me with the name and the information I require.'

Mearchealf spat again, and this time his aim was better. The spittle landed on Arthur's boot. With a calm expression, the young man quickly cleaned it by scraping it through some melting snow.

'Very well, Mearchealf, I will allow you to have your pangs of honour and then you'll tell me what I want to know.'

Still, in the hours that followed, Arthur came to wish that there was some other way to extract the information he needed, for the torturer becomes as damaged as his victim, except that his wounds are invisible to the naked eye.

Morning came before Mearchealf's spirit finally broke. By then, he had been convinced that his ceols had managed to depart with those survivors who had made good their escape. His hopes for his own salvation had vanished and his broken body betrayed him at the very end.

But he told Arthur everything he needed to know.

CHAPTER X

FORTUNA'S LAW

Man that is born of woman is of few days, and full of
trouble.
He cometh forth like a flower, and is cut down: he
Fleeth also as a shadow, and continueth not.

The Bible, Job 14:5

Several weeks passed before the Hundings War was finally
resolved and the last stragglers were chased back into Saxony.
But the cold had come with six feet of snow, drifts that men
could never hope to cross without snowshoes, and frozen water
in the fjords that had turned into thick, blue-tinged ice.

Loki's Eye and *Sea Wife* were drawn up into coves and put
under covers in Ivar Hnaefssen's lands, as were the other ships
that made up the Sae Dene fleet. No one would be able to
traverse the treacherous seas until the spring had released them
from winter's freezing fist.

Stormbringer was torn. Arthur had brought him the name of
the traitor and, to the surprise of no one, that person was
Aednetta Fridasdottar. But Arthur's information was neither

simple nor easy to understand, for the Hundings' general had spat out several teeth and the disconcerting information that the king's witch-woman had a secret lover who supplied her with funds, the benefits of a cunning intellect and the cold reason that had served to make Aednetta such an implacable enemy. The general had no idea who this enemy could be, but he cherished the knowledge that the Dene people had a clever traitor buried deeply inside the court of King Hrolf Kraki in Heorot. Like a fat rat, a traitor was listening in the rafters, concealed in plain view and as familiar to the courtiers as the layout of the king's old building itself. Was he a trusted servant? Was he a warrior? Was he even male? Arthur had no way of knowing. Even though the general knew he was dying from the punishment he had endured during his torture, he still had enough breath and sufficient effrontery to taunt Arthur.

'I hope she fucks up Hrolf Kraki's kingship until he's useless, both as a man and as a king,' the general had muttered once he had recovered his breath after a particularly painful fit of coughing. This bout was accompanied by a clot of bloody phlegm, which warned Arthur that one of the body blows had probably driven a rib into the general's lungs. Arthur owed his superior medical knowledge to that long-dead British healer, Myrddion Merlinus. Even now, with one gentle hand on the general's side, Arthur could feel bones grinding and his eyes softened with pity.

The general saw the expression on Arthur's face and accurately interpreted its meaning. Mearchealf had no desire to die and only his fierce will had kept him alive for this long, but Arthur's pity curdled in the Hunding's throat. To cover his rage at his fate, the Saxon jarl spat bloody sputum into the earth and asked for his wrists to be cut free of the thongs that bound his arms.

'I wish to face my end like a man, rather than as a slave,' he explained with a bitter snarl.

Arthur noticed that more fresh blood was seeping into the general's moustaches from his nostrils.

'As for Aednetta's lover! She alone knows his identity, and he's far too clever to be caught or you'd have captured him by now,' the general added bluntly. He wheezed out an ugly, damaged laugh, wet and agonised. Then, with an obvious effort, he managed to stop another bout of painful coughing.

Arthur had finally made the killing blow that sent Mearchealf to the shades because, at the very end, the general had begged for an immediate death. By this time, Arthur was beginning to feel true respect for his prisoner and a certain degree of sorrow at the nature of a war that had brought this brave man to such a pass.

Without any further hesitation, Arthur granted Mearchealf his boon and beheaded him with his sword. The young man knew that Bedwyr would have understood the necessity of using the huge weapon that he had given to his foster-son, and agreed that Mearchealf was an honourable man who deserved a speedy death. Bedwyr would also have understood that this fine warrior had been defeated by old hatreds that the Hundings refused to relinquish.

As soon as the necessary rituals of burial and cremation of the dead were completed, Arthur sent out scouts to discover the whereabouts of Stormbringer's army. Once they were located, the decision was made to vacate the swamp with its ruined village. The Dene warriors who had survived could only cover the corpses of the innocent villagers with a thin layer of soil, because the earth had turned to iron in the bitter cold. Arthur felt he had failed in the task of giving the villagers a decent burial.

Snorri was the first scout to find traces of Stormbringer's force. A thousand men left scars on the landscape when they passed, even in the kinder and warmer months. Footprints in the mud and slush, broken branches and felled trees used for fires left scars on the forests for those who chose to look. To Arthur's forest-trained eyes, Stormbringer had moved through the landscape with little care for the marks of passage that he left behind him. Speed was important for, as winter deepened, his horses and oxen would become useless. Stormbringer was running towards shelter on the coast as fast as his plunder-laden force could travel.

The two forces met when Stormbringer was leading his men away from the border after starting the trek back to Ivar Hnaefssen's holding where the host intended to spend the winter months. From the Sae Dene's direction of travel, Arthur deduced that his friend was still ignorant of the state of the fleet and that the boats were landlocked now for the four months of deep winter. With his newly obtained intelligence from Mearchealf, Arthur decided that Stormbringer must be convinced to take immediate action against Heorot and its master, Hrolf Kraki.

But any movement must come from the land. The advent of winter ensured that this decision had already been made for the commander.

In a fit of jovial enthusiasm, Ivar was determined to host a feast of victory, now that the Hundings were a spent force and the Dene were masters of their world once again. On the other hand, Arthur intended to call for an immediate council of the jarls. Stormbringer solved the problem by agreeing to both, so the council would take place at noon and the feast would be held during the early evening.

For Stormbringer and his minions, feasts were debauched affairs where the strength of a man was measured by the number of horns of beer or mead he could drink in the shortest possible time. Roisterers would regularly stagger off to vomit copiously, then wash away the foul taste in their mouths with still more alcohol. Any council meeting held after the feast would be doomed to failure because men suffering from huge hangovers always became belligerent and argumentative.

Arthur had no real objections to drunkenness, but he was abstemious by nature and, like Gareth, he preferred to keep his wits sharp. Fortunately, the Dene warriors from his ship forgave him almost anything because of his fighting prowess and his passion for justice, so little idiosyncrasies with alcohol were forgiven.

Hnaefssen's long-hall had changed little in the two years of war that Stormbringer and Arthur had endured since the jarl had first offered them assistance. Neither Stormbringer nor Arthur had forgotten his generosity, for the man had also detailed one of his favourite sons to help with the relief of the besieged citizens of Skania. Such devotion and honour had earned Jarl Ivar Hnaefssen the respect of all.

Ivar's holding was covered with a blanket of deep snow and glinting icicles were hanging from the guttering and roofs of every building in Hnaefssen's small town. At first, Arthur was nervous of them, but logic told him that these very temporary knives of ice would only fall if a thaw weakened their hold. Even so, his eyes continued to steal skywards whenever he left the security of a building.

'I just like to check,' he explained to Father Lorcan as he walked quickly into the long-hall with one eye scanning the icicles above him.

Lorcan nodded with complete understanding.

During the previous winter, the priest had almost been impaled by an enormous icicle that plummeted to earth from a high tree branch. It had burst into dozens of razor-sharp shards of ice that scattered themselves over the mud of the roadway in the nondescript Saxon town. Lorcan had been shaking and nauseous for at least an hour after.

The agenda of the council meeting began with the obligatory huge horns of foaming beer and mead. However, once those present had drunk their toasts to the great victory over the Hundings, Stormbringer called on Arthur to recount everything he had learned from the destruction of the Hundings' commanders and the information he had extracted from General Mearchealf.

'So that's it,' Arthur said flatly, once he had described the details of the past few weeks. 'Aednetta Fridasdottar and her mysterious lover will continue to meddle and damage Dene society wherever they can. The reason I wanted to speak to this council is that, with an army already assembled, you have the perfect opportunity to set Heorot to rights.'

Ivar Hnaefssen looked sideways at Arthur as if he suddenly found cause to distrust the Briton, but Stormbringer smiled secretively at his friend.

'What sort of treason are you proposing, boy?' Ivar asked abrasively. 'I have no reason to like Hrolf Kraki, but the man is my king. I, for one, will never raise a sword against him.'

'I don't propose treason at all, my lord. But we must ask ourselves how we can inform Hrolf Kraki of the information we have gleaned. Or do you propose we avoid telling him that he's bedding a sworn enemy of the Dene people? That's the real treason – staying silent! Do you think that we can continue as we have done in the past? Hrolf Kraki will never forgive anyone who took part in the recent battles against the Hundings because you've shown up his cowardice.'

Ivar had never considered what might occur after the Dene victory. Deeply conservative and honest to the bone, the old man nodded his recognition of the points that Arthur had made so forthrightly. Hnaefssen would never deny the truth, and nor would he try to lie.

'You and I are outlaws in the Dene homeland because Hrolf Kraki has banished us from Heorot, Arthur,' Stormbringer interrupted. 'Perhaps you should explain to Ivar what you believe we can do.'

Arthur's face flushed with enthusiasm and he spoke with more animation than usual.

'We'll never have a thousand men at our backs again, my friends. And, as we have such a numerical advantage, I believe we should march on Heorot to force Hrolf Kraki and the jarls of the north to listen to what we have to say. I'm not proposing a revolt and neither do I propose that we commit treason. I'm aware that any true Dene could never live with the dishonour of deposing a rightful king. Treason is not the Dene way and for what it's worth, I agree with you. By all reports, Hrolf Kraki was once an excellent king who ruled for the good of your people, so I'd like to believe that he could return to being one.'

'But you've no reason to love the Crow King,' Ivar Hnaefssen muttered suspiciously, as if he doubted Arthur's motives. Ivar had some cause; deep down, Arthur knew that people rarely changed once they had strolled down the dangerous road of tyranny.

Ivar was aware of Hrolf Kraki's behaviour in recent years, but he chose to blame any flaws on the witch-woman. For his part, all hints of criticism must be excised from Arthur's voice because while the jarls might be willing to find fault with Hrolf Kraki, no outsider could, and certainly not Arthur, no matter how great his reputation might be, or the strength of his friendship with the Sae Dene king.

'I may be an outsider, Lord Hnaefssen, as all the men in your council are aware, but I count my own honour just as highly as you do. Unfortunately, I have discovered that Hrolf Kraki respects only one thing, and that is the mailed fist. If we arrive in Heorot and place our army in bivouac outside the city, he will be forced to listen to our complaints. In fact, we need only point out the obvious. We can explain that Stormbringer has received certain information of an urgent nature that caused us to be concerned for Hrolf Kraki's safety. As the Sae Dene has been banished, his warriors are only in Heorot with him to ensure that he is given a hearing. Nothing else under heaven but force will make that stubborn man listen to our grievances or alter his opinions, and this certainly applies if his emotions are engaged. I think we must assume that the witch-woman has a sensitive part of his anatomy under her control. She surely commands his head and his heart. He'll never admit to his mistakes or accept any guilt for the deaths and injuries his decisions have caused to his people. Nor will he willingly accept the guilt of Aednetta Fridasdottar, even if it is proved thrice over.'

'That's true, Arthur, but what's to be gained by bearding Hrolf Kraki at Heorot? He'll lose some of his prestige if we challenge him, and he'll not like that,' Stormbringer stated with certainty.

'It's possible that we might be able to extract the name of Aednetta's lover from her, because the Crow King may agree to her being questioned if he thinks she has been playing the game of the two-backed beast with another man. I've lost my taste for torture, even if Hrolf Kraki allowed me to touch her, which I doubt. I believe he'd try to extract the information himself. Even if he champions her innocence, the possibility of a royal betrayal will eat away at him, and sow the seeds of suspicion in his mind so that he'll act eventually. In fact, I'd prefer to suggest that the witch-woman has been duped, and to offer our assistance to find the hidden traitor. We'll never know the truth, Valdar, if we leave the investigation to the Crow King or his minions.'

Stormbringer nodded, for Arthur's arguments were cogent and logical.

'Yes, my lord!' Arthur grimaced. 'Before you raise the subject, I admit that I believe your king to be a despicable human being. How could I not loathe this man who has done his very best to have me, my friends and members of my family killed? Hrolf Kraki has been false as a human being, but he is the born king of the Dene people and must be given the respect owed to the ruler of your nation. The gods have elevated him to the throne and I have no right to argue with them. But if we choose to leave matters as they stand, what do you think Aednetta's lover will do? Do you believe for one moment that the traitor will go away? Not he! He will do his best to remove *you*! We are morally obliged to finalise this whole conflict while we can.'

Stormbringer agreed and several of the jarls gave their reluctant assent. But Ivar and some of his older compatriots were still undecided.

'Do you think that Hrolf Kraki will choose to make a further attack on The Holding if the opportunity arises, Valdar? And do you remember what his orders were? His warriors were to hang the bodies of your little girls on the outer walls of your long-hall so that their brutalised corpses would be the first things you saw when you returned.'

Stormbringer winced and made a small gesture of disgust with one hand. Ivar too began to pale at what he was hearing.

'Will the king decide to attack you and yours in the spring after you set sail for Skania, Ivar? There's no guarantee that my three friends will appear at exactly the right time to save those souls who live at your farm.'

Arthur's voice was implacable as he described what could happen to Ivar's wife and the rest of his family, and all who lived in his village.

'I now have a large stake in The Holding and I'm concerned for the safety of all who are domiciled there. My sister is betrothed to Stormbringer, and I'm fearful that Hrolf Kraki will send assassins to kill her. Hrolf Kraki must be brought to heel and the poisonous influence of the witch-woman must be crushed, for she hates my sister like poison. There are wheels within wheels here, Lords of the Mark, but all is not yet lost.'

The silence was alive with suspicion.

'And what about you, Ivar, and the problems you have been facing in recent times? Your cows graze in fields that are a stone's throw from Saxon fields and Saxon thieves. How many generations of your family have fought and died to protect your hall? Do you believe that Hrolf Kraki will come to your aid if the Jutes decide to attack your lands again in the spring? The Crow King didn't turn into a lamb overnight. If anything, he'll have lost the respect of most of his warriors because you've defeated his enemies in battle despite his absence as leader. Who will become the scapegoat for the loss of his dignity?'

Arthur paused to allow his message to sink in.

'Yes, Master Ivar. The Crow King will blame *you*. He'll wait until you're off guard and then he'll make you bleed for any imagined insults, slights or treacheries. After all, what crimes did

Stormbringer commit that warranted his banishment? He brought *Loki's Eye* back from Britain groaning with plunder, all of which Hrolf Kraki kept, including Stormbringer's share and the crew's. The ostensible reason for this punishment was that we insulted Aednetta Fridasdottar. Do you understand the implications of his actions, Ivar? We now know that Aednetta occupies the centre of the king's web of sins. She isolates the king by driving away every loyal and decent lord, and leaves the sycophants and fools behind to fill the void. And all the while the real traitor is waiting, watching and laughing at our stupidity from behind his hands.'

Ivar gnashed his teeth.

'Ask Thorketil, the Troll King, what happens to honest and loyal jarls who risk their lives in the Crow King's service,' Arthur added.

All too easily, Ivar Hnaefssen could imagine the king's response to their victory over the Hundings and knew in his heart of hearts that this young Briton was correct in his assertions. The Crow King only respected brute strength, while showing a reluctance to fight for those causes he was morally bound to champion. For a man such as Hrolf Kraki, trust was a curse and undeserving loyalty was the refuge of fools.

With much reluctance, Ivar finally nodded in agreement. He longed for a drink to wash the foul taste out of his mouth, but once given, his word was his bond.

'Very well, young man, I'll grant you that the king will be angry that we've beaten off the threat from the Hundings, even though it makes no sense that Hrolf Kraki should blame us for doing so. I can also accept that we must try to identify the traitor in his court while we have an opportunity to force his hand. Again, the best time will be while we have our whole force at our disposal outside the gates to his hall. The mere threat of an open revolt will probably force the Crow King to listen to any demands we make.'

'Thank you, Master Ivar. I only hope you'll not regret the advice I've given you. I gave this matter a great deal of thought before reaching my conclusions.'

'I also hope so! Now, can we forget our woes for the night and enjoy our feast? I've discovered I have the most prodigious thirst.'

The best part of a week was needed for the jarls to recover from the debaucheries that took place on the night of the council meeting. But much planning was also needed. Once agreement on their course of action had been reached, there was no need for hurry because the army would be forced to travel on foot in the middle of winter; deep snow would make their journey very difficult. Not only would they need skilled woodsmen and guides to help them negotiate the snow-covered landscapes, but they would also be forced to carry all their supplies and weapons with them. Their plunder could be safely left in Ivar Hnaefssen's halls, where a token force of one hundred men would guard their rear from any attack from along the borders, unlikely as such an assault seemed. Arthur's caution dictated that he make these plans. As for food supplies, they could hardly live off the land in the depths of winter, so would need to bring their own. The logistics of the journey were complex, and the constant calculations kept both Arthur and Stormbringer occupied for many cold and miserable hours.

Eventually, Arthur convinced Stormbringer that they should use Roman military practices for long-distance travel as their guide, and these tried and true tactics were then wedded to hard-headed Dene practicality. The warriors should be grouped into pairs and, between them, would carry dried provisions wrapped within their tents. Dried meat, fish and lentils were far lighter than fresh rations and an efficient system of cooking was devised whereby small groups elected their own cooks. These simplified arrangements avoided the need for wagons and oxen, animals that would inevitably become bogged or trapped in the snow-shrouded landscape.

The most efficient means of moving supplies and weaponry seemed to be the ancient practice of sleds mounted on skis. Arthur had never used this form of transport before, but he'd seen peasants use sleds and sleighs often enough in the Dene lands, so he understood the principles of this mode of transport.

Arthur was forced to devise the most efficient organisational model possible to facilitate the movement of the column. He again decided to fall back on the practices of the Roman legions and use centuries, or cadres of one hundred men, each of which would use two large sleds to carry the excess rations and heavier items of equipment and armour.

He determined that twenty sleds would be sufficient to meet the requirements of the column for supplies alone. In addition at least one more sled would be needed to transport the injured and sick, and medical supplies. Finally, Arthur decided that if Stormbringer was to retain the high moral ground in his discussions with Hrolf Kraki, he would need to give a share of the spoils from the Hundings' campaign to the king, although he suggested it should be lightly taxed to cover expenses.

All in all, twenty-five sleds were eventually purchased from Ivar Hnaefssen's subjects.

The frames on the sleds were far larger than anything that Arthur had ever seen, and attached to wicked iron skis that permitted them to slide easily over the snow and ice.

With long leather harnesses attached to their shoulders while walking on large snowshoes, up to twelve men at a time would tow the supplies for the whole group. As each group of warriors began to tire, other men were detailed to take their place in a rotation system.

Arthur and Stormbringer were determined that the army should travel as lightly as possible so they could minimise the time and energy expended while crossing the unforgiving landscape. Arthur had never experienced such cold and snow, although he had lived at The Holding and spent time in Skania during the past few years; on the islands, the sea provided some measure of warmth to the land. Meanwhile, Stormbringer laughed at his friend's awe, and described how the cold in Noroway would take away a man's breath and how unwary travellers had regularly been known to drown in the worst snowdrifts. Fortunately, the landscape along the route of their march was mostly flat.

As the long journey began, Arthur prepared his furs and leathers with obsessive care, for his life and health depended on warmth. Meanwhile, he prayed that he'd not disgrace himself during the trek into the frozen north and his dangerous tilt at fate.

The journey itself was very slow and was agonisingly drawn-out in the grim weather conditions; in spite of the relatively flat terrain, the snow was twelve feet thick in some places and only the use of snowshoes made movement possible. Even so, it was thanks to Ivar's skilled guides and woodsmen that made the journey feasible for such a large group.

The land was criss-crossed by a network of streams now choked into silence by ice. At least, as Lorcan dourly noted, they didn't need to swim, although they had to be well balanced on their feet. Small injuries were commonplace during the journey, for the snow concealed low bushes and tree branches which caught out the unwary. So far, none of the men had broken bones, but Arthur was prepared for the inevitability of such injuries as, on some mornings, the murky darkness was impenetrable, while even torches did little to light the way when the gusting wind threw snow directly into their faces.

For three straight days of blizzard, the host was unable to move at all; men were forced to huddle in their hide tents while trying not to think of being buried alive.

Stormbringer showed Arthur how walls of packed snow around the tents could insulate the men against the cold, and keep them alive and healthy in even the worst of conditions. Arthur's respect for the dogged stubbornness of the Dene character increased tenfold and he saw why nature had determined that there would be very few short Dene men. In the coldest of cold winters, they tended to flounder in deep snow and often died young before they could breed.

When the host finally emerged from under the blanket of white that covered the landscape, the warriors' first thoughts were to forage for precious firewood. One thought was predominant throughout the column: war should never be waged in winter. Somewhere in Arthur's agile brain, an idea stirred and twisted, then returned to its restless sleep until needed.

After the storm had finally abated, Arthur gazed out on a landscape that was pristine and other-worldly. His breath caught in his throat at the loveliness of what he could see before him. Only Gareth, also awed by what God had wrought, stood with him to enjoy the wonders of the landscape.

The snow had been carved into waves and troughs by the

wind, so it was firm and crackling with icy particles underfoot. A thousand diamonds or stars seemed to be dancing in every branch of every tree, tinkling with frozen ice crystals. The trunks of the forest giants were large and heavy, for willows and smaller species would be torn out of the ground by the weight of snow. Even so, many branches had fallen to earth and would be burned in the army's temporary fire pits. Fire was life here, so some fuel was also carried on the sleds if room existed. Various small groups within each century constructed communal fireplaces, and all the warriors shared cooking pots to collect the snow used to soften their dried meat. Snow heated for cooking was safe for drinking, so no man could die of thirst in such a landscape.

Apart from their thick clothing, the most important item of equipment that each man carried was his snowshoes. These flat and ungainly paddles permitted the warriors to slide over the surface of the snow at a greater speed than normal walking, although the shuffling movement could exhaust a novice.

And so, under skies that were either startlingly blue and clear, or white with patches of charcoal from distant storms, the army of the Sae Dene continued on slowly towards Heorot. During the trek, the sagas of the north were recounted around the fires and various warriors told tales of their own experiences. Arthur told one eager audience of the massacre at Crookback Farm in Arden Forest when, as a young lad, he had come across the corpses of a farming family murdered by a secret cadre of Saxons. He recalled the horror he had felt when he saw the body of the farmer's wife. She had been repeatedly raped, and then her throat had been cut. Afterwards, her corpse had been cast away like a useless husk of dead flesh; the men had even killed an innocent infant, and tossed it into the snow.

The young Arthur had killed his first man on that terrible day and could still remember the face of his victim. Sometimes the dead Saxon came to Arthur as he slept and would gaze at Arthur with silent, accusing eyes.

Although Arthur's reason told him that he should feel no remorse for having survived the confrontation, he still felt twinges of pain for the man's wife and children who had been left behind to suffer after his death.

Stormbringer had listened to Germanus and Lorcan as they described the boy's night in the tree tops of Arden Forest with only a rescued kitten to keep him awake, so the king of the Sae Dene looked at his friend with sympathy. In the long night, when it seemed that daylight would never return again, Arthur told other stories of his youth and then, when those were finished, he recounted all the tales that Bedwyr and Elayne had told him about his father.

Arthur had a deep, rich voice and a talent for story-telling, so Stormbringer could visualise the curved walls of Cadbury Tor as it rose up to repel all enemies. He could stand with Bedwyr on the shield wall of Moridunum and feel the sticky coating of congealing blood cover him from head to toe. And he could hold Caliburn, Artor's great sword, just as Bedwyr had done when he cast it high into the air so that it fell into the impenetrable darkness of the tarn at Caer Gai. Thus Bedwyr had ensured that no hands other than those of King Artor would ever wield that blade.

Sagas such as these made Stormbringer's heart ache and dance by turn whenever he heard the bitter history of the Britons and their struggle for survival, and he learned to appreciate why his friend felt such guilt when he acted in ways deemed to be dishonourable. Arthur had referred to this weakness as the poisoned blood of his grandfather, Uther Pendragon.

'The dragon is truly the totem of your forebears, my friend,' Stormbringer said reflectively as the firelight danced in his eyes. Snorri was drowsing in a corner of the tent, weary from pulling the sled but unwilling to close his eyes in case he missed more of the wonderful tales. Father Lorcan and Germanus drank from a small leather bottle brought with him from the south, and Arthur swore he could smell apricot brandy on the Frank's breath.

'Aye, Arthur! As the Last Dragon, I fear that you'll have to return to your homeland sooner or later,' Germanus said sleepily, filling the hearts of both Stormbringer and Snorri with dread.

'Yes, I suppose the day must come when I'll want to return to Britain and I'm given permission to end my service to the Dene people. I still have unfinished business with my nephew, King Bran, who is interfering in the lives of anyone who threatens the future accession to the throne of Ector, his son. Bran tried to have me killed on at least one occasion; such a murderous man has lost his right to rule, even if he is my kinsman.'

'I remember,' Stormbringer said and stirred the fire with a piece of wood. 'You found your kinsman's torc among the spoils I collected in Britain and your words upset Hrolf Kraki mightily. Yes, I told you at the time that your kinsman – I forget his name – had been assassinated on the orders of King Bran.'

'It was Gilchrist, the grandson of King Gawayne, my uncle. At least I think he was! My kin are very difficult to determine because King Artor fathered me late in his life. In fact, I discovered that my sister was a woman of fifty when I was seven years old.'

Stormbringer smiled with a sad finality. 'So you think you'll eventually leave us? I agree, but that will be in the future, and I'd like to discuss the matter with you. Many of the Dene and their families may wish to migrate to strange lands with you on your ship. If anyone can carve out a successful kingdom in a strange land, my friend, it is you.'

'But Britain isn't a strange land,' Arthur protested. 'Britain is my home!'

'When I travelled down the east coast of Britain, I found that all the lands belonged to the Saxons. You know this is true, for you travelled through the towns of the east coast of Britain with Eamonn and the girls. I think you'll find that your Britain is a cold and unfriendly place, now that the Saxons have pushed west as they pursue the Celtic peoples.'

'Aye, I understand. Still, who knows what can happen in the future? Perhaps I might be permitted to return to some place in Britain with warriors of my own and longboats at my back. It may even be possible to carve out a new Dene kingdom along the eastern coast.'

'Who knows?' Stormbringer responded with a knowing grin.

'Who knows?' Gareth echoed. If Arthur should desire to establish an eastern kingdom, then Gareth would happily die to give it to him.

Arthur's friends looked thoroughly charmed at the direction of the conversation, so it was probably best for everyone's peace of mind that the fire suddenly exploded with the shattering of a log.

Snorri drowsed, Lorcan continued to sip brandy and Gareth began to nod off. But Germanus, Stormbringer and Arthur were all too busy with complicated thoughts of power to feel any weariness. Another day was drawing to a close and they would reach their destination on the morrow.

* * *

After weeks on the move, the long dragon of men labouring through the snow saw the scar on the landscape ahead of them that was Limfjord. A mighty lake gleamed grey and silver in the weak sunshine and, even at a distance, Arthur could recognise the landscape that he had last seen years ago when, frightened and ignorant, the young Britons had been dragged up the hill to the king's hall of Heorot.

'How the world changes!' Arthur muttered as he put his back into the struggle of dragging the long sled out of a deep drift of snow. In Dene society, the jarls and commanders were also expected to take their turns with such tasks.

In the distance, he could see a small group of men coming quickly towards them on long wooden skis.

Arthur dropped the harness and caught Stormbringer's attention.

'They seem to be men from Heorot town, brother,' he called urgently, but Stormbringer had already been warned.

Six young men were effortlessly sliding towards the advancing army. Within half an hour, the men were clearly visible as warriors, muffled in heavy furs and armed to the teeth.

Stormbringer had ordered his men to continue the advance, stopping only when the warriors did so. One of them released a makeshift white flag which he attached to a ski pole and waved vigorously above his head. Almost every man in the advancing vanguard of the Dene army could see the black figure of a crow painted on the stark white foreground.

'Now that Hrolf Kraki has attracted our attention, we might just find out what he wants.' Stormbringer addressed Arthur, although his sharp gaze never left the threatening group waiting on a slight knoll.

'Hrolf Kraki, King of the Dene and your lawful master,

demands that you halt your illegal and treasonous advance towards his town and his hall, or else he will be forced to kill you all.'

Several of Stormbringer's warriors laughed raucously at the envoys, who bridled angrily at the insults. But Arthur stepped forward to act as Stormbringer's voice.

'You have made your ridiculous threats, so you can now carry our response back to your master.' Arthur's words accentuated the powerful situation that Stormbringer enjoyed.

'This is treason,' the largest of the envoys snarled with contempt. 'The Sae Dene mongrel comes to Heorot with an army at his back and attempts to make demands. I am instructed to tell you that you are ordered to turn back and disband your host. Then, perhaps, Hrolf Kraki will let you live.'

'Valdar Bjornsen, whom real men call the Stormbringer, is a brave man. He is not a mongrel who can be insulted or threatened with impunity, even by his king. Nor will Hrolf Kraki's envoys be permitted to speak of the Sae Dene king with such contempt as you have done. I will settle this matter at some later time when you are not hiding behind a flag of truce. Meanwhile, Valdar Bjornsen wishes to speak to Hrolf Kraki in person, but he has no trust in either the Crow King or his jarls that hide in Heorot and refuse to assist those true Denes who fight off invading forces. Hrolf Kraki's cowardice has left our people to perish unaided. Valdar Bjornsen refuses to accept the word of a king who banished him unlawfully and confiscated the plunder of Britain out of sheer greed. Finally, knowing that the Sae Dene king was not present at his estates, the Crow King sent a force of assassins to torture and murder everybody at The Holding.'

The faces of the envoys flushed with mingled shame and fury; their fists gripped ski poles as if they were spears and the men around Stormbringer stirred uneasily with their hands on the pommels of their swords.

'Your insults serve no purpose, sir, and I will happily face you personally at some future time,' the tall envoy snapped. 'It is my duty to inform you that if you enter Hrolf Kraki's personal territory with an army at your back, your actions will be treated as a declaration of war.'

Arthur smiled lazily, but no humour reached his grey eyes. 'Our army would never permit the Sae Dene king to set foot within Heorot alone, after Hrolf Kraki's perfidy in the past. Our men do not wish to raise their swords against God's anointed king, but they will not permit Valdar Bjornsen to face the hostile fury of the Crow King without their support.'

So tell that to the Crow King, you fuckers, Arthur thought viciously.

'And who might you be, you ingrate?' one of the warriors demanded.

'I am Stormbringer's deputy, and also the Briton who is known as Arthur, the Last Dragon. It was I who defeated the king's champion, Thorketil, a fine man foully cast off by your king after he was defeated in fair combat. Thorketil fights with us now.'

The name obviously meant something to the envoys because they whispered to each other while staring, surprised, at Arthur.

One of the warriors shouldered his way through to the front of the small group. 'I saw you fight the Troll King in the forecourt of Heorot,' he volunteered. 'You've changed in the past years. Even in Heorot, we've heard tales of the exploits of the Last Dragon who travelled through Skania. I'd regret being forced to kill you, Arthur of Britain, for I won coin betting on you when you fought Thorketil. It's sad that issues should divide good men, but I'll be forced to take offence with you if you continue to curse my master.'

'And I remember you,' Arthur replied. 'You told me much that was of interest about my opponent, and it all proved to be true. And so, my friend, I would be sorry to have to kill you, but I will give no mercy to men such as Hrolf Kraki, who sought to kill my sister and my friends, all of whom were innocents. However, I will refrain from lifting my blade against the Crow King. My friend, the Stormbringer, and his faithful ally, Ivar Hnaefssen, have made me promise to stay my hand, and so I have vowed.'

The warrior who had been on guard duty in Heorot a few short years earlier was a golden-haired, leonine man with a bluff, open face. Had Arthur not been able to see the faint white lines at the corners of his eyes, he would have judged the man to be no more than thirty years old.

'What is your name, good sir? I'll remember your face the better for knowing who you are.'

'I am known as Heoden, the son of Helm, whose mother's fathers were of the Wulfings. The wolf is my totem, and some men call me Snow-wolf because I'm quick and proficient with my skis. I'm sworn to serve Hrolf Kraki for as long as we live after an oath given by my father when Hrolf Kraki was forced to flee during the reign of the imposter. There is much that we cannot know about what has brought him to this pass. I can say without hesitation that the king's father was noble ... as was Hrolf Kraki ... until ...'

Heoden's voice faded away as he struggled to justify his master's excesses.

'Return to Heorot with us, and you can explain to your master what we have said,' Stormbringer suggested. 'It is my intention to see the king in his hall whether he likes it or not. I wish no harm to the king, but he must be forced to hear the intelligence we have discovered from captives who were taken in the south. We will not permit him to cover his ears and ignore us any further, or the Dene people will fail. The Hundings were almost knocking at the doors of your halls before my intervention, and they'd not have been as polite as we are.'

The envoys were given no choice.

'I would appreciate your advice on places where we can bivouac our warriors. Is there a convenient place near Heorot? I can ask the king, of course, but I doubt that he'll be disposed towards finding warm accommodation for close to eight hundred men.'

The leader of the envoys glared at Stormbringer with a non-committal shrug of his shoulders.

'Of course, Heorot itself would be perfect for our requirements, but I do believe he'd refuse. In the meantime, we are quite prepared to surround his hall and camp around the palace in our tents. My men will be disappointed at his lack of generosity but, if necessary, they can forage for themselves.'

Heoden could hear the threat underlying Stormbringer's casual conversation, as could most of the envoys.

Stormbringer turned back to Arthur to issue his orders.

'Very well, Arthur. I grow weary of the snow and am eager to see Frodhi, my cousin. Let's leave this damned plain and move on to Heorot. Our destination is now in sight.'

The tall outline of Heorot could be dimly seen as it hunkered over the highest point of the fjord. The mists of the afternoon had been pierced for a short moment by a shaft of brilliant sunlight.

'We'll be inside Heorot in less than an hour,' Arthur told his friends, as he pulled the harness over his shoulder once again.

'Let's hope we're able to leave with more ease than last time,' Stormbringer retorted as he indicated that the column should resume its march.

The great dragon's tail of men began to move once more as the warriors dug deep to drive abused muscles onwards, after weeks in an unforgiving and frozen landscape. Each man anticipated different pleasures at Heorot, but all shared one wish – to feel warm again.

And so Arthur returned to Heorot. This time, the Crow King would discover that, of all the winged creatures of the past, the Last Dragon would prove to be the most fearsome of all.

THE HALL OF HEOROT

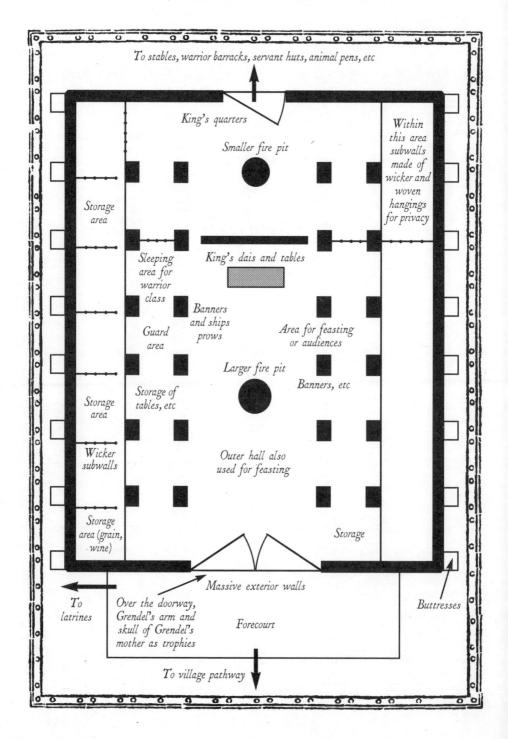

To stables, warrior barracks, servant huts, animal pens, etc

King's quarters

Smaller fire pit

Within this area subwalls made of wicker and woven hangings for privacy

Storage area

Sleeping area for warrior class

King's dais and tables

Guard area

Banners and ships prows

Area for feasting or audiences

Storage area

Storage of tables, etc

Larger fire pit

Banners, etc

Wicker subwalls

Outer hall also used for feasting

Storage area (grain, wine)

Storage

Massive exterior walls

To latrines

Over the doorway, Grendel's arm and skull of Grendel's mother as trophies

Forecourt

Buttresses

To village pathway

CHAPTER XI

YOUR SINS WILL
CATCH YOU OUT

Who is this that darkeneth counsel by words without
knowledge?

The Bible, Job 38:2

Hrolf Kraki, King of the Dene, looked out on a frigid winter's
morning at a landscape that had changed overnight. Fury turned
his eyes to pinpoints of hot, white flame and his face a dangerous
shade of plum-red.

'I want Frodhi! Find that useless bastard for me now!
And would someone explain how a whole army has bivouacked
outside my back door?' The king's voice was a hoarse bellow,
and his slaves twittered and scurried around him like disturbed
roaches.

Outside the rear door of the great hall, Hrolf Kraki
could look out over Stormbringer's army. The Crow King had
occasionally seen larger armies, but never on his own doorstep.

Tents stretched densely across the large snowbound fields, in summer normally dotted with black and white cows. The vast collection had appeared like freshly grown mushrooms; closely linked and encircled by walls of hard-packed snow for insulation.

The disciplined, unfamiliar configuration made Hrolf Kraki's belly feel like it was suddenly boiling with acid.

The hour was early but the warriors were awake and busy at their fire pits. Throughout the large camp, the Crow King could see well-organised, disciplined and alert men, all warmly dressed, and outwardly unscathed by a hard autumn campaign. The king's heart sank.

The obvious discipline of this host nagged at him, so he chewed at a thumbnail and tried to puzzle out what disturbed him so much.

Then he realised. Stormbringer had never laid out his camps in this fashion, and had never demanded this type of discipline; someone else was organising this army and implementing strategies that Hrolf Kraki could never hope to understand.

Even more alarmingly, those warriors who could see that their king was watching them deigned to bow in his direction, but the obeisance was neither deep nor respectful. For the first time in many years, Hrolf Kraki tried to think rationally and logically. As he waited for Frodhi to join him, he demanded a large horn of beer to chase away the night demons that came to disturb his rest more frequently, now that he relied on Aednetta's anodynes and potions to get any sleep at all. Any rest won through her doubtful charms was unsettled, disturbed by half-remembered horrors that left him more tired when he awoke.

Now Hrolf Kraki hugged his belly with one hand as his hunger disappeared, to be replaced by an emotion that he recognised as fear. He had almost forgotten what it felt like to be afraid.

'Sit, master, and I will order porridge with honey and warmed milk for you to drink,' Aednetta offered. 'The beer merely clouds your wits and scours your gut, my lord.'

Aednetta had entered soundlessly in her felt slippers and the king jumped in fright. Sometimes Aednetta was a burden because he knew, all too well, how much she revolted his staff, his warriors and his jarls. Yet, just when he had decided to send her packing out of Heorot, his body began to protest. She was an addiction as potent as wine or the poppy or any of the diversions that obsessed men to the point of madness.

Her sinuous fingers massaged his tense shoulder muscles and toyed with the sinews of his throat and the sensitive whorls of his ears, sending shivers of lust up his spine.

Hrolf Kraki needed to think, so he roughly pushed her arms aside.

'Why are these bastards here? You said they'd die on the southern borders but, instead, my most tiresome cousin has appeared with a huge army at his back. It's winter! How did they get here so quickly? For the love of God, Aednetta, I'd need weeks to raise enough warriors to send them packing, even if such a task was possible.'

Then, despite his protestations, Aednetta led him to the section of the hall where the king slept in state. His bed was covered with a huge blanket of arctic bearskins. The pelts were lustrous and as white as snow; Hrolf Kraki had been told that five men had died to obtain this superb covering. Now he threw himself onto the priceless bedcover without any regard for the mud and wet straw from the dirty sandals that covered his feet. Even the knitted socks that he wore were filthy.

Aednetta knelt and removed the offensive footwear and the vile socks. Her hands felt the coldness of his bare feet and she called to her maidservant to heat water so she could massage his extremities. By the time the slave returned the king was already devouring a large bowl of sweetened porridge. Milk seeped into his greying moustaches, and Aednetta swallowed back an exclamation of disgust. Instead, she kissed away the milk and food stains, while he continued to gorge himself.

On her knees once again, she carefully washed his feet. Then, her face blank, she began to heat a little perfumed oil in her hands before massaging it into the coarse skin until the flesh was pink. She had seen her man's high colour and the poor movement of blood in his extremities before and, although she hungered for the day when she was free to stand beside her lover in the sight of these high-born Dene pigs, Hrolf Kraki's early death didn't suit her purposes. The Hundings had failed, so several years must pass before they could regroup.

She lived for the victory that must inevitably come to her people. In the meantime, she abased herself – and hated. So, during the long and miserable nights, as she was pressed against Hrolf Kraki's sweating and farting body, she suffered and yearned for the touch of her beloved.

Now she permitted Hrolf Kraki to caress one of her small white breasts, even when his cousin, Frodhi, strolled into the room. The king displayed minimal respect for her in front of his kinfolk so they, in turn, counted her as worthless. Only when Frodhi winked at her did she pull away from the king's touch.

'Well, cuz, Stormbringer has once again proved to be a very difficult man to kill. He avers that he means you no personal harm, but his warriors refused permission for him to attend any audience with you unless he was under their direct protection. It's a clever ploy, and quite believable considering you sent men to The Holding to kill off his family. Incidentally, those mercenaries appear to have vanished off the face of the earth, so I suppose you won't have to pay them for their services.'

His master was too irritated to care what Frodhi thought.

'Unfortunately, those untrusting bastards asked for half their fee to be paid in advance,' the king snapped.

'How very wise of them!' Frodhi was the only man in Heorot who dared to speak to the Crow King in such a manner.

'Enough, Frod! I can hardly execute Stormbringer while his army is sitting, watching and waiting.'

'They're not as biddable as I am, my lord. Ivar Hnaefssen might resent the fact that you didn't even bother to reply to his request for help against the Hundings. And he'd disapprove if you try to kill the one man who did answer his call.'

'You're enjoying my troubles, aren't you, Frodhi? Sometimes you can be a complete snake.' Aednetta tried to be invisible, knowing that she'd suffer later, when he realised that she was privy to much more sensitive information than was wise.

'I recall warning you not to take that action against Stormbringer's home. I also advised you to send a token force into the south to defuse your problems with the Hundings. You'd have gained considerable respect from your jarls and none of those men who guard the marches could have accused you of deserting them,' Frodhi replied, unruffled by his cousin's insults. 'That old stickler, Ivar Hnaefssen, is making these same statements this very morning to any of your subjects who will listen. Many of them are sympathetic to his words, cuz.'

'That's treasonous!' the king snarled, feeling his stomach begin to burn.

'Just keep your head and try not to lose your temper.' Frodhi had almost reached the door when he turned back.

'By the by, the Briton you tried to have killed by Thorketil is the self-same warrior that the Geats have come to admire as the Last Dragon. Be careful of him, cuz, because he's a dangerous tactician and a capable warrior.'

Frodhi bowed to Aednetta Fridasdottar, and his voice was filled with admiration despite the mischief that danced in his eyes. 'As always, my lady, your beauty stirs my hardened and ancient heart.'

Then Frodhi disappeared before the king could invent a distasteful task for him.

Arthur stared hard at the doors of the king's hall and considered that they must have shrunk in the past three years. From his memory, the twelve-foot-high doors had seemed to soar to heights that could accommodate the ancient gods of the northern tribes. Now, while they were still impressive and gruesome with the remains of Grendel and his mother hanging off the huge planks at the entrance, their scale seemed more human, albeit they were larger and more impressive than the entrances to most royal palaces.

Stormbringer and Arthur stood together, shoulder to shoulder, with their bodyguards in tight formations behind them. Gareth had convinced Arthur to wear the distinctive armour that his servant had lugged through Gaul and into the north during his long search for his master. A fitted breastplate over his chain mail had been constructed in the Roman tradition. Replicating a male torso, it had been covered with silver and decorated over the heart with an enamelled red dragon modelled on the Dracos and the Roman legion of the same name.

Arm-guards, shoulder-guards and shin greaves complemented the breastplate, while a skirt of leather pieces plated with silvered iron covered his genitals, which were also protected by a special cup-shaped guard. Arthur also wore his old trews, polished, cleaned and with new laces that secured the material to his legs. His boots were made with the fur retained inside them for warmth.

A cloak of leather that had been beautifully tanned by his sister, Maeve, covered his broad shoulders and warmed his neck with its thick collar of arctic fox. Maeve had laboured for almost a year to produce two similar cloaks that would illuminate the personas of both her men. The most striking differences between them were the pins that bound the cloaks together at the throat and the wool linings. Arthur's was scarlet, while Stormbringer's was of a bluish-green colour.

Once again, the design on Arthur's brooch pin reflected the image of the Dracos Dragon, enlivened with brilliant red enamel, but Maeve had charmed The Holding's metalsmith into a prodigious artistic endeavour when he wrought Stormbringer's. A stylised wave in blue enamel covered half the field, divided by a branched and jagged shape that represented lightning made of electrum polished to a mirror-like brilliance.

In a world of tall men, these two warriors were exceptional specimens, for male physical beauty, strength and confidence radiated out of them.

The older man, Stormbringer, bore the tracks of time easily. In an age where, at thirty-five, many men had lost most of their teeth and were sliding into old age, Stormbringer still sported his own white teeth, straight limbs and an illusion of youth, while Arthur's gravity added years to him. The two men could easily have been brothers.

Arthur's three attendants and Snorri stood behind him as a rather rag-tag set of bodyguards, while Stormbringer had his own personal guard of six jarls including Ivar Hnaefssen.

Gareth's Romano-Celtic armour, Germanus's obviously Frankish equipment and the presence of a priest with a most ungodly-looking sword of eastern workmanship had already attracted considerable attention from the curious crowd gathered quietly in Heorot's forecourt. Lorcan's robe was clean and brushed, and he had even worked on his leathers until they shone, but the years of tragedy and hard living were written deeply in the scored fissures on both sides of his mobile mouth.

'Are you ready, Arthur?' Stormbringer asked as the huge doors swung inward to summon them into the presence of the Crow King.

'As I'll ever be,' Arthur replied as two heavily armed warriors stopped them on the threshold.

'We are charged with taking your weapons, gentlemen. No one but the king goes armed in Heorot.'

'No!' Stormbringer replied evenly.

The guard had not anticipated Stormbringer's reply, and was immediately nervous.

'You heard me, man! We will not stand unarmed in front of the Crow King when we don't trust anyone in his court, including you. I will gladly give my parole that our weapons will remain sheathed unless treachery is attempted by some other person.'

The Crow King could never be believed again after the treachery he had displayed over the past two years.

The two guards were caught in a conundrum: if they permitted armed men to enter Hrolf Kraki's hall, they would be guilty of failing to carry out their master's orders and would be punished accordingly. But, if they refused, the interlopers might take offence and kill them out of hand. Either way, they were in diabolical trouble.

Stormbringer understood the guards' dilemma and knew they would lay down their lives for their master if they were forced to do so. He glanced across at Arthur who responded almost too fast for the eye to follow. Using his mailed left hand he shot out his fist and caught one of the men squarely on the temple. The guard dropped like a stone, but Lorcan was there to soften his fall with uncharacteristic speed and sympathy. The other guard was caught, flat-footed and gape-mouthed, before he suffered the same ignominious fate. Gareth and Germanus had the two men securely bound within moments.

Stormbringer and Arthur pushed open the doors to their full extent and the party stalked into the hall without looking to right or to left. Arthur strode out impassively, recalling a younger, more naïve self who had stared in amazement at what the Dene carpenters could construct out of timber. Now, Heorot seemed smaller, more grimy, and pretentious with its trophies of long-gone triumphs. Like its master, the hall was falling into decay.

Armed men moved to block Stormbringer's way, but Hrolf Kraki shouted an order allowing the strangers to pass. The warriors reluctantly allowed their weapons to drop to their sides. 'My cousin, the Sae Dene king, would never assassinate me in my own hall, would you, Valdar?' The Crow King's voice was as hoarse as the call of his namesake.

'Never, my lord! I leave such actions to those churlish beings who display no honour.'

Several guards bridled at the tone of Stormbringer's voice,

but prudence kept their hands away from the hilts of their swords.

'Now that we have insulted each other, what brings you to Heorot? More to the point, why do you bring an army to hover around my heels?' Hrolf Kraki frowned in wrathful indignation. Arthur noted his unhealthy high colour.

'I've come because Arthur, the Last Dragon, uncovered certain snippets of information when he captured one of the chief generals of the Hundings after a recent battle. We would be failing in our duty as loyal vassals of our king if we ignored what that general told us, because it threatens you and the people of Heorot, if not the whole Dene nation.'

'Your friend isn't a Dene! It's my belief that he'd gladly assist our enemies to destroy us.'

Arthur stepped forward with his fists clenched by his side. 'My sister is betrothed to my lord and brother, Valdar Bjornsen, so I am now duty bound to the Dene cause for as long as she lives. I've been fighting your battles for the past three years and I've helped save many thousands of your subjects by my efforts. You, sir, may disabuse yourself of any claims regarding my treason. That excuse will no longer disguise your lack of concern for the welfare of your people.'

Hrolf Kraki's face remained blank at this pointed insult, but Arthur glimpsed an angry flash of chagrin pass through the man's pale eyes.

For his part, Stormbringer sensed an opportunity to gain the initiative. 'Where's Aednetta Fridasdottar? The information we obtained from General Mearchealf implicated her in the treacherous plot revealed by our informant. She should be present to answer any allegations that will be levelled against her.'

His words had a ring of confidence and authority, so Hrolf Kraki resisted an impulse to bluster.

Instead, he prevaricated.

'Why should my wisewoman be the subject of uncouth discussion between the Hundings and a bastard Briton?' The Crow King looked around the hall to assess the mood of his jarls. 'Both the Briton and Stormbringer have little incentive to tell the truth, for I have banished both of these men to save Aednetta's honour on an earlier occasion. Where is her accuser?'

'Mearchealf is buried in the marches on the undefended borders of your lands,' Stormbringer answered with almost tangible sarcasm. 'He was the only survivor of a battle group of Hundings who were annihilated by Arthur's warriors and ultimately put to the sword. The general only revealed his source of information after he had been sorely wounded and then tortured without mercy. He was an honourable man who died well. Sadly, all men will speak the truth when under severe torture.'

'Who would believe the oath of one of the Hundings, least of all one who will only speak under torture? I'll not expose Aednetta Fridasdottar to such slurs.'

'Then she can face our charges of treason without the opportunity to answer any of our allegations,' Stormbringer stated in a calm voice. 'I don't really care, one way or the other, because much of the truth had already been revealed for all to see. You can bury reality in the deepest and darkest caverns of a frozen mountain, but a freak summer storm will melt the ice one day and scour the surface till it is clean. Your jarls are here to listen to the charges we have laid against your witch-woman. Regardless of your wishes, the real villains of the last few years are about to be dragged from their dark hiding places into the sunlight.'

Stormbringer turned away from Hrolf Kraki's burning eyes and called on Ivar Hnaefssen to explain why he had been at war with the Hundings at the start of what would be an unforgiving and murderous winter. In the process, Stormbringer spoke of Ivar's advanced years and how he had spent a lifetime defending the border lands and safeguarding Heorot's back door from the Hundings' incursions.

Thus the northern jarls were inclined to view Ivar Hnaefssen as a man of honour and good reputation even before he was given an opportunity to speak.

'Lord King and notables of the Limfjord, I am honoured to speak to you but, before I begin, I must praise Stormbringer, King of the Sae Dene, who remembered a debt and an oath, and helped my people when they were in dire need. The rest of you left us to survive as best we could.'

The sound of awkwardly shuffling feet and a number of indrawn breaths suggested some jarls present knew they were at fault. A shiver of guilt filled the air and, as Ivar launched into the details of the Hundings' campaign, many of the nobles leaned forward in the hope of gaining some justification for their lack of support. They would have liked to believe that the south hadn't really needed their help, because the Hundings were poorly organised and badly led. But Ivar Hnaefssen had no pity, and left no room for excuses.

The Crow King gazed around the room in a desperate search for support.

'Frodhi?' the Crow King bellowed. 'I don't choose to hear more of these maunderings! So the great Stormbringer saved you? Wonderful! What do you want of me, Ivar Hnaefssen?'

Frodhi suddenly appeared out of the shadows, a sinuous, golden cat in a room full of fighting hounds.

'Frod!' Stormbringer advanced and hugged his cousin passionately. 'I've missed you! I can say before your peers that the warriors and ships you sent to me in Skania made all the difference. My only regret was that you had to act in secret, for you have always placed the welfare of our people above your own needs and ambitions.'

Hrolf Kraki glowered from his throne. This was the first time he had heard of the support that Frodhi had given to Stormbringer. Frodhi had been extremely careful.

'I couldn't ignore a legitimate request for help, could I? I don't want to see our land raped and then cut up like a juicy titbit.' Frodhi slapped Stormbringer squarely on the back. 'Be assured, cuz, that I'd never raise a hand against another kinsman.'

'If you've quite finished, Frodhi, please send a messenger to find my wisewoman and bring her to my hall. It seems I have had no allies in this confrontation, and I now find that you have given tacit support to a war that I refused to countenance, so I need Aednetta's advice on how to deal with you.' The Crow King's mouth pursed unattractively.

'Frodhi is my kinsman,' Stormbringer protested. 'But he is also a loyal Dene who has demonstrated a lifelong faithfulness to his people. He was entitled to answer my request for assistance to fight in the battles being waged against your enemies.'

'Frodhi is also my kinsman,' Hrolf Kraki countered. 'So why didn't he obey his king?'

As the messenger went to find and deliver Aednetta into the Crow King's presence, Arthur decided to regain the initiative and guide the discussion back to the purpose of their visit.

'Thank you, Ivar, for your description of the battles that led to the defeat of the Hundings. I might add that when their high command attempted to flee by boat to the safety of their borders, we were able to isolate them in a small coastal village. The general we captured not only gave me the name of the traitor that had been their informant for years, he confirmed that this source of intelligence had allowed the Hundings to foment trouble throughout the Dene lands in the south. I formed the impression that this same traitor instigated further dissension among the Geats who attacked our allies from their safe havens in Gotland.'

A shiver of apprehension filtered through the long, high room. The whispers of the jarls and warriors at the gathering rose like the noise of insects, but the comments were muffled, lest Hrolf Kraki should single out an individual on whom he could vent his growing irritation. In the firelight the Crow King slouched on his throne and tapped his feet with obvious nervous energy, while he glowered with anger. Somehow, Hrolf Kraki's authority was being leached away.

The king determined to counter Arthur's calm authority with bluster. 'I repeat! Why should I believe the words of a man who has been tortured to death? He'd do or say anything to make the pain stop, as every man here understands.'

Hrolf Kraki smirked as if he had won a major point.

Arthur sighed. He should have known that dealing with the devious Crow King would never be easy.

'Mearchealf may have been our enemy, but he was a man of honour,' Arthur responded stiffly. 'One thing is certain. With a sword that was gifted to me by one of the great heroes of Britain whose name will resonate down through the ages, I'd never contemplate contaminating it with base blood.'

Blood such as yours! The unspoken words hung in the air; some of his contempt must have been revealed in the curl of his upper lip, for Hrolf Kraki stirred on his throne and gnashed his teeth.

The Crow King turned as Aednetta Fridasdottar was ushered into the hall. She swayed up to greet him, her white robe stirring sinuously. As she turned to stand beside the throne, the eyes of all the warriors and jarls caressed her small waist and embraced the long, slow sweep of her flesh that terminated at the rounded fullness of her buttocks.

Arthur was probably the only male present who was totally immune to her glamour. He had lived his whole life with women of beauty and intelligence who scorned to use their femininity to blind the lustful eyes of men.

The king was the first person to find his voice, enjoying an almost overwhelming chance to gloat.

'My lovely Aednetta! I'm sure you remember my cousin, Valdar Bjornsen, and this uncouth Briton who was fortunate enough to defeat my champion some years ago. He has just been telling me how he tortured a Saxon general who told him that my court harbours a traitor. Yes, you might well look surprised, my lady, since Heorot has never suffered pain at the behest of the Hundings.'

'I surely remember this Briton, for his sister accused me of all manner of vile crimes.'

After the passage of almost four years, her white hair was still as shocking a contrast to her other features as ever, while her eyebrows and eyelashes remained equally colourless. However, Aednetta had heightened her striking appearance by using a black cosmetic around her eyes, much as the Romans had.

In sharp contrast, she had stained her nails and her mouth a vivid red, accentuating her pallor. On one forefinger, she wore a massive ring of gold with a carved carnelian stone. As carnelian was rumoured to be the jewel of spirituality, Arthur felt his lips twitch with unexpected amusement. In some ways, Aednetta was very predictable, using every trick at a woman's disposal to win the king's sexual favours, while still employing the trappings of a seer. Here in the Dene lands, women were a source of prophecy and wild magic, so Aednetta was seeking the automatic respect given to those women who possessed the Sight.

'My sister accused you once in the past, but I now accuse you anew,' Arthur snapped, weary of prevarication. His mood darkened further when he glanced up at Frodhi and watched in amazement as the Dene aristocrat winked impudently in his direction.

'The general swore that you were the direct source of all the information they gained from Heorot, and that an unknown lover was pulling your strings,' Arthur explained bluntly. He could tell that Stormbringer was less than pleased at the crudeness of Arthur's personal attack.

'How can you have the effrontery to tell such lies?' Aednetta blenched, while two red blotches appeared on her cheeks. Her fingers toyed with the hem of her sleeves. 'By your own admission, Stormbringer wasn't present at the interrogation. Nor was Jarl Ivar Hnaefssen or any of the southern lords. You're not a Dene, so why should anyone here have faith in your words?'

Arthur turned to summon Snorri, who was nearby. He had been expecting such accusations.

'This good warrior, Snorri Nilsson, was present at the death of Mearchealf and heard the general's last confession. Any number of other Dene witnesses were present at the time. You, Aednetta Fridasdottar, stand accused of being a servant of the Hundings, but he didn't know the name of the lover who is your puppet-master in Heorot! How I wish he had!'

Snorri reported the exact words spoken by the Hundings'

general when he was near to death. In order to force some reaction from the jarls, Arthur called on the testimony of every influential Dene who had been present in order to underscore the truth of the report.

'Your claims are part of a plot by the Hundings to tear the Dene population apart and start a civil war between the Dene and the Sae Dene,' Hrolf Kraki whined. Arthur resisted an urge to shake him.

Ivar Hnaefssen stared at his king, thunderstruck with disappointment.

'Stormbringer came to the aid of the southern Dene when you wouldn't get off your arses to help us,' Hnaefssen protested. 'I'm sorry, my lord, but if the Hundings wanted to drive a wedge between our people, they've gone about it in an idiotic manner. The Dene and the Sae Dene in the south will now be allies forever. We fought together in complete amity in my lands, just as the same combatants did in Skania. I'm proud to say that the southern Dene answered their calls for help to ensure the Geats were driven back to where they came from. But what of you, my lord? We saw neither hide nor hair of your jarls when your people needed your assistance.'

Stormbringer abruptly interrupted Ivar Hnaefssen.

'Your jarls are living in isolation here and your throne is imperilled – but not by the Skanian Dene or the Sae Dene, or even the Southern Dene. Your throne, Hrolf Kraki, has been imperilled by *you* – by *your* recalcitrance, *your* conservatism, *your* superstition and by the woeful advice that *you* have chosen to accept from your sycophants.'

The Crow King struggled to avoid answering the simplest of the questions thrown at him. Why had he refused to give aid and encouragement to his allies? Likewise, the faces of his warriors spoke eloquently of how bitterly they resented the inability of their king to explain why he had led them down these dishonourable paths.

'Shite!' Arthur's patience was stretched to breaking point. 'Every man here believes that Aednetta Fridasdottar has you ensorcelled so that you have driven away Valdar Bjornsen, the Sae Dene who has long been your strongest ally. You have also refused to assist the Dene jarls of Skania and the other states lusted after by the Geats. Finally, you have gone on to refuse aid and succour to the southern jarls at a time when the Hundings, an ancestral enemy, made their foray into Ivar Hnaefssen's lands.'

Arthur paused momentarily to assess the effect of his words on the audience around him.

'You sodding liar!' the Crow King screamed. 'Why won't any of you defend me against the slurs of this Briton?'

He was on his feet at last and spluttering with fury. Aednetta was forced to drag him back to the throne by his cloak.

'Finally, and most telling of all, it was the witch-woman who counselled you to attack innocent women and children at The Holding in an ill-conceived attempt to destroy Valdar Bjornsen's family while he was absent on a national task that was morally and legally your responsibility to pursue.'

Arthur's facial expression spoke volumes of his lack of respect for the Dene King.

'I regret the need to be so blunt, Valdar, but I claim certain privileges as a warrior who has served the Dene nation. How can anyone of any decency devise a plan whereby one of the Dene's trusted leaders will return to his home after conducting a mission on behalf of the entire nation to find that his home has been destroyed and the raped bodies of his children have been nailed to the doors of his hall? Those were the direct orders given to his mercenaries by the man who sits on that throne.'

He paused and allowed his words to sink in.

'We have toyed with the parlous situation of this cowardly ruler for too long. I have no doubt that this serpent-woman will whisper in his ears once again and he'll send an even larger troop to destroy our kinfolk in his next raid, considering that his last attack was unsuccessful. Incidentally, my lord, I was pleased to see the return of Valdar's property, *Loki's Eye*, which had been left in your harbour when we were banished. It has since been placed in safe hands for the use of the Sae Dene. I'm afraid your other ship was sunk with all hands on board.'

Hrolf Kraki had stridden the length of his dais as the young Briton began to list his deficiencies, but Aednetta managed to restrain him. The action seemed to involve little force, but Arthur noted the strained tendons of her wrist and elbow when her wide sleeve fell back. Hrolf Kraki was still on his leash, but barely, so Arthur decided to stretch that bad temper even further until it snapped.

'You bastard! I should have killed you and your hell-born sister when I had the chance.'

'I'm not a friendless slave anymore, Hrolf Kraki, so I have no reason to bow to you or to give you the respect you believe is your due. Surely respect must be earned! You left your people in Skania and in the south to fend for themselves against savage enemies, but you also demanded taxes from them that you continue to increase, which is strange when one considers that you've given nothing in return. It seems that any man who calls you to account loses his tongue, if not his life. These men are in your service, but look at their faces.' Arthur gestured at Hrolf Kraki's jarls and guards. 'They obey you out of fear, because you are a worse tyrant than Snaer, the other traitor who killed your father and usurped your throne.'

Every word struck into the heart of Hrolf Kraki, but the last accusation left him spluttering and almost incapable of speech. Stormbringer turned to hold Arthur back, but Arthur threw off his friend's restraining hand.

'How dare you compare me with that animal? How can you suggest—'

'I dare because I'm an unbiased outsider. And my responsibilities are such that I must ask why you ordered your warriors to destroy a small village of peasants at a faraway place called World's End? Your only reason was that the villagers might have offered us shelter. The name Crow King has been well chosen, given your taste for carrion and a desire to hide among large groups of your own kind. If I had my way, you'd be deposed and a far better man would be crowned in your place. But, unfortunately, Stormbringer is far too generous and far too loyal to put you down like the diseased dog that you have become.'

'What do you mean, Briton,' one of the northern jarls asked tentatively.

'The true enemy in Heorot is Aednetta Fridasdottar, who has whispered in this craven man's ear that he will offend the gods if he takes part in any war. You've heard the tales and listened to the sagas. She must be taken, tortured and forced to reveal the names of her confederates.'

Aednetta wailed as her confidence leached away with every word that Arthur uttered. 'Don't cast me off, my lord. These traitors lie! I alone have been loyal.'

Hrolf Kraki winced as his eyes swivelled from the suspicious and confused expressions of his own jarls to the hardened stares of the southern Dene, and then back to Aednetta's obvious panic and terror.

'Let me think,' he mumbled, and Aednetta could divine that he would blame her for every ill. Her expression hardened and her hands clenched into fists.

'Beware, King of Crows, because you are toying with the thought of casting me off. How will you survive without your only spiritual and magical support? Who will care for your health? Who will share your secrets without betraying them?'

Aednetta Fridasdottar was clearly threatening the king with exposure, and the jarls recoiled. For his part, the Crow King's mouth snapped shut aggressively. 'Instead of threatening me, woman, find a servant to bring me some mead. Now stop blubbering! I loathe tears!'

Aednetta flounced out of view while Hrolf Kraki used the interval to gather his thoughts.

'Damn you, Stormbringer! It would be better to call you the Stormbird, because you bring trouble with you, just like that fucking bird that cries out its warnings of bad weather. Gods, but I'm so sick of being locked inside this fucking hall. And I'm sick of the fucking winter and the whole fucking world. Nothing has gone right since the day I stole the treasure from that Geat king and was cursed by the bastard. We flounder miserably when the gods turn their gaze away from us.'

Most of the men who stood and waited for Hrolf Kraki to make up his mind silently wished he would stop whining.

Making a great show of not touching the wine jug that was carried into the throne room by one of the servants, Aednetta presented a goblet and the wine to her master.

'I won't be accused of trying to poison you, my king, so I refrained from touching this wine jug. I know you asked for

mead, but the wine was more readily available.' Aednetta's voice
was cold and clipped.

Hrolf Kraki grabbed at the jug, splashing the dark-red liquor
onto the floor and down his robe as he poured a generous
quantity into his goblet. With shaking hands, he raised the vessel
and drank deeply, pausing only to draw breath. As soon as it was
emptied, the king refilled it once more.

'The bastard's trying to get drunk,' Arthur hissed in
Stormbringer's ear.

'That ploy won't work,' Stormbringer replied, casting an
experienced eye over the anxious Aednetta.

The third cup was almost drained when Hrolf Kraki gave a
little cough before staggering back to his throne and falling into
its hard embrace.

Arthur noticed that his lips had darkened to a distinct shade
of blue. But, before he could take any action, the king coughed
once again and Arthur knew he was having breathing difficulties.

'The king is ill,' Arthur stated loudly. 'Master Frodhi, please
send for a wisewoman or whoever you use as a healer. The rest
of you stay put and keep an eye on the witch-woman. She must
remain inside this hall!'

Arthur and Stormbringer approached the king, who they
could see was panting like a dog in hot weather, while his
eyes were bulging as he attempted to drag air into his tortured
lungs.

'Lie back, Majesty,' Arthur ordered, but Hrolf Kraki shook his
head.

'Can't breathe . . . it burns . . . what was in . . . the wine?'

'Try not to talk, cousin,' Stormbringer urged. 'Frodhi will be
here soon and your healer will know what to do.'

'Would it be helpful if he was forced to void his stomach?'

Arthur asked Lorcan who was hovering behind them. 'You're familiar with poisons. Is there anything we can do?'

The scratching in Arthur's head was becoming more and more insistent; danger was very close, and death was imminent for the Crow King.

'If the poison is acid in nature, it will burn his stomach and throat when he regurgitates it. I'd be inclined to feed him some milk if we can get it into him. And then we'll need to give him a strong emetic.'

'It's worth a try,' Stormbringer decided. 'Snorri, we need milk from the kitchens. Immediately!'

He glanced across at the priest.

'Can you think of anything that can be used as an emetic, Father Lorcan?'

'Salt will suffice if there's nothing else. But we must hurry! His fingernails are turning blue even as I look at them, so his circulation is starting to shut down.'

As Snorri arrived back with a large bowl of milk balanced precariously in his arms, Frodhi was ushering a lean old woman into the hall. This woman took one look at Aednetta Fridasdottar and immediately made the warding-off sign used to drive out evil.

Frodhi persuaded the king to lean back on his throne so his airways could be kept open. Then Lorcan held a cup of milk up to Hrolf Kraki's mouth.

'You must drink this, my lord, for it will ease your stomach. I am a priest and you will have to trust my assurances that I'll do no harm to you.'

Perhaps it was the robes of Lorcan's office, but Hrolf Kraki obeyed like a child while his breath remained loud and laboured in the appalling silence. Then, once he had swallowed all the milk he could force into his stomach, the old woman took the bowl and added a vile-smelling powder to the remnants of the milk and mixed up a paste which she began to spoon into Hrolf Kraki's protesting mouth.

Suddenly, the king seemed to weaken visibly, so the old woman massaged his throat to assist him to swallow while he continued to cough and splutter. Lorcan found a large wooden bowl beside the fire pit, and Stormbringer and Frodhi persuaded the king to lie on a makeshift bed that his guards had brought into the hall. Kept high on pillows, Hrolf Kraki continued his struggle to breathe. His eyes remained the most alive part of him, for they still snapped with vigour and passion.

Then the king began to vomit, great wrenching spasms that hurt him a great deal and left him exhausted between bouts of nausea. Arthur wondered if the purging served any real purpose, for Hrolf Kraki was obviously growing weaker and weaker with each attack.

'There's no other choice, lad,' Lorcan sighed. 'The poison will surely kill him if we can't cleanse him. And even then there's no guarantee that he'll live. I've seen this poison before, although I can't remember its name. The Fathers of the Church of Rome were forever plotting and persisted in murdering each other for preferment and power. This was one of the favourites used by my cardinal.'

'Germanus! Lorcan! Watch the witch-woman for me,' Arthur ordered crisply. 'Make sure she neither eats nor drinks. In her place, I'd want to kill myself before I faced the prospect of torture. Still, this poisoning has been a very public crime, because Aednetta Fridasdottar has had ample opportunities in the past to kill Hrolf Kraki without any real risk to herself. She even told us she had refrained from touching the wine, and surely the whole point of using poison is so the murderer can be elsewhere when the victim dies.'

Germanus grinned evilly. 'I'd only use poison as a last resort if I chose to murder someone. Then I'd make fucking sure that I was far away when my victim became ill. I'd also have a bevy of witnesses to swear that I was nowhere near the scene when the victim died.'

'Exactly,' Arthur agreed.

On his makeshift bed, twisting with convulsions punctuated by periods of induced vomiting, Hrolf Kraki begged for one of the Dene priests to attend to his needs.

He had been a brave man once, but self-indulgence and overweening power had eroded the decency in his nature, so only the most terrible of circumstances could have caused such a change in his personality.

One of the Dene priests was soon found, so he and Lorcan both commenced the stately and sonorous last rites.

Arthur approached the tray on which the ceramic jug had been placed. The goblet had dropped from Hrolf Kraki's trembling hands and rolled under the throne, so he retrieved it and carefully sniffed at the few drops that remained in the base. There seemed nothing out of the ordinary. The half-empty wine jug also yielded no clues.

'There's no way of telling what's in there, short of drinking it. Personally, I've no desire to die in convulsions, thanks very much,' Arthur stated, as Frodhi clapped him on the back and caught Arthur's eye with a knowing gaze.

'Do you believe this illness has resulted from a deliberate attempt to kill Hrolf Kraki?'

'Aye! What other reason could there be for such a sudden debilitating illness? But the poison is obviously odourless, and is probably tasteless. Hrolf Kraki didn't show any concern about the taste.'

'True! I don't believe in coincidences, so sensible men consider rational explanations for things they don't understand. This illness is too opportune for my liking. Someone seems to be trying to cover their tracks.'

Arthur nodded slowly. 'So keep your eyes on Aednetta for me. She's the key, for she's the only person who knows the identity of the traitor in the service of the Hundings.'

'Are you quite sure that you believe in a shadowy villain standing behind the witch-woman?' Frodhi asked in a bland voice. 'Could it be that the accusations are a tissue of lies designed to protect the king from his own wickedness and then pass the blame on to Aednetta?'

'Perhaps! If I've learned one thing in life, it's that few men have the imagination to guess at the full scope of the evil within the human heart.'

Just then the attention of both men was drawn away from their conversation to the tableau around Hrolf Kraki. His body was suddenly afflicted by a convulsion so brutal and terrible that his feet began to drum on the planks of Heorot while his whole body, except for his head, was curved upwards like a great bow. His lips were drawn back in a rictus of terror and agony, and his eyes reflected the horror of a man who was unable to take deep breaths. But he still seemed able to recognise the details of every process that was occurring in his own death. He cried out his woman's name through clenched teeth before moaning in a great exhalation of breath that stretched on and on, further and further, until the lungs were stilled. The chest rose, struggling feebly to draw in a little precious air, but nothing could save him. Hrolf Kraki's face became congested and his tongue began to protrude, as if a great invisible hand was encircling his throat and choking him. Finally, the chest fell, and did not rise again.

Aednetta began to scream, shrilly and crazily. 'The king has been murdered! He's been poisoned! Someone has murdered my king!'

But other eyes were boring deeply into hers, impaling her with their suspicions of guilt.

'Not me! I'd never harm my king! For heaven's mercy, if I was a traitor in the pay of the Hundings, the last thing I'd want would be the death of Hrolf Kraki.'

In her desperation, the witch-woman ran to Arthur and gripped his cloak with both hands. 'You do believe me, don't you, Briton? Your sister knew me, and she'd believe me now. I've done many things that were wrong, but I'd—'

But before she could finish, Frodhi pried Aednetta's hands away and wrenched her off her feet.

'Take her away and lock her in some secure place with trusted guards to watch her,' Frodhi ordered firmly, as he singled out a young warrior. 'You will remain with her yourself, young man, and you'll keep her under constant watch. Your men will take turns to guard her door and no one is to enter the room unless they have my specific permission. You will keep all means of causing self-harm away from her, because I don't want her to commit suicide and cheat justice for the foul deed she has committed. We have a number of scores to settle with this woman!'

Aednetta Fridasdottar was dragged away, weeping and crying out for her dead lord, but Arthur felt an unease that he could barely put into words. Something was wrong here. He knew it, and the silent watcher in his brain knew it too.

A shocked silence followed before Lorcan folded Hrolf Kraki's hands over his chest.

'Well that's the end of that,' the priest said. 'Whatever he knew of these matters has gone into the shades with him.'

'But we still have Aednetta,' Arthur said in a firm voice that belied his inner doubts. 'Everyone talks under torture, so it might only be a matter of time!'

THE KING'S ROOMS

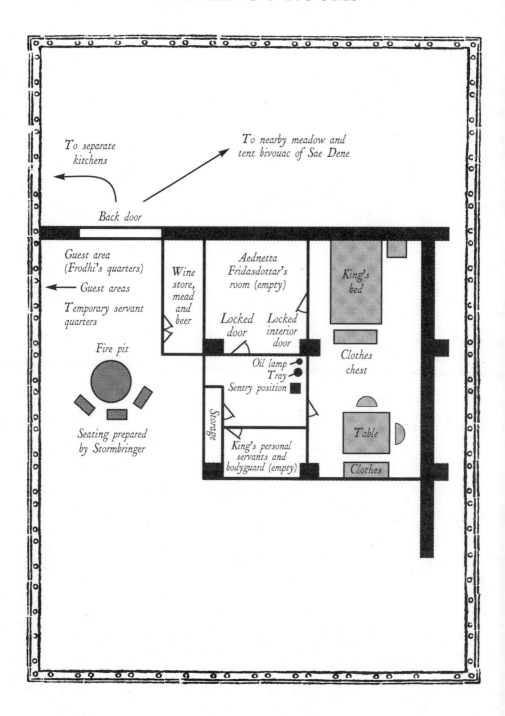

To separate kitchens

To nearby meadow and tent bivouac of Sae Dene

Back door

Guest area (Frodhi's quarters)

Guest areas

Temporary servant quarters

Fire pit

Seating prepared by Stormbringer

Wine store, mead and beer

Aednetta Fridasdottar's room (empty)

Locked door

Locked interior door

Oil lamp
Tray
Sentry position

Storage

King's personal servants and bodyguard (empty)

King's bed

Clothes chest

Table

Clothes

CHAPTER XII

ENDINGS AND BEGINNINGS

Vanitas vanitatum, dixit Ecclesiastes; vanitas vanitatum, et omnia vanitas.
(Vanity of vanities, said the preacher; vanity of vanities, and everything is vanity.)

The Bible, Ecclesiastes 1:2

'Shite! Shite! Shite!'

Arthur cursed freely as he paced back and forth. Hrolf Kraki was dead, which was a blessing for the Dene people. But, although Aednetta Fridasdottar could be forced to reveal the name of the traitor, Arthur was appalled at the prospect of extracting information from a woman under physical duress. He took comfort in the possibility that he might be able to convince the witch-woman to reveal the name of her confederate willingly, now that the king was no longer alive and able to offer his protection.

'What else can go wrong?'

In the frigid morning that was beginning to feel endless after the dramas of the previous night, Stormbringer and Arthur stood in the forecourt outside the king's hall, stamping their frozen feet and watching their breath as the vapour escaped like smoke in the semi-darkness. The two friends surveyed a silent crowd of townspeople who waited patiently in the light snow. The wind had died during the early morning, so thick cloud was obscuring the stars now, and the falling flakes created a strange and supernatural silence.

'Sir,' one old woman asked as she hobbled forward. 'Be it true? Be the Crow King truly dead?'

'Aye, Mother, Hrolf Kraki has perished this morning.' Stormbringer ignored the manner of Hrolf Kraki's death; the villagers were edgy enough already. 'Although the jarls must make the final decision, his heir is Frodhi, whom you should all know well.'

'Be he murdered?' one of the usually boisterous boys asked in a voice cracking with the onset of puberty. 'We heard that the king choked to death from poison, but I don't believe it. We thought the Crow King were too strong and clever to be killed so easily.'

'Yes, lad, the rumours are true. Your king has been sent to Valhalla before his time.'

Then Stormbringer raised his voice so that the entire crowd, easily a hundred souls in all, could hear him clearly.

'Go home now, people of Heorot. The jarls and the king's guard will be investigating the crimes that have been committed, but you'll be safest if you are snug in your homes or about your business. Of course, if any of you know anything that is important to the investigation of your king's death, I expect you to do your duty and speak to one of us in private.'

Gradually and solemnly, the crowd began to disperse. Only two people remained when the forecourt was finally emptied, an old woman and a young fisherman who was recognisable by his long knitted cap and a fishing knife attached to his belt.

'What do you know that will be of use to the new king, Mother? Tell me now, for you can be certain that I will permit no person to harm you,' Stormbringer assured her as he helped the old woman to make herself comfortable on the steps of the hall.

The old woman was a crone indeed, lean and stringy, as if time had eaten away all the soft flesh on her body, leaving a tough and fibrous carapace. Her sharp knowing eyes almost disappeared in heavy crows' feet and deep pouches, while her mouth was a seamed slit that protected her inflamed gums. Even so, she radiated an aura of strength and vitality, as if time did not have the power to harm her.

'I'm the herb mistress for the town, Master Valdar. People come to me for simples if they've got a cough or if a child has broken a limb, although sometimes there's not much I can do. Of course, some lads and lasses want help for illnesses of the heart, while other customers sometimes come in the dead of night for other . . . potions.'

'I understand,' Stormbringer muttered grimly. He realised that women occasionally wanted to remove an unwanted pregnancy or ensure that a drunken husband would be encouraged to sleep soundly throughout the night rather than use his fists on his wife and children. Although he cringed from the thought, he knew too that some women sought a permanent cure to the problem of an awkward husband.

Herb lore was sometimes used to speed the ends of elderly parents during times of famine. This was no secret, for the grandparents usually insisted on a painless death with their family members around them to give them comfort and courage during their passage to their new life.

But there were other persons as well, and a wise herb-woman tried to refrain from asking too many questions of these visitors who called during the dark hours, with their faces hidden behind hoods.

'I have received visits from a woman who was wrapped in a heavy cloak. Her face and dress were disguised, but I saw a lock of her hair, so I knew that my patient was Aednetta Fridasdottar. She asked for a poison for her aged parents, one that acted quickly but for which there was no antidote. I won't say the name of the poison lest I should give other persons sinful ideas that will further blacken my soul.'

She paused and carefully considered her words before she continued. 'Her purchases were most peculiar, Lord Valdar, for most daughters in her position desire a painless death for their parents. On the contrary, she didn't seem to care how much pain was inflicted but only asked for speed and certainty. I felt some unease in my dealings with her.'

Then the old woman burst into tears and Arthur was forced to comfort her, while he learned her name and discovered where she could be found. He wondered at her sincerity. This old woman had a sly look about her and Arthur decided she wasn't to be trusted.

'I'm afraid, Master Valdar. Now that I've heard your words, I believe that I might have killed my king, although I swear I never meant to do any such thing.'

When he finally calmed the old herb mistress, she stumbled away a little happier for she was well aware that her confession had helped her to avoid any punishment for her complicity.

The fisherman, Sven, soon regretted his spontaneous decision to tell all he knew. Unfortunately, he was unable to extricate himself at this late stage, as Stormbringer gripped him by one muscular arm when he tried to depart.

'I be a fisherman in the Lake of Limfjord, and I have been for my whole life. Now that I be a married man . . . er . . . I struggle to earn more silver than I make with my nets. I be telling you this . . . because my wife told me the whole thing were peculiar from the beginning . . . not that she were complaining when we paid our debt to the net-maker . . . but she thought . . . I mean, been thinking . . . I should explain.'

Sven was far from half-witted, although his speech was crude and what he was trying to describe so execrably was largely a mystery to him. He understood the ways of the shoals of fish and where the best catches were found, but he was less than twenty summers in age and knew nothing of the wickedness of his betters.

Now, having tied himself into mental knots, Sven retreated into incomprehensible mumbling before he finally fell silent.

'Take a deep breath, Sven. No one here will harm you, but we have to understand what you're talking about. How did you earn this extra silver?' Stormbringer made his voice as calm and as reasonable as his sense of urgency would allow.

'A strange woman turned up at the door of my house about two years ago. She must have known me, but I had no idea then who she was. She had wrapped her whole body in a thick cloak and she came at dusk so I were unable to see her very well, but my wife were watching her very closely all the time that I have served her as a messenger. My woman says the lady is the king's wisewoman and whore. I begs your pardon, Lord Stormbringer, but Aednetta Fridasdottar is called the Crow's Whore by the whole town, her not being very well liked and all. I can't say things about her for certain . . . but she's young and she smells good.'

'What did she want, Sven?' Arthur interrupted, while the young fisherman shied like a frightened horse at Arthur's crisp tone.

'Don't mind my friend, young Sven! Just tell us the truth! You'll have nothing to fear and much to gain, including the gratitude of your new king.'

Stormbringer grinned engagingly at the young fisherman and Arthur watched as the lad began to relax. He could see that Sven must have been very easy for Aednetta to manipulate.

'She asked me to deliver a piece of cloth to an old man who lives on the other side of the fjord. It seemed innocent enough, but I looked at the cloth and there were strange marks on it in some kind of paint. They weren't runes – I know them well enough – and the paint didn't wash out if the cloth was wet. I couldn't make head nor tail of the whole rigmarole. She paid me a finger of silver every time I delivered a strip of the cloth.'

'Did you ask her what the cloth was for?' Arthur spoke as gently as he could, but the nervous fisherman still edged as far away from him as he could.

'As I said, master . . . I unwrapped the cloth and looked at it during the first trip across the fjord. It was just a piece of rag that was covered with strange patterns of lines, dots, crosses and dashes. It must have meant something to someone, but I had no idea what it could be. When I asked her why I were paid so much for delivering such trifles, she told me to mind my own business, so I made certain I did only what she asked of me and nothing more. She were a hard woman, were Aednetta Fridasdottar, and she were threatening to curse me if I were difficult.'

Stormbringer nodded in understanding. 'Did the old man give you anything to deliver to her before you made the return journey?'

'He gave me a rush basket filled with fish laid out on fresh grass. It were truly strange that I was paid good silver to deliver fish – but how could I ask them what they were doing? I'm a simple man, my lord, so I kept my mouth shut.'

'But you're a fisherman,' Arthur replied.

'Aye, master! It seemed daft to me, but we owed coin for the new nets and we barely made ends meet by the time I gave the net-maker a share of my catch. I were concerned about what I were doing for this woman, but I tried not to think about it.'

'One final question, Sven,' Stormbringer asked. 'How many times did you make the voyage across the fjord?'

'I never kept count, my lord, but I suppose I've seen the old man about fifteen times in two years. I told myself that it weren't really a lot. Tell me, master? Will me and mine suffer for the tasks I carried out for the king's whore?'

'I don't think so, boy, but you'll have to show the new king's warriors where the old man lives,' Stormbringer explained in a sympathetic voice.

Eventually, Arthur also took pity on him. 'You've been very wise to speak so frankly to the Sae Dene king about this matter. Had your activities been discovered, the jarls would have presumed, quite logically, that you were prepared to betray your king and your people for fingers of silver. In such an event, I can guarantee that you would have been executed. But, now that you've told the truth, you'll be lauded as a good Dene who has acted in his master's best interests.'

The fisherman appeared to be thoroughly confused by Arthur's courtly speech, so Arthur explained more simply.

'You'd have been executed for treason if you hadn't come forward, Sven. Instead, I'll make sure that you'll be considered a hero.'

'Do I have to give back the silver, Master Dragon?' Sven asked, his hands busy as he nervously threaded the hem of his tunic. 'We've already given the net-maker his share, but I used some of the coin to buy some land next to my house. My woman has a yearning to have sheep and cows – and a vegetable patch, and she would fair murder me if I gave it back. What should I do, Master Dragon?'

'I don't think King Frodhi will require you to gift him the coin, and I'm certain that it is of no further value to the witch-woman.'

Once Sven went on his way the two friends watched his rapidly retreating back and thought furiously.

'Aednetta Fridasdottar is as good as dead.' Stormbringer spoke with some regret, for the death of a strong, clever and fertile woman was always a loss in the Dene lands.

'Someone has been very, very clever in this whole conspiracy, for the only person who has been visible throughout this whole mess is Aednetta,' Arthur said. 'She is the one who buys the poison and she organises the communication links with the Hundings. Without her aid, we'll never find this invisible traitor.'

'There's no doubt in my mind that Aednetta murdered Hrolf Kraki,' Stormbringer replied. 'I know that she denies touching the wine and the servant agrees that she didn't touch the tray, but the wine had been left out for some time. She could have poisoned it earlier in the evening and enacted a complicated ruse to divert any suspicion. She would also be certain that none of the servants would steal Hrolf Kraki's wine, so there would be no chance to warn the king of the poison.' The thought that someone he knew could be a traitor filled the Sae Dene king with horror. How could he possibly have missed such duplicity within the king's court?

'Unlike you, I'm beginning to think that Aednetta had nothing to do with the death of the Crow King. She could have killed him with impunity at any time during the past few months and never been caught, so why would she select the very day that we turn up with an army behind us to murder her paramour? The woman might be venal, but she isn't stupid!'

The Sae Dene stared at Arthur for some minutes and then shook his head like a large and very wet dog. 'Why isn't *anything* simple? She'd have to be drunk, crazy or terrified to kill so blatantly and I've never considered Aednetta to have any of these failings. She's got enough gall for ten men, so terror only goes so far with her. We'd have noticed if she was drunk. Damn and shite! She's far too convenient to be our regicide!'

'Isn't she! No one would shed a tear for her if she was executed, including you and me. But I'll be annoyed if anything should happen to the lady *before* we have an opportunity to question her.'

'Agreed!' Stormbringer said sadly, because torture was as abhorrent to him as it was to Arthur. He smiled thinly. 'Well, let's be about it then. I know how much you hate this business, so we need to get it over and done with.'

Stormbringer despatched a slave to fetch Snorri and the witch-woman from her quarters where she had been confined under guard. At the same time, another messenger was sent to find Frodhi who was trying to establish the source of the poisoned wine and discover why the mead requested by Hrolf Kraki had failed to arrive.

Then Arthur and the Sae Dene king set up comfortable seats and a stool for the woman to use. From the position they had selected for her, she would have to look upwards into their eyes, giving them a psychological advantage during their questioning.

Snorri clattered into the hall at a panicky run and Arthur immediately steeled himself for trouble.

'Master! The wisewoman has been attacked . . . and she's like to die!' Snorri was panting with effort, so neither man asked questions immediately. They could see that the helmsman was deadly serious. Something had managed to pierce his usual phlegmatic calm.

'Tell me what you've found, Snorri, and leave nothing out,' Stormbringer ordered.

'The new king had ordered that Aednetta Fridasdottar should be tied to the bed and locked inside Hrolf Kraki's room,' Snorri told them as they strode to where she had been held. 'A guard had been placed outside to ensure that she stayed put. It has no windows and the walls are at least twice the height of a man, so no one could climb in without being seen by the guard or sleepers in any adjoining rooms.'

'So the woman was secure. I want nothing more, Snorri! We'll speak further when you report to me in the privacy of the king's room.'

The corridor was short and dim, but Arthur took in a myriad of small details as the three men approached the king's bed-chamber. A small oil lamp burned on the floor near a wooden tray bearing a plate, several mugs and a large jug. A guard was standing at attention beside the thick door. Arthur's voice and hands registered his impotence that Aednetta might have passed beyond the reach of his questioning.

Just before they entered the range of the man's hearing,

Arthur pulled Snorri to a halt. He wanted to hear as many details of the crime as possible before they entered the dead king's inner sanctum.

'You can continue now, Snorri!'

'I ordered the guard to let me in, and we found the witch-woman tied to her bed by one wrist. I ordered the guard to find King Frodhi and a healer while I stayed with her. Then I ran to fetch you, for I knew you'd want to speak with her before she died.'

Snorri wanted to pass on everything he had seen and heard to his masters, and then bolt from this stifling hall into the clean air.

'Show me exactly what you did, Snorri,' Stormbringer said carefully.

The Sae Dene followed Snorri's unusually nervous form down the shadowy corridor. A miasma of intimidation lingered in this grim building with its chilly interior and its dark history.

At the doorway, the guard insisted on holding them back from the developing chaos. The corridor boiled with activity as men milled in disarray, unable to act without direct orders from their superiors. The air thrummed with tension. Ignoring the guard, Arthur brushed past warriors who tried to ask questions of him, and ploughed towards the door in the heart of the hall, the place where the spirit of the Crow King still hovered, alone and lost, somewhere between the promise of Valhalla and the cold endlessness of Udgaad.

Once he reached the door with its inner and outer locks, Arthur took a deep breath. A simple strap of leather had been devised to secure the door to the frame, for this heavily planked entrance was to protect those people who were *inside* the room. Once he had opened the simple mechanism, he paused to examine the inner security provisions, including a large slab of oak that was strong enough to prevent easy access to Hrolf Kraki's last line of defence in the event of attack. Currently, this door was unlocked on the inside.

Arthur took a moment to plan the best course of action. He had not yet glanced at the bed and its occupant, but some premonition forced his eyes to remain riveted on the smooth oak, ready to be slammed into position if the need should arise. He saw nothing, but his mind was busy as a terrible and unexpected suspicion seized him. It caused him to gasp with consternation.

Please, God, let me be wrong, Arthur thought. Will Aednetta tell me that the traitor was a lusty young warrior who had been suborned by the Hundings and acted as her lover and confederate in this treason? Anything but the unpleasant suspicions that have finally stolen into my head.

'What's in there?' Stormbringer demanded from behind Arthur's shoulder. 'Let me in, Arthur.'

Then finally he looked towards the great bed that filled most of the available space in the end of the room. His stomach lurched, despite years of experience.

'Keep everyone out, Stormbringer – except for Frodhi, a healer, my three friends – and Snorri. The helmsman has been here already so he can enter at will.' Arthur's orders were delivered in a voice that his friend had never heard before. 'For God's sake, Stormbringer, do as I say! And then I'll lock us all in here together.'

Stormbringer obeyed.

Then, with Snorri at his back, the Sae Dene king slid through the narrow gap that Arthur's strong arms allowed, and saw a new violence that lay in the dead king's bed.

'Help . . . me!' a barely audible and grossly distorted voice begged. Stormbringer turned away as Arthur slammed the oaken bar home on the door before he began to vomit in a corner of the room.

THE KING'S BED CHAMBER

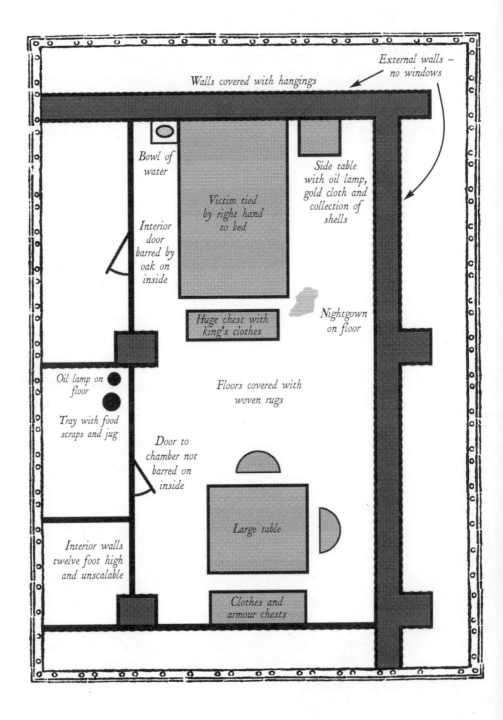

External walls – no windows

Walls covered with hangings

Bowl of water

Side table with oil lamp, gold cloth and collection of shells

Interior door barred by oak on inside

Victim tied by right hand to bed

Huge chest with king's clothes

Nightgown on floor

Oil lamp on floor

Floors covered with woven rugs

Tray with food scraps and jug

Door to chamber not barred on inside

Large table

Interior walls twelve foot high and unscalable

Clothes and armour chests

CHAPTER XIII

TO STARE INTO THE ABYSS

What I say is that *just* or *right* means nothing but what it is
in the interest of the stronger party.

Plato, *The Republic*, Book 1

Stormbringer hesitated at the foot of the Crow King's bed with
Snorri standing protectively behind him, while struggling to
avoid staring at the abomination lying on the luxurious fur
covering. The room smelled of fresh vomit, dried blood, musk
and a strange woody scent that Aednetta had left in her wake.
The vague reek of fish coming from a guttering oil lamp smelled
fresh and clean by comparison.

The sleeping chamber was much as Snorri had described it.
Within these sturdy walls an aura of luxury and sensual pleasure
was suggested by woven rugs of cloth, knotted and braided, on
the smooth floors; a beautiful massive table; a huge clothes chest
made from exotic woods and, incongruously, a collection of
shells on a small stool beside the bed.

'The new king doesn't seem to have arrived!' Arthur observed
while staring hard at the workings of the inner door. The latches

and the saddle that held the door-bar in place had been there for a long time, long enough for the few nails that held it in place to begin to rust. Out of curiosity, Arthur unlatched the door and checked the leather strap that secured the door from the outside. The materials were very new and Arthur supposed that this temporary lock had been constructed to ensure that Aednetta Fridasdottar had no chance of escape.

The hubbub of voices and the demands for entry made little impression on Arthur, who instructed the guard to stand directly outside the door.

'You will let no one enter the room, do you hear? If you do not obey these instructions to the letter, you will answer to the Sae Dene king and the Last Dragon. There are only five exceptions! The first of these men is our new king, Lord Frodhi. In addition, I've requested a healer who will attend on the witch-woman when she arrives. Finally, the three Britons who are part of my staff. No one else – regardless of their birth or their reputations – will be permitted entry on pain of your life. Do you understand?'

'Aye, lord!' the guard responded, gripping his sword hilt determinedly, his face serious.

'Fasten the bar once we are inside, then open this door only if I give you a direct personal instruction.'

'Aye, master!'

Then Arthur vanished back into the king's bedchamber. Those closest to the sentry heard the sound of the heavy bar falling into position, leaving the horrors inside the room hidden from view.

'It is certain that Hrolf Kraki was nervous of everyone and everything inside his house,' Arthur said to himself, and then turned his attention to the abomination lying on the bed. 'But he seemed to have no fear of Aednetta Fridasdottar.'

'. . . phirshy!' A voice like the rasp of iron against a whetstone made Snorri jump with fright. The voice had lost all its sexuality, even its humanity, as if a mummified larynx spoke from its sarcophagus. The mouth that framed each sound so carefully was broken and barely recognisable, for its lips were torn and bloodied from smashed teeth and the savage blows that had split and bruised tender flesh.

Arthur moved swiftly to tear a long strip of cloth from a night robe lying in a puddle at the foot of the bed. Rather than move the woman's body with its terrible patterns of bruising all over the torso, Arthur soaked the cloth in a bowl of water that had been left on one of the larger tables. He gently placed one end of the dampened cloth in that terrible mouth and the woman sucked and slobbered at it in desperation.

How long had this poor woman lain in her own faeces, urine and blood, barely able to breathe and pallid with thirst, as her lifeblood slowly and inexorably dripped away.

When she could suck at the cloth no longer, Arthur removed the fabric and laid it to one side. The woman's eyes, huge and blank, followed him with a mute appeal. For his part, Stormbringer gazed across at Aednetta Fridasdottar, appalled at the ruination of her beauty.

Someone powerful had obviously attacked the witch-woman with his fists. It had been a man, because of the size of the contusions that had smashed the woman's delicate cheekbones and the eggshell-thin bones around the eye sockets. A huge knot of swelling had deformed the jaw and her nose was split and spread to one side of her face. Even the bones of her head seemed to be misshapen.

'She must have known him, or she'd have alerted the guard.

Surely!' Stormbringer kept his eyes riveted on Aednetta's face.

Not content with smashing away her beauty, the unknown assailant had pummelled the slender body. One arm flopped unnaturally from a dislocated shoulder and a broken forearm, while her half-naked body was covered with black and purple contusions. Arthur could clearly see that several fingers on the bound hand had been snapped like twigs. Even if she managed to survive, Aednetta Fridasdottar would never be beautiful and seductive again.

As Arthur eased open her white robe, the full nature of her suffering was made clear. Even the perpetrator must have been ashamed of his actions, because he had re-tied her robe over her injuries so that only the bloodstains warned of injuries far beyond the damage caused by the perpetrator's fists.

Someone had kneeled on her small body, for bruising was evident on her naked thighs, he belly and her upper arms. Not only was all her skin marked by bruising, bite-marks or scratches, but her attacker had also carved slices from her flesh.

'He's cut away her nipples!' Stormbringer gasped. 'How could anyone who calls himself a man and a warrior do such a despicable thing?'

'Shut up, Stormbringer! She can hear you and she understands.' The ruined voice tried to cry and the eyes opened wide with the nightmare realisation of how much she had been disfigured.

'Lie still and try to rest, Aednetta. When the healer comes, she will know how to make you comfortable. I hope we can make you well and beautiful again.'

Aednetta obediently closed her eyes. Arthur eased away the fabric from her loins and Stormbringer saw a deep narrow knife wound in her abdomen where her womb should be. The symbolism of this wounding was unmistakable.

Arthur carefully covered her again. The wounds were scarcely bleeding, an ominous sign for her belly was distended, which meant she must be bleeding internally. There would be no saving Aednetta Fridasdottar.

Pity prompted him to lift a long hank of white-gold hair from across her face where it had been glued to her skin with dried mucus and blood. Gently, he straightened her twisted body into what he considered a more comfortable position. She sighed in appreciation without opening her eyes.

Then Arthur left the ruined woman and prowled the four corners of the room in search of evidence; all was quiet except for the sounds of breathing.

Aednetta's eyes suddenly snapped open – those strange, pale eyes that were now cloudy with agony and fear. She blinked rapidly as she tried to focus, and screamed.

At least she tried to.

Sickened, Arthur closed his eyes for a moment to block out the hideous sight. Her attacker had attempted to cut out her tongue at the root but, as the awful wound attested, she had struggled with all her might. Fully half of her tongue had been sheared way, which explained her difficulty in speaking. Her attempts to curl her tongue to scream had set the gross wound to bleeding once again.

Quickly, too quickly, her mouth began to fill with blood and Arthur was forced to raise her, causing fresh agonies, while Snorri attempted to wipe away blood and mucus. Once again, Arthur offered her the damp cloth and she suckled at it greedily.

'I . . . I . . . I . . .'

'You're hurting? Yes, I know, Aednetta, I know. I'll try to make it better for you as soon as the healer arrives. There's a good girl.'

Arthur realised the girl was lapsing into unconsciousness.

'The bastard tried to make sure she'd never speak.' Stormbringer's eyes were sick and glassy at the thought. 'He'd have had to smash her vocal cords to do that! But by the gods, he tried.'

'I don't know how she has managed to stay alive,' Arthur murmured, overcome by the urgency of the situation. 'And I've no idea what's happened to that fucking healer.'

The sounds she was making now were guttural grunts like those of a wounded and dying animal. In her short periods of consciousness, her pale eyes seemed to be glazed with agony.

'Your lover did this to you, didn't he?' Arthur continued. 'I know you can't speak easily, but just nod if what I say is correct. While you and I have had our differences, I promise that I'll find who harmed you and I'll do my best to make him pay!'

Two large tears escaped from her bruised eyes and, for some inexplicable reason, Arthur forgot the hurts that Aednetta had tried to inflict upon him or the harm she had brought to so many other innocents. She had loved a man who had played upon her hatreds. In return, he had used her links with the Hundings to assist him to walk the crooked paths of treason; he had revelled in her fair flesh and had asked her to seduce the king; and then, when she had obeyed him in all things and imperilled her immortal soul, he had beaten her and knifed her to the very edge of death. The final stab wound to her womb had been more than an obscene gesture of his scorn. It had been symbolic of a twisted mind.

Arthur could see in her eyes that she still had difficulty accepting that her lover had inflicted these terrible injuries on her body.

'Did you kill Hrolf Kraki – even if it was on the orders of your lover?' Arthur's lips were hovering close to her ear, so he felt her shake her head.

'Did your lover kill Hrolf Kraki, and do this to you?'

She responded with the slightest nod.

Arthur decided to whisper the one name that had teased his mind for months, praying that he was wrong, even as he asked.

She nodded her head, so he sighed despairingly while he tried to gather his thoughts; the sound of Aednetta's breathing was the only noise that could be heard in that charnel house.

So much time had passed! Who would believe him if he blurted out the name of Heorot's traitor? Arthur closed his eyes and his heart broke for Maeve. How could he leave her in a land where deceit and violence ran even deeper than in Britain?

Arthur recalled a tale related by Bedwyr whereby Artor, High King of the Britons, had exacted justice on his own warriors for the torture, rape and murder of a pregnant woman. His own mother, Elayne, had also confirmed that the High King had never regretted this decision. In old Britannia, at least, such extreme crimes were anathema.

Just as he began to despair, Gareth burst into the grisly room. He was followed by Frodhi, the old woman herbalist and a healer with dark, oily hair and a supercilious expression. Behind them Lorcan and Germanus pushed their way through the throng. The priest was carrying his worn satchel.

Aednetta made a terrible sound and her eyes almost started out of her head in her fear. Arthur took her shaking body gently into his arms; he could feel her reaction when her brazen attacker entered the room.

'You shouldn't move her, Arthur. You know better than that, boy,' Father Lorcan chided, as his hands began to ease her back onto her pillow. 'There, there, darling girl! I know it hurts, but I'll have you feeling better in a trice. All you have to do is obey old Father Lorcan.'

She whimpered. 'Don't be afraid, lass! I'll not let anybody hurt you.'

Lorcan's hands were busy, as he measured some powder out of a small glass bottle he had taken from his satchel. 'I want wine,' he demanded in a voice that had no trace of kindness in it. Nor did he bother to look at the men who clustered at the foot of the sumptuous bed like black crows of ill omen.

Snorri thrust a crude mug into Lorcan's hands, but the priest treated it like purest gold. The powder was dropped into the wine after Lorcan had drunk almost half the liquid in one careful swallow.

'Don't fear to drink this medication, lass, because it isn't poisoned. Not only have I tasted it myself, but I'd already be dying if the wine was bad. This powder will make you sleepy, and it will take away the pain so I can put you to rights.'

Arthur opened his mouth to protest that even God would baulk at healing such terrible wounds, but Lorcan shook his head to silence his charge.

Then, with infinite gentleness, he helped the girl to sip at the wine. The process took a long time but Lorcan was very patient. Eventually, Aednetta's head was beginning to loll. Arthur imagined that the white powder was a powerful narcotic taken from the poppy flower.

Lorcan barked for hot water and Snorri braved the melee in the corridor to fetch some from the kitchens while Stormbringer and Frodhi remained, essentially useless, at the entrance to the room. The Roman-trained healer had left in a huff, having been dismissed by Germanus. The herb woman would have fled as well, for every line of her body suggested panic. Gareth, however, quickly barred her exit with one brawny arm after a curtly worded order from Arthur.

The man who was exercising command in the small and sumptuous room was the Last Dragon. The Dene King and the Sae Dene ruler held no control over the loyalties of the three travellers and even Snorri would obey Arthur, unless he was ordered to cause harm to Stormbringer. Arthur could feel power settling over him like a heavy cloak of duty, while the voice in his head continued to purr and warn him by turn.

'Do what must be done,' the voice instructed. 'Expose the traitor! But you must first make certain that there's no doubt about his guilt.'

As Lorcan carefully straightened the broken limbs and began the heart-breaking task of cleaning the savaged face, he clucked his tongue and his eyes grew darker.

'She has three nasty body wounds,' Arthur said to Lorcan, with so much mingled pity and disgust in his voice that the priest raised one grey and bushy brow.

'I don't know the rights or the wrongs of this poor girl's sins, but treason would surely earn a clean execution rather than bringing her to a filthy end on a bloodstained bed. Someone is determined that this girl mustn't speak to anyone, so he mutilated her tongue. She tried to fight him off, but far too late, so she must have known her attacker. It seems our murderer is a cool customer, just the type of man to play the lover and the loyal servant, while plotting the Crow King's downfall. I'll even wager that he thoroughly enjoyed his game.'

'Aye, he must have enjoyed the subterfuge,' Arthur added, and a single pair of eyes in the room sharpened at his deliberate choice of words. Danger made the air in the bedchamber vibrate and the herb-woman, an obvious sensitive, began to weep with a peasant's lack of inhibition.

'This girl was patently guilty of treason and she caused the deaths of many men, women and children. But I would never wish such unnecessary suffering upon any human being. Whoever tortured her is as freezing inside as your northern winter skies. He won't be diverted until he achieves his ambitions, and should be hunted down like the beast he is. But beware! This man can kill a lover as if she was a crude and unwanted toy.'

'But how did the assailant enter this room, master?' Snorri asked. 'The guard is alert and I checked the room very carefully to see how he entered once I found the— her.' Snorri stumbled when he realised he was speaking of Aednetta as if she was already dead, flushing hotly with embarrassment.

'The next room has a common doorway but it's barred on this side. So is the exterior door. There's no way an intruder can get into that room except through the king's bedchamber. Aednetta always uses it when the king is tired of her presence,' Stormbringer explained.

'Let's keep these doors barred then, shall we?' Arthur added enigmatically.

'Bring the guard in, Snorri. He's not guilty of anything, so let him know he's not in any danger. I want to question him in a safe place where we can control the comings and goings of everyone who might have been responsible for this crime.'

Snorri tried to open the door, but fumbled a little with the heavy oak bar before Gareth helped him. Ultimately, Gareth was the first man through the door, and then the guard was convinced to enter the room for questioning. Outside, the crowd was still milling and the jarls were particularly strident in their demands for information but Gareth ignored them. When he finally entered, the terrified sentry took one look at Father Lorcan and his blood-spattered patient, and paled visibly.

Arthur beckoned him forward. His eyes searched for Frodhi

and Stormbringer, familiar faces in a room filled with frightening strangers. But any appeal was futile and the guard knew it. An influential prisoner in his charge had been attacked; both Arthur and he knew that the woman must have screamed or made some sounds of distress, and begged for mercy from her assailant. But the guard was adamant that he had heard nothing untoward.

Arthur's next question threw the man off balance.

'When did you come on duty?'

The guard had been prepared to swear that no one had entered the rooms while he was on watch, so the question surprised him. 'Er . . . Just after midnight, master. I was supposed to have been replaced two hours ago, but King Frodhi asked me to remain at my post.'

'I want to know everything that happened! Who did you replace? Could the girl have been unconscious for your entire shift? She was tied to the bed, and her tongue was gone. No blame can be laid on your shoulders if she was attacked before you arrived.'

Presented with an opportunity to pass on the blame, the guard was tempted but his basic honesty prevailed.

'No, master! Karl, the man I replaced, is a good man and unlikely to have even closed his eyes for a moment, least of all the length of time needed to wreak havoc like this. It's not possible! Karl was very tired when I came and he was eager to go to his bed. He can't have slept during his watch. I know him well and if he'd even heard something untoward, he would have mentioned it to me.'

'Very well, you may go.' Arthur nodded towards the guard with a measure of respect for his good character.

'Snorri, find this guard called Karl. Again, he is not guilty of any crime of which we are aware, so be diplomatic with him.'

Snorri trotted away, although he was unable to resist darting a look of triumph in Gareth's direction. As far as he was concerned, tasks such as these errands should be his prerogative.

Arthur caught Gareth's expression and sighed with irritation.

'Gareth, Snorri knows exactly where this man is likely to be found and he speaks the language far better than you – so stop sulking.'

Somehow, most of those present knew that Arthur was the only man in the room who would dare to address Gareth in that tone of voice and live to speak of it.

Lorcan's commanding voice dissipated the last of the tension that remained in the room.

'Stop bickering, you two, and hand me my holy oils and the packet in my satchel that contains my crucifix and a folded piece of black cloth. This child is gravely ill, and she has need of my ministrations.'

At this all those present quietened. As Aednetta lay, propped up high on pillows to assist her breathing, every man in the grim room could hear the ominous rattle in her breathing and the moist, sodden sound of every indrawn breath; the girl was drowning in her own blood. Her lips were blue, and the pallor of her clammy skin was even more pronounced than usual. Her flesh seemed transparent, as if her life force was shining through the fragile barrier of her skin and dissipating into the darkness that enveloped Hrolf Kraki's sanctuary, even in daylight.

As Lorcan gave Extreme Unction to Aednetta, the Christians in the group crossed themselves, even though the Latin was incomprehensible to them. Only Stormbringer and Germanus seemed comfortable in the presence of rituals that brought redemption to a dying soul.

Aednetta momentarily surfaced out of her stupor during the

performance of the rites, probably because she was suffering from surges of agonising pain. Even poppy juice could fail dismally if the wounds were severe. As soon as he realised she was partially awake, Lorcan switched to the Dene language which he now spoke with a far greater facility than either Germanus or Gareth, and arranged the ritual in such a manner that she was able to give an almost imperceptible nod of her head in response to his questions.

And so Father Lorcan completed the Last Rites and Aednetta was permitted to show her contrition for the sins of her short life.

As they waited for Snorri to return with the guard, those present in the king's bedchamber tried to avoid thinking about Aednetta's fate. The dying are entitled to privacy, but Arthur wanted these men, especially Stormbringer and Frodhi, to bear witness to the death of the witch-woman. Father Lorcan ordered more wine, although he was aware that another dose of poppy juice would probably prove fatal. But, as he explained later, if the potion accelerated her passing, then such a fate was kind rather than murderous.

Once Aednetta was unconscious again, the audience began to breathe easier. At least one person in the room was glad that he had been freed from the accusations emanating from those terrified eyes.

The warrior, Karl, entered the room a few moments after Aednetta took her last breath, as Lorcan was straightening the dead girl's limbs to give her remains a semblance of the dignity that the murderer had taken from her. Karl stared at the body, sickened and appalled.

'When did this assault happen, lord?' Karl asked, his face screwed up like that of a small child hovering on the brink of tears. 'I had a feeling there was something wrong during my time at the door, but I had no idea what had happened until now. Rumours are rife.'

'Why would you feel so uneasy?' Arthur asked, frowning.

Karl struggled to find the exact words he needed, but Arthur could read no guilt in his open and uncomplicated face.

'I . . . I . . . don't remember the time ever passing as quickly as it did last night. I remember the early hours of my guard duty when the servants of Heorot were about their master's duties. I heard old Poul, the kitchen slave, when he was hauling wood into the main hall for the fire pit . . . and I swear I heard someone stirring the embers in the room when more wood was added to the fire. I had slept for several hours before taking up my duty because Lord Frodhi had explained how crucial my duty was to the safety of the realm. He told me that no one, including himself, was to enter the Crow King's room until I was relieved from my task – for any reason!'

The lad was visibly upset, so Stormbringer patted his shoulder with a large, callused hand.

'I'm sure I didn't go to sleep when I was on watch. I couldn't have – or I'd have remembered it, wouldn't I?'

'Did you drink or eat anything while you were on duty? Come, Karl, there's no sin in drinking a mug of beer or eating a slab of cheese during the long reaches of the night. Could you see clearly from your post?'

Karl clenched his fists as he struggled to remember.

'Yes, I could see quite well. An oil lamp was burning on the floor.'

Snorri made his way back through the door, while the young warrior continued to wrestle with his memory. The helmsman returned with a pottery lamp; Arthur could smell the dregs of fish oil inside and a fragment of dark flaxen wick still sat in place at one end to provide a dim light. Someone, probably the second guard, had extinguished the small flame when Snorri arrived to rouse Aednetta as the first light of dawn came over the horizon. A similar lamp sat on a small bench beside the luxurious bed where Aednetta had met her grisly end.

'The lamp seems harmless,' Arthur decided, and Karl cringed at the gleam reflected in the Last Dragon's strange eyes. 'Now, did you eat or drink during the night?'

The young man's eyes suddenly sharpened and he cursed with excitement like a peasant.

'I remember now! I *did* eat! A tray with food and beer had been left for us. Just a jug of beer and a couple of pieces of dried fish and some nuts, but I remember the tray was beside that oil lamp. I didn't fancy the nuts, but I ate one of the pieces of fish and I drank a full mug of beer.'

'And?'

'And what, Lord Arthur? I don't understand.'

Arthur sighed with exasperation. 'What do you remember next, Karl?'

'My feet were cold! I sat down on the floor to rub some life into them and then put my boots on again. The sheepskin seemed warmer once I'd done that . . . I noticed that my shadow made odd patterns on the wall, and I recall thinking that I could have used my hands to make children's shadow pictures.' The young man paused. 'You know, master! Like the rabbit or the hound!'

Arthur realised Karl had been doing his utmost to remember every detail of the disastrous night that had just passed. With a visible effort, which only succeeded in flustering the guard into silence, Arthur stopped himself from cuffing Karl across the ears to jog his memory.

'And ...' Stormbringer put in gently.

'And ...' Karl's open face was distraught. 'Nothing! I have dishonoured my name and I've shamed my father! I must have fallen asleep on duty, so this poor creature has died because I failed to follow the orders of my king. I am beyond forgiveness ...'

The words that tumbled out began to trail away as the full enormity of his dereliction of duty sank in.

'Snorri! Fetch the food tray!' Arthur ordered.

'The lad has done his best to remember the events of the night, Arthur,' Frodhi exclaimed from the bed where he had been standing quietly, as if he wished to protect Aednetta's corpse from any further indignities. 'He isn't at fault here!'

Arthur said nothing because Snorri had returned with empty hands. The helmsman shrugged expressively. 'It's not there!'

'Then find it, Snorri. And give no explanations to anyone, even if they outrank you.'

Snorri padded away once more without complaint. He guessed that the young guard must have been drugged and his master was seeking proof of this. As he hurried towards the separate building where the kitchens were located, he wondered at how easily his master had assumed control of this investigation while the uncrowned king and the Sae Dene ruler remained passive spectators as the events of the night were unfolding.

He's destined to become a king himself one day, Snorri thought, as he approached the servants who were clustered around a small fire in their spartan living space. A man could do well if he was prepared to follow in the footsteps of the Last Dragon.

He spent a few moments finding the old woman who had been ordered to prepare the food and drink for the guards, and have it delivered to the guard post. A few more moments were spent discovering that a kitchen-hand had gathered up the tray in the hubbub of the discovery of the dying Aednetta and had washed and cleaned everything. The rheumy-eyed old man finally confessed that he had eaten the single remaining piece of fish left on the tray. He added that he hadn't liked his first taste of the beer so had thrown the rest away.

'Did the beer smell strange? Come on, old man, the great ones are waiting, so don't fuck me around. You'd have drunk that beer in an instant, frightened or not.'

The old slave cringed as if he expected to be beaten. 'It smelled funny. I only had a taste, but I thought it had gone off . . . please, master, I meant no harm.'

With a curse to show his displeasure, Snorri retraced his steps and reported his findings to Arthur.

'So now we know!' Arthur's voice was cold and hard, like the ice that covered Heorot's roofs on that bitter and cheerless morning. 'Snorri, Lorcan and Germanus, I need you to guard these doors and keep everyone away. I don't care how you do it. This room is to be kept private until such time as I tell you otherwise. Is that understood?'

'Arthur, this poor child must be laid out and prayers said for her overburdened soul,' Lorcan protested.

'She's not going anywhere, so we'll allow the rites for the dead to wait. Do what I say, and take Karl with you.'

The older men left the room and its palpable horrors with a sense of relief.

'And now I know what was done,' Arthur whispered as the door closed behind his friends' retreating backs.

Silence! Had they chosen to listen, any of the four men in the room could have heard the scuttling vermin in the straw of the roof. Black eyes peered down from the shadows as rats stalked the rafters while they struggled to find a way to reach the bags of grain and the dried meat that hung there tantalisingly. And then the sound of an icicle breaking loose from the roof cracked sharply like a breaking bone.

The long period of mute accusation was far too long and too suspicious for at least one of the men there, but every man present had some secrets in the darkest corners of their souls that they would prefer to keep private.

'Well, Arthur?' Stormbringer demanded. 'I hope you can throw some light on what's happened here, because I'm completely flummoxed. You say the guard was drugged, but how?'

'How long would it take to drop some powder into a jug of wine? Or beer? Someone other than Aednetta knows how to kill and to send grown men into a state of unconsciousness. I noticed that the guard's pupils were still dilated by some form of drug even as he was talking to us. He was still confused.'

Stormbringer lapsed into silence as he tried to think his way through the puzzle. Soundlessly, Gareth moved into a position where he could protect Arthur from a sudden attack, even from his Sae Dene friend.

The silence was almost agonising as Arthur turned to face Frodhi.

'Why did you plot against your cousin, Frodhi? Did you desire to be king so badly that you could betray your honour so easily? I was convinced that you were the guilty man from the very beginning, Frodhi, because I understood the ways that you had trained Aednetta to think.'

'What are you raving about, Briton? Who among us has been more loyal to the Dene cause than I have?' Frodhi's voice was hoarse and Arthur wondered how he had ever thought this

Dene was charming. Even the new king's handsome face seemed to have coarsened and no humour remained in his blade-sharp eyes.

Part of Stormbringer's mind could easily follow Arthur's logic, but a lifetime of friendship and adoration of his older kinsman made it almost impossible for the Sae Dene to accept his cousin's guilt.

Arthur turned to address him.

'Aednetta lusted after power, Valdar! You knew her very well, my friend. Would she have betrayed Hrolf Kraki for a man who was less aristocratic than a member of the royal family? Never! Aednetta placed a very high value on her flesh. And who is the only other man of your status who is as handsome and as charming as yourself? Your other cousin, the man who happens to be Hrolf Kraki's heir. Frodhi was an eminently suitable lover for any woman of good taste. I believe she loved Frodhi without reservation, because he was able to strike the first of his blows without alerting her to his intentions. Only a man such as he could have manoeuvred her into purchasing the poisons and relaying treasonous messages to the Hundings in person. I suspected him from the moment that Hrolf Kraki died. Quite simply, Frodhi had more to gain than you or, for that matter, anyone else in the Dene kingdom.'

'Me?' Stormbringer yelped. 'I'd never stoop to poisoning! How could you have considered that I'd do such a thing?' He was more shocked by the possibility that he had been under suspicion than if Arthur had accused him directly of the crime of murder. Yet the revelation of Frodhi's complicity caused him little surprise.

'Personally, I'd never be prepared to commit murder, but you both had much to gain in committing these crimes. Men kill for power or wealth, or both, but they rarely kill for love – do they, Frodhi?'

'Aye, Arthur. You are quite correct in your assumptions about me, but there's nothing you can possibly do about it. I'm the king now, whether you like it or not. As the king, I have all the trappings of power at my fingertips, but I'm loath to use them on you, my young friend. You have served the Dene cause well, and the kingdom has survived Hrolf Kraki's stupidity. You're inconvenient . . . but you can't touch me.'

Frodhi lifted his chin and smiled slowly. Even Stormbringer flinched as those blank eyes swept over him.

'That's generous of you,' Arthur replied in a voice dripping with sarcasm. 'I expect that too many questions would be asked if I were to die suddenly.'

'I don't believe it!' Stormbringer protested. 'You sent aid to us, Frodhi. You saved us from the Geats and the Hundings. We could never have defeated them without your ships and your warriors.'

'Of course he did,' Arthur explained patiently. 'The last thing that Frodhi wanted was to inherit a ruined kingdom. The Sae Dene warriors protect the islands and the coast of the mainland. No land army can totally protect the Dene Mark from attack; he made sure you escaped from Hrolf Kraki's banishment because he needed you to keep the kingdom safe. Perhaps he even loves you as his kin . . . but I never entered into his plans. He never expected you to return from your voyage to Britain with noble captives, so I was merely a happy accident who helped him with his ambitions.'

'You were a valuable asset until this morning, Briton, but you're too damn sharp by half! I probably should have neutralised you after the Battle of Lake Wener, but you were out of my reach and to attack you was to weaken Stormbringer. I couldn't permit *that* to happen.'

'But you'd have allowed my sister and my daughters to perish at The Holding,' Stormbringer whispered in a voice thick with shock and misery. 'She's your *cousin*! And my daughters are also your kin.'

The king's eyes dropped, seemingly with shame. Daughters were valued within Dene society, but Arthur began to realise that Frodhi might actually have an aversion to women. He had never wed and, except for this dalliance with Aednetta, had never been known to take a mistress.

'They're only females, cousin, so what can they really matter? As it turned out, the British bitch with the black hair managed to keep your kin safe, so there was no harm done.'

Frodhi was almost pleading with Stormbringer, and Arthur realised that a genuine affection still existed between these two strong men.

But Stormbringer was nauseated at Frodhi's callous words.

'No harm?' the Sae Dene asked in a soft and controlled voice. 'I loved you, Frodhi!'

With deliberation, Stormbringer turned his back on his cousin in an attempt to blot out the beloved and hated face as if such an action would excise Frodhi from his life.

'What are we to do with this monster, Arthur? And how can the kingdom be set to rights?'

'We can do nothing to Aednetta's killer, Valdar,' Arthur replied with some regret. But his eyes never left Frodhi's face as he spoke. 'You haven't flinched from regicide, Frodhi, so would you also want Stormbringer's death on your conscience?'

'Of course I don't want Stormbringer dead. He's an asset to any king, which is something that Hrolf Kraki never understood.

In fact, I'll go so far as to say that the Mark would fall if Stormbringer wasn't here to hold us together. The Crow King would have turned the Dene people into slaves because of his superstitions, cousin, so I did you a favour by removing him from this world. Wouldn't you agree?'

Stormbringer shook his head violently and his plaits flew like serpents around his head.

'No, Frodhi! No, by God! I cannot bear the thought of the traitorous and dishonourable things you have done on this terrible day . . . and I cannot tolerate the stain you have inflicted on the honour of our family. But I can't think of a remedy.'

Arthur finally decided to reassure his friend and end the discussion. The politics of the situation were a coil that could not be unravelled, only cut.

'What has occurred here is unfortunate, Valdar, but you must remain silent and endure the pain of what you have seen and heard today. The Dene kingdom cannot survive a civil war, because the Hundings and the Geats will lick their wounds while you tear yourselves apart, and then they'll gladly accept their shares of the ruins that remain. Do you want to lose The Holding? Would you choose to go to war against your cousin? Many good men have been forced to live with far worse secrets than those you'll be obliged to bear.'

'But, Arthur, how can you expect me to continue to speak with him, and to serve him, while I know that he's a regicide and a coward who'll beat a harmless woman to death? He would have permitted that foolish boy, Karl, to be killed for dereliction of duty, and he'd not have turned a hair. He's a monster!'

'Certainly! But Frodhi is the monster that your people need at this time in their history. You'll have to do what needs to be done because you're the Lord of the Storm and Frodhi . . . well, Frodhi's just another petty king.'

'I love you too, Arthur!' Frodhi retorted with a contented smile. 'You're presupposing I will allow you to prance out of here unscathed. I'm perfectly capable of removing all of you – and I would if I had to. I've come too far to turn back now when the prize is so close.'

Arthur watched as a number of emotions passed across Stormbringer's face, but the Briton knew his friend would eventually make the sensible choice. The Sae Dene's family, his seamen, his friends and his kinsmen all depended on it.

But Valdar Bjornsen would never again be the untroubled and honourable man he had always been, although long years of rule would stretch out before him.

Arthur watched sadly as Stormbringer bowed his noble head and knelt on the stone floor of the king's bedchamber. With the corpse of Aednetta Fridasdottar as a silent witness, the Lord of the Storm took his cousin's hand, kissed his ring and offered his fealty to Hrolf Kraki's murderer.

CHAPTER XIV

GOING HOME

No tyrant need to feel fear till men begin to feel confident in each other.

Aristotle, *Politics*, Book 5

Spring came slowly and reluctantly to Heorot, while Stormbringer's warriors ate and drank Hrolf Kraki's long-hoarded stores of grain and beer with gusto. For long frigid months, Old Man Winter had enjoyed his time in Limfjord and famine came to the population before the thaw began, so the children began to know the pangs of empty bellies. Only then had Frodhi, the newly crowned king and a fine fellow if you ignored his murderous nature, opened the last of his grain-houses to his people. The citizens kissed his hands in gratitude.

Day after day, Arthur's position in Heorot became more and more untenable, while he continued to ache for skies that were misty and soft. Here, the blue of these alien heavens hurt the eyes when seen against the white dazzle of the latest snowfalls. He turned to women gladly to dull the inner ache, but no number of willing bodies could warm the deep and long-buried coldness of the spirit. Waking and sleeping, he hungered to once again be warm inside, to be Arthur; and to have friends and family around him.

Stormbringer observed his friend's suffering and his heart ached for the younger man. But what could he do? Arthur would never accept pity. That could never be the warrior's way and God had made Arthur a warrior from birth.

'But he's more than that!' Stormbringer exclaimed one dark afternoon as he sat over his beer and warmed his feet at the front of the fire pit. Surprised, Snorri almost dropped his sword which he was sharpening on a whetstone with long, practised strokes.

Normally, a master would never speak candidly with a crewman, except during sea voyages where all men had a measured degree of equality. But something of Arthur's easy camaraderie with people of all classes had begun to rub off on the Sae Dene king. Arthur treated Snorri like a friend and a brother, and the death of Aednetta Fridasdottar had proved how profoundly Arthur trusted the helmsman, for he was the only Dene, except for Stormbringer, who knew the whole truth of Hrolf Kraki's death. Such trust prompted Stormbringer to speak freely with this remarkable sailor.

'I've been dwelling on the qualities of Arthur, your master,' Stormbringer began. 'As well as being my friend, I've discovered he's more than just an exceptionally capable warrior. You were there at the death of Aednetta and you saw how well he controlled a potentially disastrous confrontation with our new king.'

'Yes, master! I was there, but I try very hard not to think about what took place on that particular morning. Begging your pardon, my lord, but your cousin will have my tongue ripped out if I so much as mention a single word of what I heard. I suspect he may have me killed anyway, truth be told.'

'Yes, I know,' Stormbringer replied blandly, a response which made Snorri grunt with displeasure. The Sae Dene king was already falling back into the patterns of a lifetime, drinking and casting dice with Frodhi and sharing the rich background of common experiences that made them both laugh even if at times he remembered the twisted corpse of Hrolf Kraki. Snorri accepted that the Sae Dene king, his commander, had returned to a comfortable and easy friendship with his cousin, but as a Dene warrior and the helmsman of Arthur's longboat, his loyalties were torn.

Try as he might, he couldn't forget the battered body of Aednetta or the death pangs of the Crow King.

'Our friend longs for his homeland so I, for one, believe he will leave us when I marry his sister in the spring. Arthur has all the instincts of a king, including a ruthlessness that allows him to say what must be said. But he made his future in the Dene Mark impossible when he exposed my cousin's sins, even though I believe he understands me when I tell him that Frodhi wasn't entirely motivated by personal ambition. By the gods, but I wish I knew what to say to him. For that matter, where is he now?'

'He walks in the snow, my lord, so he can seek the trees that help to ease his loneliness. He was born in the deep forests in his homeland, and the trees give shape and meaning to his life, just as the sea does for you.'

Snorri pondered whether he dared to speak the unadulterated truth to his lord and master. 'He's trying to decide how to return to his homeland with nothing but his three friends to aid him. He knows that Britain is full of avowed enemies, and as the Last Dragon, his life will be eagerly sought by kinsmen and enemies alike.'

'But Arthur is a rich man now!' Stormbringer protested. 'His share of our successes on the field can buy him many acres anywhere in the wide world.'

Snorri made a snorting sound which caused his master to raise one questioning golden eyebrow.

'Arthur plans to achieve his destiny in his homeland, master, and nothing else will do for him. Gold and silver alone won't bring him the vast acres of good earth that he plans to farm in that far-off place. From our discussions, I've learned that northern invaders have forced Arthur's kinfolk to retreat into the more remote corners of Britain, so the original Celtic lands are now owned and ruled by the Saxons, Jutes and Angles. He accepts that the old days have gone forever, so he intends to carve out a new homeland on the eastern and northern shores of his great island, in a place where people can raise their families and live in peace and prosperity. To fulfil his promise, Arthur needs warriors at his back and families of good stock who are prepared to stand beside him and resettle their children in a strange land, even if he must do it as a Dene.'

Snorri, a landless man whose family survived through Stormbringer's generosity, could understand how Arthur yearned for a land that he could call his own. He hungered for the same dream.

'Would you follow him, Snorri?'

Snorri pondered the question, visibly weighing up the pros and cons.

'Aye! I would gladly follow him with everything I have, as would any of the landless men in our crew. But our numbers are too small to carve out a kingdom. From what Arthur has told me, the Saxons have burrowed into the hide of Britain like ticks, so that neither flame nor knife can remove them. Only the sword and a total dedication to strong and forceful leadership can set him on the pathway to becoming a king.'

Stormbringer's face began to clear.

'Then I must give him what he desires. He has already given me a precious gift in the form of his sister, who has become my heart's desire. Would you be prepared to follow him in *Sea Wife* if I commanded him to raid the Saxon and Friesian coasts in the north? Would you and your men be prepared to brave the north to win gold and silver from our cousins in Noroway? He will gain much from these raids, but he needs men behind him who will be prepared to challenge the gods of wind, water and ice.'

Both men understood this referred to the fabled lands to the north and north-east where the ice never melted. Stormbringer had heard that half the year in these lands the sun never rose above the horizon, while the remainder was filled with perpetual sunlight and the darkness of the night became a distant memory. There, a longboat could easily be crushed by the living ice as if it was made of eggshells. Should the stories in the sagas be true, then Arthur would visit a world never braved by Dene sailors and he could win a great name that would last forever.

Snorri thought carefully. Would he risk his life for such a dream? Ultimately, his answer came from the heart.

'I will gladly go with him, master. He's already given my family the chance of a better life with my share of the spoils of our past forays, and I know many other landless men who wish to fight under the banner of the Red Dragon. One thing is certain: Arthur is not a Dene, but he's no longer a Briton either. He has become something other than these races, as he'll discover when he sets foot on British soil and breathes the air of his childhood. I'll follow him, for he offers the best chance for the future of my sons and the Dene people. And, master, I'm not alone in my ambitions.'

Stormbringer chewed over Snorri's wisdom and knew he had just received wise counsel.

'It's decided then! Arthur must seize his destiny and challenge the will of the gods.'

And I've always considered you to be a Christian, Snorri thought. But he said nothing.

Spring came suddenly, with torrents of water beginning to run down the cobbled road from Heorot to pour into the lake below. The fields were chocolate and green with spear-points of growth, so Arthur took pleasure in this tangible proof that life continued. Flowers began to spring up in every nook and cranny in stone walls, and weeds flourished. Girls wore garlands in their hair, while children squealed with joy as they played in thick puddles of mud.

Finally, after a winter of silence, Frodhi called an audience for Stormbringer and his entire officer corps, for the time had come when the Sae Dene army should be disbanded to allow the warriors to return to their farms. The arrival of spring demanded that men should take over the farm work from their womenfolk. Meanwhile, those men whose lives were unhampered by family responsibilities would sharpen their weapons and prepare to go roving, for such was the way of Sae Dene warriors. Their cousins who came from Heorot and other settlements along the peninsula might be content with their broad acres, but the unfettered sailors were always eager to explore the wild and turbulent waters of distant seas.

Of all the souls who spent their days and nights in Heorot, Father Lorcan was the only concerned person who prayed with all his strength that Justinian's Disease would pass the Dene population by, although he knew in his heart of hearts that such scourges were rarely deflected by prayers. Fortunately, only two other people were familiar with the contagion, and Lorcan was certain that neither Germanus nor Gareth would discuss the matter with *anyone* in the Dene lands, other than Arthur.

Stormbringer, Arthur and the other officers gathered in the familiar hall, now bright with strengthening sunlight that streamed through unshuttered windows. They met in the late morning, a time of day when the fire pit glowed with coals, but left the air in the hall untroubled by thick smoke. Arthur dressed with considerable care and carried the wolf-fur cloak that had been brought from the Forest of Arden by Gareth. Whenever he felt its heavy folds fall from his shoulders, he imagined that his father, Bedwyr, was rewarding him with a paternal embrace. In his father's cloak, Arthur cut a barbaric figure in Heorot's ancient, echoing space.

For his part, Frodhi had dressed with the care expected of a new king who must build a reputation for statesmanship. Golden armbands adorned his wrists and arms, while a heavy golden chain that had once belonged to the Crow King was hanging around his neck and shoulders. The new king had elected to dress in the style of a warrior, perhaps to emulate the men who, by their presence alone, had created a situation whereby Hrolf Kraki could be removed. Perhaps Frodhi chose this mode of dress to warn Arthur that he, too, would be prepared to use the sword to enforce his rule. Whatever the reason, Frodhi rejected Hrolf Kraki's ostentatious, gold-edged armour in favour of good, highly polished iron and chain mail, while his sword was both ornamental and workmanlike. Arthur held no doubts that Frodhi would use his weapons and his regal power against anyone who stood in his way.

'We have come in compliance with your demands, my lord,' Stormbringer announced in a voice that rang through the rafters. His choice of words was a subtle warning to his cousin that any show of force would be unwise. But if Frodhi recognised any external threat, he chose to ignore it. The king smiled broadly with a flash of perfect canines, an unusual characteristic in warriors who had their teeth knocked out regularly during physical combat.

'Welcome, one and all. I have asked you here to discuss our plans now that spring is with us and the thaw is well advanced. Although I am grateful for your presence and your service during the past winter, our supplies are running desperately low, so I'd be a poor king if I didn't take action to renew our food stocks. I await your thoughts and your advice.'

How easily Frodhi adapted himself to the formal language of rule while mouthing platitudes and showing the outward trappings of friendly interest! He had proved to be a man of infinite patience, prepared to wait for his machinations to bear fruit.

Dammit, Stormbringer thought with regret. Arthur is right! I'll never be able to trust Frodhi, even if I continue to love him like a brother. Can I rely on him as I once did? His loyalty to others will always depend on his immediate needs. He needs me during these difficult times in which we live, but that state of affairs could easily change.

'I have developed plans to march my forces back into the south before the week is out, my lord. Once we have reached our ships and the waterways are free of ice, the army will be released to return to their homes, their farms or, alternatively, to sail with Master Arthur into the far north. Those men who are eager for plunder will be invited to take ship under his command.' He smiled broadly. 'I hope these plans meet with your approval, my king.'

King Frodhi gave a grunt of approval, but Stormbringer saw scarifying thoughts surface out of the deceptive blue of Frodhi's eyes.

'Why is he travelling to the north?'

Arthur decided that there was little profit in this particular ruler knowing his exact intentions, so made an immediate decision that he would always travel by a far different route to any suggested by the new king. As he responded to the king's request, Arthur gave vague descriptions for, to be honest, he was unsure himself. One thing was certain: he wanted to remove himself from Heorot and its dubious charms.

Frodhi was quite avuncular by the time the audience was over. The Sae Dene's army would no longer be eating his store-house bare; he would be able to deal with the cleaning up of the Crow King's rule without Stormbringer peering over his shoulder; and the one man who could do him harm would be far off in Noroway and other points in the distant north. With luck, the Briton would die there.

'Hopefully, he'll make a fatal mistake outside my borders, and then I'll be done with him without any cost to myself,' Frodhi remarked to the spring breeze later that evening. The air held just a promise of chill at its edges to remind the king of dark winter storms. 'It's strange! I rather liked the Last Dragon too, so it's a pity he outlived his usefulness.'

Two days later, Stormbringer's army departed from Heorot and the Limfjord with few signs of regret, having scrounged whatever provisions they needed without even a modicum of apology. Once so disciplined, his warriors remained loosely within their assigned crew-groups but their imminent return to their women and children took priority over almost everything but the speed with which they could reach their homes. A hundred of the single warriors opted to go with Arthur, so he robbed no wives of their menfolk.

For the first time, he had the leisure to view the green fields of the Dene mainland. The country spread around him, bright with wildflowers, grain that burst through the rich soil and cattle that grazed on a patchwork of industry. Streams were bountiful and Arthur washed himself daily in the icy water. With a sharpened eating knife, he scraped away at his chin and cheeks to free them from the fledgling beard he had grown during the colder months.

And so, with the next year planned, Arthur felt a tentative sense of satisfaction and hope.

Still, the young man's nights were filled with dark dreams that were quickly forgotten after waking. Nights found him drenched in sweat and shaking with vague horrors but, by and large, the days seemed to pass swiftly.

Home! Every time a warrior spoke of the impending joy of spending time with their kinfolk, Arthur felt as if a long spike had pierced his heart. In the Dene lands, he had learned the precious, ineffable wonder of kin, so he was now longing for his mother, his brothers, Lasair and Barr, and his other sister, Nuala. Deep inside, Arthur was reasonably certain that Bedwyr would have passed into the shades by now, and he would never again know the warm embrace of that fine old man. When he slept, he found himself running once more through Arden's forest branches in the depths of a freezing winter. Although there were no pursuers that he could see, he knew with the certainty of dreams that something frightful sniffed the air to catch his scent.

One slip, even one minor error of judgement, and he would fall to earth where the pursuing horrors would have him at their mercy.

Although Stormbringer had urged Arthur to take ship once spring was upon them, the prospect of his friend's absence dented Stormbringer's feelings of well-being. He had lived and fought beside Arthur for more than four years, and knew the Briton better than he had ever known his father or his uncles. He had come to depend on Arthur's cold logic. Although at times he found the chill in Arthur's nature to be alien, he was also aware that it was the well-spring of his remarkable gift for strategy. Like his ancestors, he could crush his feelings so as to act with the ruthlessness that all kings must possess.

All too soon, *Sea Wife* and its two consorts, sweet of line and graceful in the waves, left the eastern coast of the Dene Peninsula and headed into the north. Stormbringer stood on the beach and raised his sword so that the morning sun caught the blade as if it was wreathed in a sudden burst of flame. As the longboats set their sails once they had reached the slow sea swell, a small figure standing in the stern blew on a horn taken in plunder, so that a full-throated roar came to the Sae Dene king over the grey-blue waves. Stormbringer was comforted by this masculine salute, but bereft at the same time. He stood alone on the beach until the horizon was bare and empty under the rising sun.

Summer came, and then autumn, but Arthur did not return to The Holding. Maeve wept for him, although she consented to wed Stormbringer in her brother's absence when she found herself with child. Stormbringer was both shamed and elated by her condition, because he had been unable to bear her beauty and had seduced her under a warm summer sun. But after Maeve had gazed up into his face with green eyes that were clear and beautiful to tell him that she was quickening with a son, his happiness knew no bounds.

'Arthur will refuse to return until he finds his place in the world,' she told her husband one night after the marriage rites had been conducted by Father Lorcan. The priest had chosen to remain at The Holding to protect Maeve and Blaise after Arthur had begged this boon of him. Germanus and Gareth had gone with Arthur, although the younger Briton fully expected to be seasick during every moment spent on the water. Despite his disappointment, Lorcan knew his old bones couldn't survive the rigours of such a voyage.

Still, when winter came with a bitter and brittle early frost, even Lorcan began to feel the sharp edge of anxiety. Although he was convinced that Arthur's preternatural gifts would protect him, the long period of silence depressed Lorcan's usually ebullient nature.

When summer came and went in a haze of flowers and fruit, and Maeve's son began to crawl after his father while chortling baby talk, Ingrid and Sigrid also began to worry. They were slaves without a master, and Sigrid was now fifteen and lovely, for all that her temper was mercurial and her manner remained imperious. The passage of a second spring and summer seemed to bode Arthur's death and their hearts were sickened at the suggestion that they might require a new master.

At first, the two slaves had refused to fret. They knew their master very well and both women were certain that he had decided to remain in the north and make his fortune. 'He'll be searching for plunder that will allow him to leave the lands of the Dene, or he will die,' Sigrid stated with finality. Her face said nothing, but Maeve sensed a deep longing in her and wondered what her brother meant to this awkward, difficult, but lovely young girl.

Eventually, Frodhi began to forget that the Last Dragon had ever existed. But then, at the same time as a forlorn Stormbringer was beginning to look at his wife with saddened eyes and Ingrid's son, Ingmar, had just commenced his training with weaponry despite his tender age of five, a mass of huge sails suddenly appeared on the horizon.

'I told you!' Maeve accused her nonplussed husband, and then patted the beginning of a paunch on Valdar Bjornsen's belly. 'No northerner could ever kill my brother! He's obviously been preparing to meet his destiny and become the ruler of those lands across the seas.'

'Perhaps they aren't Arthur's ships! Perhaps they are enemy vessels who wish to attack The Holding,' Stormbringer retorted, but he grinned to let his wife know that he was speaking in jest. Nor did he remind her that she had been fearful of disaster for nearly three years. Valdar was too fond of her and too experienced in diplomacy to fall into that particular trap.

'You idiot!' she protested, and pinched him hard on the arm. 'Can you see the sail on the horizon, the one that is ahead of all the others? If that's not the red dragon sail of *Sea Wife*, then I'm going blind.'

The citizenry of Stormbringer's island were already on edge. Father Lorcan had sat the Sae Dene king down during the last winter and had explained the dangers of Justinian's Disease to him in detail, much as he had warned Stormbringer's sister some two years earlier.

Cautious as always, Stormbringer had barred all traders from landing on the island during the past two years, for he preferred to take no chances with such a fierce disease. He could still recall the warning given by an old seer at World's End, a no-name village that had taken in Stormbringer, his captives and the crew of his ship after Hrolf Kraki had declared them to be outlaws. The frail old woman, almost certainly dead by now, had told him that Maeve, his Maeve, would one day place her own safety at risk and would save many Dene lives after the onset of a great evil. Although three springs had come and gone, and no disease had stirred the sweet peace of their lives, the Sae Dene king continued his embargo on foreign ships when spring eventually returned to the north.

Only two weeks earlier, a courier had arrived from the estate of his nearest neighbour with fearsome news. With his usual caution, Stormbringer had instructed the man to remain distant from the houses and barns and he had avoided close contact with the man while they spoke. Suddenly, he had been struck by a feeling of impending doom.

The man's memorised message had travelled from the king's hall in Heorot.

'*Since you choose to lock yourself in your estates, I must petition you like a peasant to come to my aid in Heorot,*' Frodhi's words were repeated. '*A deadly disease has come to the halls of Heorot and the people sicken and die like cut flowers. They are alive in the morning, deathly ill at noon, and dead by evening. I insist that you come at once to our assistance, on pain of death.*'

'This message came from my cousin, King Frodhi?' Stormbringer asked the courier, filled with a growing fear that his young family was under threat from a new and dangerous foe. Maeve had responded immediately, for she believed that she and Father Lorcan, who was experienced with this disease, should travel to Heorot. However, she had been convinced to wait until such time as little Sven was weaned.

But any decisions would now be deferred by Arthur's arrival at the head of this huge fleet. Already, Stormbringer realised that many of his warriors would choose to take ship with Arthur and remove themselves from the terrors of a disease that killed its victims at random.

'So, our boy returns triumphant!' Father Lorcan said, his Hibernian lilt a little more obvious than usual. As Stormbringer turned, a small figure atop Lorcan's shoulders burbled at him and held his arms wide.

'Dada!' Sven had recently discovered names. 'Lorka,' he added. He giggled then, and his red-gold curls bounced disarmingly.

Lorcan lifted the boy down and tickled him on the belly with his whiskery chin, producing more giggles.

'Enough, Lorcan! Between you and Blaise, our boy will be spoiled rotten. I swear he'll lose the use of his feet if she continues to carry him everywhere he goes.'

Lorcan changed the subject. 'There are a great number of ships in his fleet, so I'm wondering where they could have come from. That's it! I'm becoming an old fool in my dotage! Arthur's planning to return to Britain! The whole purpose of this voyage was the acquisition of men and ships rather than plunder.'

Stormbringer had arrived at the same conclusion, even as Arthur was planning his voyage into the freezing north lands.

'His plans have been long in the making,' Stormbringer agreed. 'I suppose you're correct, but this news comes at a dangerous time for me and mine. Shite! Why can't anything ever be easy?'

'If life was truly easy, we'd live in a state of constant boredom. But I agree with your concerns, especially over the disease that Frodhi is battling in Heorot. Justinian's Disease has been waiting to come into the north for some time, my lord, and its onset will definitely solve any problems of overpopulation. When we were travelling through the Frank lands during our journey into the north, the plague had gone before us, and only one person in ten managed to survive its kiss. Perhaps the cold winds that come down from Noroway have delayed its onset in these northern climes, but I fear the message you received from Heorot bodes badly for your people.'

The old man sighed and handed the wriggling child over to a hovering woman who served as the wet nurse and surrogate mother whenever Maeve was busy. Stormbringer fondly considered how well his wife had done and how she worked amicably with Alfridda, who had been mistress of The Holding for so long that she could easily have resented sharing.

But Maeve had been diplomatic, and she assumed her duties with such gratitude that Alfridda was charmed. So life had become a pleasant experience for the entire household until the news of this mysterious illness had abruptly surfaced.

'Our boy returns to us at an opportune time, for I must be going to Heorot to give whatever aid I can to those affected by this illness,' Lorcan added. He sighed softly, reluctant to give up his quiet and fruitful life at Heorot. 'I'm fearful that your girl will be determined to journey to Heorot with me. I could never deny her anything, not even when she was no larger than young Sven. But she's your spouse now, so I hope you might be able to talk some sense into her. I wish you luck in this regard, for the children of Bedwyr and Elayne are laws into themselves.'

'Me? How could I change Maeve's mind about anything? Even her love for me will not prevent my girl from doing exactly what her conscience dictates.' Stormbringer had resignation clearly etched onto his face.

Valdar could see that Father Lorcan had aged significantly

during Arthur's absence and his hair had whitened, even as it retreated to a fuzzy fringe around his tonsure. Although his eyes were as sharp as ever, they were buried in heavy wrinkled bags, much like those of an ancient tortoise. His bushy black brows, however, still bristled with life as they had always done.

Lorcan walked with the assistance of a cane, for the cold of the north wind and the damp climate exacerbated the swelling in his joints. Old sword wounds and injuries incurred during his disreputable middle years had come back to haunt him too. Yet, typically, he was still able to joke about his increasing weaknesses.

'You're too old to undertake a task such as this, Lorcan, and little Sven would never understand why you would ever want to leave him.'

'I'm immune to the sickness, so I can't contract it – and who in the community would threaten a healer with physical harm when Death stalks the land? I'll be safe in Heorot, as you know full well. I can understand your position! You don't want Maeve to risk herself, so you're hell bent on convincing me to stay put.'

The old man patted Stormbringer's hand and his eyes were suspiciously damp. 'I don't want to leave this place. I've found peace at The Holding after a lifetime of strife, and I'd not lift a finger to help that Frodhi bastard. He deserves to catch the disease himself.'

Lorcan paused to regain his breath.

'I'm not searching for vengeance. I'm a man of God and my place is to heal! God can bless the most unpromising persons and He has given me an opportunity to do His works and save as many innocents as I can. In days gone by, I was a sinner, a murderer, a mercenary and a lecher, yet God has given meaning to my life and has granted me an old age where I can still be of use to others.'

Stormbringer, unable to find logical objections to this, held his tongue.

Meanwhile, the approaching fleet sailed ever nearer to the cove beyond The Holding, so Stormbringer could no longer doubt that Arthur had, indeed, returned. He made his way to the nearby sand dunes.

Sea Wife drove its bows into the sand of the cove as her rowers raised their oars above the slow wavelets. This flamboyant manoeuvre was completed flawlessly. The rest of the fleet landed with more decorum and The Holding's master felt a momentary doubt that they would have sufficient stores to feed all the crews. Then, berating himself for his cautious reaction, he strode over the dunes to greet Arthur as he stepped through the shallows with his usual athletic grace.

'Arthur! You've returned at last. Maeve has been demented with worry over you for the past few months. She feared the worst, although she also reminded me constantly that her *voice* would tell her if anything had happened to you.'

Arthur and he embraced, so that Stormbringer could feel the young man's hard muscles and his callused hands.

'I've come with men from the northern lands who are eager to travel with me to build a new life in Britain.' Arthur's whole face was browned and handsome and he was smiling joyously as he greeted his friend. 'I have supplies aplenty so we won't eat you out of home and barn while we're sampling your hospitality. Come, my friend! I've a great desire to see my sister. Have you wedded her yet?'

'She's wedded, bedded and she's now the mother of my son and your nephew. He is called Sven Bedwyr, a lad with two names that honour both sides of his lineage. He will be eager to melt your heart, as will Father Lorcan, who has fretted for you during your absence. Gods, Arthur, but you look the very picture of a Dene warrior.'

It was true. Arthur had filled out a little and he was now so powerful and tall that few warriors would willingly choose to face him in combat. His shape, wide in the shoulders and narrow at the hips, was so perfectly proportioned that the women in the fields stopped their labours to follow him with hungry, appreciative eyes.

His skin was burnished to bronze, which threw his red-gold hair into prominence, while the changeable eyes, more green than grey, were startling within the setting of his polished face. At almost twenty-six years of age, and clean-shaven, Arthur was at the very peak of his physical prowess.

Snorri, Gareth and Germanus laboured up the dunes behind the two friends.

'Does Gareth still become seasick?' Stormbringer asked with a laugh.

'If he did, he would've starved when we departed near to three years ago. He suffered an initial bout when we first left, but then began to improve. He thrives on the sea now, although he still burns in the sun, even when the cold is a live thing in the far north. Oh, Valdar, even you would have been impressed by the marvels we saw during our voyages through the north.'

When he greeted Gareth, Stormbringer immediately saw the changes in the younger man. He was strong and healthy, although his nose was peeling, his skin ruddy brown.

Germanus, on the other hand, seemed to have cast off any semblance of old age during the voyage, unlike his old friend who had remained behind. His close-shaven skull was smoothly polished and his skin was still ruddy with good health, while his face was covered by a network of fine white lines where the sun had failed to penetrate. But his back was unbowed, his stride was long and powerful and apart from a smattering of age spots and freckles on his skull and his hands, his joints showed none of the encroaching swellings and feebleness of advancing years.

Stormbringer gripped the sword arms of his friends in greeting, and threw his left arm around Snorri's shoulders to show his liking and respect. The helmsman was unchanged and, if possible, seemed to be carrying more weight than before.

'Come one, come all. We'll find beds for some of you, while we'll set up tents in the large field near the hall. Your crews will be able to rest comfortably and we can share whatever supplies are available.'

Stormbringer spoke with uncharacteristic vivacity. Arthur smiled a little to see the Sae Dene's obvious contentment; his little sister had chosen well.

And so the Last Dragon and his warriors returned to The Holding where joy, good food, singing and dancing would embrace them.

As if she could read her husband's mind, Maeve was hard at work erecting tents in the hall field. Here, a bullock had just been killed and a huge spit had been set up over a large fire grate used for special celebrations. Stormbringer swelled with pride at the efficiency of his workforce.

Good luck seemed to sail with his young friend; the obvious good health of Arthur's warriors, their energy and their wide, honest smiles spoke of contentment and joy, especially on this momentous day.

The master's friend had returned to the fold. And, in an optimistic state, even strong and intelligent men can delude themselves, as Valdar Bjornsen was soon to discover.

* * *

'We've seen islands of ice that are higher than the hills of Noroway as they sailed by us like ships, while huge expanses of underwater ice that are larger than Heorot and its village float just below the surface of the midnight-blue waters. We were lucky to experience no more than a gentle tap from one of the monsters,' Arthur said in a hypnotic voice that transported his rapt audience to those lands where the sun was still shining at midnight.

'In these lands, the little dark people make homes from ice in the winter and go out in hide canoes to hunt for the seal people. Then, when they kill their quarry, they pray to the souls of the seals, who are their brothers, to grant them forgiveness. Every part of these beautiful animals is used to keep the tribal members alive in their hostile and unforgiving homeland.'

Maeve's eyes filled with tears; she had watched on many occasions as these creatures came to the seas near The Holding and played in the shallows with their pups like sleek, black dogs. Arthur smiled to see her compassion.

'Sometimes, these brave men challenge the impossible and paddle their fragile canoes out into deeper waters where they hunt for the great blue whales that are the size of whole villages and are as clever as any man. If the hunters are successful with their sharp harpoons and they manage to pierce the outer skins of the whales, the great fish bleed inside and will eventually weaken and perish. Many men die during the chase and the ensuing kill, but their tribes are greatly enriched by the capture of one of these creatures.'

'Surely it is wrong to kill such great sea dwellers,' Maeve protested. She had seen some of the huge creatures on her first voyage across the seas; by chance, one of the behemoths had been accompanied by its calf and the sight of mother and child frolicking in the ocean waters had touched Maeve's soft heart.

'Perhaps hunting a whale might seem to be an unfair contest, Maeve, but the Inuit hunters rarely attack healthy beasts. Even so, many men perish because the waters are so cold that a human being cannot survive in them for even a heartbeat. Most of their village inhabitants are either older men or women and children. Life under the midnight sun can be terrifying for those who live there.'

Around him, rapt eyes followed his every movement and keen ears were eager to hear more of the marvels he had seen during his voyages. The Dene people were always captivated by story-telling; tales of love, heroism and battles thrilled them, so Arthur responded to their interest and sucked his audience into the very core of his tale. They could picture five or six tribesmen as they struggled with an enormous white bear that was almost twice the height of a tall man as it stood on its hind legs. The creature had claws like scythes and teeth that were white spikes of death. Arthur's audience could smell the blood of the four tribesmen who had died before the white bear succumbed to the many barbed spears that were planted deeply into its flesh.

'Behold the coat of the snow bear,' Arthur cried out with a dramatic flourish as Snorri threw open a huge cloak of fur so thick, so lustrous and so long and snowy-white that Maeve cried aloud in admiration.

'The chieftain of these fine people gave me this cloak in thanks for a blue whale we killed for them – but that's another story,' Arthur teased.

'I have seen the night sky awash with coloured stars in waves of luminescence, as if the heavens were weeping the very soul of light. Such a display was never seen in Britain or in the Dene lands, but I was struck by the wonders of many-coloured ice, pure white snow and a sky that was rainbow-hued. I could write the story of these wonders on a piece of vellum by the light of these gifts from God.'

Then Arthur described the fierce men of the fjords in Noroway who were as adept on the seas as the Sae Dene. Arthur was forced to risk his three ships in a sea battle, but the use of a battering ram had resulted in the capture of one of the enemy longboats and, ultimately, won him the friendship of these hard-bitten and fierce seamen during the truce that followed. Not for the first time, Arthur had cause to thank the long-dead Myrddion for his scrolls and memoirs describing Caesar's wars, from which he had gleaned so much useful knowledge of warfare and strategy.

His small fleet had swollen to eight after the first season, so the sea wolves were able to harass the coasts of the north and the north-east for a whole summer, plundering not only the Geats, but the Pomeranians, the Estonians and the Lithuanians, all of whom fell prey to the lightning-fast attacks from the Skandian raiders. The combined force returned to Sognefjord in the north-west of Noroway for the winter. And so Arthur's fame spread quickly in a hard land that valued its heroes.

When the spring released the fjords from the ice, Arthur's fleet surged out of Sognefjord to harry the Friesian coast where many of the settlements had been appropriated by marauding Saxon forces. Much gold and silver was taken in these raids, most of which had been stolen from the original Friesians who were increasingly being starved for land by the invading Angles, Saxons and Jutes.

Then, when the longboats had returned and had been emptied of their heavy cargo of treasure, Arthur decided to use the rivers to strike ever deeper into Saxony. As he approached, the villagers frightened their children with horror-filled tales of the Last

Dragon who had stripped the thanes of their wealth. Deep within the Saxon heartlands, Arthur and his allies from Noroway realised what wealth and provisions awaited daring and determined warriors. He only laughed when his men accorded him superstitious awe and he explained that both Loki and Fortuna favoured him against the complacency of the barbarians who had preyed on the common folk for generations.

'I saw the strategies used by the Saxon and the Angles in my homeland, so their thanes hold no fears for me. Our enemies fight in the same manner as their ancestors who invaded Britannia a century or more in the past, because they see no need for change. The northerners are fierce and ruthless fighters, but their weakness is, as always, their predictability.'

Out of respect for Germanus, Arthur decided that his horde should let the Franks be, although several petty kings to the north of their lands offered vast sums in gold and slaves to Arthur if he would pass them by. He accepted their offerings, and another summer passed with the accumulation of even more wealth, men and supplies.

During the long winter in Sognefjord, Arthur recruited several hundred young warriors from among the Noroway population, men who were prepared to sail across the seas to Britannia where they could carve out a kingdom in lands that were rich and bountiful. Captured slaves, too, added to his numbers; all swore their allegiance to Arthur in blood and many cups of mead and beer.

One more season of a'rovering: one more store of gold and slaves to be set free so they could willingly enter his service. Arthur was content.

Then he smiled across at his friends to show that he had completed his tale.

'I'm ready now to make my final preparations for our journey to Britain. I have decided that I will make my landfall in the Otadini lands along the north-east coast, an ideal base for the creation of what will become a new Skandian kingdom.'

He paused to allow his words to sink in.

'The Otadini king is my kinsman and, if his tribe still exists, I believe he can be convinced to help us in our quest to build a new homeland free from the Saxon yoke. Then, once our fortifications have been built and the first crops are sown, I'll send our longboats back to Skandia for our women and children, as well as any livestock we want for the new settlements. Most of what we need will be available in the new lands and will be obtained either by conquest or by purchase. If our neighbours wish to integrate with us in peace, then we will live together amicably. If they oppose us, my people will do to the Saxons what they did to the Britons.'

Under his noble words, Arthur accepted that he was a thief who used a mailed fist to win his fortune.

Lorcan furrowed his brow. Despite the good news that Arthur had delivered regarding his forays into the north, the Dene lands were still under threat from an invisible enemy that killed without remorse.

'Did you see any evidence of Justinian's Disease in the northern lands, Arthur?'

'No, Lorcan. We did see some derelict villages in Saxony but I assumed that the reason for the absence of villagers was fear of my forces. Gareth told me that Justinian's Disease has dissipated during recent years, at least in the last sailing season, while Germanus speculated that the extreme cold might kill the illness.'

'Well,' Stormbringer exclaimed slowly. 'The disease has come to the land of the Dene and Frodhi has demanded that I return to Heorot and help him to control the epidemic, although I don't know how. He wants us to bring our healers from throughout the islands to Heorot, a plan that would rob the islands of any treatment if our own people should become infected. Like Hrolf Kraki before him, he is asking a great deal of his subjects.'

He paused to allow his message to sink in.

'I have refused to risk The Holding, so I have stripped the outlying farms of our workers and kept them and their families close to our homestead. We have also banned all contact with outsiders who might have been in contact with the disease. Your people are a different matter entirely, because you have come down from places where the illness has not yet been seen. Unfortunately, your sister and Lorcan intend to go to the aid of the villagers who are at risk in Heorot. I've tried to explain that we owe nothing to Frodhi, but they won't listen to me. Perhaps you can talk some sense into them.'

Arthur's face became very stern and still, while Germanus uttered a vicious oath.

'But you can't go anywhere near Heorot, Lady Maeve. You have no idea of the savagery and pestilence that this disease creates,' Gareth tried to explain. 'I could never permit a woman to walk into such a charnel house as those places I've seen during my travels. Please don't risk yourself so foolishly.'

But Maeve's mouth was set in mulish lines, so Germanus in turn attempted to dissuade her and his oldest friend from casting their lives away.

'I know you believe you are immune to this scourge, Lorcan, but remember what we saw on our journey through the Frank lands. That Jewish family crucified, tortured and left to die because their neighbours thought they brought the disease to their village? Yes, you'll save lives in Heorot, but you'll also have many failures and many citizens will perish. Please don't go, Lorcan! If you remain here, Maeve will also be forced to stay.'

'If I must, I will walk towards Heorot until such time as my feet are bleeding,' Maeve answered for them both. 'And then I'll take ship in whatever ramshackle craft that dares to make gold of the troubles there. You'll need to tie us down if you wish to keep us here, and I don't believe that you'll go to such lengths.'

Then she turned to her husband with eyes that were wise, soft and pleading.

'I know that you cannot go to Heorot and obey your king, Valdar, because someone must stay here to protect The Holding. But I have always been bound by a solemn promise that I will alleviate suffering, if I have the tools at my disposal. And I do! This oath is one that I will always try to keep, no matter the cost. If it should happen that I don't return, tell my son how much I loved him and ask him to forgive me.'

'I would never cast you off, my love, even if you're acting foolishly. But how will you reach Heorot? The fjord is closed to all ships, so you'll have difficulty finding a captain who is willing to take such a dreadful risk.'

'Arthur could take me when he leaves for Britannia, couldn't you, Arthur?'

Valdar knew he could order Maeve to obey him, but if he did so their relationship would be poisoned beyond repair.

The room became silent as every eye turned towards Arthur to hear his response. The hall itself seemed to be listening, for its old wooden walls creaked slightly in the autumn breeze.

'Aye!' Arthur agreed after a long pause. 'I'll take you, Maeve, but we'll have to trust in Bedwyr's luck to save us all. We can only hope that the spirit of the Arden Knife will protect its own.'

And now the silence was even longer, as every person present began to wonder if and when they would sit together once again.

Somewhere in the depths of the building, Sven laughed happily as Stormbringer's eyes began to fill with hot tears. The decision had been made, so there was nothing more for a fond husband to say.

CHAPTER XV

WHEN LUCIFER SMILES

Probable impossibilities are to be preferred to improbable possibilities.

Aristotle, *Poetics*

The land slid away behind *Sea Wife* and her two sister vessels, all manned by Dene warriors who would act as bodyguards for Arthur and, to a lesser extent, for Snorri, the helmsman who knew too much of events that had taken place in the palace of King Frodhi. Steady on her feet and eager to reach Limfjord, Maeve stared out towards the dark horizon, although she knew her eyes should have been fixed on the dim shapes of her husband, Alfridda and Sven Bedwyr, who had been held high to wave his farewells. Instead, her eyes bored into the dark shadows towards Skania.

'We will be in Limfjord within three days, sister. Did you ever think to see that hellish hall again?' She started in fright, but only for a short moment, and then stared directly into eyes that had changed from those she had known so well in childhood.

'Ah, brother, I have always known I would eventually return

to Heorot, but I had no idea when or why. One thing I'm certain of is that I will also return to my home at The Holding after we've helped the villagers to survive this illness.' She slapped at the side of her head with one hand. 'Do you get strange feelings about places and people? Odd, familiar thoughts come unbidden to me. They're never strong and never clear, as if I'm seeing a blurred scene through a misty veil. I hate it! I don't even know if they are real or imaginary. Is it the same for you?'

'No, I never seem to have any kind of visions. However, I sometimes have dreams which seem to be parables for something else. Apparently, men rarely have the Sight, even imperfectly, and from what I've been told I don't want it because those poor women who do are often driven mad.'

Maeve shuddered. 'To know if my Sven was going to die . . . or my dear Valdar . . . or you . . . would be a curse that no rational person would want to contemplate. I can understand why a woman's brain would crumble if she had such terrible fore-knowledge.'

'My only gift is a warning when danger threatens, and it scratches at the inside of my skull even as we speak. You're dancing with the devil, Maeve! Frodhi can take you captive and force Valdar to obey his every command. I'm still unsure of his intentions but be prepared, because that snake'll have something in mind. Understand, too, that there is an utterly ruthless brain behind his charming smile. He'd happily allow other unfortunates to perish if it's to his advantage.'

The sea surged around the prow of *Sea Wife*. Above them, the massive sail caught the wind and billowed out so that she seemed to be flying over the waters. The crew rested in the sunshine, cleaned their weapons or chatted, while their imaginations drifted to the prospects of their new lives in the lands of Britain.

Vague speculation on the horrors of Justinian's Disease and the uglier whispers of Frodhi's murderous route to the throne fuelled their suspicion and anxiety. None of the Dene warriors really wanted to venture close to Heorot.

'How will you avoid the contagion, Arthur? I've heard tales of ships that were full of dead men, drifting on the currents for years. Greedy thieves and fishermen who have stolen from these bloated corpses are believed to have caught the disease and died not long after. I'm fearful for your safety, brother. I know you well: you won't stay quietly in *Sea Wife*.'

'Don't be! I've developed a strategy that should ensure that I don't carry any contagions back to my ship. My men will stay aboard the longboats and won't be permitted to come ashore. My archers have already been instructed to kill any person who tries to board our vessels. It would be better to kill at a distance, but they can take any action they feel is necessary to ensure that my orders are obeyed.'

Maeve looked much happier after hearing of Arthur's sensible arrangements, but her face creased in concern when she wondered how her brother intended to ferry her to dry land.

'Don't fret, little sister! I plan to land you, safe and sound, in the village below Heorot. We shall take you ashore by canoe, just like the ones used by the men in the Land of Eternal Ice. You and Lorcan will land and, once the way is cleared, you'll approach the great hall in company with Germanus and me.' He smiled into Maeve's eyes. 'You're staring at me as if you're frightened for my welfare, dear heart, but I beg you not to be over-concerned. Germanus is immune to the disease, and I intend to wear gloves and cover my mouth, nose and ears with clean white cloth. I don't intend to take greater risks than are absolutely necessary.'

Maeve knew her brother far too well to believe that he was even half as casual as he sounded. She hugged herself around the waist and rocked gently with the movement of the longboat. Then, when Arthur lifted her chin, he could see fat, sluggish tears rolling down her cheeks unchecked.

'I wish Blaise had chosen to return to Britain with you. I'm afraid that she'll never marry in the Dene lands for she developed a fearsome reputation for carnage during the defence of The Holding. She says that she has no need for a man in her life. I believe she regularly takes lovers, but she has refused to accept any offers of marriage.'

Arthur shrugged. 'Have you ever thought that she would be reluctant to leave her brother's ashes in an alien land when he was killed so far from his hearth and home? Perhaps she also wishes to remain unwed so she's not under the control of a man – even one who loves her. I can understand her reluctance to relinquish her freedom.'

'Really?' Maeve considered this proposition, then nodded. 'That would be just like her. What's to become of her, Arthur?'

'She'll live and she'll decide. God doesn't promise that life will be an easy road. Father Bedwyr told us on many occasions that we should live our lives as well as we can, while hurting as few people as possible when we follow our chosen paths.'

Maeve gurgled, somewhere between a laugh and a sob. 'But I know you've killed many men during your life, so you've left women and orphans aplenty behind you. How can you bear those stains on your soul? Don't you have regrets?'

'I can't weep for my way of life as you do, Maeve. Men are tied down by their masculinity just as inextricably as women are tied to family. I just follow the pathways that all men of honour should travel. I attempt to kill my enemies from the front and I damn no man who faces me fairly to unnecessary pain or suffering.'

Maeve cursed her foolishness for she had heard rumours of how Arthur had extracted the full measure of Aednetta Fridasdottar's treachery through torture and she regretted the conversation that had brought shadows into her brother's eyes.

'I wish you good afternoon, brother. If I've brought you any pain with my gibble-gabble, then I am sincerely sorry. I'll sleep now so I don't think of little Sven and how much I will miss him during my absence. I'll miss you when you return to Britain, but I'm not sorry in the least to offer aid to the Heorot villagers. They were generous to us at a time when we needed help. And now children no older than Sven are suffering and dying. I hope you understand, Arthur, because Valdar doesn't.'

Arthur lightly kissed her soft mouth, and tasted the sweetness of wild honey. His little sister was an extraordinary young woman.

'If there was another maid in my life half as good as you, little sister, I'd be happily wed by now.' He was joking, but his laughter failed to reach his eyes.

Maeve turned back from the stern where Arthur's female slaves were minding young Ingmar or trying to sleep under the pleasant warmth of the sun. She could see that Sigrid's skin had browned to the shade of pale gold and the same colour glistened in her pale-ash hair.

'Perhaps a suitable maid might be closer at hand than you think, brother.'

Arthur briefly looked struck by an unexpected pang. Then he strode away towards the prow of his vessel where he could watch the heaving flow of water passing under the hull in an unending, blue-grey reel.

* * *

Limfjord loomed as grim and as forbidding as Arthur remembered it. In light rain, the crew huddled in their oilskins and rowed through the narrow entrance to the safe mooring that lay between the soaring walls of the fjord. This time, no ram's horn trumpeted out a warning to Heorot that vessels were approaching.

'If all goes to plan, the bulk of my fleet will meet me at the entrance to Limfjord in a week or so. This allows time aplenty to gauge the situation in Heorot when we make landfall. I can still override you, Maeve, and I will send you home if conditions in Heorot and its village are too dangerous.'

Maeve began to protest but Arthur cut her short. 'I'll insist that you comply with my wishes. If Heorot should prove to be unsafe and violence imminent, you'll never set foot on its soil. I've given my promise to Valdar, and I keep my word. Risking your life by pitting your limited knowledge against a deadly disease is one thing, but attempting to fight a crazed populace is a totally different proposition.'

'But I'll have Father Lorcan to protect me in Heorot,' Maeve began, but her brother shook his head vigorously.

'Four or five years ago, I would have left you with Lorcan without any hesitation, but he's not as fast or as strong as he once was. I'm sorry to be blunt, Father, but I'm speaking the truth.'

The old man rubbed his whiskery chin and grunted his agreement. 'I'd like to say I could protect you in any situation, Lady Maeve, but Arthur's right – damn him! Sword play is beyond me.'

Arthur knew that this admission was made at some cost to the elderly man, so he honoured Lorcan for his courage.

'A man's worth isn't measured by the strength of his arms, Lorcan, as you know. Courage is worth much more than the ability to lift a sword.'

'I know, lad, but growing old is a fair bitch.'

'Germanus and I will explore the village and the hall. If we haven't returned by nightfall, I've told Gareth to abandon us and take the canoe out to *Sea Wife* from his position on the shore. Once there, he will prepare for a quick departure if necessary. However, he can remain at the mooring for some days in case we are simply delayed. Don't come after us, Maeve, I beg you. After all, the only reason I won't return is because I have contracted the disease.'

Maeve reluctantly agreed. Meanwhile, Germanus and Gareth had assembled an odd contraption of willow wands, light pine and pliant leather to form a long, narrow canoe. Three sets of paddles were laid out on the bench seats.

'Stay here until we return, Maeve,' Arthur repeated.

The canoe was carefully lowered into the water and held close to the longboat by two crewmen as Arthur, Gareth and Germanus seated themselves inside. Arthur dipped his paddle into the waters and the canoe began to scoot over the waves.

Ahead of them, the village was silent and empty. Arthur knew that small boats and coracles would normally have been thick on the sheltered waters closer to the shore; instead, the various craft were drawn up neatly on the shingled beach. Dry nets hung tidily from frames, and the usual bustle of the paved area close to the shore was stilled.

Even the sea seemed to be breathing softly, yet the soft whirl in his skull was warning Arthur that this village was in terrible trouble.

With a sigh, he shoved his suspicions into the back of his mind. They would know the worst when Heorot's village was reached.

The unconventional vessel must have been seen from the

village at the foot of the low hill, yet no souls were stirring in the houses that staggered along the slopes of the hill. As the three warriors pulled the canoe above the high-tide mark, they could feel hidden eyes boring into their backs. Silence surrounded them, as if the inhabitants were holding their breath.

'I don't like it here, Arthur,' Gareth muttered. 'If any place can be haunted by wights, then this is it.'

'There's a stink of burning in the air, but none of the outward signs of a town that's been attacked by the contagion,' Germanus observed. Somehow, the normality of the situation was more frightening than if dead bodies had been piled in the streets.

Arthur opened the door to a simple house that he remembered as belonging to a fisherman. As soon as he did a putrid reek flooded out from the interior, making Germanus and Gareth reel back, coughing and choking. Behind his protective scarf, Arthur paled but forced himself to advance into the room.

The smell of putrefaction suggested that all persons inside the cottage were dead, but a woman was sitting beside the house's fire pit while rocking the swollen corpse of an infant. Around her, two more children and a man, all dead and in various stages of decomposition, were neatly tucked into sleeping pallets. Except for the foul odour, the cottage was unnaturally neat and tidy.

Gagging, Arthur tried to remove the infant from the woman's arms but she resisted him with determination, so Germanus helped him to break the terrible death-like grip. As he dragged her out of the cottage her eyes were like empty holes of madness within her skull.

'Remove this woman, and set fire to the cottage, Arthur. A cleansing fire is the only answer when a place is as contaminated as this structure,' Germanus instructed. He, too, was sickened.

As the flames caught, a few people began to appear in the streets. Arthur recognised a face here and there, especially the battered nose of a smith he had met during the long winter in the first year of Frodhi's rule.

'Smith? Do you remember me?'

The man nodded warily, although he glanced nervously towards the longboats in the bay, as if Arthur had brought an invasion fleet with him.

'Aye, you're the Last Dragon.' His voice revealed that the young man was terrified.

'You may tell your friends and neighbours that we've come in answer to a call from your king. He asked us to bring healers to your people during this time of terrible sickness. Lord Stormbringer couldn't come in person, but he has sent his wife, Maeve, who is also my sister. You might remember her from our first visit to Heorot. Maeve is very skilled in the art of healing and she is accompanied by Father Lorcan, a priest who is familiar with this disease and understands its onset and symptoms.'

'Was your lady sister the girl with the black hair? We've heard word of her brother, the young man who died during your battles with the Geats.' The smith's face had cleared slightly at the welcome news.

'No, my sister has red hair. She is the one who insulted Hrolf Kraki's witch-woman to her face.'

The villagers nodded, for they remembered the brave and beautiful girl. The smith spat on his hand and offered it to Arthur, who accepted the risk, for the man appeared to be hale and strong.

'My name is Knut Hard-hand and I have served as the king's smith in recent years. I've never known such terrible times as those we have suffered since the murder of the Crow King.

Perhaps Hrolf Kraki has cursed his people from the cold halls of Asgaad.'

'How many souls are dead in this village, Knut, as distinct from those who have died in Frodhi's hall?'

'At least half the villagers are dead, lord. The old folk seemed to catch the illness first, then the children began to sicken. Now . . . well, we wait to see what new horrors come to us with the start of each day. Any help you bring will be welcome, because our herb-woman doesn't know what to do.'

'Can you find a clean cottage which we can use as a hospice? It must be outside the village boundaries, somewhere the contagion hasn't visited. The priest and my sister will treat the sick from this building once they have made their preparations. We intend to treat your villagers first, so I'll send for the healers as soon as you find a suitable house for them. They will also require the assistance of your herb-woman, so she must be ordered to follow the instructions of my healers without comment. You can tell her that her own life will be forfeit if she doesn't obey. Maeve will need a good supply of clean water – and I mean *clean* water – from a supply uncontaminated by human contact. She will also need all the soporifics that your herb-woman possesses, including poppy and henbane. Can you provide these needful things?'

'Aye! And gladly! I'll take the herb-woman with me to collect her stores. As for this poor bitch, she is scarcely twenty years and she's lost everything of value, including her kin. But if she was going to die from this disease, I think she'd have caught it already.'

The blacksmith took the grieving woman held by Germanus from the Frank's grasp and pushed her into the welcoming arms of his wife.

Germanus beckoned the men of the village into a small group.

'Have you been burning your dead? If not, you must do so immediately, along with all bedding and clothing in the infected houses – even if there are survivors living there. When I caught the disease, I was bitten by something, probably a bedbug. I don't know for certain if these small creatures cause the illness, but I've always wondered. You cannot be too careful. The herb-woman must also dispose of her clothing, in case she should contaminate our treatment house. I know winter is coming, but we must wash fire over all suspected objects within the affected areas and leave the houses empty until the snows arrive. Justinian's Disease hates fire, and it hates cold weather.'

Knut nodded. 'We will follow your instructions, my lord. The king has been hiding in Heorot and totally ignores our suffering. Thanks be to God that someone has finally come to relieve us in our time of troubles.'

'I can't guarantee that my sister and Father Lorcan can stop all of the deaths, but they can help those who are ill. This disease doesn't care if you're a king or a whore, it devours you just the same.' Arthur's words brought nods of agreement from the crowd.

'Gareth, could you fetch Maeve and Lorcan? Germanus and I are going up to Heorot to speak with Frodhi.'

Gareth refused to budge until Germanus assured him that Arthur would be safe; finally, he ran off down the hill to the canoe.

'Be careful up there, my lord,' Knut advised. 'No one has come out of Heorot for two days and we've no intention of going up there to see what's been happening.'

Arthur was silent as he started the steep climb to the platform on which the forecourt of Heorot was built. Here, he had fought the Troll King who was now waiting on one of Arthur's vessels to undertake the long journey to Britannia.

It was here too, that his friend, Eamonn, had battled Rufus. Arthur recalled the foolish boy he had been, so concerned with duty and honour, but so ignorant of how to lead men and how to make his way in a strange land. He owed everything he had become to Stormbringer, now his kin by marriage.

He had learned to lead men in the deadly and strategic games of war; he had won a great fortune that would buy him a kingdom, and he had amassed a small army of loyal men who stood at his back but, as yet, called no living man their king. He was their leader because of his fighting prowess; he accepted that the day would soon come when they would kneel before him and call him king.

Looking out over the village, he could see the scene that had lain before him on the day of his mortal combat with Thorketil. On that day, the landscape had been misty and half-seen. It was clear and silent today, for the trees wore their autumn leaves like a cloak of bronze and gold. The waters of the fjord were still rising, for the occasional skeletal branches of trees could be seen below the surface.

'I have stood here on a previous occasion, dear Lord, but this will be the last time. Please allow me to survive this test so I can return to my kinfolk in Britain,' he prayed. 'I'll try to do what is right, or I won't deserve your mercy. Protect me, give me strength and allow me to help these people in their time of need.'

THE BARRACKS BEHIND HEOROT

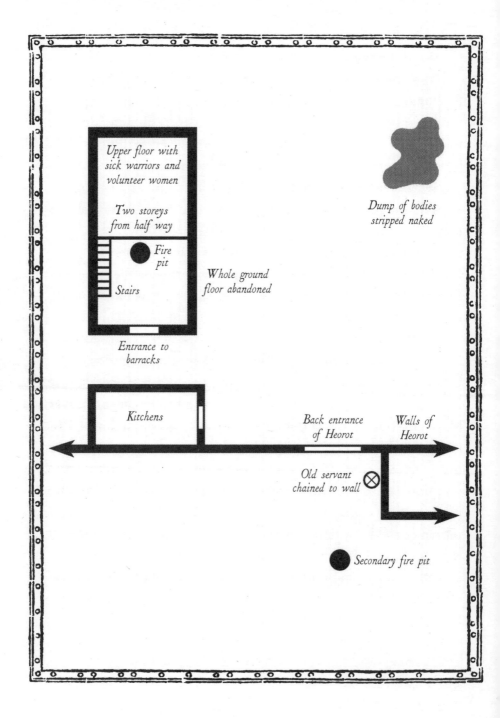

Upper floor with
sick warriors and
volunteer women

Two storeys
from half way

Fire
pit

Stairs

Whole ground
floor abandoned

Entrance to
barracks

Dump of bodies
stripped naked

Kitchens

Back entrance
of Heorot

Walls of
Heorot

Old servant
chained to wall

Secondary fire pit

CHAPTER XVI

GRENDEL'S CURSE

Natura dat unicuique quod sibi conveniens est.
(Nature gives to each what is appropriate.)

Auctoritates Aristotelis

Only the rising afternoon wind gave the appearance of life in the vicinity of Heorot. In the field behind it, Arthur's large army had camped when he forced Hrolf Kraki to accept that Aednetta Fridasdottar was a traitor, but their presence had only served to trigger the regicide of the Crow King. The traitor and murderer, Frodhi, ruled over Heorot now, assuming he was still alive.

'We'll circle around the building first, Germanus. If in doubt, we should go in through the back door,' Arthur suggested.

Germanus agreed. Something about the stillness, the early fall of amber leaves that had been left to rot against the hall and a feeling of abandonment warned the old warrior that danger lay around him.

'There's something about this place that smells very wrong,' Germanus muttered, while he searched for some sign of a threat.

Then, at the rear of Heorot, they found the answer to the eerie stillness.

Someone had used the empty space behind the building as a dumping ground where the bodies of the dead from within the barracks and the hall could be piled. Sun-bleached, swollen, and with split abdomens and empty eye sockets, the naked corpses stared into an unheeding sky. The huge pile contained well over fifty bodies and writhed with life from the insects and larvae that were feeding on them. Larger scavengers – crows, ravens, shrikes, dogs, cats, and especially rats – gave the corpses an obscene parody of movement.

Both men felt their gorges rise. In days gone by, only the worst of felons were abandoned after such a grisly end to life. Northerners were prepared to pay rings of gold and silver to recover their dead killed in battle so their warriors could be accorded clean and noble passage to Valhalla.

'What animals could have left them like this? At the very least, burning would have given them a decent ending to their lives – but this is an abomination.'

No worse fate could await a warrior than to have their remains cast away like rubbish. Far worse for those who survived the illness would be the knowledge that their compatriots' remains had been desecrated by scavengers. The bodies of female slaves had been permitted to lie among the abandoned sprawl of death, a further insult.

'I think we'll look inside the barracks first, Germanus. For some reason, I'm afraid to enter Heorot itself. Those fucking bones from that fucking Grendel and his fucking mother seem to have poisoned the air around the king's hall.' Arthur laughed shakily. 'Grendel and his bitch of a mother, whoever they damned well were, were accorded more respect than Frodhi's own men, noble warriors who were loyal to a man. Frodhi has much to answer for.'

Arthur avoided unpalatable duties so rarely that Germanus was surprised. He was a little chary himself now that he had seen his charge's reaction. With some reluctance, he padded after Arthur towards the separate barracks, which were built without the usual stone bases designed to elevate the floors above the chilling earth.

Steeling himself against thoughts of finding a barracks building filled with corpses and dying men, Arthur strode towards the main entry with his shoulders squared manfully. He noticed that moss had been stuffed into the gaps between the building's timbers to repel draughts. Even so, the wind had been rising as the afternoon advanced, and had begun to whistle through the rafters with a mournful cry that sounded like high-pitched moaning. Fleetingly, Arthur wondered if the barracks was mourning its dead inhabitants.

The emptiness of the first half of the barracks was an anticlimax. The main room, filled with sleeping pallets that encircled its central fire pit, was otherwise utterly bare. Because of the height of the roof here, the footfalls of the two intruders were unnaturally loud in the emptiness of its bleak spaces. A steep staircase along one wall indicated that an upper floor had been raised over the back half of the building.

At the far end of the room, a set of folding walls and doors had been built across its width, leaving a narrow gap in the middle just wide enough for a man to squeeze through.

'I suppose we must enter that room and go to the second floor as well,' Arthur said, looking at the rough stairs. 'The barracks are quite sensibly laid out; our officers were billeted here three years ago.'

He pointed to a series of tables that had been pushed against the half-wall as screens. 'This was where they ate until the men became sick. Someone has tried to separate the sick warriors from the well.'

'There's no sense in putting off the inevitable,' Germanus decided manfully and marched up to the screen which he pushed aside carefully. Feeling like a coward, Arthur joined him.

They could clearly see evidence that the room had been used for the treatment of deathly ill patients, but no one had chosen to clean up the detritus: bowls of water tinged with blood, soiled bandages tossed into darkened corners. Similarly, pallets had been stained with dried sweat and vomit, while several bowls of congealed stew indicated recent occupation.

Then both men heard a moaning sound that grew louder and louder until it was suddenly cut off as if a suffering man's mouth had been clamped shut. As they tried to identify the source of the noise, another, deeper series of cries told them that the rooms above were inhabited.

'Damnation!' Arthur swore as he raced back into the first room at a run. The stairs were sturdy, but the hand rails were rickety, and would be dangerous if anyone threw their whole weight upon them.

'Keep close to the left,' Arthur warned his friend and took the steps two at a time.

As he reached the top where a shuttered window was the only source of light, Arthur's second sense screamed a silent warning and he unhesitatingly dropped onto all fours. A sword blade sliced through the air; he felt the breeze of its passage as it narrowly missed his head. The figure on his left was only a dark shape muffled in a cloak, so Arthur charged at it and struck the body with the full force of his shoulder. He heard and felt the expelled air as it was forced out of an invisible abdomen. Then, with a wail, the figure fell to the ground.

Arthur drew the Dragon Knife and had it pressed against the assassin's muffled throat with blinding speed. He would have rammed the eager blade home, but the figure coughed and moaned with a distinctly female voice.

'Gerda?' a voice called from the semi-darkness. 'Who is it, for the gods' sake?'

'Peace! Peace!' Germanus shouted as a number of hunched figures tried to rise and several others, women to judge by their skirts, clutched besoms, spears and knives in their hands. They were ready to defend their menfolk with their lives.

'This man is Arthur,' Germanus continued. 'He is the Last Dragon, and he's brought healers to those of you who have been afflicted with the disease. Can we find some light in here? We're likely to fall arse over tit and accidentally hurt someone if we're not careful.'

One of the women attempted to raise a spark in a small bowl of tinder. A prepared torch was leaning against the wall, evidently guarded for an emergency.

With much heaving of an ample bosom, the woman under his knife on the floor was trying to catch her breath. Arthur apologised profusely, just as the tinder caught and the head of the torch was thrust into its feeble flame. Once lit, the scene was much as Arthur had been expecting.

Some thirty men were crammed into a space which covered half the length of the entire barracks block. Positioned right under the roof, and with the single window at the southern end shuttered and covered, the patients were unable to enjoy any light or fresh air. Arthur ordered that this window should be opened wide. The torchlight also revealed a small group of women who were striving to care for the sick, their faces strained as they started to clean the filthy floors. Some men in rough night shifts were helping; their pallor and extreme thinness indicated that these happy few had managed to survive the illness.

Before Arthur had time to speak a word, a harsh voice ordered them to drop their weapons. Five armed men were standing behind them on the stairs with swords bared and eyes that were hard and suspicious.

'Who are you and why have you come to Heorot? The longboats in the anchorage are obviously yours so I'd suggest you think again if you intend to rob us while our defences are weak.'

Arthur bared his head and lowered the Dragon Knife.

'Don't you recognise me? I'm Arthur, the Last Dragon, and I'm here on the orders of Stormbringer to bring your town back to good health. Surely the last few years haven't entirely robbed you of your memory.'

One of the men responded from the stairway, even as another pushed his way through to stand upright under the low rafters.

'I remember you, my lord. I was the guard who fell asleep when the witch-woman was murdered. My name is Karl, but I'm also called The Owl as a punishment for that dreadful night. God alone knows why, but the foul disease has decided to pass me by. I still see you in my sleep when the night horrors come to me. But you were kind to me when every other jarl turned away; Lord Frodhi permitted me to live with my shame and to consider my failure throughout the remainder of my life. I've often wished I'd been executed on the spot.'

'But an owl is also a raptor, Karl, the most dangerous night hunter of them all.' Arthur spoke quietly and respectfully. 'And I'm prepared to state publicly that you were never at fault in the death of Aednetta Fridasdottar,' he went on firmly, making certain that the whole room echoed with his response. 'You were drugged as part of a larger plot so that you couldn't hear the cries of the victim. Your reputation was deliberately besmirched by a man who saw you as having less worth than a favoured hound. I cannot speak the name of the culprit for reasons of state, and I cannot call the guilty person to account for the suffering endured by the Crow King, his witch-woman and yourself, for you are as much a victim as they were. I, for one, could bear death more easily than the loss of my reputation.'

Karl, who was still very young and obviously deeply wounded by his experiences during the past few years, continued to hang his head as if he was a convicted felon.

'Stand up straight, Karl, so we can speak plainly about this situation.'

Arthur turned to face his audience. 'Listen to me, both sick and hale men of Heorot. I found that your companion was innocent of sleeping on guard duty at the time of your erstwhile king's death, so nothing more should be said of this matter. For now, we must attack the dreaded disease that has afflicted your people. I'm sent to you by the Sae Dene king who has tasked my healers to relieve the suffering in this hall and in your village. Put up your swords. Immediately! I've no desire to kill you, but I'll tolerate no more nonsense.'

Shamefaced, the warriors sheathed their weapons while Arthur pulled the winded woman back onto her feet.

'Explain the conditions of your remaining patients, woman.' Arthur was smiling at the plump matron, despite having to suppress his natural anger at the conduct of King Frodhi. He knew that any show of anger would frighten the already terrified patients and their carers.

As the woman gave him her assessment, she admitted that her knowledge of the incidence of the disease in the village was minimal.

'My own man is dead now, but how could I not try to save as many boys as I could? All of us women have loved ones here, or we had them before they died.'

There was no answer to this, so Arthur set about imposing some form of order on the barracks. He ordered three of the men and two of the women to go to the kitchens to prepare hot food for those who could still eat. Similarly, pre-boiled water was a necessity for washing and drinking. Fresh milk would also be needed, if they were to save those citizens who had any chance of survival.

'While we are at it, I want three of our survivors to collect all the firewood they can find. They can use timber from the hall itself if they must. Then I want them to erect a large bonfire over the remains of those good warriors in the field at the rear of the king's hall. Once lit, the fire will be kept burning until all the bodies have been turned to ash. Good men should not be permitted to rot where their corpses are at the mercy of carrion birds and other vermin.'

Arthur's voice was so scornful that Karl excused himself and tried to explain the charnel house in the fields.

'Our king instructed us to place our dead outside the rear of the barracks. His servants collected the corpses and piled them up, exactly as you have seen. We are forbidden to enter the great hall on pain of death, even if we're searching for food or supplies. As you can see, Lord Arthur, we have no food stored here, for the servants of King Frodhi took everything when the first warriors became ill. We've been forced to live on the charity of the villagers and any supplies we can beg, borrow or steal. We'll be cast out if we attempt to obey you, just as we'll be killed if we take any of Heorot's timber supplies to despatch our companions in the flames.'

Arthur made an exclamation of disgust. 'Come, Germanus! We'll see if this king has the balls to stop me from taking what these good men need.'

Then he turned and moved down the stairs through the warriors as if they were as insubstantial as smoke. The two women and the armed men hurried to catch up.

Fury powered Arthur's legs as he strode to the back entry of this cursed place. He swung the door open with the heel of his hand, surprised that no one had sought to lock interlopers out of the building.

The interior was pitch-black, causing Arthur to stub a toe on a large chest placed on the floor near the entry. It had been dragged this far, as if someone was attempting to steal it. He felt the hair rise on the back of his neck, while his second sense scratched at his brain with a sharp claw.

Germanus had found the stump of a torch, so he carried it with him as they searched for the smaller fire pit where meals were cooked by the king's servants. Above them, the vast rafters were only dimly lit by light from the shuttered window in the rear wall. Even close to an open doorway, the hall seemed to reek of death and decay – overlaid with sweaty fear.

'I hate this fucking place, Arthur. I didn't like it when I first saw it, and I like it even less now.'

'Shhhh! The king's assassins could be standing behind us for all that we'd ever know.'

Germanus cursed and darted a quick glance over his shoulder, relieved to find that only breeze-blown shadows seemed to be dancing on the smoky walls.

'Ah! The fire pit! But it's almost dead. Where is everyone, Germanus?'

Almost on cue, something moved in the corner of a partitioned storeroom wall, so both men spun to face the tiny sound. Germanus thrust the remains of the torch into the almost cold coals of the fire pit and it gradually caught alight as it drew the dying heat from the embers. Arthur drew his weapons with a hiss of iron.

'Who are you? Stand forth so I can see you,' he ordered a bundle of rags that stirred with something resembling life.

'Please?' A cracked voice answered. 'I need water!'

Arthur ensured his mouth and nose were well covered, and then leaned down toward the shrouded figure. He held out one hand wordlessly towards Germanus who found a jug of water and a horn mug which he filled. Arthur handed it to two claw-like hands which raised the mug to a hidden mouth that greedily drained the fluid.

'More!' the grating voice begged and Arthur complied. Finally the figure waved the cup away and Arthur used his gloved hands to bare a grey-haired visage.

In the same instant, the torch leaped into vivid light as the oil-soaked rag finally burst into a generous flame. Germanus raised it and the face below Arthur became clear. It was female, and old before its time.

Her deep-set eyes were surrounded by a network of fine lines, while the cheekbones in her thin face were as sharp as knife blades. Her mouth was sunken, indicating that she had lost most of her teeth.

'Who are you?' Arthur smiled in as friendly a manner as he could muster.

'I'm a nothing, a slave who has seen things come and go at

Heorot. You can call me Asa. I can't tell you why I'm still living, except that the good Lord must have some purpose for me, one that I can't understand.'

'Where is everyone, Mother Asa? Where is the king?' Arthur's voice was persuasive as he searched for the old woman's hands and discovered fresh injuries around the wrists caused by very tight bonds. She had painstakingly removed the ropes over many hours. Then, when he searched for her feet, he discovered that they were both manacled to an iron ring set into the wall. The old woman would have died of thirst had they not come to her aid; her cracked lips spoke of a day or two without any liquid sustenance at all.

Asa coughed and Arthur realised that her voice had been ruined by hours of screaming for help that never came. Germanus found a wooden bucket of milk and she drank the thick liquid with every appearance of relish. The milk was old, but had remained drinkable in the cool autumn weather.

'I don't know where them stupid-arse soldiers be! I've not seen a soul for more than a day. The disease struck the hall a few days ago.' She paused, obviously trying to count the number, while Germanus started to prise apart her manacles with various tools he had found.

Her index finger on her right hand pointed out one finger after another on her left until eventually she stopped at seven.

'Seven?' Arthur asked, and the woman nodded.

'Yes, the king was still well at that time and he had all the sick people thrown into the great hall and had the doors locked. He ordered that none of the servants should go near him, no matter how much they begged, and we didn't know if we'd be joining the sick patients if we became sick ourselves. The king spent his days drinking and carousing with his women until he found the first swellings under his arms. He became angry and ordered everyone into the hall, whether healthy or not, and his warriors locked the doors from the inside. We slaves were the only people left free. Then, when the king started to go mad, the cook decided to steal some of his gold and, when I asked him what he intended to do, he said I could rot with the rest of them and chained me to the wall. Until you came, master, I thought I would die of thirst in there.'

'And you've seen no one since?' A growing and unpleasant suspicion had roughened Arthur's voice.

'I could hear them around the king's throne, for they were all drunk and singing at first. But they began to cry then when they started to sicken. We servants feared for our lives so the others eventually decided to run away. The cook thought I'd be too slow to keep up with him, and he was also worried that I might tell the villagers about the gold he had stolen.' She laughed raucously. 'Gold! Let's see if the plague gives a fuck about that!'

Then the manacles binding her to the wall gave way with a sudden tearing of metal.

'Go outside now, Mother, and make your way down to the village. If you haven't caught the disease by now, I'm certain that you will be spared from it. At any rate, this hell-pit isn't for one such as you.'

The servant gazed at Arthur's silvery eyes and something in them gave her a strength that surprised her. She was almost running as she left.

Arthur and Germanus wound their way through the half-rooms of Heorot until Arthur recognised the central door that led into the main hall. They put their shoulders to the doorframe until the crude fittings pulled away.

Now, as they entered the blackness of the unlit room, the

smell became suffocating. Germanus held the torch aloft to reveal a room full of corpses in various stages of decay. Some figures still stirred and moaned pitifully at the centre of what had been a hellish banquet.

The tables and benches had been set for a sumptuous feast. Containers of beer, wine and mead had been placed all over the tables, while the remains of maggoty food covered the table. The seated men seemed like a ghostly group of revellers caught by death in their drunkenness. Still others had curled up in the straw where they were lying in their own filth. The manner of their deaths beggared Arthur's imagination.

'I'll go to them, Arthur,' Germanus offered. 'It's perfectly safe for me to offer them some assistance.'

'Open the front doors first, if you can,' Arthur called after his friend. 'This pest hole begs for light and fresh air.' The sound echoed in the empty rafters where the only other sound was the busy patter of rats leaving their own banquets for the safety of darkness. Arthur shuddered at the thought.

A cackle of maniacal laughter further agitated the vermin within Heorot as Arthur spun to face the dim light that surrounded the throne. Then, with a crash, Germanus raised the long wooden bar and the doors of Heorot swung open in all their barbaric splendour.

To describe Frodhi and the two trollops who lolled at his feet on the dais as human beings was to take one step too far, given the sight that greeted Arthur when a cruel shaft of light arched towards him and exposed the king's rotting face.

'May God have mercy on you,' Arthur muttered softly. He recalled what Lorcan had told him about the disease when it was in its worst form, and looked closer at the horror-made-flesh sitting on the throne before him.

That Frodhi still lived was a miracle; Arthur wondered whether his constant recourse to alcohol had helped prolong the king's life. Two of five women still lay alive at his feet, but this pair were lolling with disease and drunkenness while struggling with a thirst that no amount of ale could quench. Nerveless fingers were unable to lift cups and they had descended to lapping like dogs drinking water. One of the women did so in front of Arthur, who turned away in horror and vomited into the filthy straw.

The light must have returned a short burst of sanity to the living corpse on the throne and the noise that came through the suppurating lips and nose sounded sane and suave once again.

'I always took you for a man with a girl's stomach, Arthur. Huh! It's always a pleasant experience to watch the squeamishness of an enemy. I suppose Stormbringer has finally stirred his farmer's arse and sent you and the healers to clean up this mess. I expect to be treated as quickly as possible. But first I want you to fill my mug.'

'What will I fill it with, Lord Frodhi?' Arthur managed to answer, once he readjusted his cloth to block his nose against the vile smell.

Germanus took the utensil from his master. 'Let me do it, Arthur,' he hissed with his back to the throne. 'You can't trust this man until such time as he's dead and past inflicting harm.'

When Germanus placed the mug in Frodhi's hands the king spat at him, the spittle landing on the Frank's cheek. The king then tried to spit at Arthur, but Arthur was too far away.

'I might have missed you, Arthur, but at least your hulking Frank will die now . . . and it will be your fault.' Frodhi giggled then, a sound far more terrible than any death rattle.

'You're a vicious man,' Germanus responded, and wiped the

spittle away with a torn piece of his shirt. The fragment of cloth was thrown into the cold fire pit. 'You're not a king's arsehole, Frodhi, unless you're prepared to answer to the title of Master of Corpses. You'll be pleased to know that I'm immune to Justinian's Disease, for I've survived it in the past. You can't hurt me, and I won't allow you to harm Arthur in any way. I must offer you my sincere felicitations on your kind thoughts towards us, my lord.'

Fear scudded through Frodhi's still-handsome eyes, but their expression finally matched his stomach-wrenching appearance.

'You wouldn't dare to touch me, you Frank bastard, for I'm still the King of the Dene. My warriors will have your head.'

'Are you speaking of the warriors you left without food when they were locked in their barracks? Or perhaps you are speaking of the warriors lying around you on the floor in their piss, shit and vomit? Perhaps you expect your jarls who are guarding your borders to save you. I'll warrant they're standing on the dykes that separate them from the Saxon lands and thanking their gods that you're far, far away from them.'

Arthur halted his diatribe to draw breath and to stare with loathing at this man who had caused so much death and heartache among the Dene people.

'You'll die soon in your own piss and shit,' Arthur continued mercilessly. 'I don't give a fuck how you feel except to pray devoutly that you suffer every moment until death takes you. I want you to die slowly for the death of my friend, Eamonn; for the Dene warriors of Skania who starved to death at the Vagus River; for the children who were sold into the brothels of the east; for the many innocents who died at Lake Wener and, finally, for those warriors who perished in the marshes beyond the border lands, the Daneverke whom the Hundings killed before we brought their depredations to a halt. Ultimately, your

suffering is because of the crimes you inflicted on Hrolf Kraki
and Aednetta Fridasdottar. As the ancients once swore, the gods
should never be mocked – and now you must pay the price.'

Then Arthur turned to face Germanus.

'Instruct the able to remove the warriors and women who are
still alive. Have them placed somewhere central where we can
assess their chances of survival. On pain of incurring my severe
displeasure, they are not to touch King Frodhi on his throne.
Poison is dripping from that man, and he can remain there until
he passes into eternity. Warn the servants too that they must not
come within spitting distance of this creature. It's best that he
dies alone and untouched . . . and I now need some fresh air
before I vomit again.'

Arthur hurried out into the clean air. The sun was sliding behind
a bank of clouds, as if nature itself might be shrinking from the
visions of festering flesh. Certainly, Grendel and his mother
would be laughing beyond the shades at the justice that had
been dealt out to their avowed enemies.

Then the sun disappeared and only the sound of high-pitched
laughter disturbed the crows nesting in the highest branches of
the pine trees. Even the scavengers of the night scorned to enter
the dark maw of Heorot; evil dwelled in this place, and only
cleansing fire could erase the old wickedness from the Limfjord.

The night was dark and very still.

LANDFALL

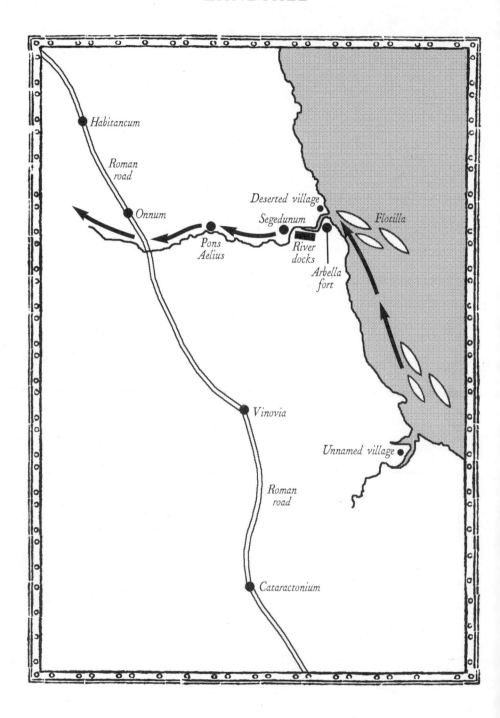

CHAPTER XVII

A FOOTHOLD

Nemo bonus Britto est.
(No good man is a Briton.)

Decius Magnus Ausonius, *Epigrams*

The long, grey waves stretched ahead of the flotilla that followed the sail with the red dragon emblazoned on its vast surface. Winter was coming and the slate-coloured British skies were streaked through with charcoal, dove-grey and silver, while the sea's hues shaded to midnight-black in places. For the first time on this journey, gulls were screaming for scraps to squabble over as the ships approached their disembarkation point.

'We can't be very far from land now,' Arthur said to Ingrid who was standing beside him. The wind lifted her white-gold braid until it was a banner streaming behind her. Several men from the crew were gazing lustfully at her matronly body.

Arthur knew that such proximity would be a trial for any man with red blood in his veins, forced to live cheek by jowl with Ingrid and Sigrid for weeks on end.

'Is there any sight of land, Snorri?' Arthur called to his

helmsman who was acting as lookout as well. From his position high in the stern, Snorri had been scanning the distant horizon.

'Aye, master, can you see the grey line in the distance? It's landfall at last!'

Arthur gazed over the prow, forced to squint against the glare thrown up from the sea and the intermittent sunlight. But then he recognised it, a thin line of charcoal with an irregular edge.

'Aye, it's surely Britannia . . .' Only Ingrid heard; she began to reach out to touch his stiffening shoulder but then thought better of it. Her master's profile was showing the stiff, unrelenting willpower that had brought this fleet into dangerous and alien waters to a land that was beyond her understanding.

'The first snows will be here soon and we must have palisades and shelters built before then. We must also ensure the fields are ploughed before the earth turns to iron and next year's crops must be planted. Time is marching on and it will drag us in its wake if we aren't ready.'

Snorri nodded his understanding as *Sea Wife* ploughed on with a fresh breeze filling her enormous sail.

A week had passed quickly at Heorot as Arthur forced some degree of order out of the chaos caused by Justinian's Disease. Drunk and raving, Frodhi sat on his throne for three days as the strength departed from his legs and all reason fled from his brain. When he breathed his last, none of the warriors, servants or villagers would approach the swollen and menacing corpse, either for silver or any other reward. Germanus, Lorcan and two other survivors eventually took on the distasteful task so that Frodhi's remains could be burned without ceremony, and the throne could be cleansed for the new king, another of Stormbringer's cousins.

Meanwhile, the land was bereft; for now, the fields would lie fallow and cottages would rot until such time as new generations of younger Dene farmers replaced those who had died.

Under Maeve's ministrations, the number of new victims declined sharply and more patients seemed to be surviving. Clean air, nutritious food, bathing and plentiful pre-boiled fluids saved many lives, as did the care given by the women who provided the bulk of the nursing. Father Lorcan carried out lancings and amputations, using the techniques he had first learned when treating Germanus in the land of the Franks.

Maeve quickly began to organise the care of the sick warriors who had been abandoned in the barracks. She provided the upper rooms with nutritious foods, milk and clean water, and most importantly the fire pits on the floor below were kept alight.

The last survivors of Death's Banquet, as Frodhi's mad feast had been called by the peasants, were removed to a central downstairs room where their kinswomen could nurse them. Unfortunately, most died because of initial neglect during the early stages of the illness.

Arthur's eyes had filled with tears when his sister had looked up at him after he called her name at the entrance to her hospice. Her hair had come down, her eyes were glowing and she was flushed with exertion after boiling a huge cauldron of rags to use as dressings. What a woman she was, a worthy queen of the Sae Dene who would become a superb mother of fighting men.

Then, as Arthur glanced up at the menacing façade of Heorot still bearing its grisly trophies, something snapped in his head.

'Take down those fucking bones, Snorri. You can collect the gold and give it to the widows, although it's no recompense for the loss of their kin. Then add those hideous relics to the fire to join the remains of King Frodhi; with luck, Heorot's curse will burn as well. Afterwards use whatever labour can be found to scour that building until it's clean – we should let the new king, Halfdan, begin his reign without the bad luck that has preyed on the Dene kings since they began to display their arrogance.'

Father Lorcan had watched as Snorri climbed a tall ladder to reach those grim bones. With a curse, he tossed the relics onto the cobbles of the forecourt where several shattered within their net of shining gold.

'I don't see myself as a coward, but my heart quails at the thought of even touching them,' Germanus stated with a deep shudder.

The skull fell to the ground, cracking across the crown like a smashed egg.

'I'll collect the pieces, Arthur,' Lorcan suggested. 'I'm a man of God, so no curse laid by pagans can harm me. Let me perform this small chore out of the love I hold for you, my friend.'

'No, Lorcan. If any objects on this earth come from your Satan, then it's these ancient relics. I can't allow you to soil your hands on them.' Arthur was adamant and Snorri, who had leaped down from the ladder, used his cloak to scoop them up.

'I'm not afraid of a few fucking bones. Grendel can have me, if he wants to be kept from the flames,' Snorri joked, before striding off to the funeral pyre with his unholy spoils.

'Is there anything else I can do for you, dear boy?' Lorcan asked wistfully. 'I'm fast becoming an old man, but I'll try to help you in any way I can before you sail off to God-knows-where.'

The priest's eyes were suddenly tearful. 'How else can I show the love I have felt for you, Arthur? You'll be leaving this wicked place soon, and we'll not meet again in this world.'

Because his heart was breaking, Arthur took Lorcan in his

arms and held the fragile old man close to his heart. 'The best gift you can give me is to pray for me whenever I enter your thoughts, Father, for I'll need your help during the months and years that lie ahead. I didn't think that parting from a lifelong friend could be so hard.'

And so the bones of Grendel and his mother were consigned to the cleansing flames, but heartened as he was by Lorcan's demonstration of love, Arthur could still smell the stink of corruption from the funerary pyre.

Gradually, the charcoal-grey land became clearer and clearer, and Arthur arrived at a decision. Although the eastern coastline of Britain was largely unfamiliar to him, he had passed through these lands years earlier, but at this particular juncture, he had no idea where he was.

'Instruct the fleet to move to the north and wait for us off that headland over there,' he instructed Snorri. 'I'll take the canoe to one of the local villages and establish our exact position.'

Snorri looked at him doubtfully.

'I'll be careful, Snorri. I speak Saxon and Celt, with Latin as a back-up, so I'll discover where we are fairly quickly. Look over there! I can see smoke rising in that little bay, so I'll head for there in the canoe and rejoin you as soon as I can.'

'At least take Germanus with you, master, for we'll be in all sorts of trouble if you are killed or injured.' Snorri was looking thoroughly alarmed at this prospect, so Arthur agreed. Then he decided to take Gareth too, rather than endure the younger man's protests. Gareth had steadfastly refused to let Arthur out of his sight in times of danger.

'Is that better, Snorri? I'll have two men at my back which, I admit, seems a sensible idea. You can't come with me because you're acting captain of *Sea Wife* in my absence. Take good care of her!'

Snorri grumbled and commiserated with Sigrid, who shared his concerns. But both knew that their master only listened to one voice, the one that lived deep within his brain.

Arthur, Germanus and Gareth climbed nimbly down the side of *Sea Wife* and into the canoe. Once they were settled into position and had readied their paddles, Arthur loosened the rope that bound them to the longboat and the three friends began the two-mile paddle to reach the shore.

As they drew closer they saw the floating detritus of a swiftly flowing river and the evidence of habitable land. A tree branch proclaimed itself to be pine, still with some of its cones attached. Arthur lifted one of the smaller offshoots out of the water for a short moment and inhaled the resinous smell, overlaid with salt. The northern climes had pines aplenty, but Arthur imagined that this one had a special smell that Britain alone could produce. Gareth agreed with him; Germanus, who understood that the aroma of these needles was the same as elsewhere in the northern lands, nevertheless sympathised with the expressions of joy on their glowing faces.

As they rounded a small headland near the mouth of the large river, Arthur saw the first signs of habitation. 'There! We'll seek out information at that little village to the right of the dunes where the smoke is rising. If there's a village, there must be a larger town further upriver.'

They paddled on, almost flying across the open waters. The night was coming in rags of darkness across a setting sun as they passed by the village, because Arthur had decided to find a sheltered spot where they could hide the canoe *before* confronting the inhabitants.

Once on land they quickly hid the canoe in the copse of low shrubs that proliferated above the high-tide mark.

'The villagers will consider us to be barbarians when we arrive, heavily armed, on their doorsteps, and they'll be scared.' Arthur suddenly realised how odd the three warriors would look to the Saxon or Celt inhabitants. 'Well, it's far too late for us to hide the fact that we are outlanders, so it's probably best to simply tell them the truth of our intentions as far as possible.'

Germanus grinned sadly. 'Now would be the perfect time for Lorcan to make one of his bad jests about the things that lie before us. Aye, but I'm sorely missing my Hibernian friend.'

'I know how you feel,' Arthur said. 'It's strange to make a journey such as this without him at our heels, talking and talking. I miss his incessant chatter.'

'And his rotten jokes,' Gareth added as he grasped clumps of grass to climb the dune.

'But my friend was ageing towards the end, and he told me that he was enjoying his life at The Holding. He'd put down roots there and was happy. It's odd, Arthur! I left a wife and two sons at home in Arden, and I set off in pursuit of you without a second thought. I hope they'll be there when we return, because my wife is a good girl.' Then Germanus sighed.

'He's happy with the choice he made,' Arthur agreed, as he joined Gareth on the lip of the dune. 'He sees himself now as the protector of Blaise and Maeve. He'll teach young Sven to read and write, and he'll do his best to ensure that a new Sae Dene king will be ready to fulfil his destiny after the death of his father. I can only hope the plague doesn't visit The Holding.'

'But will it?' Gareth asked, frowning.

'We'll find out when we send our trading vessels back to collect the women and children and our goods and chattels.

There might be other volunteers seeking a new life in other lands. Of one thing I am certain, Germanus. Many Dene men, women and children will die as a result of this scourge. In the past, Stormbringer has worried that the burgeoning population would outgrow the arable land available, but Justinian's Disease will put an end to those fears. I suspect it will be generations before the Dene will be forced to sally forth and find new homelands.'

'What are we doing then, Arthur? Why have four hundred Norwegians, Denes and even some Geats chosen to follow you into what seems to them to be a wilderness?' Gareth was honestly confused.

'Don't be such a dolt, boy,' Germanus reprimanded him. 'They have a leader in whom they have confidence, and Arthur represents their best chance to obtain riches beyond their wildest dreams.'

'I meant no offence,' Gareth replied. Although he was a grown man now, one with a slew of female admirers and a goodly portion of gold in the hold of *Sea Wife*, in some respects he was still the boy of eighteen who had followed Arthur into an impossibly dangerous and foreign world with such determination.

As the sun lowered towards the horizon, the three men could see the village fires becoming brighter in the fading light as women added extra firewood to the fire pits and hung huge cauldrons over blackened iron tripods.

The autumn air was already showing the first signs of the coming winter; Arthur could smell snow in the air and recognised its presence in the colour of the distant cloudbanks. But while this northern part of Britain was cold, the sky, sea and earth were softer and gentler than the jewel-bright skies and deep snows of the Dene lands.

'There doesn't seem to be a public house of any description,' Germanus noted. 'Then again, I suppose six cottages don't merit such luxury.'

'They're fishermen,' Arthur replied shortly. 'There's a path leading into the interior which could pass as a road for market days and the local fairs at some larger town, but without a thoroughfare there's no need for an inn. Be prepared, gentlemen! We're going to cause a stir, so just follow my lead.'

The three men strode down the low hill overlooking the village as if they were newly arrived gods who had come to earth to be worshipped. Several of the women squawked and dropped their spoons and brooms before scattering with children clutching at their skirts. The fishermen dived into their huts and came out carrying primitive hoes, fishing spears or clubs, prepared to guard their homes and their families with the last of their blood.

Arthur's gaze took in the fishing nets laid out on primitive racks to dry. Smokehouses indicated the thrift exercised in this poor village and the scant returns from their vegetable patches bore mute testimony to the quality of the soil. The day's catch had already been cleaned, gutted and strung up through the gills on sharpened spikes of willow.

'Is there a headman among you who can speak for your village? We mean you no harm, good sirs, but we require information from you. We are Britons who have been far away in distant lands in the north for far too long.'

Not surprisingly, the fishermen viewed the three huge warriors as a threat. They raised their makeshift weapons as menacingly as they could, although the full complement of five middle-aged men, two elderly grandfathers and four boys aged between ten and fifteen hardly presented any danger. Arthur silently congratulated them on their courage. With little to lose, they were nevertheless prepared to die to protect what was theirs.

'I repeat to you, good sirs, that it's not our intention to harm you or yours. Nor do we wish any harm to your village and your livelihoods. We only wish to converse with you and obtain the information we need. We will then be gone.' The Saxon tongue, so similar to the Dene language, felt awkward and rusty on his tongue.

The headman lowered his weapon a fraction.

'And then you'll go?' he asked in a doubtful voice.

'You have my word on it as a prince of the Britons,' Arthur replied. 'Are you a Saxon? A Jute? A Briton? I only ask so I can speak to you in your own language.'

The headman looked puzzled.

'We have lived in this village for time past counting, my lord. The Saxons and Angles leave us be, as long as we pay the thane's tribute in coin or kind. Our people were here when the legions first came, so we know one master is much the same as any other. None of them worry us as long as we accede to their demands.'

Arthur promptly switched to the Celtic language and the surprised villagers stirred with a sound like rustling leaves.

'Where are we, master? What is the nearest large town, and where does it lie?'

The headman launched into a rapid explanation in Celt, while further lowering his spear. He drew a rough sketch of the surrounding area in a soft patch of earth to indicate the relative positions of various landmarks. Meanwhile, the other villagers sighed with relief when Germanus and Gareth straightened up from the fighter's crouch that they had unconsciously adopted when the fishermen had drawn their weapons.

'The nearest town to us was called Vinovia for many years. It is two days' march away on one of the northern rivers. Our thane rules from the old Roman town of Cataractonium. Do you know these towns, master?'

Arthur grinned happily.

'I travelled through Vinovia years ago to reach the lands ruled by my uncle. The Otadini tribe used to rule the broad acres that lie on the other side of the Wall, as I'm sure you'd know.'

The headman looked grave and shuffled his feet.

'What happened to the Otadini tribe and the kin of King Gawayne of blessed memory?' Gareth asked bluntly. He was certain from the demeanour of these peasant fishermen that their tidings would be sorrowful.

'Most of them are dead, my lord. Llyr Marini Gul, who is the son of the Celtic king, Meirchion Gul of Rheged, came out of his fastnesses in old Verterae with a horde of warriors and killed every Otadini tribesman they could find. They killed and tortured their victims until they could find no further enemies to destroy. They hated Lord Gawayne, although he was long dead, because he fought alongside the great Artor, who had been an avowed enemy of the Brigante. Gul's warriors waited until the Otadini were isolated from their allies, and then crushed the last of Gawayne's line. I hear tell they even dug up his bones so they could be scattered to the winds. The Gul clan is allied to one of the kings of Powys, a man called Ector, so I suppose there were old wrongs to be settled in the slaughter that took place.'

The headman laughed drily.

'But the descendants of Gawayne are hard to kill and some of them still prey on the Angles. These warriors are outlaws all, or so I hear tell. At any road, the son of Meirchion Gul set up a fiefdom in Bremenium after they had smashed the Celtic palaces and churches into so much kindling. They are now in control of the southern lands abutting the Wall. Even our own thane treads carefully around this kinglet who likes to call himself the Dragon Slayer, because he's plain crazy.'

Arthur had lowered his head to concentrate on what he was hearing, so the villagers watched him narrowly, in case he should blame them for any unpalatable information. When he raised his head again, his eyes had paled with anger.

'So old wrongs and unseemly ambitions continue to colour my family's name. Bran and Ector! I'd not have thought them guilty of such shame.'

The headman and the other villagers, puzzled, feared they could become the objects of his wrath.

Eventually, the headman screwed up his courage and reached out a tentative hand towards the tall warrior. 'What is your name, lord?' he asked shyly. 'We have no reason to speak to our thane about your visit, even if he chose to speak with us – which he would never do! I would like to know what nobles have come to our village.'

'I am called Arthur! I am known as the Last Dragon, and I have travelled from the lands of ice and snow so that I could return to my homeland once again,' he answered ambiguously. Then, with a slight smile, he bowed to the fisherfolk and left the circle of light. Night had fallen during the discussion, so Gareth and Germanus followed Arthur into the darkness, while praying that they wouldn't fall among the dunes and injure themselves.

'Who was he? He told us he was the Last Dragon, whatever that means,' the old man mused. 'I thought he said his name was Arthur, and he came to us from the Land of Ice. Perhaps it was a dream? I've seen no sign of boats being beached nearby, so the gods might have sent them to us as an omen of things yet to come.'

The villagers agreed that the Last Dragon was a man to watch out for because he was courteous and well behaved. But the headman still thought that his new friends were obviously warriors, who could have killed them all.

The three were forced to paddle hard and fast to reach *Sea Wife*, which had lagged behind the rest of the fleet in anticipation of their arrival.

The canoe reached the longboat just after midnight and Arthur dragged himself up onto the deck before offering his hand to Germanus to manoeuvre the exhausted Frank over the side of *Sea Wife*, where he proceeded to curse in several languages about incipient old age.

Finally Gareth pulled himself over the side to fall in a crumpled heap on the boards. He was forced to endure some good-natured joking from the crew as they sat at their rowing benches, for they were ready to resume rowing as soon as Arthur issued his orders.

Gareth cheerfully acknowledged his own weariness, while mentally praising the crew for their tact in not making jokes about Germanus's exhaustion, thus allowing the elderly warrior to retain his dignity.

'We'll sail into the north, Snorri. The next deep river flowing towards the coast marks the end of the Wall and we'll find excellent landing places there that will meet all our requirements, just as the Romans did. Once there, we will assess the terrain, construct a beachhead and then select a defensive perimeter that can be held with the forces at our disposal. Is that understood, Snorri?'

Arthur waited as the helmsman and the nearest banks of rowers chewed over his instructions.

The helmsman nodded. It was part of his duties to disseminate information and relay Arthur's orders to the rest of the fleet, which he did as *Sea Wife* sailed close to any of the other vessels. Arthur sometimes dwelled on the inadequacies of this archaic system, but something always seemed to prevent him from developing a better solution.

Given the slight onshore breeze, *Sea Wife* had been forced to tack to keep her sail filled. Arthur expected the wind to drop even further, so the rowers would be forced to labour throughout the night if the fleet was to continue its journey up the coast. Perhaps it would be better to down oars, lower the great sail and then wait until dawn; he had no idea what shoals and reefs existed in these waters and was fully aware that his good fortune might not continue if they pressed on in the darkness.

Deciding, he issued an order to the flotilla that the fleet should stop and maintain their positions overnight, so the longboats slowed and eventually came to a halt. Since the sea was too deep to drop anchors, sea anchors were allowed to trail out into the dark waters.

Meanwhile, the spirits of those aboard the longboats were high because their long and dangerous journey was over and the Last Dragon had done what he promised. A new land stretched out before them, a world of soft skies, gulls and, from what they had experienced so far, peace. No ships came to intercept them; no warning pyres lit the skies with messages of alarm exchanged between shore-based defenders, and the waters fairly teemed with fish. To the warriors under his command, everything Arthur touched turned to gold.

In the morning, after eating mouldy flat cakes, dried apples and strips of raw fish covered with a piquant sauce that Ingrid seemed to have conjured out of thin air, Arthur ordered the fleet to continue cautiously towards the shoreline. He soon realised that the fleet had drifted closer to it than he would have expected and his calculations convinced him that their passage along the coast had been affected by totally unexpected tidal currents during the night. The shoreline seemed innocuous and relatively harmless, so he ordered Snorri to steer closer and then sail parallel to the shore. He wanted to remain as close as he dared during this reconnaissance, so he was depending on Lars to carry out depth measurements every ten minutes or so. Another crew member was perched perilously at the top of the mast as lookout. From this position, the changing colours of the waters would warn him of shallows, while flocks of seagulls hovering and diving indicated the presence of reefs where the birds were feeding on surface fish. This lookout was also searching for rocky outcrops along the beaches that might be hiding otherwise safe areas where the fleet could make a landfall.

An hour passed, then two. Finally, the sailor aloft sighted a large, sheltered cove protected by two rocky headlands. Arthur quickly recognised that it could be an almost perfect landing place; the beach in this cove was creamy-white with mixed shingle and sand that would give the crews every assistance to drive the prows of their vessels above the high-water mark.

But first, Arthur ordered Snorri to carry out a brief reconnaissance to check the security of the cove and determine whether there were obstructions below the surface. The cove and headland were on the far side of a large river mouth that would be suitable for the shallow-drafted boats to enter once the security of the locality was established, but Arthur knew they would have to winter in these sheltered waters. With this in mind, he insisted on checking thoroughly before committing his flotilla to a landing.

Under oars and with Snorri at the helm, *Sea Wife* drove its bows towards the white sand while the other vessels held back and awaited Arthur's orders. The longboat cut through the grey waters like a dolphin until, on a prearranged signal, the rowers raised their oars.

Cruel, ship-tearing rocks slid past *Sea Wife* on the port side where a headland reached out into the waters, and Arthur reflected on the possibility of building a fortress here in future. But then the rocky outcrop disappeared behind them to be replaced by a regular sandy bottom. If sets of stone walls were erected, defenders could control the entire cove and hence the fertile lands beyond.

Arthur was the first man to leap over the bows as *Sea Wife*'s keel drove effortlessly into the sand and shingle. Her practised crew used brute strength to haul the superb vessel into the softer sand where the jealous sea would be unable to steal her.

After a quick reconnaissance by speedy scouts, Arthur was advised that there was no sign of human habitation in the immediate area. Then, and only then, Snorri drew out a long, red-dyed pennon and attached it to the mast where it unfurled like a tongue of fire. The signal had been passed to the fleet to make their own landings.

The sturdy trading vessels made their way to the shore, their broader draft making their landfall less graceful than the beaching of *Sea Wife*. Meanwhile, the other longships guarded the entry to the cove. As Arthur watched his flotilla finally land, he experienced a sense of accomplishment that his will had prevailed. He had brought his people to a new and wonderful world.

Now for the establishment of a beachhead. Having sent out a number of scouts to further explore the immediate vicinity, Arthur issued instructions for a horseshoe faced defensive perimeter to be set up some four hundred yards inland. A location such as this fertile strip begged for human habitation, and one of his scouts returned quickly to report the presence of an abandoned village on the banks of a broad river flowing past the headlands, no more than a mile from their landing point. The scout also told Arthur of a small stream that fed into the river, which meant his forces would have a plentiful supply of clean fresh drinking water.

As the other scouts returned from their forays they reported that the terrain in their district seemed rich and fertile from silt laid down by the flooding river. Rough paths ran from along the banks of the river, bisecting other paths that seemed to be heading west towards the hinterland behind the village. One scout had seen evidence of dressed stonework near the river, but the village had clearly been abandoned for some time.

We'll carry out a more detailed survey of our surroundings once we set up a base camp beyond the dunes, Arthur thought. There were none of the usual fishing boats and coracles he would have expected from a village by the mouth of a major river. The only signs of life were the footprints of a few mangy dogs that could be seen from a distance as they were slinking among the stone buildings.

From where he stood at the top of the highest dune, Arthur's gaze followed the path of a straight road that led into the west. Perhaps there was an abandoned Roman settlement further inland; if so, such a settlement would be an ideal base for the winter.

'This is a perfect spot for us to make our landfall, Snorri,'

Arthur said happily. 'We can establish a secure compound here where our people can spend the winter, and we can prepare the lands surrounding our encampment for farming by our settlers. By the time that spring comes, we'll be ready for the arrival of our women and children.'

Snorri had followed Arthur like a faithful hound, eager to investigate this new country where he was preparing to transplant his family; he longed to spirit his wife and young sons away from the Dene lands now that Justinian's Disease was ravaging his people.

'Master?' he asked. 'Will we be able to return to The Holding before winter sets in?' Snorri could smell snow on the wind.

'No, Snorri. These parts of Britain can occasionally be as cold as Jutland, but winter finishes far earlier here than in the northern climes. When the last of the winter snows have thawed and the northern ice has begun to melt, we'll be able to bring our women, children and chattels to Britain. By then, we'll be well and truly dug into the landscape, and we'll know if we're likely to suffer any attack. I'd not have innocents arrive during a war.'

The winter months would be long and lonely but, at the very least, Snorri could savour the knowledge that his labours would benefit his family.

'That will be a good day for us, Master Arthur.'

'Aye, Snorri! It will indeed.'

The perimeter was established on the landward side of the dunes where the grass was sweet and deep. Enough supplies for several days were unloaded, while guards and wandering scouts were tasked to patrol the lands within the perimeter and maintain a watch over the tents in the newly prepared encampment. Unlike many of his companions, Arthur found tent-living pleasant for it reminded him of long summers in Arden where he had received his first lessons in woodcraft, trapping and fishing.

Then he had believed that his life's path was set in stone: to protect Bedwyr, his mother and his siblings and to provide guidance and protection to the people of Arden Forest until his eventual death. So simple a dream now seemed unimaginably narrow.

The land around the base camp showed evidence of abandoned agriculture. A stand of fruit trees crowned one low hill and unpicked apples were scattered on the ground. In the same patch of ground, stalks of grain raised heavy heads ripe for harvesting, and wild herbs and vegetables had been left to seed and regrow for several seasons. Some of the provident Dene warriors were already hard at work harvesting the bounty.

'Volunteers,' Arthur barked at his crew. 'I need ten men to investigate a village on the river, about a mile distant. You can actually see it if you climb to the highest point of the dunes. I won't feel comfortable until we know its importance.'

Snorri was the first to leap to his feet, and Arthur chose nine men at random to carry out the patrol under the helmsman's command. Meanwhile, he gave Germanus and Lars the task of arranging a series of fire pits. Germanus was also instructed to allot permanent positions along the defensive line for the crews from the various vessels. With an order of battle firmly fixed in their minds, Arthur's warriors would always know who was on their left and who was on their right, essential knowledge if a pitched battle should test them, especially at night.

Lars proved his worth during the hours that followed. Recently promoted to the post of longboat commander, the young man had asked Arthur for permission to join the Briton's crew during the voyage from the Dene lands, when Arthur had taught him long-distance navigation, a skill that he had learned from his expert mentor, Stormbringer. Using the fixed stars in the heavens as reference points was invaluable when the Dene ships were far from land.

Now Lars could be used to communicate Arthur's orders to the large number of northerners in the fleet.

Arthur and his group set out over the dew-wet grass at sunrise the next morning on what seemed to be a beautiful day.

The journey was uneventful, and the column found the remains of a village community that had once thrived from the bounty of the river, the sea and the commerce that had come with traders who sailed inland to the Saxon and Angle settlements, as the old Roman docks along the river banks demonstrated. The river had narrowed a little over the years, and the waters had deserted the docks, leaving rich land for agriculture and vegetable patches now full of weeds.

Now, Arthur and his companions drew their swords and searched cottage after cottage as they made their way into the village. Each home was deserted, and had been picked clean of furniture, stoves and food. Even the rats had left, having devoured everything that was edible. Arthur found a small carved wooden fish that had been chewed on the tail by baby teeth, its surface smoothed by the fingers of many small children over many generations.

On a whim, Arthur slipped the toy inside his tunic, where it could lie against his heart.

'Master! There's something odd over here that you must see,' Snorri called from the edge of a small stream about fifty feet away. The streamlet had cut its way through soft deposits of silt from an underground spring that was trickling from the earth.

Rain, thaws and flood had eroded a trench into the upper bank of this streamlet. But some enterprising soul had filled in the ugly scar on the landscape, allowing the water to run free. Arthur felt a stab of irritation.

'I don't see anything, Snorri. What are you talking about?'

'Look closer, master, in the bottom of the stream!'

Arthur strode into the streamlet, surprised to discover that it came to mid-calf. It certainly wasn't deep, but its clarity was deceptive. The mosses that waved idly on the bottom were viridian and as soft as velvet in the nest of onyx, chalcedony, agate and quartz pebbles, all of which had been smoothed by the waters until they glowed like gems.

Within the nest of pebbles, something white and unexpected waved at him. A child's body lay in the bottom of the stream; tendons were still holding the delicate, articulated bones of the hand together. Like a flower carved from ivory, the fingers opened and closed in a strange and lovely parody of a flexing movement, as if a babe was learning the magic of his own fingers.

Alarmed, Arthur stepped back abruptly, stirring the silt between the stones so that the hand disappeared. Looking up, he saw the scar on the earth caused by the erosion of a shallow grave. The waters seeping from an underground stream had exposed the child's rotting flesh to the elements. Doubtless more remains could be found downstream of this place.

'Buried corpses!' he grunted. 'How long since this hole was filled do you reckon, Snorri?'

'The grass is thick, master, but it's only about twelve inches long. Several months, I'd guess! Do you think that these villagers have been murdered?' Snorri wasn't particularly afraid for, as a Dene warrior, he understood the cruel ways of nature. Children were born, they flourished for a time and then violent men, illnesses or wars cut them down like flowers in a storm.

'If they had died by human hands, these perfectly habitable cottages would have been claimed by other kin or landless men. This village is deserted, so disease is the unseen killer.'

'Is it the plague?' Snorri's question caught in his throat as he looked back at his companions who were searching industriously through the overgrown vegetable patches.

'Say nothing about this graveyard, Snorri, until I discover the truth of the matter. Whatever the case may be, disease will die in long-abandoned places, and it can't affect vegetables that have been pulled from the earth. I'll consider the whole situation first.'

When their patrol returned to the encampment at the cove with their booty, Arthur was pleased to see that other groups had harvested some of the native wheat and other produce from the fruit and nut trees that surrounded the village. The settlers were collecting winter supplies far more easily than they could have expected.

'Truly, Arthur,' Lars said with a laugh. 'This land seems determined to make me fat. Your slave has even found a cow with a young calf.'

Ingrid had chanced on a cow and its calf as the animals were cropping grasses only a stone's throw from the shelving beach, and she had already borrowed an adze from one of the farmers to cut down saplings and lash a fence together that would separate the cow from her calf, a youngster long past the time when it should have been weaned. Several sailors eyed the calf and licked their lips in anticipation of fresh meat, but a quick check revealed that the calf was female and far more valuable as a breeding heifer.

'It's fresh milk, Ingrid. Ingmar has probably forgotten the taste of it,' Arthur said with a wide smile, but the six-year-old boy took his words seriously.

'No, I haven't forgotten, Master Arthur. Mother told me we would be able to make butter and cheese from the milk and, once we've threshed the grain, she'll show me how to grind it for flour. And then we'll be able to have freshly baked bread.'

'I thought you wanted to become a warrior, young man, rather than a cook or a farmer.'

Arthur could see the boy testing and rejecting answer after answer. 'Mother has told me that a clever man should master many skills, my lord. Even warriors must eat and, sometimes, they must make do and live off the land. I wish to be a man of many skills so I can serve you well.'

Pleased, Arthur swung Ingmar onto his shoulders and proceeded to point out the remains of the Roman road that scarred the landscape. His good mood lasted all the way through a scrappy meal, after which he held a meeting with his captains to determine the disposition of his vessels during the coming winter. Then, tired after a full day of effort and excited discovery, Arthur rolled himself into his sleeping furs in the tent he shared with Germanus and Gareth.

But, try as he might, he was unable to sleep. Eventually, he made his bed in a nest of grass near the perimeter where he could gaze up at familiar stars. The constellations wheeled around him and the night seemed more like summer than autumn. Though Arthur knew that this fine, warm weather was one of winter's jests on unwary Britons, he felt embraced by the earth, as if his homeland was choosing to welcome him home with fair weather and good fortune.

'Long may it last, dear God, long may it last. The encampment is secure and the night is dry and warm. What more could a man want?' He lifted a drowsy hand in salute as a sentry drew his sword at the sound of an unexpected voice.

But an icy rain began to fall just before dawn, and drove Arthur back into his tent. Outside in the coppice, he heard the flapping of great wings and knew that an owl was on the hunt. He began to say his prayers like a frightened child.

SEGEDUNUM

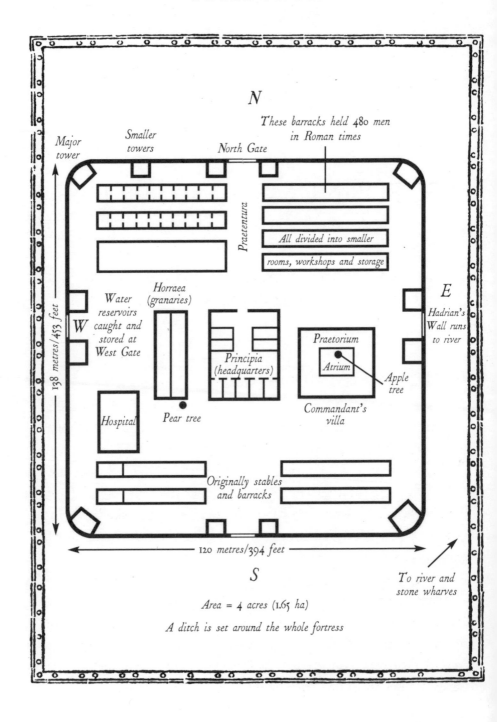

N

These barracks held 480 men
in Roman times

Major
tower

Smaller
towers

North Gate

Praetentura

All divided into smaller

rooms, workshops and storage

W

138 metres/453 feet

Water
reservoirs
caught and
stored at
West Gate

Horraea
(granaries)

Principia
(headquarters)

Praetorium

Atrium

E

Hadrian's
Wall runs
to river

Apple
tree

Commandant's
villa

Hospital

Pear tree

Originally stables
and barracks

120 metres/394 feet

S

To river and
stone wharves

Area = 4 acres (1.65 ha)

A ditch is set around the whole fortress

CHAPTER XVIII

SEGEDUNUM AT WALL'S END

For in every ill-turn of fortune the most unhappy sort of unfortunate man is the one who has been happy.

Boethius, *De Consolatione Philosophae*, Book 2

'According to Myrddion Merlinus, the one quality that the Romans had that overrode every other consideration was their predictability,' Arthur said drily as he looked out at a miserable rain-drenched day. Lars's nose was red with a cold, the Troll King was bitching about the pains in his knees and Snorri was observing the weather with his usual jaundiced eye.

'What are you talking about, Arthur?' Gareth asked for the edification of all the members of the council who were huddling around a small fire.

'The Romans built fortresses wherever they were likely to be attacked. They crossed the mountains and fought their way through Gaul and then sailed over the waters to Britannia. The same strategies were always followed: capture an area and then build a fortress to control it. As far as the south-west and central areas of Britannia are concerned, this rule held true. I've seen it often enough. And they had enemies to spare here in the north of this island, so they built a defensive wall that stretched from sea to sea just to keep the blue-faced Picts out.'

'You're probably right, Arthur,' Lars replied. 'But what are blue-faced Picts? And I don't see what old Roman building methods have to do with us.'

When Arthur and his British friends were in the Dene lands, he had been ignorant of ordinary matters. But now that they were in a place where his local knowledge held sway, he rather liked the feeling.

'The Picts are a violent and barbaric tribe of people who used to control all of Britannia. The British Celts defeated them in numerous battles and eventually drove them into the in-hospitable northern parts of the island, which became their new homeland. As I said, the legions built a wall, in fact two, and numerous fortifications to keep them out of Roman Britannia. They are called blue-faced because they tattoo themselves with woad dyes.'

The Dene jarls looked vaguely appalled. 'Why would any-one want to fight for a country that constantly drips with moisture?' Lars muttered darkly until Snorri kicked him on the shins.

'Don't be a dolt, Lars. The rain will stop sooner or later.'

'Promises . . . promises,' Lars grumbled, wiping his streaming nose on his sleeve.

Darting a warning glance at Snorri, Arthur interrupted the whining complaints.

'I believe we are close to where the first wall ends. It's called the Vallum Hadriani, and it's the larger of the two constructions. You'd think that a stone fortress would guard the earthworks at the very end of it, wouldn't you? How effective would these fortifications have been if the Picts could simply walk around the earthworks and attack the rear of the Roman defences? The Romans didn't make all that effort for nothing, so I think we'll find that there is a great fucking fortress at the end of the wall. In fact, I'd be prepared to bet my balls on it.'

The other men nodded their understanding, if not their agreement. As usual, Arthur's ideas were certainly logical, although Thorketil grinned at the idea of anyone collecting on a wager involving Arthur's manhood.

'So that great fortress will have been constructed at the end of that overgrown road heading west from the village.' Arthur pointed out through the pouring rain. 'If we should decide to follow it, there might still be enough of the fortifications left for us to use.'

'But won't the local thane have taken that fortress for himself? Surely, he'd be using it to his own advantage.'

'You'd think so, wouldn't you? But the Saxons and Angles tend to tear down Roman forts and replace them with their own timber buildings. Other solid defences have been left to rot. I, for one, don't understand their reasoning, but if the local thane has acted like his contemporaries, we might find a safe and dry fortress in which we can spend a comfortable winter.'

The council members examined Arthur's proposal from every possible angle. Eventually, they agreed that a small patrol should carry out a reconnaissance mission to search for the old Roman fortress and, at the same time, determine whether any lands in the vicinity were populated. With his usual decisiveness, Arthur announced that he would lead the patrol.

He knew that Snorri, Germanus and Gareth would expect to travel with him, but he had no intention of taking all the fluent Celt-speakers on this journey. If something went wrong, the

Dene could lose all their people with local knowledge in one engagement, tantamount to suicide.

Arthur allowed Gareth to join him, aware that he would refuse to remain behind.

As well as Gareth, Lars had the quick thinking, intelligence and flexibility needed for such a dangerous enterprise. To flesh out the group, he needed brawny men from other ships, so he selected Harald Leifsen, a tall, red-bearded warrior with a nasty adze in his belt that he used with the facility of an axe. The fifth man, a Geat called Ragnar Sigurdson, was darker than most Dene men, but he stood at six foot eight inches in his bared feet, and was dwarfed only by Thorketil, whose hamstrung leg made him unable to withstand the rigours of such a journey on foot. Finally, to ensure that most of the disparate members of their small mission were represented on this important patrol, Arthur selected a fiery cousin of the southern Jarl, Knud Thorvaldsen, to round out the group.

As soon as he made his choices known, there was an immediate outcry of protest, but Arthur's concise explanation of the reasons for his selections was soon understood and accepted by the pragmatic Dene leadership.

'But what if you meet strong resistance?' Snorri demanded with the usual complaint that the Dene settlers would be lost if Arthur was killed or wounded. But Arthur had heard this tedious argument before and was prepared to counter it.

'Do you speak the language of my people, Snorri? With the exception of Gareth and Germanus, none of our people can. Nor does anyone have the knowledge to make the command decisions needed if we are to find permanent bases. These are assessments that only I can make, so I must undertake the journey. I can assure you that I don't plan to be killed, not now that I'm about to establish our presence in these lands.'

'Humph!' Snorri's opinion was crystal-clear, for he was almost as protective of Arthur as Gareth. However the rest of the council agreed with Arthur, so Snorri was forced to comply. Germanus was as sullen as his disciplined nature would allow but, like Thorketil and Rufus, he knew his age was an insurmountable handicap.

Snorri was incensed when he realised that Lars had been invited to join the reconnaissance party. Acidly, he pointed out that Lars was a sea captain and essential for the sea voyages that would return their longboats to the Dene homeland in the coming spring. His loss in a land battle would be a catastrophe.

'Can't you see my reasoning, Snorri? You're the helmsman of *Sea Wife*, the flagship of the Dene fleet, so you're responsible for the entire flotilla. In that regard, you're far more important than I am, or Lars, for you will be the only man among us who can successfully lead our people home to the Dene Mark if a disaster besets our expedition.'

'I'd prefer you don't fuck around with me, Arthur. That decision was hardly fair!'

Snorri sulked for hours.

By the morning, sullen rain was still falling when Arthur, Gareth and the four Dene warriors set out to determine what lay at the end of the Roman road.

'This dribble isn't real rain,' Lars complained, as he huddled inside his arctic furs. 'This piss is a drip, drip, drip, like an old man with a limp dick. I wish it would really pour down – and get it over with.'

The cold rain was the first indication that winter proper was just over the horizon and the Dene had started to believe that snow, ice and deep cold might never come to this green land.

When the patrol reached the Roman road, they found it was straight and true, but overgrown with weeds. It soon became obvious that the road had only been used sparingly, if at all, during recent years. Despite this, Arthur ensured that all six companions remained fanned out and alert for a possible ambush.

At one point where the road ran parallel to the fast-flowing river to the west of the village, they discovered an overgrown crossroad which would have normally taken traffic over a bridge, now ruined. Across the flooded stream, Arthur spied dressed stone rising out of a natural mound of earth and realised that a thick-walled building of some kind had once guarded the river mouth.

'Gareth! Lars! See? What did I tell you? The Romans built a small fort here that would guard the northern banks of the river. See, Knud? But the bridge has been destroyed by marauders and the fortress is derelict now.'

'So? What do we do now that we've found this fortress?' Lars asked hopefully, keen to evade the steady drizzle. Ragnar had covered his long hair with a hood of hide and was trying to find his comb; like many Dene and Geat warriors, he was extraordinarily proud of his hair and beard.

'This road must go to a place of some importance, so we'll continue till we reach the end.'

The group continued to follow the roughly paved way. As they walked, Ragnar took the opportunity to neaten his beard with the assistance of a comb of walrus tusk.

The road moved parallel to the general windings of the river, despite the curves and loops followed by the waterway as it snaked its way through to the coast. Arthur noted the depth and width of the stream, which would easily accommodate the vessels in his fleet. The road gradually widened, and the going seemed easier, regardless of the cold downpour which showed no sign of abating. The land was rich, but the few cottages they saw revealed no signs of life, so Arthur became increasingly certain that plague had come to these lands from trading ships. Wherever the vessels landed, death must have followed quickly.

Squelching in damp boots was an almost welcome experience for Arthur since he could still remember how he had plodded through the mud to build the Warrior's Dyke in the south-west long before he even became a man. By comparison, the boots used by the Dene warriors were constructed for warmth in fine weather. They were very soft when compared with the sturdy ox-hide specimens worn by Arthur and Gareth, and ideal for fighting because of their flexibility. Unfortunately, they failed to keep out heavy rain and slush.

When the men became hungry, the patrol stopped and ate the food that Ingrid had prepared for them. Then, as night fell, they hunkered down in a barn beside an abandoned cottage. The hay smelled stale and possessed the distinctive reek of rat, but the roof was watertight and enough dry wood was piled in one corner to light a fire. Gareth took some time to strike a spark from the flint because his hands were trembling and stiff from the cold. Once it was coaxed into life, the spark was protected and nurtured until the tinder and crushed-up leaves from the corner of the barn leaped into vivid tongues of flame.

The night proved to be both long and wearying for Arthur. He was so close to his dream that he railed against every small hiccup that slowed his inexorable march toward the home of his heart, even as he recognised that it might not be the haven he sought. On the one hand, he wanted a kingdom so he could stand within the halo of Artor's fame and be a fitting son. On the other, he knew that he would never be acknowledged as an heir to the High King.

He longed to clasp his parents in his arms and know the sweet belonging of his boyhood, but inexorable years had passed since he left his home. Yet he was still determined to return to Arden Forest, but only when his Dene followers were safe and secure and had been reunited with their families. His hubris had dragged these followers from their northern homes; he could never abandon them to chase his own desires. Only in the distant future could he consider riding off to Arden to discover what jokes Fortuna had played on him for his sins.

Curled into the straw like a child, Arthur slept in complete exhaustion, still harried by dreams that crumbled into dust through his fingers and a green she-dragon that laughed at him from her undersea ossuary.

'Do you think you've escaped from my reach, earthworm? Do you think that your fires will be stronger than mine when you are on land?' Her tongue flickered as it licked her malachite lips. *'Men are such fools! The primal powers of fire and ice remember their forging by the gods, and only a fool seeks to escape his destiny. You will be remembered as the Ice King, and the scrolls will shout your name as the father of a great kingdom.'*

Then the she-dragon giggled like a young girl. She was so captivating and flirtatious that Arthur had wanted to vomit.

'The name that will echo down the ages is not yours, Arthur. And nor is it the name of Artor. You will be lauded as an Anglii barbarian, one of those northern warriors whom your birth-father struggled so hard to defeat and, through your strong and just rule, the Dene will come to rule the British lands as the last act of betrayal against the Celtic peoples. Ah ... but you are a foolish little man! You would have been more content if you had remained in my ossuary.'

Then Arthur awoke with a start as a new day of sleet and intense cold spurred him on to greater efforts of will.

There it was!

There lay the fortress that protected the eastern end of Hadrian's Wall. The name stirred Arthur's memories of Lorcan's lessons. Segedunum, the great fort! It would live in the history of men until Myrddion Merlinus's predictions came to be, and the great healer's *cities of glass* would rise into the sky like spires of ice.

The patrol arrived as the afternoon of the second day lengthened towards night. Seeking a semblance of cover, they had spotted traces of stonework ahead through a curtain of stubborn gorse and copses of aspens.

The Roman fortress was unmistakably constructed in the classical military style of the legions. It appeared to cover an area of about four acres and showed obvious signs of deterioration. The southern gate, a structure of large planks, was gaping open and, when Arthur's patrol approached, they discovered that it was frozen into position by the growth of young trees and shrubs. However, some judicious tree lopping and minor excavations would remedy that.

So far: so good!

Lars was stunned into silence by the sheer size of the structure. Three times the height of a grown man, it was surrounded by a protective ditch; at the gateway, Arthur pointed out the thickness of the walls that had been designed to survive, and had, for generations. At each corner, towers provided added height and protection, and four gates were laid out evenly to allow entry from all sides.

'Peasants may have been taking some of the stones from the

walls for use on their farms,' Lars noted, for parts of the fortress wall and the Vallum Hadriani seemed to have been nibbled at by giant mice.

'Aye! What a splendid structure this fort must have been in its prime,' Arthur replied, his face shining with admiration for the long-dead Roman engineers.

'If you discount the forests that are growing out of the ramparts,' Gareth replied dourly. The young warrior could usually be depended upon to be glum in any situation. Grass and shrubs had indeed seeded where stones had been stolen, giving the walls the odd appearance of having sprouted large swathes of dried brown hair.

'It's nothing that a winter's labour can't put to rights,' Arthur said bracingly and forced his way through the underbrush at the entrance to survey the interior of the fort.

A road had run through the fortress between the gates on the eastern and western walls, but the eastern gate had obviously remained closed since the Romans had marched away from the Wall, and from Britain. He retraced his steps around the building to what he now realised was a path flattened out over two hundred years earlier by the feet of peasants as they pillaged the structure. When he reached the eastern gate, he saw at once that someone had tried to burn down the gates at some time, so the timber was scarred and splintered. The metal bindings and fittings had been torn off for re-use, but the legions had certainly built this fortification to last.

When Arthur rejoined his companions, he discovered they had found a stone pedestal once obviously topped by some kind of commemorative statue, long since stolen or destroyed. Lars was scraping at the clinging green lichen that blurred the lettering, but once it was cleaned away, all five men scratched their heads, for the inscription was written in Latin.

'The legionnaires of the Second Augustan Legion were the original builders of this fortress,' Arthur told his warriors. He pointed out the letters and numbers carved into the stone. 'The carving tells us that the words are *LEG II AVG*, and the Latin script tells us that it stands for *Legion Two in the reign of the Emperor Augustus*. This cohort of Romans built it, and they took pride in their work.'

There were many more inscriptions scattered throughout the enclosure, far too many to explore before the onset of darkness. Arthur tried to remember everything he had ever been told about Roman defences. He climbed to the top of one of the four corner towers designed to protect bowmen and house other unpleasant weapons as well as providing a view of the whole of the inner sanctum. Driven by curiosity, Gareth and the Dene warriors had followed him, for they had immediately grasped the towers' purpose.

'The timber is still sound,' Lars observed. 'It will hold for a year or two at any rate, although most of the roofs are in need of serious work.'

'From memory, the ornate building in the centre of the fort was called a *principia* and it was used as the regimental head-quarters. There, to the right, is the *praetorium* where the commander would have lived and to the left is the *horraea* where grains were stored. I doubt if any of these buildings will be of any use to us.'

'They're under cover, aren't they?' Ragnar pointed out.

Arthur's careful description, including his use of Latin, surprised Lars.

'My master was trained by Father Lorcan, and this training covered everything that was worth knowing about Rome's conquest of their world,' Gareth explained to Lars and Knud as they looked out over the countryside below. 'So was I, for that matter, because my father, who was my tutor, had learned everything he knew second-hand in the court of King Artor. But Father Lorcan had actually lived in Rome for some years, and he's been well travelled throughout his life. What is certain is that my master was trained to rule from birth.'

'Then we're fucking lucky to have a leader who knows what he's doing,' Knut replied dourly. 'And it's stopped raining, at long last.'

Arthur was half listening as his men looked outwards over the darkening landscape. No lights showed in the steadily advancing gloom, but the land seemed tamed and was divided into a patchwork quilt of cultivated fields with walls of fieldstone separating one crop from another. Now, because of the inexorable march of winter, the fields remained fallow.

'Arthur was right about this country. If we can survive the winter, and if we can avoid discovery, and if we can plant a spring crop, we'll have ourselves a land of milk and honey,' Lars decided.

'That's a hell of a lot of guessing,' Knud retorted, but Gareth slapped his hand aggressively on the stone sill.

'Are you suggesting that Arthur would lie?'

Arthur hastily brought their attention back to their discussions on the fortress. He pointed out how easily a little thatch could repair roofs, or better still, his men could take good tiles from damaged buildings to repair others where the decay was relatively minor.

'To the north, six infantry *centuria*, or about four hundred and eighty men, would have been housed in four barracks. Can you see those buildings in the southern section of the compound? The stables were situated there, and also accommodation for about one hundred and twenty horsemen, about the normal number for the cavalry unit which would have been stationed here. We have stables, something that looks a lot like a bathhouse and, by my reckoning, there would have to be a temple and a hospital.' He smiled companionably at his men. 'So, where would you like to spend the night?'

Lars grinned impishly. 'I vote we sleep in the commander's house. I always wanted to be a master or a jarl, and this might be as close as I ever come.'

'Why shouldn't you become a jarl?' Arthur responded. 'This is a new land, Lars, with many possibilities for men of courage. There's no reason you can't become a jarl, and it might happen sooner than you think.'

Lars was dumbstruck by Arthur's words, for he had never considered the possibility.

While Lars pondered a glowing future, Arthur pointed towards a row of large stone tanks positioned just inside the walls of the compound.

'See over there, gentlemen! Those huge water tanks you can see have sealed covers and I believe they are still holding plenty of water. Because they are sealed, the water should have remained fresh and clean, even after all the time that has elapsed since the fort was abandoned. The Romans used a system of sandpits to filter the ground water until it was pure enough to drink and they collected rainwater which, as we've noticed, Britannia doesn't seem to lack. With luck, that system will have been built into this fortress.'

Arthur could see at once that the Dene warriors had no idea what he was talking about. They asked a number of questions that he tried to answer, but eventually he wished he'd kept his mouth shut.

'Why would the Saxons and Angles destroy a defendable fortification where the water was safe to drink?' Ragnar asked.

Arthur had no answer to that.

'I'll examine the entire water system tomorrow, but I'm certain that I'll have no reason to be concerned about it. The Romans always made certain that they had permanent sources of good water and food so they could survive long sieges. Even if the Picts surrounded the fort, the Romans would have thumbed their noses at their enemies for months, perhaps years.'

'That was clever of them,' Gareth put in as he tried to recognise the water tanks. But the deepening shadows had become too inky.

'Tonight, my friends, we'll take our rest in the commandant's house,' Arthur decided abruptly. 'That is, if it's sound enough to accommodate house guests.'

The six men clattered down the stone steps of the tower. The once well-tended gravel paths between buildings had been destroyed by time and now supported a veritable forest of growth, but Arthur mentally removed the undergrowth and repaired the ravages. Yes! Given the availability of labour, this fortress could live again.

As night fell, a colony of bats rose from the nearest granary and flew out of some of the gaping holes in the structure's brick walls. Then they rose in a long spool of leathery wings to change places with some of the birds who had found ways to enter other buildings where they lived in the rafters. In one of the barrack blocks where a whole section of rafters had collapsed and the tiles had shattered on the stone floors, whole families of birds had lived and died for generations and left deep drifts of guano that encouraged the growth of several trees whose roots were embedded in the floors.

Fortunately, although the commandant's house had been picked bare of everything of value, it still retained its roof and the interior walls that revealed vestigial traces of a rich, brick-red paint. The first requirement for the warriors was to build a fire in a safe area.

During his youth, Arthur had spent many happy hours poring over scrolls that described his father's childhood at Aquae Sulis, so he expected to find an atrium within the commander's house, even though the building was situated inside a working military fortification. The Romans had considered an open courtyard in the centre of a living space to be essential for civilised living, so the last rays of daylight led the patrol into an open area at the centre of a rabbit warren of small rooms. After clearing pieces of broken tiles and stones, the six men quickly fashioned a protected fire pit, and a comforting fire was soon lit in the space under the roof's overhang.

Fires always lifted the spirits of tired men. Better still, an apple tree had been planted in this atrium in its early days, still sufficiently fertile to bear misshapen fruit. The earth below the tree was thick with the remains of fallen fruit that, over the years, had acted as a perfect fertiliser to keep the tree alive.

Fallen boughs from the tree sweetened the fire smoke and the least-bruised apples from the current crop were scavenged for the feast to come. Roasted apples, impaled on stakes of wood, made their mouths water.

Then, wrapped in their furs in the snug confines of the inner room, the companions settled down to the simple joys of full bellies and warmth. Mercifully, the she-dragon remained silent within the coils and tunnels of Arthur's brain.

Sometime before dawn, a hound bayed loudly in warning, an

alarm that instantly brought all six to full consciousness. Arthur rose silently to his feet with his fingers to his lips, while gently unsheathing the Dragon Knife.

In the pitch darkness, the warriors stood with their bared blades at the ready. Their senses were totally alert as they listened for any alien sound in this silent ruin. Arthur pointed at his feet and they shrugged their way into their boots.

Something grated on the stones at the entrance to the commandant's house. Arthur visualised the large flat stone at the entry; the scraping sound was so obviously caused by leather soles crossing that uneven surface that Arthur motioned to his companions to move back into the shadows.

'Pwyl! Where are you, you stupid mutt?' The coarse voice uttered the words in the Anglii language. Arthur understood perfectly.

A shadow appeared on the wall of the colonnade surrounding the atrium. To judge by the reek, someone was carrying a rough torch soaked in fish oil. A long double-sided axe was dangling from the other hand, making the shadow appear monstrous.

Arthur gestured to Lars and one of the others to encircle the figure who had slipped through the atrium, apparently without noticing the cold fire pit. Arthur and Gareth followed the bobbing torch and the other two slid out of the rear doorway in order to approach the figure from behind.

Without any obvious alarm, the figure stopped and paused to shake a young aspen that was growing out of a crack in the paving near the stables. With a satisfied grunt, he began to chop at the lower trunk of the tree with quick and efficient axe strokes. As the severed trunk fell to the ground, the shaggy form found another and then another, until three small trees had been felled. Then the man began to trim off the useless twigs and leaves. When he had completed his task by the light of a small torch that he'd rammed into a crack in the nearby wall, he began to chop the trunks and larger branches into usable lengths of firewood.

'Why is he cutting firewood now?' Gareth hissed in Arthur's ear. 'He can see far more clearly if he waits until dawn.'

'Shhh! He'll hear you! I think he's cautious because he's thieving firewood ... but I'm guessing, mind,' Arthur hissed back.

Perhaps the intruder would have slipped away with his ill-gotten gains had he not brought his hound on this particular foray. Arthur heard the scrape of clawed pads on stone, a rumbling growl and then the concerted rush of a charging animal of considerable size that howled at the thought of gaining some easy prey. The dog launched itself at his throat in a blur of shaggy fur, red-rimmed eyes and white teeth. Its sheer size should have caught Arthur off guard, but he had expected the hound to sniff them out. The white teeth snapped impotently as Arthur gripped the massive neck with his large right hand and the Dragon Knife gutted the beast.

As if a light had been extinguished, the dog's eyes clouded over and it fell to the ground with its heart sliced in two. It twitched twice, then lay still.

The man with the purloined firewood was fast on his feet. As the hound began his attack, the intruder turned and ran with inordinate speed towards the western gate. Obviously familiar with the fortress, he skilfully dodged every tree and depression in the foundations.

'Don't let him escape,' Arthur shouted, as his warriors set off in pursuit.

Only seconds behind their prey, the Dene warriors forced their way through the narrow opening of the western gate and into the trees and undergrowth as they followed the noise of the intruder's retreat.

'He must be stopped,' Arthur shouted again, his voice ragged with effort.

Within minutes, they had reached a small clearing where a mangy horse and cart waited. Unfortunately for the Anglii peasant, he had no time to mount the wagon and make good his escape; fearing for his life, he dodged and weaved his way through the thick growth of forest at the edge of the wall.

But luck eluded the peasant on this dark and wintry morning. Lars anticipated his escape route and ran on a tangent, hoping to intercept him.

Then, as the dark figure reached an old oak tree that had been spared by the Roman engineers some five hundred years earlier, Lars stepped out from behind its trunk and stood in the peasant's path. The man skidded to a halt as his panicked eyes searched for an escape route, but he was swiftly trapped inside a cordon of armed warriors.

'I didn't mean no harm, master,' the fugitive whined. 'Lord Eoppa has banned us villagers from entering the ruins for fear of angering the gods and the wights that live there. But what's a man to do if he needs firewood? Our master would cut off my hands if he caught me in there, but that's better than seeing my children freezing when the snows come. Please, master, I didn't mean no harm to the wights. Why would they want firewood anyway?'

Arthur responded to his pleas and lowered his blade marginally. The man's eyes burned redly for an instant with a sudden hope that he might still survive this confrontation.

'Surely there must be some firewood close to your village? Why in hell's name would you come here, especially if you have to make sure you aren't seen?' Arthur's voice was clipped and the peasant knew his life might depend on his answer.

'The king has forbidden all movement along the roads because of the Yellow Death, so the land's been picked clean of firewood around my village. But I decided to brave the wights to collect some wood and a little food for my family. Apples are always good, even though they might be a little soft. Please, masters, don't hand me over to Lord Eoppa. I only wanted to protect my children from the cold.'

Somehow, this Anglii peasant had failed to realise that his captors were neither Angle nor Saxon. In his fear, he continued to gabble and weep till Arthur eventually felt a grudging pity for a man whose only real crime was his poverty.

'Tie him up until I decide what to do with him,' Arthur snapped.

But, aware of his likely fate if his lord, Eoppa, was informed of his attempts to steal firewood, the peasant took a dreadful chance, opting to strike quickly and then flee back along the route that had brought him to the oak tree.

He launched himself at Arthur's back while his right hand extricated a long, thin blade from where it had been secreted inside his sheepskin leggings. Arthur could have been impaled, but the voice in his head had screamed a warning and he ducked below the arc of the blade's downward sweep. Nevertheless, Arthur still felt the hot sting of the man's knife as it skidded against a rib.

Gareth's reaction was immediate. Stepping forward with lighting speed, he removed the head of the Angle with a single blow from his sword.

For one short moment, the corpse remained upright with its neck fountaining blood, but then the knees buckled and the body folded slowly as if its bones had turned to jelly.

'Damnation!' Arthur swore. 'Why did you have to do that? The bastard will be missed now – and his absence will draw suspicion to the fortress.'

'Thanks, Arthur, it was nothing!' Gareth responded sardonically, but his master ignored the irony. Feeling a little light-headed from his wound, he leaned against the oak to rest for a brief moment and press a pad of cloth to the free-bleeding area.

Gareth stepped over the Angle's corpse and bared Arthur's wound. 'You'll have another impressive scar, master, but it's only a narrow slice. It's more blood than anything else, so you're lucky your leathers are so thick and your voice gave you some warning. As long as the wound doesn't become infected, it'll cause you no trouble. I can stitch it up as neatly as Father Lorcan would have done.'

'We'll have to solve the problem of what to do with this man first, Gareth. We'll need to take his body, his dog's, his cart and his horse as far as possible from here. With luck, no one will think to look in this area if his remains are found somewhere along the Roman road. Our whole venture could be wrecked if a search finds us before our friends can bring the fleet up the coast and moor the boats at the fortress.'

As Lars bundled the corpse into the cart and his comrades hunted for the severed head, a solution to the problem suddenly occurred to Arthur.

'Fill the cart with firewood. I don't care where we get it from, but we'll find a highly visible spot to the west of here where the wagon can be found by searchers. The corpse can be placed close to the wagon so our friend will appear to have met his death at that spot. We can dump the body of the hound at the same time. When his people find them, they'll assume that our unfortunate friend was thieving wood that belongs to his king and was put to the sword. We don't want any visitors coming to the fortress until we're good and ready to receive guests.'

How quickly the world could change. One moment, they were safe and fast asleep in the ideal winter camp and, in the next, the whole enterprise had been put at risk.

'When we were on the tower last night, I could see the remains of the Roman wharves. I'm convinced that this fortress is the perfect jumping-off point for our people to annex the whole area where we intend to build a permanent settlement. The wharves will serve for the flotilla during the coming winter, while we can moor the smaller vessels under the willows along the banks of the flood. I doubt that the Angles or their allies have vessels that can attack our ships from the seaward side of the coast, so the moorings can be easily defended.

'I want you to hurry back to the base camp, Lars! Your task is to pass my orders on to Snorri. Tell him he is to sail the entire fleet to the moorings at the Segedunum wharves immediately, with all of our people and whatever supplies can be stripped from the land around the cove. He must bring any stores that have already been unloaded and leave the cove as untouched in appearance as possible. While we await the fleet, we'll begin assessing what can be done to turn the remains of the fortress into a bastion that will protect us in the months to come. God speed, Lars.'

Arthur clasped the young man's arm in the Roman salute. 'Get the body of that damned dog, Lars, take our Anglii friend and his wagon with you on the first part of your journey, and abandon them some distance down the road where the Anglii searchers can easily find them. Uncouple the horse and hobble it so it can feed, then leave the bodies on the ground close to the wagon. I'm hoping they'll think he was taken by outlaws if they have doubts about their thane putting him to the sword. Meanwhile, take Ragnar and Knud with you in case you run into any trouble. You must scatter if you come under attack. If that happens, make your separate ways back to the cove. At least one of you must reach the base camp to ensure that Snorri receives his orders. Understood?'

Lars, Knud and Ragnar nodded their understanding. Ragnar strode off to load the grisly bodies into the cart while the remainder of the patrol set about cleaning up the small clearing and the area in the vicinity of the oak tree, flushing away the worst of the blood spill with river water collected in helmets. Arthur thanked the heavens that the river was so close. Some judicious spreading of soil where the ground had been churned served to return it to its normal wild tangle of vegetation. The first rains would wash away any residual signs of combat and bloody death and, as the smell of moisture in the air indicated, rain was already near at hand.

Lars and his two companions set off with the horse and cart while the others made a final, careful search of the area before returning to the fortress. But, before Arthur would permit Gareth to treat his wound, he insisted on stacking the cut firewood over the bloodstained stones outside the commander's house where the dog had died, so that the supply of fuel would be ready for burning in the fire pits. Then, once he was satisfied that their confrontation would pass some form of scrutiny, Arthur finally agreed to strip to his torso, have the wound washed and allow Gareth to stitch the cut together. Fortunately, Gareth always carried a small medical and surgical kit; he had promised Lorcan years earlier that he would keep this small kit filled and close to hand, for one of Father Lorcan's greatest fears was that one of his friends might succumb to some minor cut or illness.

Arthur endured the stitching and the application of a salve spread onto a length of clean rag. Then, once the ministrations were completed, a pad was tied in place around his back and chest.

Perhaps Arthur should have rested, but his first priority must be to prepare the fortress for the imminent arrival of several hundred people, clearing the inner sanctum of the forest of young trees and underbrush that impeded access to the various buildings. The same trees would provide firewood, and logs to repair any gross holes in the walls or roofs. The deserted countryside worked in their favour, because the Yellow Disease, whatever that was, had killed almost all the local population. The survivors had fled.

Methodically, Arthur set about planning the use of the precinct. With a determined glint in his eyes, he pointed out a bathhouse and, when they checked the subterranean levels of tanks, pipes and drains, they found that the hypocaust could be made operational.

'I had a Roman bath many years ago,' Arthur crowed at Gareth. 'I know you grew up with them at Aquae Sulis, but they're a luxury that's almost dead in Britain.' He smiled happily. 'I can't wait to have my first bath here.'

Gareth had almost become used to the realities of being filthy for weeks at a stretch, but he could still remember how pleasant a long, hot soak had been in the bathhouse of the Villa Poppinidii.

'Other priorities must come before bathing, Arthur. We'll need barracks to house the men, so we need to decide which buildings to repair. Once the ships arrive with more manpower, the work will progress much faster.'

'Still, we can make a start,' Arthur retorted amicably as he set to work.

Gareth, Arthur and Harald used the few tools that were available to them to begin the preliminary work of converting these ruins into a fully serviceable fortress. Arthur had never become used to the array of ironware carried by all Dene warriors, but these weighty tools now came in handy. In their first day of labour, they managed to clear the entrance to both the southern and eastern gates, to allow their companions an easier passage when they arrived at the fort. Not only were the trees chopped down, but the remnants were cut into firewood and stored in the old hospital. Then the three men set themselves to the task of digging out the centuries of earth and humus that had built up against the gates.

And so, four days passed in heavy labour, although Arthur's wound remained an irritant. Happily, the lands outside the fort were rich, green and ready for the Dene settlers to begin cultivation. All they needed were ploughs and seed.

Arthur knew the Dene presence would eventually be discovered, but he prayed each night for the leisure of time. Time would see them dig into the landscape and make it theirs; time would provide the comforts of a winter-proof camp; time would permit them to pick the countryside bare of the resources they would need in the months to come and allow them to plant crops; and time would give them a harvest to secure their futures and the lives of their wives and children.

Then, if the gods were kind, he would fight to hold this land in his mailed fist. He would forge a new kingdom here, or he would die in the attempt.

A happy man knows what he is meant to do with his future, and Arthur should have been elated as he saw ship after ship row up the river. The dim autumn light danced on the metal shield bosses and shimmered in droplets on the oars as they rose and fell like glistening diamonds in the bright waters. His heart caught fire in his throat as he looked out over the arrival of his fleet. He was truly home!

CHAPTER XIX

AN ENEMY IN THE FOREST

They answered that they were called Angles. 'It is well,' he (Pope Gregory the Great) said, 'for they have the faces of angels, and such should be the co-heirs of the angels of heaven.'

Bede, *Historia Ecclesiastica*, Book 2

Winter had been hard for the members of the fledgling colony, not because the weather was particularly cold, but because their lack of supplies forced them to scavenge and hunt throughout the countryside, while still attempting to disguise their presence. When they had left the Dene lands, Arthur had packed as much grain as possible into the ungainly trade ships that had been used to transport their livestock, but the supply was far too small for them to depend entirely on this staple. Arthur's long-dormant trapping skills must once again come to the fore.

There was much to do. The Dene warriors settled into the fortress as if it had been their home for many years. For security's sake, no effort was expended to open three of the gates that were sealed shut and limited access to the fortress. Any passing

Angle or Jute would notice such changes, but the half-open gate at the southern end must be addressed first for their safety. Arthur allotted one group of men the task of working to clear paving, doorways and entry areas, while another group was given the task of making buildings watertight. One other group became fishermen, trappers, hunters and scavengers and, finally, the fourth became scouts who were instructed to move beyond the local area and discover the politics and power structures within the local population. These men had some knowledge of the local languages and could fit seamlessly into the landscape.

The devil makes work for idle hands. Father Lorcan had often preached this simple axiom; now, in a late autumn and early winter when the snow had come early, the winds blew chill and the shallower parts of the river were freezing over, Arthur came to appreciate its aptness. Far from home and with nothing stimulating to challenge their minds, men quickly lost patience with each other, or harboured grudges and became irritable and difficult. However, the shared responsibility of patching roofs, felling trees, sawing and constructing shutters and making buildings snug kept the crews of men occupied and left them pleasantly tired at the end of the day. Further, Arthur allocated maintenance responsibilities for individual buildings to crews and turned what should have been hard work into competitive activities. As a reward, the winning crews were permitted to labour on repairs to the hypocaust and its promise of hot bathing if they ever managed to get the facility working again.

'Typical fucking Britons!' Lars grunted, deadpan. 'We work hard and win a prize from Arthur – the right to work even harder! And, if we work extremely hard, we'll be allowed to take a bath. Only he could think of rewards like that!'

'Are you insulting my master?' Gareth asked mildly, his

forefinger toying with the small leather strap that secured the pommel of his sword to its scabbard. Lars heard an edge of insult under the silky voice, so he shut his mouth firmly, although his jaw jutted out aggressively.

'Stop jesting, Lars,' Snorri ordered.

'My apologies, Gareth,' Lars said with apparent contrition. 'Arthur is our leader, so he's entitled to decide who does what, where and when.'

Gareth ran a forefinger over his prickly jaw with a menacing rasp. 'We're all a little on edge, Lars, but I warn you not to criticise my master in my hearing. He's already made you rich by inviting you to follow his banner. His journey has only just begun, so you're destined to have lands of your own if you follow him with patience and loyalty. Who else would do that for you?'

The awkward moment was permitted to pass, but only the love that Arthur's men felt for him had prevented certain disaster.

In the evenings, knowing the Dene love of story-telling, Arthur would search his memory for tales that would explain to his eager listeners the martial qualities of the Roman military machine in bygone days. Already the stuff of legends, the legions had developed a gloss of near-invincibility, so Arthur's stories often surprised his uneducated audience.

'The ordinary Roman soldier was about this high,' he explained, indicating what five and a half feet would look like compared with Ragnar's standing form. The warriors were unable to imagine how such little men could have conquered and ruled their world.

'I'm sorry to gainsay you, Arthur, but that couldn't be possible,' Lars said, shaking his head. 'My son's that tall, and he's only just turned eleven.'

'In fact, many of them were much shorter,' Arthur continued.

'But they beat the Franks, the Goths, the Germans . . . everyone! It doesn't seem possible,' Snorri exclaimed.

Leaving his men to mull over this strange information, Arthur bade his jarls a good night and retired to his room to sleep.

Germanus and Gareth, in company with Thord, a willowy warrior who had been a contemporary of Stormbringer in the Sae Dene's youth, eventually found signs of habitation that caused Arthur to re-evaluate his plans.

A small township comprised of defensive ditches, a familiar long-hall built of pillaged stone blocks and a number of small rectangular cottages straddled the smallish river but, although it was close to Segedunum as the crow flies, there didn't seem to be any roads linking the fortress to the township.

However, when the scouts ranged further afield, they found a partially serviceable Roman road, a thoroughfare that indicated the town was probably old Onnum, once famous as a waypoint on the route running through the Vellum Hadriani to the agricultural lands beyond – lands that were full of savages, Celtic tribes and the weakening influence of the thane called Eoppa. The scouts knew what Arthur would expect of them, so they followed the road into the north.

They were two days from the fortress when they sighted a trail of early-morning smoke rising from a township that lay astride the road.

'Better that we greet them now, rather than have a confrontation when we aren't expecting each other,' Germanus said pragmatically, as the three companions strolled through a copse towards a track leading into the outskirts of the grubby little township.

The road had once been paved, but was now little more than

a track and was covered with slush and debris from traffic. But there was some evidence that efforts had been made to keep it serviceable, so Germanus checked the edges of the paved area where chipped and broken stone channels drained water away from the thoroughfare. Some fifteen feet away, a stone emerged from the fresh snow and Germanus pointed towards it. Gareth responded with a slight nod of recognition.

Thord was annoyed by his own ignorance. 'What does that stone mean?'

'It's known as a distance marker and it tells a Roman traveller the distance from the nearest town of any significance. We're a little north of the Wall and I wouldn't have expected too many signs of Roman construction here, but it shows that this town must have been of some importance in the past.'

'Oh!' Thord noted that the ruler-straight path pointed directly at the distant signs of habitation. Germanus was certain that the handsome Dene was filing this evidence of Roman administration away so he could recall the knowledge if the opportunity should arise again.

'Do we wait for nightfall before we enter the town?' Thord asked, pointing towards the deep cluster of shanties and huts that surrounded the walls on all sides.

'I expect that the gates will be closed and locked at dusk. We'll draw too much attention if we try to enter at night, so we'll go in now. All three of us speak Saxon, so there shouldn't be any trouble over language.'

'So we just stroll in then?' Thord asked, surprised.

'Absolutely!' Germanus looked positively perky at the prospect. 'I feel the need for a warm bed tonight and a good beef stew.'

As the trio strolled along, they came upon several farmers with carts who had obviously been into town for the markets, although what they could be selling in winter was a mystery. Germanus greeted them with courtesy and pleasant inquiries about their day. For his part, Thord watched in amazement at the easy conversation that the two Britons struck up with their enemies, and was agog at the wealth of information that they learned before they reached the outskirts of the town that had the unprepossessing name of The Rising.

The road eventually bisected lines of shacks that obviously plied their trades on market days. Crude drawings on wooden walls indicated what was for sale and, sometimes, indicated price. In a world of illiterates, a picture was far more powerful than any number of words.

Gareth sensed that this town was teetering on the very edge of collapse. The shanty village and cottages outside the obviously once-Roman township were filthy, and many dwellings were abandoned. Those still in use were surrounded by churned mud paths, while obscenity-shouting children ran between the structures like small feral beasts.

Germanus noted that the children were undersized, lousy and swollen-bellied from malnutrition. Even more distressing were the young girls and women who were idling outside the doorways, trying their very best to look seductive despite being forced to don as many filthy clothes as they could wear to try and keep warm. Gareth was approached by one red-haired girl whose hair parting was visibly crawling with lice and whose smell took away any thoughts of sex as soon as he breathed it in. Whatever the town had once been, it was now a rat-hole, and it would remain a visible blot on the landscape until it was scoured clean by a new and vigorous master. Even the whores were thin to the point of emaciation; winter was almost over, but anything that could be eaten was long gone.

A hunchbacked peasant in a greasy cowl was already closing one side of the northern gates when the three travellers reached it. Thord recoiled visibly when he saw the man's diseased face; the man flinched under Thord's appalled gaze and, sensitive about his appearance, was trying to hide behind a rough woollen hood.

His breath whistled through two crude holes in a face that was a mass of scar tissue. His upper lip was mostly gone, exposing his teeth and gums in a gruesome parody of a permanent smile, while half his lower lip had been cut away, as if nibbled at by a voracious rat. With a gut-wrenching stab of pity, Gareth noticed that several of the poor man's fingers had been amputated. No doubt some of his toes had suffered the same fate.

'Well, gents,' the peasant whistled, his voice forever rendered comical by the horrors of his deformity. 'Yer only just made it into the town. Good thing yer did, for I've heard wolves howling these past few nights. The peasants say it's been a hundred year since the wolf packs came out of the north, but what can yer expect? These be bad times.'

'Plague?' Germanus asked, studiously keeping his face bland.

'Aye! We hopes it's been and gone! Two-thirds of our people died, so Lord Eoppa has banned all movement through the countryside to stop any new outbreaks. The farmers still come to market, but they live close-like. We'd have no food at all without them, so the thane's man closes his one good eye and lets them come and go whenever they've got something to sell.'

The grotesque face grinned amicably. 'Be careful, gents! The thane's like to order your throat cut to make sure you're free of disease. Since his son died, Eoppa's been ...' The peasant twirled his forefinger round his temple to indicate the universal sign of madness.

'We know nothing of what you speak. My friend here is Thord, and he's a recent arrival from Friesia, with some training as a healer. My other friend is Gareth, a part-Roman bastard out of Aquae Sulis. Before you get nervous about him, he's a mercenary who hires his sword to the thanes for gold.' Germanus rubbed his finger and thumb together suggestively.

'I'm a Frank, but I'm a bit long in the tooth for blood work, son. I've been looking for a new master, since my last thane died of the plague in the south. We'd be interested in getting any advice you could give us, perhaps over a drink or two?'

The universal language of alcohol cured the peasant's wariness and he hastened to pull the gates into position, a difficult task with his ruined hands. His new friends helped him with the task.

'And now, what's your name, good sir? If we intend to share some beer or wine with you, it'll be good to know who we're drinking with.'

Flattered, the peasant attempted to straighten his tunic and voluminous cloak to neaten his appearance. 'I'm Ludic No-Nose,' he said proudly. 'I know my face would fair frighten children, but I survived that damned disease, and not many men can say that. Men look at me now, and they know I'm not likely to pass it on to others.'

Thord wondered at how bleak life had to be when survival from a grim disease could be considered a measure of worldly success. What had he got himself into by travelling to this far-off land and leaving behind everything he knew and understood?

Then Germanus showed his mettle and his manhood. He extended his hand to Ludic, man to man. Ludic stared for a short moment, but then stood a little taller in his run-down boots. He extended his own paw.

'That makes two of us who've survived this terrible disease, friend Ludic. You might not know it, but I've discovered from experience that we're both safe now. The physicians have assured me that you can't catch the illness again once you've survived its first onset. I was one of the lucky ones!'

Germanus caught Ludic staring at his unmarked mouth and nose. The mutilated peasant could also see that the Frank had ten good fingers and bore no obvious signs of the disease. His face expressed his chagrin at his own appearance.

Germanus sighed softly to show his sympathy.

'The healer that treated me knew a little something about that bitch of an illness. As I said, I was lucky. He massaged my face and all my extremities, so the sickness didn't take them. He kept the blood flowing continuously around my body, and I even managed to keep my prick!'

'Me too!' Ludic giggled, as he realised that an odd friendship had formed between them.

Later, as Gareth and Thord watched Ludic and Germanus drinking companionably in the filthy inn, both men felt a little ashamed at their want of compassion.

When the three scouts returned to the fortress, they were able to give Arthur a valuable insight into Anglii motivations. Arthur was especially pleased to hear about Eoppa, a canny old Angle who had risen to his full height not only because of his intelligence, but because he understood the fallibility of men.

But time cursed Eoppa when the Yellow Disease killed his last surviving son, a stalwart warrior called Ida. For years, Eoppa had survived sustained attacks from the remnants of the Otadini, the Picts and several Celtic armies who had penetrated into the north from their lands in the south and the west. He had given three living sons and several daughters to these lands, so his blood was hand-fasted to Britain forever. But love it? Never!

Thord attempted to put his understanding of the complex political situation into words. 'Eoppa's determination keeps him here. That and the fact that this is the final resting place for his sons. The Yellow Disease appears to be the same plague that we know so well and it seems to have wormed its way through northern Britannia. The sickness came here with trading ships that crossed from Friesia and Saxony to Dubris and made their way up the coast. The disease spread like Greek Fire at every place where the traders stopped.

'From what we heard, the Britons have suffered even more casualties than the Angles, but that news is the stuff of rumours. What is certain is that Eoppa's people have borne the full brunt of it.'

He paused, and allowed his message to sink in for a few short seconds.

'Some of the survivors we met were badly scarred but they were still grateful to be alive. One thing's for sure, the onset of the illness has denuded these lands of farmers and labourers.'

Thord continued to explain the situation as patiently as he could, but he was constantly interrupted with questions that had little bearing on the subject in hand.

'Give Thord a chance, friends,' Arthur ordered quietly, his fingers drumming on the table top. The hubbub subsided with remarkable speed.

'Thane Eoppa rules lands that stretch from the coast to positions well south of the Wall and extend along the Roman road leading to the fortress town called Habitancum. In recent times, this town has been called The Rising because of the sloping terrain in the area. He's not a true king, but his ancestry is as regal as any Anglii lord's can be in these difficult lands. At this time, he is surrounded by enemies who would happily destroy him, and this danger is compounded by the remnants of the Otadini tribe and the other British kings who wait to the north of the Wall and hide among the inaccessible mountains. To these enemies can be added those Saxon outlaws and blue-faced Picts who steal whatever plunder they can find. He has been at war with different enemies for too many years now, and he's turned into a tired old man.'

At the use of the Otadini name, Arthur's face twitched and he massaged his chin. His raised right eyebrow asked his next question without any need for words.

'I was told that Eoppa is the nephew of Ine, the king of Wessex, which is a vast tract that lies far to the south. Historic-ally, Eoppa's ancestors were kings in Jutland, but they were displaced by the Dene. Eoppa has an excellent pedigree and I would have to concede that his capacity for ruling his people is considerable.'

Thord went on to explain how the thane lost his sons during the battles that had been fought to maintain control over the land. The new rulers of the British tribes were his greatest enemies, men who remained arrogant and unbending because of their descent from King Gawayne and King Artor. They refused to cede a single inch of their ancestral lands, and waited to pounce on Eoppa at the first sign of a chink in the old man's armour.

Arthur felt his throat constrict. 'What happened to the Otadini?'

Thord could think of no way to soften his news.

'From what I was told, master, their kings are long dead or they've fled north and west to continue their resistance with the remnants of the other British tribes. Our informant told us that the Picts have tried to kill off the survivors, so heaven knows how strong they are now.'

Arthur thought of Blaise who was living in safety at The Holding, and how fortunate she had been to avoid the certain death that would have awaited her if her planned marriage into the Otadini ruling class had taken place. Her betrothed had been murdered by stealth, possibly by Arthur's own kinsmen.

'Who killed off the Otadini? Was it this Eoppa? He must be a clever strategist if he achieved what so many Saxons and Jutes failed to do.'

Gareth took up the tale smoothly, but his brow was lined with perplexity. He guessed that these questions were intensely personal.

'According to a disreputable Angle called Ludic No-Nose, the Otadini rulers were betrayed from within by one of their own kinsmen.'

Gareth's use of Ludic's name was followed by soft titters from the jarls.

'The man's name seems humorous, but he has lost his nose and most of his lips to the Yellow Disease,' Gareth continued. 'But Germanus found him to be a knowledgeable sort of fellow. He was likeable too. He told us that a kinsman of the Otadini, domiciled in the south, had brokered an arrangement with Eoppa to kill off the tribe's ruling family. When Eoppa quibbled at the use of treachery to gain control of the Otadini lands, this man, who is apparently called Bran, left Eoppa in no doubt that his alternative plan was to take the Otadini lands by making a pact with Pict mercenaries to assist him in an invasion of the north. At the completion of this campaign, Bran threatened to put all of Eoppa's men, women and children to the sword. Ultimately, Eoppa was forced to comply with Bran's demands.

Ludic, of course, was just repeating rumours, and I heard several other names mentioned as being among the perpetrators of the plot.'

Gareth stared directly at Arthur. 'I know it sounds bizarre, but Eoppa's position is tenuous and is centred on a place on the Wall called Onnum. If the Angles were to survive and prosper, the thane would have to make treaties to deal with this Bran, a prospect he found unattractive. Is this the same Bran who is your kinsman?'

'Do you think so, Gareth?' Arthur's voice was controlled, but his eyes were an ugly shade of wintry grey.

'Lord, you know how unreliable gossip can be. Everything Ludic had ever seen of Britons suggested they would die before they would give up a foot of their ancestral lands. He warned us to be careful of what we came to believe – and what we passed on to others, especially if Eoppa's men were listening.'

'Yes! Eoppa submitted,' Ragnar interrupted cynically. 'But he didn't surrender out of fear. Such a course of action suited his purposes at the time.'

'As it turned out, you're right,' Gareth answered. 'But everything we've learned of Eoppa indicates that he is a brave man who's tried to act with honour and decency during most of his reign in Britannia. I don't see him as a murderer or a barbarian, for the orders he issued to save his people from the Yellow Disease were sensible and would have saved many hundreds of lives. He confiscated the coastal lands of the Otadini out of the same rational acceptance of a bad situation.'

'But he is an Angle, so he must be an enemy!' Knud rumbled from the end of a long table.

'That kind of thinking shouldn't apply here,' Arthur said diplomatically in an attempt to avoid alienating the impulsive

Knud. 'By your rules, I'd have to consider all of you as lifelong enemies because you're aliens in my homeland. Besides, we have a number of Angles among the settlers we brought to Britannia with us, so we shall have to accept that all these people are worthy of inclusion in our plans for the future.'

'Real men like my friend, Conn Long-Jaw, don't count,' Knud mumbled, shame-faced. 'He might be an Angle, but he's already committed to living with us.'

'That doesn't make much sense, my friend,' Germanus stated, and Snorri, who had been very quiet, nodded.

'We're strangers in this land, so where we come from doesn't matter to most of the people who live here. We'll have to start thinking of ourselves as Britons, because to go home in failure and disgrace is unthinkable,' Snorri explained. 'We need to leave our prejudices out on the grey seas from where we came. You too, Arthur, because you've never been over-fond of Saxons.'

'I agree, Snorri! Their forebears have lived here for well over a hundred years. Much as I hate to say it, they are Britons now. In fact, my grandfather was half-Roman and most of my ancestors were aliens here too.'

Arthur was bleeding inside. He had been prepared to go to war against Eoppa with a cheerful heart because this unknown thane had supplanted and decimated the Otadini. But he found himself cut to the quick by these rumours of Bran's involvement, strategies so overt that even the peasants gossiped about them. Still, there would be time to think these horrors through. Right now he only needed the evidence of his scouts' eyes and ears.

'Enough! We'll return to the here and the now. Tell me everything you can remember about the town.'

Thord lurched into nervous speech. 'Aye, master. The town walls were once the walls of a Roman fort. We could see the towers and the four gates, just like here. One of the Roman roads runs northwards through the walled town, and the whole area inside the walls has been filled with rickety wooden structures. You'd be hard put to get a wagon into the smaller streets. I could just recognise the main Roman buildings, although the townsfolk of today use them for other purposes.'

From Thord's description Arthur could imagine how the Angles and Jutes must have used the extra space bequeathed to them by the Romans. The security of the thick walls would have contributed to their successful occupation of the town.

'There were a number of buildings clustered outside the Roman walls, filthier and more decrepit than others I've seen, although it's hard to tell what the place was like before the plague visited. Most of the buildings are deserted now and there's a real stink of failure about the place. I discovered the name of the fortress from a commemorative pedestal at the city gates,' Gareth added. 'The word on the stone was *Habitancum* but, as Thord says, everyone we spoke to referred to the town as The Rising.'

'It'll be years before I forget the bed in that inn,' Germanus interrupted, shuddering. 'I stripped off my clothes before I had the courage to lie on the floor, and I could still see the lice as they crawled around on that pallet. I don't think I brought any of those little buggers back with me, but every stitch of clothing I wore is boiling away as we speak.'

'All three of you should take every precaution to ensure you're clean again,' advised Arthur. 'Burn all of your clothing if you have any doubts, because one of the things we know about the plague is that it travels with lice. Meanwhile, Germanus, is there anything else you learned that might be of use to us?'

'Eoppa controls the coastal area around the Wall and his

influence extends a little way into the north. He is also in control of a Roman road referred to as the Dere Path in those parts. But he leaves much of the inland area and the hills to the Britons, the outlaws and those landless men who eke out the barest of livings up there. The thane is pinned down inside an area that is relatively wealthy, but he can only further his ambitions if he can acquire further tracts of land. From all that I heard, I'm convinced that Eoppa will have to relinquish any dreams of glory now that the last of his sons has passed into the shades. I was assured that the Briton, Bran, is just waiting for an opportunity to attack him.'

'So! What can we do to protect ourselves?' Ragnar asked. How bad could their luck be? They had landed in the area where a kinglet had carved out a small, wealthy, but precarious kingdom. Eoppa's external threats would have made him very vigilant to the presence of strangers.

'The plague came at exactly the right time for us,' Arthur stated baldly. 'With luck, it will remain dormant throughout the winter, so we must work hard to prepare for spring and the arrival of our families and livestock. Meantime, we don't invite the plague to turn on its tracks and revisit this place. We shall keep the fortress clean! Eoppa will be licking his wounds throughout the rest of the winter months, and we know he's ordered his peasants to stay within their villages, so I'm hoping we can remain undiscovered until spring. By then, it'll be too late to dislodge us. Like the ticks in Germanus's tunic, we'll be too deeply embedded to shift.'

'I pray you're right, master,' Snorri added. The circle of captains seemed a little happier.

That night, before sleep overtook him and he was forced to endure another visitation from the she-dragon, he made a ruthless decision. If Bran had destroyed Gawayne's descendants, then he and Ector were the last survivors of the line of King Artor. The destruction of the whole Otadini tribe was an unimaginable solution to the thorny problem of succession to a throne. But the Britons were outnumbered, so even Bran's grandiose dreams could hardly delude him into believing the Celtic kings could defeat their many enemies. At best, Bran and his son would be the undisputed leaders of the Western Alliance centred on Cymru; but Arthur hated to think that Bran had grown so deluded.

As the Last Dragon, Arthur was now presented with a conundrum where he must be divorced from his family forever. His living kinsmen were men of straw and Bran would be of no use to him in a new world that was about to be born out of the ashes of northern Britannia. Except for his immediate family, Arthur would throw his lot in with his Dene followers. The redoubtable Taliesin wanted to use Arthur to carve out an impossible kingdom from the old rags of glory; Bran wanted him dead for obvious reasons; the other kings wanted to control him like a puppet; and most of the noble lords would choose to use him as a bulwark between themselves and their enemies.

Like his father, he would be goaded into an early death, driven by forces that cared not one jot for him as a man or as a king.

Arthur made his decision. He would build his own kingdom, but he would never use his father's name to achieve this ambition. If Bran got in the way, then Bran would die.

Thorketil was in his element during the winter. His bow brought down so many deer and wild oxen that the warriors, under the tutelage of Ingrid and Sigrid, were kept busy smoking, salting and drying meat. In the few weeks before the winter solstice,

Arthur had ordered the soil broken by the two ploughs they had brought with them, and the warriors uncomplainingly took the place of horses or oxen to draw the heavy ploughshares. They had all known that the earth would freeze once the snows came. The first steps in agriculture had begun and every man felt his heart begin to lighten.

The winter that year was particularly vicious, with snowfalls deeper than the height of a man. But the Dene warriors, used to even colder winters, were unperturbed. Snowshoes, skis and hastily built sleds were quickly constructed and the men roamed ever further through the forests and the snow-covered agricultural lands.

The few women in the fledgling settlement were all slaves who had accompanied their owners. For one reason or another, their owners had been reluctant to sell them and had opted to bring them on the voyage, forcing Arthur to place them under his personal protection. Aware of the difficulties, Ingrid ensured that the women stayed out of sight once the light was gone and kept them working hard within the confines of their own secure area. Courtesy of a few wild sheep that had been caught, Arthur was surprised to hear the comforting thud of a loom and the whir of spindles. There was little enough wool to keep the slaves occupied on this task, but many other preparations needed to be made before the ships sailed for Skandia in the early spring. Arthur grew more and more impatient to find his family.

Meanwhile, the warriors had little time to fret for distant kin during the hours of daylight. Roofs must be made sound after every rafter had been checked and, if necessary, replaced. Soon, room by room and building by building, the fortress was being dragged to some semblance of order.

The clearing of paths had provided enough firewood to last

throughout the winter and spring months, except for some sturdy fruit trees that had grown up in the most improbable of places. As for the floors in the barracks, the patient Skandians found coarse terracotta paving lying under the several feet of guano and earth that had accumulated since the Romans deserted their fortress. Arthur's warriors were amazed at how the buildings seemed to have escaped the ravages of time.

The curative powers of nature were remarkable. Like the apple tree in the atrium of the commander's residence, one resilient pear tree had forced aside several fired bricks in the foundations of one of the granaries and its skeleton now awaited the warmer months. Arthur lacked the heart to chop it down, for good fruit trees were hard to find.

The bats were another matter entirely. The Dene shared an intense dislike for bats with the local population, so the small nocturnal animals had to go. The deep guano deposited in the granary during their long occupancy was remarkably fecund, and Arthur was eager to shovel up the mucky wealth. For some time, he feared he would have to kill the whole colony before they would relinquish their hold on this warm and dry resting place. Eventually, he realised the granary would have to be sacrificed if the humans were to force the bats to move to more amenable quarters. And so, after ensuring that every entrance to the fortress buildings was barred, the granary was left open to the winter weather. Affronted, the colony of bats left at dusk and failed to return.

'Will they die, Arthur? I'd hate to think that we've sent them off to perish in the cold.' Sigrid's face was wet with tears as she watched the final bats fly off into the west.

Arthur took her determined little chin between his thumb and forefinger. 'Don't worry! They'll find a deserted barn or another set of Roman ruins to colonise before morning. They're flexible little buggers!'

'So they'll be safe and well? Even the little ones?'

'Even the little ones!' Arthur felt the urge to kiss her upturned nose, but he resisted. He could hardly enjoy the pleasures that had been forbidden to his own warriors.

Scruples can be painful constraints, he reflected as he left the girl to her own devices. Nearby, her mother smiled knowingly.

Life in the fortress was peaceful and uncomplicated, and even Snorri was convinced that Arthur's settlers had escaped discovery. The Dene scouts had seen no evidence of strangers by the time of the first spring thaws, so Arthur ordered the captains to select skeleton crews and make their preparations for the return journey to collect the warriors' families and their worldly goods, plus whatever staples were needed for those who remained at Segedunum.

But Fortuna is black-hearted, and the man who trusts her is a fool.

Shortly after the fleet left, Arthur had taken his snow shoes and left the fortress several hours before sunrise. He took no food and no light on his lone night patrol, trusting to the Dragon Knife and his mailed shirt to keep him safe. The men on sentry duty watched as their master slid through the southern gate; Arthur had insisted that sentries should remain silent in case their positions were discovered by infiltrators. One of them secured the gateway as soon as he was safely into the line of trees.

Arthur had no idea why he chose to leave a warm pallet behind him and risk freezing his backside off on a one-man patrol during the dark hours before dawn, but he had been insistently taunted by the warning inside his skull throughout the night, so he eventually decided that to ignore it might be more foolhardy than responding to it.

Memories of Arden Forest came back to Arthur as he slipped from shadow to shadow until he found a tall oak tree that would allow him to observe the area to the rear of Segedunum. Hoping he hadn't forgotten his climbing skills, he began the noiseless ascent.

Halfway up the tree, he reached a secure fork that was hidden from below. If he sat still with his back against the trunk, he was virtually invisible.

One hour passed. A second hour drifted by, while he tried to ignore his cramped leg muscles. A third hour had almost passed when a shape moved in an adjacent tree, only thirty yards from his hiding place. The silent screaming in Arthur's ears was very loud now. The figure seemed to unroll itself from its perch until he could see a man as he slide, to the ground and followed the spreading roots towards a long fissure in a streamlet where his footsteps would be disguised by running water. In the stillness of the dark morning, muffled Anglii curses sounded quite clearly when the dark shape took a sudden step backwards into the water.

'By the black tits of Don, why do we have to keep getting our feet wet all the time?' the man snarled.

Another body appeared from a position near the narrow waterway, while the first man cursed again with alarm. 'Aethelthred, you shit! I almost pissed myself! Can't you give a man a bit of warning before you appear from under his fucking feet?'

'Shut up, you babbling fool. I've had to endure your blathering for three weeks and I'm growing very tired of it. If you don't like your duties, you can tell Eoppa about your problems and see where *that* gets you.'

The second voice was lighter and crisper. Arthur guessed that the second man was probably of a higher caste than the first.

'Fuck you, Aethelthred! I hope you catch the lung disease and *die*,' the first scout complained.

'Has there been any news from the fortress?' Aethelthred demanded.

'Nothing! It was nothing last night, and it'll be nothing again tomorrow night. This whole business has been a waste of time. For great, hairy savages, this lot are surprisingly stupid.'

Arthur held his breath in shock because he couldn't understand why he hadn't been intercepted and killed. But suddenly he realised. Thanks be to all the gods, but you've been sleeping when you should have been awake and patrolling this area. You should have seen me, you arsehole, and now you're lying to your jarl to cover up your damned incompetence.

'Let's hope they're truly stupid and aren't here to mount an attack on us. We could find ourselves in a hopeless situation. What's the latest death count from the Yellow Disease?'

'Two hundred, at the last and best guess.'

'Sweet Jesus of Nazareth! Have we lost that many? Let's pray there aren't too many more. Now, pick up Egbert and Harald and report back to the captain. Then you'd best get yourself some sleep while we have the chance.'

'Oh! And before I forget, the bats seem to have gone!'

'Sometimes I think you have porridge for brains, Ingwy. What fucking bats?'

This idiot has been in that tree since nightfall, Arthur thought furiously. But he's alert enough to notice that he hasn't seen any bats during that time. Shite! How long have we been under observation, and why haven't our scouts spotted their tracks?

Then Arthur was forced to be fair. These scouts were using

the stream to disguise their footprints, and seemed to be using basic woodsmen's precautions to hide their movements. The closeness of his escape made his hair rise at the nape of his neck.

Ingwy hissed out his observations to Aethelthred. Cursing Ingwy's sudden bout of caution, Arthur strained to catch their words.

'They're up to something in there . . . but only Wodin knows . . . most of them speak bad Anglii . . . I think they're probably Denè because I heard the word Heorot, and something called Justinian's . . .'

Aethelthred replied but Arthur missed what he said. Fortunately, Ingwy wasn't so careful.

'Are you deaf? Fuck me! What is it about you Wessex Angles? You said to count the number of boats – or whatever they are – moored down near the old Roman wharves! There's at least a dozen vessels that are missing from the earlier count.' Ingwy was almost shouting as two more scouts materialised from out of the watercourse.

The words were suddenly cut off as the four figures disappeared like wraiths into a line of black willows.

Arthur waited almost half an hour, just to be certain.

Finally, satisfied that the landscape was utterly still, he unfolded his numbed legs and climbed down from the oak.

He limped for several paces while his blood began to flow down into his feet. Then a chorus of birds sounded in the hidden crown of a tree high above him. The first burst of feeble light had reached their roost and the small creatures carolled their joy at the advent of a new day.

Arthur felt his heart lighten; he was in his homeland and would soon find solutions to their problems.

Is this Eoppa a man of common sense? I'll swear allegiance to the devil himself if such a promise wins us the right to any empty land we can use. I'll not despair until all hope of a reasonable solution is lost.

Almost jauntily, he strode through the small wood. He had no intention of weakening now, not when everything he wanted was so achingly close.

Even so, he decided to re-organise his defences so that his command could cope with a prolonged siege. As a first priority, he decided to restore the protective ditch and to prepare his warriors for the prospect of a major skirmish. Nor would it hurt if the jarls were told of their failure to notice infiltrators in their midst.

Several birds broke from cover in front of him with a great clatter of noise as he approached. The tendrils of light caught the red-gold of his hair in an aureole of fire. Like some ancient sun god, Arthur approached his fortress with purposeful foot-steps, his heart suddenly light. Something fortuitous was surely coming their way.

Mercifully, the warning voice in his head had become totally silent.

CHAPTER XX

TO DANCE WITH THE DEVIL

The most hateful torment for men is to have knowledge
of everything and power over nothing.

Herodotus, *Historia*, Book 9

Well into the morning, the Dene ships negotiated the river in a
long serpentine tail as the north-eastern towers came into view.
The cry went up in the fortress as soon as the first ship hove into
view. They had come: the women had come!

The ships carried sails woven with bright emblems and, as he
gazed down at them, Arthur wondered if those brilliant symbols
had been touched up especially for this triumphant moment.
The sun was bright and strong, while daffodils grew in every dell
and damp rockery. The most gifted singer would have struggled
to find a day that was more dew-washed and beautiful for the
fleet's return. Seagulls screamed, wheeled and waited for any
bounty cast out from the vessels while on the decks women and
children, wearing their best clothing, stood in huddles with
their fair heads catching the light.

'They are ever so brave, Gareth,' Arthur said to his companion who, as always, was standing phlegmatically behind his master.

'What do you mean, Arthur?'

'Look down at those women. They've left their families, their homes and everything that is familiar and safe, because their men require this sacrifice from them. Would you do the same for a *woman*? Would Snorri? Or Ragnar?'

'I wouldn't,' Gareth replied decidedly.

Arthur was certain that the fortress was under observation, so he detailed a skeleton crew of unattached warriors to man the battlements and act as lookouts while the families were reunited and the most essential stores were unloaded. Everyone who could be released was permitted to make his way to the crumbling old wharves with hands full of flowers and faces that were wreathed in smiles. Regardless of the feeling that prying eyes were watching from every coppice and the tops of every tree, the Dene warriors were determined to enjoy the arrival of their families.

But as soon as the initial greetings were completed, willing and enthusiastic hands began the mammoth task of unloading the ships and carrying everything up to the fortress. It was time for the crews and the guards to begin the back-breaking task of storing these long-awaited necessities.

Arthur stood in the tower above the southern gate and looked down on the gaggle of chattering families entering the fortress for the first time. With nervous care, the women avoided brushing against the scrubbed walls of the entrance as if they might pollute this huge old structure with their skirts. Their happy chatter was cut off abruptly by the ruler-straight paths and the refurbished buildings which Arthur's warriors had made cheerful with flowers planted beside the doorways and in elongated garden beds.

'Segedunum is a daunting place for our new arrivals, isn't it?' Arthur commented to Gareth. 'So much stone! So much order! I'd bet that there'd be at least one good wife out there who is telling her husband that this place isn't very cosy.'

Arthur and his captains had been preparing for the allocation of accommodation for the non-combatants for several weeks. Concentration on such mundane tasks took their minds away from the pressing concerns of what lay ahead. Meanwhile, the Anglii silence was nerve-racking because Eoppa had refrained from moving against the Dene. In fact, he made no sign that he even recognised that invaders had taken up residence on his doorstep.

Arthur smiled a secretive smile – and waited.

Meanwhile, barrels filled with seal oil were placed inside the ditch in carefully prepared positions, so the oil could be set alight if the Angles should be so unwise as to make a full frontal attack. Still more barrels were positioned throughout the fortress where channelled water could be stored in the event of a protracted siege. As well, the defensive ditches outside the walls had been cleared of any growth that would offer cover to an attacking army. Forever obstreperous, Ragnar had grumbled that Arthur's precautions would prove useless if Eoppa was determined, but Arthur's only response was that same sweet and annoying smile.

One of the first requirements of the new arrivals was to have their treasured possessions moved up to the fortress where they could be placed into temporary storage. Ever-thoughtful, Germanus was heard to say that the limited room available would soon set the women to bickering.

'One way or another, Segedunum can only provide temporary protection until such time as we can move out into the surrounding countryside,' Germanus advised Arthur as soon as an opportunity arose. 'Too many women close together is a recipe for disaster. I tell you the truth, boy, when I say that women are notorious for measuring each man's status by the size of his property and they'll go to war over a stool or an iron kettle if they are left to their own devices for too long. These families need to be out in the countryside where they can live in their own cottages and work their own land. Otherwise, the women will replace Eoppa as your enemy.'

One stubby forefinger pointed towards a cluster of women who were drawing water out of the cisterns, while laughing merrily at the convenience of the Roman system of water collection.

'They're happy now! But just give them a little time and we'll see what they're like!'

'I understand, Germanus. I have a feeling that Eoppa has already decided to attack us during the night, either in the late evening or very early in the morning. He'd expect that most of us would be drunk and burrowing into the breasts of our women then.'

'A fair assessment. What do the captains say?'

Germanus and Gareth exchanged glances that were difficult to read, but Arthur knew that his two friends had a healthy distrust of Dene overconfidence regarding their own skills.

'I've given orders for the unattached men to remain on duty on the palisades throughout the night. To be on the safe side, and because they'd not obey a veto anyway, I've given permission for those of our men with families to make merry during the night. However, I've extracted an oath from them that they'll drink no more than two draughts of beer or mead on this most dangerous of nights. They can resume their celebrations at some future time when their families are safe.'

'But will they obey these instructions?' Gareth replied. Arthur was all too aware that most of his men would be tempted to break their oaths after such a long separation from their families. They had wrought miracles in order to bring Segedunum back to life; they had ploughed and laboured in the fields like slaves rather than warriors; they had lived like monks; and they had served their masters cheerfully and eagerly. Arthur had no complaints about their general behaviour.

But this night was special. There was a strong possibility that Eoppa would use this celebration as an opportunity to mount a direct attack on the fortress, and only Fortuna could know what events would transpire.

As the evening meal was devoured, and after the children were led to their beds in these strange surroundings, a festive air began to set hearts aflutter throughout the ancient fortress. Knud found his pipe and Rolf took out his harp, while a number of warriors and women retrieved an assortment of musical instruments from their possessions. The musicians began to play peasant tunes until the night was filled with the rousing music, and an old, outdoor fire pit was quickly filled with timber and lit, its sparks rising into the night sky. One of the men swung his wife into a vigorous dance, followed by more and more pairings, faces sweating, plaits flying and feet stamping.

Arthur was pulled into the square of dancers by a beautiful girl, her hair russet in the firelight, and he moved as gracefully as he could to the pumping sound of the music. But then he caught sight of Sigrid's pale face as she watched him from the shadows. Inexplicably, he felt guilty.

As soon as he could extricate himself without causing offence, Arthur stopped a cheerful young warrior and exchanged places with him so adroitly that the pretty young maiden felt no slight.

They swirled off into a ring-dance of young people as he melted into the crowd.

Sigrid was in the doorway of the commandant's house, her chin resting on the heel of her hand. So engrossed was she in the revelry that Arthur was standing alongside her before she noticed his presence.

'You startled me, Lord Arthur,' she said and reluctantly dragged her gaze away from the dancing couples. 'How may I help you? Is there anything that you need?'

'Why, nothing at all, Sigrid! But isn't it nice to see everyone smiling and happy?'

Sigrid wasn't used to displays of affection or any open consideration from her master, so she had decided long ago that he disliked her.

'You're jesting, my lord, and it's not kind to play such games with me. I'm sixteen now, and a woman full grown. I'd rather you didn't trifle with me, for I know the workings of the world and the true value of a slave girl.'

Arthur was taken aback by the honesty of her response. As she watched his mind working, Sigrid's eyes were painfully sad.

'I know that I'm your slave, master,' she mumbled, unable to meet his eyes. 'I'm grateful for the respect you've shown me. I was longing to dance.'

'You're not just a slave to me, Sigrid. I never wanted to make slaves of any of you, but I couldn't guarantee the safety of your family if I hadn't taken you. If you only knew the long nights—'

Sigrid placed her hand over Arthur's mouth, as if she feared what he might be about to say. Her eyes were even more miserable than before. Impulsively, Arthur responded by capturing her hand and kissing each finger in turn, although she tried to pull her hand away from his grasp.

'Listen, Sigrid. Tomorrow night when I am once again the leader, I may not be able to find the words to express my feelings for you. But tonight, I'm able to speak the truth. I've cared for you for a long, long time, although I know that I've often been selfish. I could have granted manumission to your mother but feared that your family would suffer without a man to protect her. As my slave, I'm supposed to protect you, rather than seduce you, so I haven't known what to do with you. I haven't been happy when I've been away from you, and I've been equally unhappy when you are close, but beyond my reach!'

Sigrid had opened and closed her mouth to speak on several occasions.

'My lord! . . . Arthur, I've loved you for years, so I don't give a damn about how honourable your behaviour might be. You're such a blockhead, Arthur, and our friendship has suffered because of your stupid scruples.'

Then, to make his position even more difficult, she slid into his arms, while pinning him against the doorframe, her long brown legs and small conical breasts pressed against him. His body responded immediately, so she giggled with amusement as her hand sought him out.

'Behave, Sigrid,' he managed to blurt out. 'I cannot marry a slave. In fact, the day may be approaching when I'll have to marry a suitable woman for the sake of a throne. Think, girl! You'll gain nothing from our friendship but unhappiness.'

She had pinched him then, hard enough for the sudden pain to be a fine balance of eroticism and sadism. He felt an urge to bite her long neck until the blood began to flow and then feed off her as if he was a feral beast. Half-defeated, he closed his eyes as her hands moved and her lips found his sensitive nipples within his jerkin.

'Woman!' he warned her thickly. 'A man can only have so much willpower and mine is leaking away far too quickly. Go to your mother – now!'

'No!' she replied in a determined voice. Then, before he could push her away, she began to slide soundlessly along the passageway while leaving him in her wake.

Arthur followed her, acutely conscious of her feet padding over the tesserae floor. When she reached his doorway, she fumbled awkwardly with the latch and Arthur heard her curse like a soldier for a short moment, then the door swung open and she disappeared into the black maw. By the time he arrived, she was almost invisible within his darkened bedchamber.

Half-blinded by lust, Arthur heard the door close behind him. Sigrid stood naked alongside his sleeping pallet with the dull light from an oil lamp behind her. Despite his best intentions, Arthur caressed her body with his eyes. Shades of ivory tinted her skin; her hair was a river of palest white gold, her eyes were the bluest of blue; she was every young man's dream of perfection. She was his now and, by choice, she would never belong to any other man.

'I'm virginal, my lord, although several men have cause to speak *castrato* because they tried to take me against my will. I belong to you for life, regardless of what you may decide to do with me. If you should reject me, I am determined to die with my maidenhead intact. The choice is yours.'

What could Arthur do?

In the end, just as Sigrid and her mother had planned, Arthur took Sigrid's maidenhead in his large and rather uncomfortable bed. Ingrid had spread rose petals and small daisy flowers over the pallet and Arthur fell asleep with the scent of a garden crushed into her creamy flesh.

* * *

The warning knock at Arthur's door came at a time when Segedunum seemed to be sleeping, totally silent. Putting his hand over Sigrid's mouth, he clambered to his feet and searched for his clothes and the Dragon Knife secreted under the pallet.

'Be careful, my love,' Sigrid whispered. 'I'll wait for your return, no matter how long your business takes.'

Gareth and Germanus met him outside his room after he'd donned a mail shirt and a leather tunic braced with dragon-embossed brass plates. Arthur's chest glittered dully, but his eyes were gleaming in the semi-darkness. He was feeling warm and loved, and marvelled at how cheerful he felt to know that someone would be awaiting his return.

'We have a problem, Arthur,' Gareth began without preamble.

'A large force of Anglii warriors have taken up positions around the fortress,' Germanus added.

'How many of them are facing us? Have you alerted the captains? How about the boats? Have they been secured?'

Arthur's questions came with the rapid-fire rhythm of his heels as they thudded over the stone-flagged floor of the commander's villa.

'There's no real way of knowing yet. We only left a skeleton crew of single men on guard – remember? The captains are waiting for you in the south-west tower. That's where the Angles were first spotted.' Germanus's voice was crisp, unemotional and unhurried.

'I want Thorketil up there, and one of his best bowmen in each of the other three towers, Gareth. Carry him up the stairs if you have to. I need them all in place as quickly as possible.'

Gareth was appalled. 'I can't carry the Troll King, Arthur. The man is seven feet tall, and he's a monster.'

'Just get him to the wall, Gareth,' Arthur sighed. 'We'll figure out some way of getting him to the top of the tower.'

And then the tower doorway lay before them. Arthur and Germanus bounded up the stairs to the ramparts.

With six of his captains beside him, Arthur stared out into the pre-morning darkness. The hour was very late and the moon was sinking down into the heavens. Although summer was coming, the early morning still held a chill and Arthur could see faint tendrils of fog in the deeper hollows of the ground outside the fortress. The moon was large and full, dangerous because it shed so much pearly light. A single torch burning below the parapet of the tower allowed Arthur to clearly see the faces of Ragnar, Snorri and the others.

'Where are the rest?' he asked tersely.

'I've allotted men to each of the other towers and a number of places along the covered parapets. I know this is the only gate that opens and shuts, but I'd still like to know what's going on behind our backs,' Snorri grunted. When he had been dragged from the arms of his newly arrived wife by Germanus, the helmsman had been dreaming of his children and the farmland he had selected. Terrified by the interruption, his woman had responded by bursting into tears, so the bluntly spoken helmsman wasn't happy.

'Let's see what we're dealing with before we start jumping to conclusions,' Arthur advised. Just then he heard a commotion at the bottom of the stairs leading up to the tower. 'That sounds like Thorketil climbing the stairs.'

A series of oaths warned the captains that someone was dragging himself up the tower by brute force. When Thorketil, bright red in the face, arrived at the top, with Gareth grunting behind him as he assisted the big man, he heaved himself into the partial light like a shaggy cave bear, seemingly more beast than man.

Arthur beckoned to the man-mountain as he shouldered his way to the front of the rampart and was able to stare down into the ditch that surrounded the fortress.

'You were watching when we placed the barrels filled with seal oil in the ditch, my friend, and I agreed with you that they'd be an expensive gamble if they couldn't be used against our enemies. The time has come. You also noticed that we broke some of them open so there are pools of oil in a number of places. You and your other marksmen must rain fire arrows down and set them alight, preferably with our Anglii friends nearby. Will you summon Rufus?'

Thorketil whistled in two high-pitched patterns and, within moments, Rufus joined him. 'Where do you want him, Arthur?'

Arthur explained that he wanted one archer in each of the major towers, and what he required of their marksmanship. 'I want our bowmen to discover the enemy's concentrations around those parts of the fortress.'

Rufus nodded grimly and was gone.

'You can use the torch to light your arrows, friend, and I'm pleased to find that you've anticipated the need for them. Let your magic work again and we'll destroy these Anglii bastards.'

Thorketil lit a fire arrow from the torch, waited until the soaked lint was well alight, and then used his huge bow to send the burning arrow into a clump of long grass to the left of the southern gate.

The grass flared up quickly.

Thirteen pairs of eyes peered into the darkness, but Arthur was the first to recognise the outline of a barrel that had been tipped over and spilled to allow seal oil to spread along the bottom of the ditch.

'An excellent target,' Thorketil breathed, as he sent a second arrow to wing its way into the general area of the barrel.

The spilled oil ignited into a flare of scarlet, gold and white that panicked the clusters of men in its path who struggled to avoid the sudden trails of flame that tickled their ankles and set a good twelve feet of ditch to burning. Another flaming arrow speared down from the tower and struck a barrel that was still sealed. The heat generated from the brush around this container was such that the oil exploded outwards with a great splatter and a gout of flame that caught several men in its path. Burning, they fell to the earth, where their friends encased them in blankets and used loose earth to suffocate the flames.

One whole side of the wall was burning now, so Arthur felt justified in squandering so much of their precious lamp oil. The captains feverishly began a head count to gain some idea of the numbers of enemy warriors ranged against them.

Meanwhile, Thorketil anticipated Arthur's requirements and turned his attention to the southern section of the eastern gate. The light from one of the fire arrows exposed another unopened barrel, but Thorketil was forced to use several more arrows to set it ablaze. Meanwhile, Rufus worked industriously with his bow and most of the northern side of the ditch was now burning.

But the Angles had no intention of retreating. Their warriors merely drew back a little from the flames, seeming totally unconcerned. An older man stood at the edge of the ditch so that the light played on his grey beard; it was obviously King Eoppa.

The old man was an easy target and, for a brief moment, Arthur considered ordering Thorketil to bring him down. Then he realised that two of Eoppa's warriors were flanking their king with heavy shields at the ready to block any arrows once they saw Thorketil draw on his bow. Arthur pointed out the king and his guards and the Troll King nodded in immediate understanding.

Eoppa was neither particularly tall, nor overtly strong, nor handsome, nor noble in appearance. In a crowd of his peers, he could easily be overlooked, except for the integrity that seemed as essential a part of his nature as breathing. Arthur had expected a soldier or a barbarian, a man well used to the disciplines of power and the ruthlessness that authority brings. What he saw below him was a man who was loved by his warriors, and who loved his men in return.

'How many men does he have, Gareth? Can you check with the other towers and ask them for their head counts.'

Gareth ducked down into the stairwell. When he returned, short of breath, he looked considerably happier than when he had set out.

'We estimate that Eoppa has approximately three hundred and fifty men, give or take a score or two,' he panted. 'To be honest, I expected he'd have more, especially considering the time he's had to assemble his forces.'

Arthur stared out into the darkness. The fires were guttering and the ditch was plunging into darkness again, but he could feel the presence of the Anglii warriors as they stood and waited. He knew that they promised a red death to any men who were so unwise as to open the gates and try to escape the siege.

'The Yellow Disease, as they call it, has cost Eoppa dearly, Gareth. An Anglii warrior called Ingwy provided that item of information, so I must remember to thank him for his loose tongue one of these days.'

As one, the six captains in the tower looked at him with curiosity.

'So! What do we do, Arthur?' Snorri finally asked when his commander failed to make any further comment.

'I plan to return to my bed. Nothing's likely to happen until daybreak, unless you think that Eoppa might decide to climb the walls. Put out sentries, and then we'll rest. It would be best if our warriors remained fresh in case Eoppa decides to take action.'

Most of the captains filed away to have their own discussions with their underlings, but Snorri lagged behind, his dissatisfaction written clearly on his face.

'We are surrounded by enemies who can obliterate our ships at will, master, and yet you're content for us to go to bed until the morning. The others won't say anything, because you've led us to victory after victory, but these men have risked everything for you. Not only will they die if this adventure turns to disaster, but their women and children will as well. I feel I have the right to know if we've risked everything for nothing. Do you have a plan that I can repeat to our men and their families?'

Arthur paused at the top of the stairs. Behind Snorri, Thorketil shook his head fractionally, warning Arthur that Snorri was deadly serious. For an instant, Arthur felt anger stir, but then he realised that high-handedness could destroy his plans for the future, or break trust with his men.

He returned to the centre of the dimly lit watchtower so anyone, friends or enemies, could clearly see him in the reflected torchlight.

'I owe you an explanation, Snorri, for you've been faithful and trusted me when others might have doubted. I knew the Angles would come tonight, because if Eoppa leaves us to our own devices, his enemies will presume that the Yellow Disease has fatally weakened his kingdom and they will fall on his warriors and his people.'

He paused. 'I've been certain all along that Eoppa would wait until the women and our provisions arrived,' Arthur continued. 'In his situation, I would have done exactly the same.'

'I don't know what he's up to, Arthur. I've been hoping that you do.' Snorri's confusion could be heard in his voice.

'Thorketil?' Arthur turned to the Troll King, whom Snorri had forgotten in the heat of the moment.

'I have a feeling that Eoppa wants to hedge his bets,' Thorketil said. 'I think he's been weakened to the extent that he'd like to make an enduring treaty with you that would hold off the rest of his enemies. I believe he wants to follow the path of friendship after this initial period of confrontation.'

'It's all possible – and it's even probable! He hasn't made a move against us, Snorri, and he could have done so if he'd set his mind to the task. He's allowed our plans to proceed, so there's something that he wants from us. I'm inclined to sit back and do nothing until such time as he tells us what that is. That man standing in the torchlight didn't act like a failure to me. Eoppa wanted us to have a good look at him. He didn't fear us: he challenged us to see what our response would be.'

'I understand your words, master, but I just don't see how you can remain calm,' Snorri muttered, as he ran his hand through his thick hair. He had washed himself very carefully to celebrate the fleet's return, and his hair crackled with life in the muted light. Arthur knew that Snorri was concerned for the safety of his wife and young sons.

'Go to your family, Snorri. I intend to sleep so I can think clearly in the morning, when I must deal with a clever fox who has nowhere else to go but here in the land of his birth. Though Eoppa may be an Angle, he's as British as I am. But I can swear to you that I'm determined to secure our future in these northern lands. Within the constraints of my honour, I am prepared to do anything that will ensure our survival. If I succeed, so do you.'

Snorri felt that thrill he had experienced when he had first met the Last Dragon on the decks of *Sea Wife*. Arthur had become the star that guided Snorri's life and steered him into those waters where his hope for the future could finally be realised.

'I will follow wherever you lead, Arthur,' Snorri promised. 'I have always done so, and nothing has changed.'

Arthur nodded, satisfied at last.

'And you, Thorketil?'

The Troll King shrugged. 'I've never understood the workings of your mind, Arthur. But I swore an oath to you when you picked up what the Crow King discarded. You gave me the pride I needed if I was to become a warrior again. This land is soft and sweet, and I'm happy to become a part of this earth. I must die somewhere, and this place is better than most.'

'Thank you, Thorketil! And my thanks also to you, Snorri! Until the morning then, and we'll see what transpires. Wake me before dawn, Gareth, and we'll learn what the king of the Angles wants of us.'

Arthur was slowly surfacing from a dream in which he was entangled within a forest of seaweed as the Green Dragon toyed with his blanched flesh. One of his hands was reaching for the Dragon Knife under his pallet as Sigrid reared away from the fingers that had begun to claw towards her throat.

'I'm sorry, Sigrid,' he murmured as he returned to wakefulness. 'I was having a terrifying dream. I hope I haven't hurt you?'

She shrugged, but Arthur had already spotted the bright red

mark on her shoulder where his fist had caught her. He leaped out of bed and made a belated attempt to kiss away the growing bruise.

'Don't be concerned, Arthur. No one can control their sleep horrors, and I will learn to be faster the next time.' Then she giggled to indicate that she had forgiven him.

Later, a penitent Arthur was inclined to snap at Gareth who was, after all, only obeying his master's orders when he called his master out from the commander's sleeping chamber.

'You'll have to ignore my bad temper, Gareth, I've had a restless night. I assume the sun is rising?'

'Aye, Arthur! Germanus sends word that the Angles are awake and are breaking their fast as we speak. They seem remarkably casual for a force that is about to go into battle.'

Gareth thrust a heel of bread, cold meat and a hunk of cheese towards Arthur. 'Germanus has sent this food to you, and some beer too.'

After climbing up to the tower, Arthur looked over Segedunum and the surrounding lands under the control of Eoppa's forces. The Dene warriors were already guarding the southern entry and those watchtowers where the captains and bowmen were at their posts.

Arthur was standing on the parapet in his tunic and mailed shirt, with his golden arms bare except for his armlets. His unbound hair flowed down his back. Few warriors remained alive who had seen Artor in all his grandeur in the glory days of yesteryear; but Eoppa had, and, for a moment, the king felt the solid earth shake beneath his boots.

'How long ago was it when we were at Cataractonium, or whatever it was that those Roman bastards called home?' Eoppa asked a scarred old veteran standing beside him.

'We were youngsters then, master. Only boys! And we were far too young to be in those fucking swamps where the British king almost beat us.'

'He hurt us badly. And the Saxon lordling lost his head, didn't he? Forty years ago? It's been a long time, my friend.'

'Easily forty years, master! The Dragon King was old then and was well past his prime. Him and that bastard nephew of his had almost finished us and they would have done for us if the country down south hadn't caught fire and the bastard wasn't killed by his Brigante kinsman. Odin was with us on that day.'

The retainer at Eoppa's side was too old for battle, and Eoppa could feel their fires dimming as they both moved closer to their inevitable deaths. His own eyes were still sharp, thanks to Odin, and he was grateful that he could still recall things from the past that were as clear as the present.

'Can you see a resemblance between King Artor and the young man above us, my friend? Or am I becoming a little crazed after the troubles that have beset us?'

The retainer stared up at the tall figure standing in the guard tower with the morning light behind him. Something about that red-gold hair, curling and vigorous, jogged his memory – but the hair he recalled seeing had been of a lighter shade, greyer and shorter.

'It's not possible! These raiders are Dene, so there's no possibility of both men being kin. You're seeing ghosts from the past, master.' The servant's face had paled when he had considered what was passing through Eoppa's mind.

'But you are seeing the same ghosts, aren't you? It's possible that this young man's presence might provide us with great advantages.'

* * *

Arthur could see the two gesticulating as they pointed at him. One good spear cast would strike them down, yet Eoppa seemed to be uninterested in his own safety, although he was surrounded by fully armed warriors.

'It's time to see what Eoppa wants,' Arthur decided. A light breeze had risen and the sun was sending long shafts of light across the walls of the fortress. He walked to the very edge of the watchtower and shouted out into the morning, trusting that the wind would carry his voice to the Anglii king.

'Are we going to stand here and piss at each other, or are we going to fight? Or would you prefer to talk?'

Eoppa ignored Arthur and continued to talk quietly with his servant.

'Do you hear me, Eoppa? I, Arthur, the Last Dragon, am quite prepared to sit here astride old Segedunum until your bones take root in the soil.'

Once again, Eoppa appeared oblivious, although the old servant raised his head at the mention of Arthur's name.

That the canny old king was ignoring him made Arthur's captains nervous. Worse still, he was losing the respect of Eoppa's warriors.

'Are there any signs of treachery from around the fort or down at the river?' Arthur demanded.

Within minutes, word came back that the Anglii troops seemed to be at rest and were simply waiting, although no one could fathom why. 'We're awaiting Eoppa's pleasure,' Arthur decided gruffly. 'I'll not push him any further.'

Another ten minutes passed dismally before Eoppa finally made up his mind. The retainer was despatched to the edge of the ditch from where he delivered Eoppa's message to Arthur's waiting command.

'My lord Arthur! Eoppa, King of the Northern Angles, invites you to meet with him outside the fortress. If you require proof of our integrity, our men will retire to a point ten spear lengths from where you will carry out your discussions. The only additional Anglii warriors present will be the king's personal guard. You, of course, shall have the same number of guards behind you. We do not care if you have archers trained on us, for we do not have treasonous intentions and we aren't liars. What say you, Arthur, the Last Dragon of Britain? Do you answer yea or nay?'

Arthur was halfway down the stairs with eagerness before the servant had finished. How did Eoppa know I was a Briton? he wondered. It's of little moment now, for I can worry about that later. Calm down, fool! He'll know you're too eager.

'Gareth! Germanus! Ten men, please! In full gear! Call for volunteers, because they'll be locked outside the southern gate until the negotiations are completed, or we come to blows. You may join me, but only if you so wish.'

Gareth ran to obey his master's command. Most of the Dene warriors were eager to volunteer, but Germanus and Gareth were careful to select young, single and impressive men, although Snorri would not be denied and was added to the party.

Once the guard was assembled, Arthur ordered the gate to be opened briefly while he led his men from the fortress in single file. His inner voice remained silent.

The sound of that great and ancient gate thudding closed behind them seemed to echo through the hearts of the guards, yet not a flicker of fear was revealed in the handsome faces that gazed out at their opposite numbers among the Anglii guards on the other side of the ditch. Their faces and figures were virtually identical to those of their enemies; the Angles and the Dene were roots that fed the same tree.

Arthur paused long enough to evaluate Eoppa's position, then leaped down to join him.

From a distance of a few feet, both men carefully surveyed each other.

Eoppa's noble face revealed all the cares of kingship and a long life. Although his jaw was still strong, the flesh on his face had sagged towards the stern jawbone, while his keen blue eyes were buried in a network of fine lines. His hair was still very thick and straight, although it seemed dirty and greasy. However, in every other respect, the simply dressed king shone with cleanliness, an unusual trait among Saxon and Anglii tribesmen.

Eoppa's face expressed no sign of nervousness. This man was at home within his own skin and was comfortable with any decisions he made.

'Before we begin our discussion, young man, I have one question I would ask of you,' Eoppa said firmly. 'Would you satisfy the curiosity of an old man and clarify a memory from out of the distant past?'

'Aye! I will happily answer all reasonable questions.'

'Can you place your forebears among the kin of Artor, the Dragon King, who ruled the Britons for so many years? Your use of the Last Dragon title was evocative. That great man has been dead now for near to thirty years. I should state that I saw him forty years ago when he decimated our army outside of Cataractonium, and I will never forget him, and his wolfish eyes. In fact, I can see the delineations of the Dragon King in your face. Am I wrong?'

Arthur lowered his gaze as he thought hard on his response.

'Why should I answer you with honesty?' he finally replied.

Eoppa sighed. 'Your answer will determine the way we treat

with each other, young man. You must decide for yourself if we are to speak freely, and as honest men? We are leaders struggling for dominance while involved in difficult negotiations, so it's up to you.'

Arthur could hear what Eoppa was choosing not to say, for no treaty could hope to succeed if there were secrets between them. Arthur wanted land, and Eoppa wanted vassals. But both could only be achieved if the partners could depend on each other.

'I am the bastard son of Artor, High King of the Britons, my lord. My mother was Elayne, wife of Bedwyr, the Master of Arden. It would be unwise to think I could be ransomed to my kinsmen Bran and Ector; Bran would order you to kill me, but then he'd use my death as a rallying point to inflame the northern Britons against you. He'd never pay a reward for me, alive or dead. He would be angry to discover that I was alive and back in Britain, for he's been content to think of me as dead in recent years. The Dene captured me, used me and made me a successful leader. But I've come home now, and I intend to forge my own kingdom in Britannia, whatever others might do or say.'

Eoppa smiled with satisfaction, something Arthur had not been expecting.

'I'm a fortunate man then, as I hope you'll soon appreciate. After the death of my son and my dishonourable dealings with your Bran, I had come to believe that the loss of all my male heirs was Asgaad's judgement on me for my own perfidy. Your kinsman poisons everything he touches, of that I'm certain.'

The old man paused and carefully considered his next words before continuing.

'Perhaps you can offer me one last chance to create a great and stable kingdom here in the north of Britannia, a place where your people and mine can work together for our mutual wealth and prosperity. Your kinsman used my influence to destroy the Otadini tribe, but such treason can be revenged. Best of all, I could erase my guilt over my dealings with Bran, a man whose very name offends my mouth.'

'We're certainly in agreement in that regard. I've become tired of serving others, and I'm reluctant to rely on treaties with other rulers, regardless of their reputations. For right or wrong, I want to forge my own kingdom. A treaty offers peace and prosperity to our peoples, but any conflict between us would destroy us both. The stakes are very high.'

Eoppa reached out his ungloved hand to grip Arthur lightly on the forearm, careless of Thorketil's bow that was immediately drawn with an arrow pointed directly at the old man's heart.

'Walk with me, lad, and I'll try to explain how I believe our aims can be realised. If we came to a satisfactory agreement, I would hold my northern realm and you would succeed me as the king of all the lands where our joined people will live and mate together. In this domain we would all become Britons who are strong, clever and united as no other peoples have ever been in these isles. I offer you the north, Arthur ap Artor. All I will ask in return is that you should wed my daughter, father sons on her and take the name of my dead son, Ida. I am reluctant to allow his name to vanish from his home.'

In the wake of Eoppa's impassioned speech, the silence was complete.

Even the morning birdsongs seemed stilled as the world waited for Arthur's answer. He could clearly envisage a multitude of fair-haired people who populated a vast tract of the north and beyond to the mountain chains, where the noble dreams of Artor would finally be achieved. All Arthur had to do was to deny his own name.

He cleared his suddenly constricted throat. 'You have my attention, Lord Eoppa. Explain the details so I can make my final decision.'

Eoppa, too, had briefly seen the possibilities of the future, and he knew that Arthur would choose to follow his advice. The King of Winter was about to be born.

'Walk with me, my boy, and I'll explain my plans.'

So an old king and a young warrior strolled amicably along the winding trench. Their bodyguards remained at a respectful distance, but still close enough that both men were protected. The two men walked and talked as the sun continued to rise into the heavens and its summer rays burned the faces of the guards awaiting the pleasure of their masters.

Then, with a hand clasp, the treaty was made between two great Britons.

CHAPTER XXI

ADVENT

When the bottle has just been opened, and when it's giving out, drink deep;
Be sparing when it's half-full, but it's useless to spare the fag end.

Hesiod, *Works and Days*

The sun rose on a damp and miserable autumn morning. Falling leaves had gathered in drifts under the trees before the gusty winds sent a torrent of scarlet swirling around him as Arthur strode from his campaign tent. As bare branches rattled hollowly, a chill breeze raised the hair at the back of his neck under his helm and he felt a wight rake its cold fingers down his spine.

So much had occurred in a little over a year. Arthur gazed down the tunnel of time that stretched from the day he had extracted a generous treaty from Eoppa until this morning when he found himself standing on a bluff overlooking the green pastures of the narrow coastal strip. Around him, armies had been assembled and, in the grim hours to come, warriors would be trampled, pierced, crushed and slashed to death along that strip. In the coming conflict, enemies were friends and friends were enemies; the ironies of power stretched out inexorably before Arthur and his mailed feet.

Gareth and Germanus swung into position behind their master, although Germanus rarely fought in the front line any more. Arthur prized the Frank's clever advice and the deep well of calm common sense that always served to settle his introspective moments before the dance of death. He had believed that taking a royal wife and a new nomen would be easy, but the normal patterns of his life had been dramatically altered. Germanus had been the only adviser who had fully understood this difficult transition. Now, reunited with his wife and two sons after years of absence, Germanus had presented Arthur with a tow-headed, tall boy of ten years who had sworn an oath to serve Ida and his house forever.

The change of Arthur's name to Ida, a convention that would be adhered to on formal occasions, had seemed a mere bagatelle in the face of the many advantages that would accrue from the treaty. As well as bringing another woman into his household, the treaty had symbolically positioned Arthur as a bulwark between Eoppa and his many enemies, including Arthur's own nephew, King Bran of the Ordovice. Bran was now the avowed ally of Meirchion Gul, the Dragon Slayer, and he was the centre of British resistance to the Saxons, Jutes and Angles. As such, Bran must be defeated in open warfare if Arthur was to make old bones.

Arthur had scarcely bothered to consider the human implications of the choices he had made. Now, drawn into a war against the remnants of the British tribes of the north and the ever-present and vitriolic Picts, he must reflect on the ease with which everything he had won could be washed away. After all, time had defeated the Romans and the great King Artor.

* * *

When Arthur had explained the terms of Eoppa's treaty to Sigrid, she had wept a little, but had then placed all thoughts of Eoppa's daughter, Bearnoch, behind her. Sigrid had grown into a mature young woman with a goodly share of common sense and Arthur took comfort from the sound foundations of her love.

Her mother, Ingrid, had not been so charitable.

'Marriage without love is difficult, Arthur. Do you think this woman will be grateful that her father has exchanged her for a kingdom?'

'You will remain silent, Ingrid. You are overstepping your position!' In truth he had failed to consider the feelings of his slaves when he initially made his treaty with Eoppa. 'I agreed to marry Bearnoch, regardless of her appearance or her manners. Her father puts a high price on his daughter, just as I have put a high price on the safety of our people.'

'How noble of you!' Ingrid had sneered in mock admiration. 'Such a sacrifice! And all you get from this treaty is a throne and another woman who will become your plaything. What will you do when your new wife wants to push Sigrid to one side?'

Her words were followed by a wholly feminine snort of indignation.

'I swear to you that no one will force me to push Sigrid away and, before we marry, Lady Bearnoch will be made to understand that I will not be parted from Sigrid. From now on, Sigrid will be treated as a common law wife. As such, all offspring from the pairing have no rights in the succession, but Sigrid's children will be free-born, and they shall be raised with any other children of mine with the proviso that they will not be able to inherit any throne that I should win in the future.'

'But they won't be equal to your other children,' Ingrid snapped bitterly.

'No, they won't be equal. But her children will have lands and can recruit other men to follow them. And, if Sigrid bears daughters, these young women will be married to men of substance. Eoppa and I have already settled on plans to attack and destroy his enemies along our northern borders. Once they are secured, we intend to carve out a much larger kingdom than is presently the case, so the portions of wealth flowing to Sigrid and her children will grow as the fortunes of the new kingdom increase.'

But Ingrid was far from convinced. Her nostrils were still pinched and she remained white with fury.

'Sigrid is the love of my heart, Ingrid, and the wife of my choice. Eoppa's daughter is the wife of my ambitions, and she must be accepted if I am to achieve my destiny. You should save your pity for her.'

Then Ingrid reached out blindly to grip Arthur's arm in apology, and the new heir to Eoppa's kingdom lacked the will to shake off his slave's presumptions of possession.

Months of planning followed before any part of Eoppa's plans could be put into action. With the assistance of Eoppa's steward, a number of abandoned Anglii farms were allocated to Dene families, who moved rapidly into the countryside. Those families who missed out on the initial allocations of established farms were gifted with parcels of arable land around Segedunum that could be cultivated until the arrival of spring. A feeling of optimism ran through the old fortress when the trading ships were put into dry docks until the following spring when trade would recommence.

As autumn dragged on, Arthur sent two longboats up the remote areas of the northern stretches of the coast where they could reconnoitre the coastal waters and obtain information on the activities of those Otadini stragglers who maintained a precarious existence in the area. The crews were also given the task of testing the attitudes of the various families of Picts who still resisted the presence of outlanders. Arthur felt secure with the progress that had been made so far, but he counted the days until he set out on the journey to Eoppa's hall at Pons Aelius.

On the surface, Pons Aelius was a small settlement used by the Romans as a regional centre. However, its position on high ground along the Wall provided a good view of the flat lands that stretched away into the north, so it held strategic importance. Over time, the town had become very Saxon in appearance. Grass and small trees grew in every crevice of the Wall, so that the monument seemed to be wearing a ragged crown of scarlet leaves. Inside the town, the centre of habitation was dominated by a large thatched hall which was the focal point of a large compound.

Off to one side, pens for cows, pigs and a plethora of well-fed chickens gave a good indication of the wealth of the local population. As Arthur arrived with his cortege, he noted the dung-coloured walls of the buildings and the neat doors and roof trusses, but he was unimpressed, remembering the stone Roman towns of his past, such as Calleva Atrebatum, Aquae Sulis, Deva, Glevum, Vinovia, Ratae, and Verterae; all places of substance despite their eventual descent into ruination. He felt a twist of sadness in his heart for what had been lost forever.

'I will build my fortresses in stone!' he said in a determined voice as he rode through the gates of Eoppa's compound. Gareth looked at his master with sharp awareness. After living cheek-by-jowl with Arthur for many years he understood Arthur's need to have something permanent and tangible at his back.

'Well, Gareth, let's get these meetings over and done with,' Arthur said in an introspective voice. In the brief months of spring and summer, Sigrid had been his constant companion and she had recently informed him that she was with child. Now Arthur was about to marry another woman for the sole purpose of laying the foundation of a new kingdom. At times, the newly christened Ida wondered where this journey into the land of his birth would take him.

Arthur had given Sigrid a necklace of perfect pearls and a ring of garnets to stop her tears, but she would have thrown them in Arthur's face had he not apologised quickly, once he realised his error. Eventually, Sigrid took pity on him, forgave him for his coming absence and accepted the gems in the spirit in which they had been offered.

Arthur sincerely regretted that he would be absent for the birth of his son – Ingrid swore the unborn child was a boy, and she was rarely wrong.

An honour guard under the command of Eoppa's steward appeared with well-practised speed. Willing servants led away the horses to waiting stables, while Arthur was shown to a house that smelled aromatically of newly sawn timber and pine sap. Servants were soon on hand to present jugs of beer and mead as refreshments together with sweetmeats and nuts so that Arthur and his attendants could break their fast. A separate dwelling stood only a few spear lengths from his quarters, obviously prepared as accommodation for the jarls.

Once the Anglii attendants had left them to their rest with much bowing and deference, Arthur and his companions had an opportunity to inspect the accommodation with interest. The fragrance of the wood used in the building was satisfying to those men who had worked with timber for their whole lives, while Arthur especially liked the simple flat stones covering the floor. Although he missed the warm mosaic floors of Segedunum, he appreciated the contrast between the two styles. Other than a paved fire pit, the room had little furniture or elaborate décor save for an exceptionally fine hanging, woven and embroidered, that had been placed on the end wall.

This huge piece of art must have taken many years to complete; it depicted two enormous and heroic dragons fighting a stylised battle on a field of blue that appeared to mimic water. One of the dragons was white while the other was red. The red dragon was dominant and it reared over the exposed throat of the white dragon, whose sharp tail was wrapped around the red dragon's belly in an attempt to disembowel its enemy.

Arthur understood the message conveyed by the hanging, for he was aware of the prophecy given to King Vortigern by Myrddion Merlinus decades earlier when the High King had been convinced to sacrifice the boy. The king had been assured by his sorcerers that the newly built tower of his fortress at Dinas Emrys would never fall if the foundations were cemented together with the blood of a demon seed. The fame of the prophecy, and the resultant collapse of the structure, had been such that the tale eventually entered the realms of myth.

Myrddion had seen the red dragon of the Britons and the white dragon of the Saxons engaged in mortal combat for dominance in Britannia. This wall hanging depicted a situation where both were equally poised on the brink of either victory or defeat.

The pair were crowned and Arthur smiled at the clever sentiments embodied in the hanging. But then, when he moved closer, a small detail hidden in the background caused him to abruptly draw in his breath.

Gareth and Germanus could see that their master was upset; the Frank was the first to realise why.

Above the darker blue of the waters and the jewels used to colour the dragons, a long and sinuous shape had been stitched into the sky. Small wings fanned out from a serpentine body with vestigial legs and vicious, sickle-shaped talons.

'That figure represents the Ice Dragon, the Wurm, used in the sagas of the Dene Mark and Noroway,' Germanus said quietly. 'There are four of them, aren't there?'

Arthur nodded. 'The Jutes and Angles are probably aware of the tales of the Ice Dragon as well.'

The thoughts of all three men boiled with the possibilities that this hanging explained with such subtlety. Only a northerner would recognise the Wurm; but the weaver of this hanging believed that northerners would win the lands of Britannia.

'I'd truly like to meet the artist who made this hanging, Germanus. The workmanship is exquisite. Could I also trust to your tact to see what information you can gain about Bearnoch? I want to know something of her likes and dislikes. I have a selection of gifts for her that Sigrid helped me to choose, yet I don't even know the colour of her hair. Sigrid swears that such details are very important to women.'

'I'd guess blond, if we were to judge her by Eoppa's colouring,' said Gareth.

'So you guess! I want to know for certain, because I plan to avoid causing any offence. I want all the information about my future bride that you can glean.'

Arthur's servants nodded their heads respectfully and departed. Left to his own devices, Arthur drank a mug of beer, ate some nuts and then wandered out into the afternoon sun to see the barracks where his men were quartered.

This building had already been equipped with sleeping pallets, furniture, and the accoutrements necessary for cooking. Ragnar was already working with a store of food provided by their hosts and he had hung many of their own supplies from the ceiling out of reach of rodents. The aroma of cooking meat permeated the air and Arthur's mouth began to water in anticipation.

Snorri looked up from a dice game he was playing. 'Is there anything you need of me, Arthur?'

'Our hosts seem to have forgotten that I will need a bed to sleep in.' He laughed then, because the constant bowing scarcely mitigated the absence of a bed, a chair or a fire. 'I suppose the servants didn't expect me to arrive so early.'

Snorri rose, curious about this apparent lack in Anglii hospitality, so both men returned to Arthur's quarters. They walked into a hive of crazed activity as servants ran to move precious stools and chairs to prime positions near the fire pit which was now glowing with freshly lit flames. A bed fit for a prince had been prepared and positioned beneath the wall hanging, while a suitably regal pallet was being covered with finely woven blankets. A large coverlet of bear fur was also thrown over the luxurious bed in case of a stray draught.

Four small, fur-covered pallets were laid discreetly just outside the door to Arthur's quarters behind a woven screen, obviously prepared for servants or guards. Meanwhile, Arthur's travelling bags had already been unpacked and his possessions had been reverently laid out inside three huge coffers.

'It seems our hosts are remedying their lapse,' Snorri said loudly, for he was prepared to offend these thoughtless servants who squealed like mice whenever he glowered at them.

'It seems so. Gods, but they're well organised when they decide to get moving,' Arthur replied.

Two large male slaves approached him in company with two women, one old and the other barely beyond puberty. All four wore slave collars, much like the restraint Bedwyr had worn during his youth. As one, they sank to their knees, and then lay supine on the flagged floor with their arms outstretched in abject obedience.

'Arise!' Arthur ordered. 'I don't ever require obeisances from you. A simple bow and courtesy is all that is necessary. I also insist that you look me in the eyes when I am speaking with you.'

They stood, although the older female needed a little assistance.

'That's better! I can speak directly to you now. What are your names?'

The slaves looked blankly at Arthur, and then at each other.

The eldest male answered in a monotone, his eyes never leaving the flagging.

'My name is Banwyn and this man is Selwyn. We have been ordered to clean your weapons and look after your beasts. My master told me that we must provide for all of your needs while you are at Eoppa's court. I will polish your armour, exercise your horse and assist you to dress and arm yourself. Kerryn, here, is a good cook and will see to all your food, if you so wish. Sybell has been provided to clean this room, launder your clothing and cater for all your personal needs. We are sworn to defend and support you in all things, master.'

Arthur, aghast, seated himself on the nearest stool and left Snorri to supervise the other servants as they moved in the heavy chests that held Bearnoch's dowry. At one point, Arthur caught a glimpse of rich silks and a precious golden lamp in one of the chests before the lid was firmly closed again.

'Mark my words, Banwyn, and listen well! My foster-father wore a slave collar before he eventually became a king, so I have no liking for slavery. I will not expect any task of you that I wouldn't undertake myself, and I certainly don't expect you to die for me. For now, Banwyn and Selwyn, you will assist the two women to finish their tasks. I assume you will sleep on the pallets outside the door. Is that correct?'

'Aye, master!' Banwyn replied in the same monotone. 'Shall we collect our possessions now?'

'Yes, you may. And you have my permission to move your pallets closer to the fire pit if there's a chill in the air tonight.'

The two men bowed far too deeply and padded away on bare feet. Arthur sighed.

'Now! Ladies! Kerryn, I'll inform you later of what foods I truly abhor, and those I truly enjoy. I'll need a table and stools placed where my captains can sit whenever I need to speak to them, and I'm sure that you can persuade some of these large fellows to steal sufficient furniture for my use. I'll need at least ten more stools. One final matter! I'll need more screens to seal off my sleeping space.'

Kerryn looked startled but she bowed low and scurried off to order the loudest and most objectionable servant in the room to do her bidding. At least she has possibilities, Arthur thought drily, as he watched her deliver a set of terse instructions to the large man. She'll be using my name, no doubt, to force that oaf to obey her.

Arthur turned to face the younger woman.

'I require no bed partner, Sybell, so you are free of any concerns in that regard. Nor will I permit any of my warriors to trifle with you. You are instructed to tell me personally if any unwelcome attention comes your way. In the meantime, can you plait my hair?'

'Aye, lord,' she replied, her eyes huge in the pale light.

'Good! Later then . . . but it must be done before the feast. I'll require your help to prepare myself suitably to honour the king. Before that, however, I'll need a bath. Is there such a luxury in the town? Or any large container that can permit me to wash my body? I'm dirty from our travels and I'd not insult your master and mistress by attending their feast unshaven and covered in grime.'

'I don't know if we have such a thing, my lord. But I'll try.'

Sybell's face was creased with concern in case she should fail in the first request from her new master.

'If not, I need to know if there is a clean stream near here where I can bathe in private. Don't be afraid, Sybell. How old are you, lass?'

Arthur could tell by the trembling of her bottom lip that she was on the verge of tears.

'I'm sorry, master, but I don't know my age. Kerryn says I'm thirteen years, but I can only recall my life from when I was about ten. Everyone thinks I'm stupid.'

Arthur was afraid she was about to weep in earnest. However, she bit down on her lip and forced her head up. 'You must tell me if I disappoint you, my lord, for I've been told that I'm good for very little.'

'Not so, Sybell. Your master wouldn't have sent an idiot to serve me.'

The girl was pretty and very dark, and her eyes shone, especially after receiving such an unexpected compliment. Arthur noticed a mark on the side of her face that was exposed whenever her hair moved, so he gently lifted the locks of her hair to examine a long scar that ran down her face from the temple to below the jawline. A small indentation just below the temple showed where her skull had been pushed inwards by a savage blow to the head; it explained her loss of memory.

'You don't remember who struck you or why, do you, Sybell?' She must have been very fortunate to have survived a wound of such severity.

'No, my lord. I was too young.'

'Let's hope you don't remember, little one. At least you are safe under King Eoppa's protection, so let's see what you can do about finding a bath for me.'

Sybell ran out to do his bidding. He thought of Maeve and what he'd have done to any man who dared to wound her in such a terrible manner.

A suitable container for bathing was found and Sybell was soon producing large buckets of water, allowing Arthur to luxuriate in cleanliness. Later, after drying his body, he dressed himself in leather trews, a freshly bleached shirt, his mailed coat and a tunic of brass plates. He took up his second-best cloak, checked the cleanliness of his goatskin boots, strapped on his sword belt and then sat while Sybell combed and plaited his hair. Then, with her heart in her mouth, she shaved his chin and cheeks with his special blade. Finally, as well-dressed as possible, discounting his wedding finery, Arthur joined his bodyguards to attend Eoppa's feast.

As they walked through the darkness towards the great hall, Gareth and Germanus briefed Arthur on what the bodyguards had learned during the afternoon.

'The consensus of opinion seems to be that Bearnoch is a prickly sort of woman. She's Christian, and it's claimed that she'd rather become a nun than a wife,' Germanus began. 'There are few physical similarities between her and Eoppa and some of the Angles have made oblique references to cuckoo eggs placed in foreign nests in bygone years. One thing is for certain: Eoppa would kill any man he caught voicing such insults. Her eyes are blue, but her hair is more red than brown, and its shade is far darker than her father's. I gained the impression she had ideas and ambitions above her expected station, for the nuns taught her to read and write. It seems they decided she might become a noble abbess at some time in the future.'

'That sounds hopeful! I have no time for a stupid woman although, as a Christian, she's unlikely to take to my Sigrid.'

'Some of the men here have referred to her as the Ice Queen because she has never shown the slightest interest in any man. She is also very tall. One of the warriors joked about men who might be brave enough to scale the heights,' Gareth added. 'I eventually warned the oaf in question to keep his tongue between his teeth when he speaks of my master, or my master's wife. He wasn't pleased by the time I left him, but we had settled the disagreement between us.'

'Was it painful?'

'For him, Arthur, but not for me!'

Arthur sighed, then realised he had forgotten to bring a package containing some special gifts for Bearnoch. He turned to Germanus. 'Could you return to my room and bring me the parcel wrapped in red cloth on top of the clothes chest bearing the Red Dragon motif? Make haste, my friend. We'll wait for you outside the hall.'

Germanus returned so fast that Arthur was sure that the old man had sprinted the whole way.

'Now I'll get to meet the Ice Queen for myself. Meanwhile,

accept my thanks for your efforts to inform me of the lady's character. I'm aware that some of my men call me the King of Winter when they think I'm not listening, so perhaps Bearnoch and I are perfectly suited to each other.'

The interior of the king's hall was surprisingly sumptuous for a structure as plain and as unadorned as it was on the outside. The flagged floors were covered with the usual carpet of loose straw, but it was unusually fresh and sweet-smelling. The eating tables, scrubbed and polished, were placed in two long rows, with the head table on a dais across the end of the room; the bench seats had been softened with embroidered cushions for the comfort of the guests. Even the copper pots steaming with the aromatic smells of herbs and meats were polished until they shone.

The entry of the Dene guard made quite an impact on the assembled thanes and their ladies, who competed to outdo each other in the lavishness of their attire. Anglii women rarely had the opportunity to join their menfolk on formal occasions, but Eoppa had decided to make an exception for the first two days of feasting to celebrate the marriage of his only living child.

The next feast, to be held on the morrow, would follow the nuptials in the ancient church in the ruins of Pons Aelius.

A further ceremony on the third day would dedicate the young couple to the old gods and would be sealed through the ceremonies of the Nuptial Feast and the Marriage Bed.

Dozens of pairs of eyes ran up and down the tall, athletic figures of Arthur's guard, young men who had been chosen for their beauty, as well as their strength. Arthur had ordered them to leave their weapons in their quarters, and more than one thane noted this with approval. As one, the guard bowed to the dais, as Arthur strode through their neat lines, flanked by Germanus and Gareth, to stand before the king.

'We are here to pay homage to you, my lord, as I promised at Segedunum.'

Once more, the guard bowed as one, then stood upright with their hands clasped respectfully at their sides.

'Be seated and welcome, men of Lord Arthur,' Eoppa intoned with notable seriousness from his armchair in the centre of the high table.

The guard graciously permitted Eoppa's steward to seat them along one side of a long table opposite the warriors from the king's guard; the two groups of men examined each other with careful but not overtly hostile eyes.

'Lord King of the Northern Angles,' Arthur began in a resonant voice. 'I present Snorri, son of Sigmund, son of Sven, who is a master mariner and helmsman, and can read the stars. No seas defeat him and no storm dares to drown him.'

'Welcome, Snorri, son of Sigmund and son of Sven,' Eoppa replied with equal courtesy.

'These warriors have been my friends and closest confidants since I was a boy,' Arthur continued as he called Germanus and Gareth forward. 'They have guided my footsteps into manhood. Germanus is a Frank by birth, and was a servant of the descendants of Merovech for many years. He is a warrior *par excellence*.'

'Welcome, Germanus,' Eoppa replied and bowed his head a fraction, a considerable concession that wasn't lost on his own thanes.

'And this warrior, so young and so fair, is my friend, Gareth, son of Gareth, who served the Dragon King for his whole life. I expect that you will find such a connection vile, for the Dragon King almost defeated the Saxon and Anglii alliance. But times change, and now Gareth serves only me, so his allegiance to you is also assured.'

Eoppa marked the special nature of this particular meeting by rising and bowing to Gareth, who responded by kneeling at the king's feet.

'Truly, legends come to life before our eyes. Was your father the Sword-Bearer?'

'After the death of the Sword-Bearer, Gruffydd, my father did, indeed, bear Caliburn for his master. Then, after the Dragon King perished, Lord Arthur's foster-father cast Caliburn into the tarn of the Lady of the Lake, deep in the mountains of Cymru, so it could never again come to trouble the world of men.'

'Welcome, Gareth ap Gareth. Mayhap you will tell my singer some of your stories so that the past doesn't die.'

Arthur remained standing before the dais, although the room was very silent as the Anglii thanes attempted to digest the information presented to them. For a generation, the Dragon King had been their enemy, the fiend who had been portrayed as a monster in a hundred battles. Now, they were being asked to accept that the son of the Dragon King was trustworthy enough to become an ally. They were confused and unconvinced, but Arthur stepped forward to address them.

'My friends! Your king and I have made a solemn agreement that I will remain as Arthur ap Artor for this one day – and then no longer! By the end of this feast and by the oaths that we shall swear on the morrow, he and I have agreed to create a new kingdom that will be free of the prejudices of the past. For this last time, I shall salute you as Arthur, Jarl of the Dene Mark, the last descendant of the Roman emperor, Maximus, and the Last Dragon of Britannia.

'In the new British regime that will soon come into being, I see no delineations between Briton, Roman, Angle, Jutes, Saxons or Dene. Our people must belong to the land, this Angle Land as I have heard it called, and even the Picts are welcome to farm and fight beside us if their prime allegiance is to us and not to the ancient and pointless wrongs of yesteryear.'

It was immediately obvious to the Dene contingent that the Anglii king had convinced his vassals that his vision for the future was in the best interests of his subjects. Realising they were among future friends, Arthur's guard began to sit a little taller on their bench seats.

Satisfied with Arthur's stirring words, Eoppa rose to his feet once more.

'Welcome, Arthur. Come now and seat yourself at my right hand so you may meet your new bride.' Eoppa sounded slightly nervous. In turn, Arthur did his best to avoid staring; instead, he marched up to the High Table and placed the package in red cloth in front of Lord Eoppa.

'I wish to present this small gift to Lady Bearnoch in gratitude for my welcome today. The gift is also a pledge of my enduring respect.' He smiled directly at the attractive young woman sitting woodenly at the table, and she flushed under his searching gaze. 'And I am hoping she can tell me who it was that wrought the marvellous wall-hanging that has lent such beauty to my hall.'

A muffled voice coughed in embarrassment.

'I made the hanging, Lord Arthur, so I am pleased that it has given you enjoyment.'

'It is doubly appropriate then that you should be given my paltry gifts, which could never hope to match the beauty of your weaving. Still, I hope you will forgive the choices made by a mere warrior. The jewellery was part of a treasure horde collected in the icy north lands where the sun doesn't set for half the year.'

Eoppa passed the colourful package to his daughter, whose high cheekbones flushed with obvious pleasure. She was beautiful, but without the conventional prettiness of most Anglii women. While her nose was just a little too narrow and elongated, her face was fine but determined. Her eyebrows were dark, winged and slanted upward, while her mouth was full so that it appeared to be bee-stung.

Like a hesitant child, she opened the package with great care, conscious of the many eyes that followed every movement of her narrow fingers, but Arthur could see something wounded and vulnerable in her dark blue eyes. Their colour reminded her betrothed of deep water on a fine day, and seas that consisted of many layers. Arthur could imagine a sensitive man becoming lost in those eyes and the complex mind that lay behind them. He was intrigued, something he had never expected to feel in this loveless match.

Bearnoch had covered her hair with a length of rose-coloured silk; she looked well in this material, because her hair was almost a rich oak colour, with just a trace of red in it. It hung down her back in a thick smooth curtain almost to her knees. She had never permitted its length to be cut.

Arthur wondered why this attractive woman had remained unwed. She's obviously clever, he thought, and she's certainly accomplished. Perhaps she's not beautiful in the accepted fashion, at least not like my Sigrid, but a man could feel content and proud if he possessed such a wife.

Then Arthur amended his thoughts. No! This woman *isn't* a possession. She would demand to be an equal, not stridently, but by the subtlety of her intelligence. Bearnoch would be an eternal companion and a friend to the man who won her allegiance.

Putting aside his odd thoughts, he gazed at Bearnoch and

saws the colour rise from her collarbones to suffuse her face with pleasing shades of pink.

'How did you know that I loved pearls and amber, my lord?'

The necklace in Bearnoch's hands consisted of large, irregular pearls of spectacular refulgence strung with beautifully matched pieces of honey-coloured amber. At the end of the long double string, another large piece of amber hung, shaped carefully into an oval. Within it, a small white moth had been caught in the yellow tree-sap at some time during the distant past, imprisoned forever in a single moment of fragile grace.

'A night moth! It's perfect! This gift is far too fine,' Bearnoch breathed, as her eyes glowed with excitement. 'I should feel sad for the poor thing, but its beauty has been preserved for eternity. Long after we are dust, other women will wear this amber and be reminded that life is short and fragile.'

'No mere moth could rival your eyes, Mistress Bearnoch. Honest beauty can survive beyond time when Fortuna is just,' Arthur responded. His words were cautious, rather than flattering, for something about this woman reached out to him. He could scarcely understand why he had chosen to be so fulsome with his praise.

The king looked from one young face to the other. The young man's beauty had been hardened by far skies, glare-soaked seas and adversity. Then, with fondness, Eoppa gazed at his only living child and recognised the inner strength that was softened by her innocence. For a moment he wondered whether it had been wise to have her educated among the gentle nuns at Eburacum.

Eoppa felt a shiver begin in his lower back, which usually presaged an increasingly troublesome onset of pain, and he prayed that he had done everything within his power to protect the only things that he still loved in this wicked world.

* * *

On the morning after the welcome feast, Arthur and his jarls returned to the great hall to meet the churchman who had travelled from Eburacum to record the marriage of Eoppa's daughter with the northern heathen. An increasing number of prominent thanes had adopted the teachings of the new faith, including Eoppa's second wife. At her insistence, Bearnoch had been sent to the little nuns and it had been half expected that she might spend her life there in quiet contemplation and prayer.

Eoppa valued the teachings of the Church of Rome and took every opportunity to have his alliances recorded in the scrolls prepared by the church fathers, knowing that word of his deeds on this earth could endure for eternity within the monasteries' secure vaults. Wise men in Eoppa's position kept their feet in both camps, pagan and Christian, and there they would stay until battle for dominance was eventually won by one side or the other.

Arthur had scanned the long and excessively elaborate document quickly, his lips curling at the scholarly language that buried the unromantic details of alliances under fulsome wording.

The cleric stared at him disapprovingly.

'Can you make your mark, my lord? I will show you where to place it.'

The cleric's well-fed face displayed ill-concealed scorn, and he wore a knowing look that declared Eoppa, the Dene and the Angles to be upstart barbarians. Arthur's sense of devilry made him pore over the whole document, reading it carefully while the black-garbed cleric flapped his hands together in distress and insisted that Arthur make his mark and return the scroll into the priest's safe hands.

Grinning and mischievous, Arthur finally demanded an implement suitable for writing.

The room was suddenly silent as all eyes turned to him.

'Yes, Father, I'm very fluent in Latin. After reading some of the tortured language in this scroll, I'm of the opinion that I'm better versed in its intricacies than you are. I must say that it's hard to grasp at the meaning of some of the passages here.'

'My lord, I . . .' the cleric stammered, and then ground to a halt.

Germanus and Eoppa couldn't help themselves. Their smiles soon turned to laughter.

'Imagine that! A literate barbarian!' Eoppa chortled. 'Who could have considered such a possibility?'

While the priest sweated with embarrassment, Arthur signed the long documents that would bind him to Eoppa. He also signed the wedding agreement and, on this occasion, used his new nomen of Ida, comforting himself with the knowledge that those friends who loved and cherished him would forever see him as the Arthur of old.

If he was fated to lead the Dene and Angle people through the coming years the name of Ida would probably endure down the centuries, such was the power of the written word. I'll let Fortuna call the odds, he decided, and I'll place my trust with the goddess.

And so, Arthur and Bearnoch were wed. As they sat on their bed under the remarkable hanging, the new bride was still dressed in stiff robes and wearing a veritable breastplate of gems like an ivory idol. Bearnoch had replied to Arthur's questions in monosyllables during the feast. The only clue he had to her partiality towards him was the huge necklace of pearls and amber that was prominent on her breast.

In the half-light, Bearnoch carefully removed her garland of flowers and the heads of wheat that had been interwoven with ribbons. Her fingers began to shake in the dim light.

'Come! Sit closer to me, Bearnoch, and we shall talk for a little while. There's been scant time for us to know each other at all,' Arthur began; his new wife sighed deeply and he searched her face carefully to see if there was any sign of nerves, repugnance or fear. After all, this girl had been raised in a nunnery.

'I am, as yet, unfamiliar with the way that Anglii men and women organise their households. However, after a number of years living among the Dene, I have found that their marriages seem to fare better than those I have seen in Britannia. I believe you should rule my household and my kingdom in my absences, exactly as the Dene women do. From this moment onwards, everything I own is equally yours.'

She smiled at him, but he still found her expression was a complete mystery.

'The only people who will remain as my personal property are the Geat slave, Ingrid, and her two children. I took them as captives in a raid years ago and have developed a fondness for them. Ingrid's daughter, Sigrid, has warmed my bed and she is gravid with my child. I tell you these details for I want no secrets to exist between us. Your children will always take precedence over hers; I could never marry a slave, even one who is as well-born as Sigrid.'

'The poor thing!' Bearnoch whispered suddenly and her hands twisted in her lap with distress. 'Does she know you will return to your fortress with a new wife?'

'Yes, Bearnoch, she does. There will be no discontent in my household, at least not from her. How say you, Bearnoch?'

Arthur waited breathlessly to find out what kind of woman he had married . . .

'You'll have no trouble with me, Arthur, for I'll do my best to bring honour to Sigrid for the betterment of us both. Perhaps she will help me to learn and understand my responsibilities as the wife of a king.'

Arthur laughed self-consciously. 'I hardly think I'm a king yet, Bearnoch. As your father has probably told you, I'm the birth-son of the High King of the Britons. But your father has concluded that the days of kings may disappear into the chaos that threatens to swallow our lands.'

Bearnoch moved closer to him then and took his hand in hers.

'There is a power in your flesh that tells me you will become a king, one who will father a line of kings that will last far into the future. You are giving me immortality, Arthur. I'm a poor excuse for a woman, for I know nothing of the arts of love or the secrets of domestic organisation, but I'm loyal and I'm proud. I'll never cause you to regret your bargain with my father – or with me!'

Before she could become afraid of the ordeal to come, Arthur extinguished the oil lamp and plunged the room into darkness.

He fumbled gently with laces, buttons and ties until he finally bared her pale flesh from under the many imprisoning layers of clothing. Then, dressed only in the nest of her hair, he caressed her until she forgot what the nuns had told her of the horrors of the marriage bed.

Before the first cocks crew at the break of day, Arthur discovered that Bearnoch was a pearl beyond price.

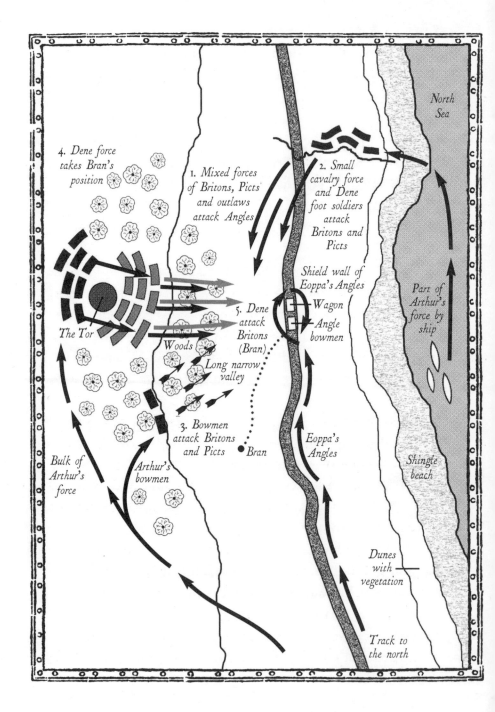

North
Sea

4. Dene force
takes Bran's
position

1. Mixed forces
of Britons, Picts
and outlaws
attack Angles

2. Small
cavalry force
and Dene
foot soldiers
attack
Britons and
Picts

Shield wall of
Eoppa's Angles

Part of
Arthur's
force by
ship

Wagon

5. Dene
attack
Britons
(Bran)

Angle
bowmen

The Tor

Woods

Long narrow
valley

3. Bowmen
attack Britons
and Picts

Bran

Eoppa's
Angles

Shingle
beach

Bulk of
Arthur's
force

Arthur's
bowmen

Dunes
with
vegetation

Track to
the north

CHAPTER XXII

BRAN'S BANE

Eternal law has arranged nothing better than this, that it
has given us one way into life, but many ways out.

Seneca (The Younger), *Epistulae*

Once Arthur was certain that his wives could live together
amicably after his marriage of convenience with Bearnoch, he
had decided to make a rapid overland journey to Arden to be
reunited with his parents. The young man knew that Bran was
restless in the south and would soon come raiding into the
distant north-east to settle old scores with Eoppa. If Arthur was
to see Elayne before she passed into the shades, the time to make
the journey was now – while relative calm reigned.

In an oilskin folder he carried a lock of soft red-gold baby's
hair. Sigrid had borne his first child, a lusty boy whom he had
named Valdar in honour of the Storm Lord, now far away beyond
the heaving seas of the north. Had he waited just a few more
weeks, Bearnoch would have been delivered of his heir, but time
pressed at Arthur's heels and he felt impelled to take to the
roads.

Bearnoch had been close to weeping because Arthur was leaving at such a late stage in her pregnancy, but Arthur took time to explain how much he longed to see his kinfolk and how he could be back in time for the birth anyway.

'I never expected to love you, Bearnoch, but more importantly, I never expected to be able to talk with you on important matters. Marriages of convenience are usually dead, chilly things. Fortunately, you understand me, so I can explain how much I need to see my family. I don't want to miss the birth of my first legitimate son and heir, but—'

Bearnoch put her hand over his mouth to still his explanations.

'I understand the duties of a lord and I know you've spent time with me as you settled me into my new life. In the process, you've neglected your blood kin. I understand how your mother must be suffering, and I can't conceive of any harm coming to the child I'm carrying, so go, my beloved. Even if you can't return in time, I'll have you for a lifetime.'

Arthur was shocked by her generosity. Sigrid had been petulant, yet he had been there for the birth of her son – barely! He counted himself fortunate in possessing a wife who was proving to be a friend and a lover too. The women were already plotting against him in matters, Bearnoch swore, that were entirely for his own good. Arthur should have been the happiest of men.

'Few men could be as fulfilled as I am in my marriage,' he had responded with complete honesty, so that Bearnoch had flushed with pleasure at the compliment. 'I even like your father.'

Yet, when Arthur rode away, Bearnoch had allowed her tears to fall unchecked as she waved her goodbyes.

Arthur was accompanied by Gareth, Germanus and Snorri. The four had discussed and planned their journey, while recalling the lessons that Germanus and Gareth had learned during their travels to the northern lands of Skania so many years earlier. They had concluded that a small group of companions would cause little comment if they rode at a reasonable pace and stayed away from the main roads and larger towns. And so Arthur's party had ridden south in easy stages with his packs full of gifts for his kinfolk and a song in his heart at the prospect of a long-awaited reconciliation.

The journey to Arden was relatively uneventful. Arthur hadn't expected so much change, for forests are eternal and the wild places had been sacred to the Britons for a thousand years.

Yet he soon discovered that many of the old fortresses were gone or fallen into dilapidation. Cataractonium, Lindum, Verterae and Ratae lay in ruins, their walls breached and the rock dragged away for use in Saxon walls or foundations. The Roman roads still existed, but only their regular use by carts, livestock and the feet of travellers prevented these ancient wonders of engineering from disappearing back into the earth. Fortunately the still-visible milestones told Arthur where he was, for the signs and landmarks of his youth had been washed away.

As he approached the margins of Arden, he felt his heart sink, for axe-men had bitten deeply into the quiet glades and groves he had once known so well. Arden had shrunk, and was shrinking further still, for men were hauling away large forest giants or burning venerable trees to make charcoal. He could have wept at the desecration.

He had almost given up hope of finding a familiar landmark when a simple well-travelled track led him into the forest's heart. What he had hoped to find at the end of his long journey was long gone; the ancient timber fortress was manned by strangers and Elayne's clean rooms were filthy with fouled straw and animals that seemed cleaner by far than their Saxon masters. Here, beds could be purchased by travellers from a new order that was stripping away Arden's beauty like a half-remembered dream.

Arthur had refused to remain for longer than one night for the beds were verminous and the stews were rancid and fatty. Of the Britons, including the Arden Knife and his family, there was no sign. Nor could the new landlords give him any word of them and spoke of Bedwyr as if he was an overrated legend from bygone days. Disgusted and heavy-hearted, Arthur decided that his small party should ride on at first light.

Bedwyr's great oak tree had been chopped down, but Arthur's favourite tree had survived. This oak had grown from a seedling that Bedwyr had transplanted, and the old man had used it to teach Arthur about paternal love. By chance, the smaller oak had been spared by the Saxon woodsmen, so Arthur paused for an hour to climb its branches and recall how his world had changed since he had left Arden a decade earlier.

Then Fortuna turned her wheel and offered him a small gift. Just outside the shrinking western margins of the forest, the party came across a British crofter and his family in a simple stone cottage and barn more Celtic than Saxon.

'We are travellers on the road, good sir. We seek word of Lord Bedwyr and Lady Elayne who were masters of Arden Forest in bygone years. I would be pleased to reward you for any inform-ation you could provide that would aid me to find my kinfolk.'

The crofter was a small man with a scarred face that hinted at battles and multiple wounds in his past. At the shabby door, Arthur could see a bulky woman with small children around her skirts.

'Mayhap I could help you, sirs. I mean no disrespect, but I recognise your friend there. He was sword-master to Lord Bedwyr's son, back when the world was peaceful and good. Unless I miss my guess, you might be the master's son.'

'Aye, good crofter, that I am,' Arthur replied, grinning in his delight. 'What is your name? I will give Lady Elayne news of you and your family, if I should be lucky enough to find her.'

The crofter flushed with pleasure. 'Aye, Lord Arthur, the good lady will remember me. She begged us to come with her and the rest of the folk from Arden, but my wife couldn't leave her old gran behind. The old besom is dead now, but I can swear that she were a tough old body. If you see your noble mother, tell her that Gwyllium of Arden still holds to the old ways. He's quiet-like now, though, for our Saxon friends rule the roost in these woods.'

Arthur nodded, for he feared his voice would betray him if he tried to speak.

'Melvyn? Fetch milk for Lord Arthur and his friends. Hurry, boy, for the sun's past noon and our lord will want to be far from here before darkness comes upon us. The outlaws will be about, sir, and them devils give no respect to anyone, warrior or king.'

A boy of no more than ten came running, while he attempted to carry a large jug of foaming milk. Another smaller boy followed, clutching four rough mugs.

Each guest drank deeply, although they guessed the children would have to do without in the name of hospitality. And so, when the visitors were offered a second cup, each man refused with such courtesy and flattery that no offence was given or taken.

'From your speech, good crofter, I must assume that the noble Bedwyr has passed into the shades,' Arthur said softly.

The crofter's face screwed up in response, for Bedwyr had

been truly loved by all the people in his community who had known him.

'Aye, I've heard he breathed his last, but it weren't afore he saw a new fortress built in the Forest of Dean. I believe them woods lack the beauty of old Arden, but they be wide and wild. It's said that it's far too difficult for any Saxons to remove their ancient trees.'

'Thank you, Master Gwyllium. Have no doubt that I will remember you to my mother when I see her. Should you and yours ever have need of me, send word to Ida, north of Hadrian's Wall, and I will endeavour to come to your aid.'

Then, as tears streamed down his plain and honest face, Gwyllium loosed the horses and his four visitors cantered away under the high sun.

The distance from Arden to the Forest of Dean was short as the crow flies, but the route through old Glevum, which still clung precariously to the Western Alliance, was thick with outlaws and wild northerners who seemed hell-bent on robbery and murder. On several occasions, Arthur's party was obliged to fight and kill small bands of robbers who were so desperate for the base coins in their pockets and the food on the traveller's packhorses that they refused to heed warnings. After several bloody encounters, the four reached the Marches of Cymru and entered the ancient Forest of Dean.

On the outskirts of the Forest of Dean, Arthur had begun to doubt the wisdom of his journey. Did he really wish to know what had become of his family?

Germanus saw his young friend's hesitation and brought his horse to a halt in front of Arthur's mount.

'You'll soon get to know the best, or the worst. At least, you'll be free of any anxiety.'

Arthur nodded. Germanus's advice was always sound.

'We can expect to meet up with sentries in the trees soon, all armed with bows. Make no sudden movement once they challenge us, for they are nervous of strangers.'

Once they entered the cool environs of these ancient woodlands, Arthur's heart felt easier. He had lived in wide, open farms and had spent many months on the equally wide seas, but his heart had been given years earlier to the dim, green lights of the forest. His horse picked its way nervously along the narrow path that was frequently breached by fallen trees, sustaining new life and rebirth from where they lay. Velvet green lichen grew lushly on trunks, rocks and decaying wood, punctuated by vivid mushrooms and branch-like strings of flowers. The horses' hooves could easily slip on these treacherous surfaces, so the experienced horsemen spent more time looking downwards than examining the road that lay ahead of them.

The four men had been travelling for hours inside the margins of the forest, following lower trails that kept them close to the sounds of rushing and bubbling waters, when a disembodied voice hailed them. The sentry warned them not to make any untoward movements, and then demanded they give an account of what they wanted.

'I am Arthur, son of Bedwyr. I was thought to be lost in the far north and stolen away.' Arthur swept away the cowl of his cloak so that his unusual curls were bared for the sentry to see. 'Germanus and Gareth you should also know. The other warrior is Snorri, a fine friend from across the grey seas. We seek news of my mother. How goes Lady Elayne?'

The silence among the trees was menacing. 'I remember Germanus,' another voice called from out of the darkness. 'And I remember Gareth Grey-Crow. You brought bad news when I saw you last. You may pass on to the next sentries, who will be warned of your approach.'

The four horsemen obediently set their horses at a slow walk while their eyes tried to piece the darkness of the trees.

They were accosted three times and Arthur gave the same greeting each time, trusting that word of his party would reach the fortress before him. At last, a curve in the track led to a sudden opening in the trees that permitted the men their first sight of the pastureland that had been hollowed out from the green heart of Dean.

Then, after passing through fields already slick with young grain heads or grazed by cows, they came to a palisade and a great set of gates. Arthur could have been in Arden again, except that Dean was surrounded by hills. Before they could ask for entry, the gate swung open and Arthur's gaze settled on the faded and wrinkled face of Elayne, the Lady of the Woods, his troubles forgotten as he threw himself from his horse to bury his face like a child in the ample softness of her breasts.

Arthur luxuriated on a warm bed after a real bath, although the hurriedly organised water was little more than tepid. His long hair had been spread out across the pillow to dry and his whole body felt as light as thistledown. He would have continued to lie there, without thought and without any particular emotions, had his mother not silently entered the room.

Elayne was very old now and she held herself with the dignity of a woman who had known legends and been loved by heroes. Arthur's fond eyes accepted the inevitable march of time. Her hair was white, with the odd streak of faded russet; her face was plump and rosy-cheeked, wrinkled only at the corners of her eyes, and in the deep lines of suffering that dragged down the corners of her mouth. Her buxom figure had thickened, yet Arthur would have known her anywhere.

She lay on his bed above the covers and made herself comfortable, so she could rest her head against his chest.

'I've longed for this day for many, many years, my darling son, but I was beginning to believe that you might have been lost in the northern snows. I often told your father that I couldn't accept your death. He had always credited me with having traces of the Sight, but it was only wishful thinking that kept me sane. I don't have the gift. I'm just a mother who would have known if her children had died. However, there was never a sense that you and Maeve had met your fates and gone into the shades.'

Her eyes filled with tears as she remembered their enforced departure from Arden and Bedwyr's strength of purpose when he led his people to a new sanctuary. Then a pleasant possibility suddenly occurred to her.

'Now! Enough of me! Tell me about Maeve. How fares my strange little daughter?'

So Arthur told his mother of Maeve's adventures with such vivid exactness that Elayne wept with happiness or, perhaps, from loss. Strangely enough, Arthur had never been able to tell what she was thinking. He took out his son's wisp of hair and described Sigrid and Bearnoch and the child that had been born to Sigrid. Her heart was elated this time, for Arthur's children weren't in the distant lands beyond the cruel sea; the promise remained that Elayne might yet see them before she died.

Elayne also asked for news of Eamonn and Blaise, so Arthur was forced to relate the dolorous tale of the Battle of Lake Wener. She grieved for the Queen of the Dumnonii Tribe of the south-west of Britain, who would never receive the long-awaited news for which she had yearned. Reports of Blaise's state of mind would be difficult for any mother to accept; that Blaise could change so much in a relatively short time filled Elayne with dread for her own daughter's safety in such a barbaric place.

'But Maeve is ecstatically happy in her marriage to one of the great men in the Dene Mark,' Arthur explained with a smile. 'Would you have believed your little Maeve would ever become a queen?'

Elayne shook her head. 'I will send word to King Bors of the Dumnonii so they can be freed from the cruelty of hope. Be assured that I will explain all that is necessary to set their souls at rest.'

She smiled wistfully and hugged her son once again.

'I have seen so much pain and glory in my life, Arthur, and methinks I have lived too long. Yet I feel no different from the girl who lay with Bedwyr on her wedding night under a bower of leaves.'

'Do you miss him, Mother? We heard on the road that my father was dead, but I wasn't surprised. I felt the lack of him in my world a long time ago, so I knew instantly that my lord had passed into the shades. He had lived so long and had suffered so much that death must have been as welcome to him as sleep.'

Arthur rested his chin on his palm and half-reclined on one elbow so he could examine the truth in his mother's amber-green eyes.

'I miss him the way I'd miss the sun if it suddenly died in the sky. But my lord was weary of living at the end of his life. Once our people were safely domiciled in Dean Forest, he took to his bed. Towards the end, it was only his desire to know your fate that kept him alive. I promised him that you'd return one day, but I only half believed my own vow. Eventually, he closed his eyes and simply drifted away in my arms.'

Two fat tears slid unchecked down her cheeks.

'I am so glad you're still alive, Arthur. Bran has tried to kill all those souls who bear the Dragon's blood, so you'll need to be extremely careful who you trust now that you've returned to your homeland. The king has become crazed in his old age and forgets the old alliances. He trusts no one, and no one understands the motivations that impel him.'

'You couldn't comprehend that man's thinking, Mother, for your heart is honest and selfless. Bran yearns for the love and approval of King Artor, something he cannot have.'

'But the High King has been dead for near to thirty years,' Elayne murmured. 'So he's chasing a mare's nest.'

'And that is Bran's torment,' Arthur replied.

Three months later, Eoppa's force moved slowly along the winding track through the pastures that hugged the land next to the beaches. 'The bastards can run, but the trap you've set will drive them towards our archers if they attempt to flee, as surely as Loki watches us today and laughs at what he has fated to happen.' Snorri was elated as he stood beside his master on the small hill above rocky cliffs that plunged down to the sea below. The sun had barely risen but the gulls were abroad already, their wicked beaks gaping wide.

Behind him, a primeval wood was filled with bright, sharp eyes. Arthur could feel the arrival of the carrion hunters of the air who sensed the blood-letting to come. He felt waves of danger vibrate out of the woods, and his inner voice warned of a large and hostile force awaiting him along the narrow road.

Ordinarily, Arthur's strategic thinking would have required him to keep his archers and cavalry to the south of Bran's army which was lying in wait near the Vellum Antonini. But he had seized on an opportunity to use his longboats to transport a small force of troops into positions to the north of the anticipated battlefield that could cut off potential escape routes if his enemies were forced to retreat.

The commander of Arthur's blocking force had been instructed to position his warriors behind a concealing ridge once the combined Pict and British force, led by Bran, had been committed to the battle. So far, Bran seemed to be unaware of Arthur's presence; he was convinced that his opponent was Eoppa, universally recognised as an elderly kinglet making one last throw at securing his boundaries. The Ordovice king was fighting blind.

'Know your enemy!' Germanus had often told the young Arthur. Now that simple soldier's adage was more important to Arthur's safety than ever.

'We'd be foolish to believe that Bran is feeble-witted with age,' Arthur began, as his jarls gathered for their briefing on the forthcoming battle.

'I don't underestimate that cunning bugger,' Germanus rumbled. 'He's in his sixties now and he's like his grandfather, the High King, so he'll always be a force to be reckoned with.'

'He should be sitting by the fireside with his grandchildren rather than going to war on the back of a horse,' Gareth added. He remembered how he'd been forced to give Bran's lands a wide berth when he had travelled to Caer Gai to seek aid from Lady Nimue and Taliesin in those early days after Arthur had been kidnapped by the Dene. Even then, Bran had sought to do harm to Arthur, although he kept his dark needs secret. Nothing much had changed in the interim, except his animosity was now open.

'Bran recalls a time when the High King ruled most of Britannia and men trembled at the possibility of attracting the

Dragon's rage. He wanted his son Ector to aspire to the throne of the west but the boy was far too soft to rule during such turbulent times. Bran's personal ambitions have grown slowly, but since the death of his mother, Licia, my elder sister, there's no one to keep him in check. Though the men in my family struggle to be wise and just, there must be an acid in our brains that drives us to achieve our desires by any available means. Truly, Bran has lived too long, and the dragon is rising within him like a poison. I believe I can predict what he will do in most situations that frustrate him.'

'And that will be?' Ragnar asked, as his seaman's eyes tried to pierce the wood and discover its secrets.

'Bran is angry because time has robbed him of his birthright. The grandson of Artor expected more from life than the kingship of a minor British tribe, no matter how large that kingdom might be. In his youth, Bran was Artor's strong right arm. But the High King took that strength for granted, while looking elsewhere for an heir. Eventually, he settled on Ector, Bran's son. That decision must have eaten into Bran's soul.'

'Is he so jealous of his own kindred?' Snorri asked, with a bewildered expression.

'Not now! But he was angry and hurt as a younger man. Unfortunately, King Artor was dead, so he couldn't explain his motives.'

The presence of his friends gave Arthur some comfort. Like Bran, he had known the flail of ambition. He had led his followers to this land; now, for the first time, he questioned his true motivations.

'Why did King Artor bypass him, anyway?' Gareth asked. 'You've never explained that.'

'Artor had experienced the deaths of his other grandsons,

Balyn and Balan, and he loved Bran too well. He told my mother of his reluctance to crush Bran under the weight of a crown. It was only when I found her in the Forest of Dean last spring that I learned this; she was with King Artor during those momentous years and had seen for herself the guilt that King Artor had felt for the deaths of Bran's brothers. He swore to her that no other grandson would die in pursuit of the British throne. So the sins of the present arise from careless small actions in the distant past. Little by little, the real and decent Bran has been devoured by his own jealousy.'

'So a High King who has been dead for some thirty years is the cause of Eoppa's struggle with the fractured tribes of the north.' Ragnar worried terrier-like at the question.

'Yes, although my father never intended that Bran should be slighted. Unfortunately, evil is often born out of good intentions.'

'How does such knowledge help us?' Snorri was ever the practical man.

'If the battle begins to swing away from our grasp, as it might, I'd only need to show myself. Such a sight would cause Bran's reason to crack, as he believes me to be lost,' Arthur answered bluntly. 'He fears and hates me more than any other man on earth.'

The silence that followed this statement indicated how helpless his captains felt.

'Right, let's get on with our planning! Where is Bran's main force, and how many men do the scouts estimate are at his disposal?'

Ragnar pointed towards a bare hill just visible above the thickest part of the wood. 'Bran's men are in bivouac at the base of that tor, and he has dispersed a number of scouts throughout the woods. Some of them are armed with bows, and they seem to have been ordered to give him plenty of warning if Eoppa decides to attack.'

Ragnar bent and roughly sketched the terrain he had scouted on a bare patch of earth.

'The scouts estimate that there are about two hundred Picts in Bran's force, plus a contingent of some two hundred highly trained warriors from the south. The local tribes of Meirchion Gul, the Dragon Slayer, have contributed near enough to three hundred and fifty men too. That's a sizeable number of warriors by any estimation,' Ragnar added. 'I think your Bran is playing a very hard game. He intends to destroy Eoppa, because he must believe that the Anglii contingent on the coast road is the total force at the old man's disposal.'

'I agree, Ragnar, so you can send word to Eoppa that he is to remain in his present position for one more day, and then march up the coast road as if they haven't a care in the world. In the interim, I'll send our cavalry north on longboats and then put them ashore to the north of the area patrolled by Bran's scouts.'

Arthur's instructions were clear: Eoppa's force would endure the brunt of Bran's initial thrust because the Anglii force was expected to be in that position. Bran would believe that Eoppa was moving blindly into an ambush with a limited number of warriors at his disposal, and would mount an immediate attack.

'Eoppa's three hundred men will be outnumbered by almost three to one,' Snorri said, as he drew a large cross on the ground to indicate the spot where Eoppa's troops were likely to trigger the ambush.

'Eoppa and I have decided that he will form a shield wall as soon as Bran's forces spring their ambush. If they perform the manoeuvre speedily, the Anglii warriors will withstand whatever force is brought against them from that point onwards, even if

Bran commits his cavalry to the battle. Bran has brought his cavalry with him, hasn't he?'

'Yes, he has,' Germanus answered with his usual calm. 'But only forty horsemen. I suppose he believes the terrain isn't suitable for cavalry manoeuvres.'

'Mnnnn! The land is relatively flat once you leave the forest. Still, we'd be fools to argue against the will of the gods, or fate, or Jesus if he's on our side. Forty cavalry is a third of what I expected Bran to throw at us, but no doubt he has some reason. I'll think on it.

'Well, gentlemen, that's our plan and it's all we can do for now. I'll take ship shortly and will join the northern troops on the longboats. Our fifty cavalry will more than match the horse soldiers used by Bran and, in any event, he won't expect barbarians such as Eoppa to be using cavalry. A hundred foot soldiers will follow us in the same ordered ranks that we used at the battle in Smaland. Once our northern forces engage with the enemy, our warriors may fight at will, but we must seal off all escape routes to the north and to the south. I will personally command the cavalry attached to this contingent, and Snorri will command those warriors who are afoot.'

He gave his commanders a reassuring grin.

'You, Ragnar, will command our battle group. I require your men, supported by the archers, to infiltrate the forest and penetrate the area behind Bran's army in their bivouac. You have the best part of a day and a night to position your men, and this time will allow Eoppa to move his contingent up the road. Then you will wait for as long as it takes for Bran to unleash his men at Eoppa. You must use your scouts to avoid detection, Ragnar, and your force must remain hidden from Bran's picket lines. Your part in this deception is critical, so Gareth and Germanus will assist you with the deployment of your men, one on each flank. The warriors know and trust them! When Bran attacks, Thorketil will move his archers forward to the edge of the forest where they can unleash their arrows.'

Ragnar grimaced. 'You've given me a task which will involve a great deal of walking if we are to position our men behind Bran's force.'

'Are you complaining?' Arthur countered. 'You have two good legs.'

Ragnar quickly apologised.

'Sorry, but I want to be certain that I understand my responsibilities. What role will my force play in the battle? It will be difficult to hide two hundred and fifty warriors who are blundering about in the woods.'

'I'm sure you can manage,' Arthur retorted silkily, certain that Ragnar would arrive at a solution.

'There is one final matter to be addressed, Ragnar! When Bran's cavalry and infantry move against Eoppa's force, I want you to select suitable men to release Bran's s spare mounts, scatter his baggage train and set fire to any stores that can be destroyed. Let's leave them with nowhere to run to.'

Arthur paused.

'After that, Ragnar, you will wait! Bran won't commit his infantry with his cavalry, but he'll use them to mop up Eoppa's last few living warriors. But, if all goes as I plan, when I attack Bran's cavalry with mine, and he sees who I am, he'll panic and commit all of his infantry. He will want to smash me. Only then should your land attack begin. We will each deal with our own separate tasks as best we can. You and your men must crush Bran.'

Ragnar looked much happier now.

'What do you want from Thorketil?' Gareth asked. 'Does he need to enter the woods?'

'Only so far! He'll need to be concealed at the edge of the forest before the battle. However, he must hold his fire till Bran's cavalry is fully exposed. His presence must be a surprise. We don't want small groups of Bran's people rampaging around the woods to threaten those warriors we are holding in reserve. I'd also prefer his archers to hold their fire during my cavalry charge. After that, my friend, Thorketil can kill every warrior who isn't showing either our red dragon symbol or Eoppa's white horse.'

All four men grinned, knowing full well that the Troll King was too experienced to fire on his own cavalry.

'So the battle is a three-pronged affair,' Arthur summarised. 'Firstly, Eoppa comes along the coastal road and draws Bran's forces out of the woods. As soon as Bran's army leaves their bivouac, Ragnar will destroy Bran's escape routes. Meanwhile, my cavalry attacks Bran's horsemen when he charges Eoppa's position. My foot soldiers will follow and they will lure Bran's full force out in the belief that he outnumbers us.

'In the centre, Thorketil's bowmen will be inserted into the battle once Bran is committed. At this point, Ragnar will join the attack to cut off Bran's retreat and complete the encirclement. Are there any questions?'

Arthur looked at his commanders. 'Then we shall meet again after the battle, if Loki is kind to us. I pray to God that we will all be alive to drink ale together.'

Dismissed at last, the captains dispersed and left Arthur to gaze out over the small cliff. His careful gaze noted that the road, really a narrow cart track, was the only sign that humans had meddled with nature. No smoke stirred the air in all four directions, and the land waited patiently to have its price paid in blood.

Arthur's thoughts seethed. The plan was complicated but Bran was too clever to attack, breast to breast.

'Dear Lord,' Arthur prayed. 'I hope I've thought of everything. But if I haven't, let it be my body that bears the blame for my errors.'

Eoppa's force moved slowly along the winding track through the green pastures that hugged the land adjacent to the pebbled beaches. A long baggage train slowed their pace considerably, for their passage was impeded by camp followers and heavy wagons. Nevertheless, the mid-morning sun shone brightly on mailed shirts and helmets and shields. Above them, a large banner snapped and curled in the wind. Bearnoch's clever fingers had made a wonderful flag for her father, showing a white horse at full gallop on a green background against a bright blue sky. Several crows took flight in the wood and filled the air with their harsh cries as the army of the white horse marched into the north.

Eoppa rode at the head of the column, wearing the helmet gifted to him by his son-in-law. In style, it was much like the Anglii versions, but a long nose-guard gave a threatening aspect to the polished ironwork decorated with bezels of brass coated in gold.

With his guard clustered about him, Eoppa felt steadier and more confident. The weariness that comes with age and a growing deafness were the only ills that time had laid upon him, but on this particular morning he could feel a heavy presentiment of his own mortality.

Yet Eoppa was content. His daughter was happy in her

marriage and was the mother of his only male descendant, a sturdy little boy. When Arthur had gone away in search of his parents and left Bearnoch alone and heavily pregnant, Eoppa had considered killing the lad. But Arthur had returned, much to Eoppa's surprise, and the boy now used the name Ida on every official occasion. If the King of the Northern Angles should die in the coming battle, he would be content with his fate.

Meanwhile, another old man waited impatiently for Eoppa's arrival; Eoppa could feel Bran's menace for he knew the British warriors waited in ambush within the forest.

The Anglii troops were deep into the pastures by noon and the air had that peculiar vibration that comes before the arrival of a summer storm; Eoppa wished passionately that something would happen so that the conflict could begin and the tensions would be released. Arthur had assured him that Bran would respond to his presence.

The Angles had seen Arthur's flag with its strange scarlet dragon, and the common soldiers were gambling even now on the subject of Bran's standard.

On the very edge of the forest, Thorketil and his archers were concealed in their hides. Several dozen archers had clambered into trees and had settled themselves into comfortable positions in the crowns. Their bows were strung and ready to fire, their iron-tipped arrows laid out within easy reach. Several more archers had been positioned in a fold in the earth adjacent to the tree line. These men would be invisible to Bran's warriors when they eventually entered the pastures, but their targets, the Britons and the Picts, would find themselves caught in crossfire when the killing began. Eoppa's force also included another small contingent of archers who were hidden inside the wagons that would remain inside the shield wall once battle was joined.

'Be prepared! I can smell Picts in the forest,' Thorketil hissed to the man next to him on the ridge. A gnarled forefinger pointed to a spot several hundred yards to the north where several low shrubs seemed to be moving without the benefit of a breeze. Suddenly, the woods were full of hundreds of stealthy men.

'Pray God they break cover! And pray God that Bran has no archers here. The Picts will charge soon enough, according to what Master Arthur instructed us to do. They hate us too much to sit and wait prudently. Our men know what's required, but send the word down the line again anyway. We don't fire until Bran's army is out of the woods and committed to attacking Eoppa's warriors.'

Arthur saw the movement in the forest from his position on a ridge that ran diagonally towards the sea. It was little more than a fold in the earth, but the terrain gave him a perch on higher ground that provided a clear view of the forest, the sloping ground and the narrow road leading into the north.

As he watched, the movement among Eoppa's contingent became more pronounced, so the watching Dene cavalry on the ridge could see that one edge of the wooded tree line had suddenly become alive with men.

A warning horn sounded from within Eoppa's force and the Anglii warriors scrambled into the shield wall position; Arthur felt a thrill of pleasure as those figures that had appeared to be camp followers were revealed to be reinforcements who rapidly joined the front line.

As they waited for Bran's forces to attack the shield wall, the reinforcements took the opportunity to release the horses which were then frightened clear of the defensive area. Then, at a command from one of the thanes, a number of defenders lifted one side of each of the wagons to roll them onto their sides to make a barricade of sorts in case Bran had access to archers.

The time for subterfuge was over now. Out of necessity, Eoppa's troops faced the expected attack by the Pict and British warriors with a side of the shield wall containing six elongated rows of defenders. The side of the square that faced the sea was less likely to face the full brunt of a charge, so the line required fewer troops.

Even so, the other sides of the fighting square seemed to possess significant depth, giving Arthur confidence in the Anglii ability to hold the line against overwhelming odds.

'Eoppa's jarls are showing that they have cool heads,' Arthur said over his shoulder. 'Here they come! Bran has unleashed his army, and the Picts are in the vanguard.'

The forest erupted as Picts began to run wildly towards Eoppa's position, screaming shrilly, the blue tattoos on their faces and bared arms giving them a fearsome corpse-like appearance.

'They scream and wave their weapons to engender fear in the hearts of their enemies,' Arthur explained to Snorri. 'Don't allow your men to be afraid of them. Picts die as easily as any other men, and I've never commanded a Dene who'd be frightened of screaming savages.'

The Picts had reached the Anglii lines by now and the defenders used their shields to brace for the shock. But the British cavalry had emerged from the forest and was moving in the same formations that Arthur remembered so well from skirmishes he had seen when he was a very young man.

'Bran still uses the same tactics he always adopted in the past. He really has become old and tired,' Arthur went on.

When the Britons finally broke cover, Arthur could see from the rag-tag mixture of tartans and dress that warriors from a number of the British tribes had been brought together under Bran's banner. Bran was personally leading the charge. He recognised the armour from Bedwyr's descriptions and he felt doubly ill. Bran had donned Artor's distinctive battledress and was sitting atop a black stallion, hoping to spark a memory of the Dragon King. Even his standard was a direct copy of the Dragon Banner. The disciplined British cavalry carried banners that spoke of old conflicts, including ragged flags that fluttered in the wind to remind the horsemen of past glories. They charged past the Pict infantry towards Eoppa's lines at full gallop so, when the two lines collided, the noise from the impact was deafening.

For one short moment, Arthur thought Eoppa's resolution would fail and the line would break, but the Angles were fighting for survival, so they swung back into position as soon as the lines of defenders had absorbed the force of the charge. Any Briton unlucky enough to break through the first line, horse or not, was immediately despatched to the shades.

Eoppa's men, though, had no idea if Arthur was close and their hearts were weakening from fear at the numbers aligned against them. Then, just when they began to imagine the shame of surrender, Thorketil brought hell down on the Britons with a rain of arrows.

Armed men are difficult to kill as individuals, but arrows seek out the softest parts of horses and can bring them down with relative ease. Thorketil concentrated his waves of arrows on the vulnerability of the beasts and the sound of screaming battle-steeds, high and shrill, came to Arthur on the breeze like the keening of frightened women.

'On my mark, Snorri!' Arthur's roar rose over the stir of his eager warriors. 'Attack! Let's kill the bastards!'

The Dene cavalry rode over the crest of the low ridge like a breaking wave of bronze, iron and scarlet. Arthur's warriors had chosen a red item to wear, in acknowledgement of the Last Dragon, the legend who was their leader.

Bran's forces were surprised to see an unexpected wave of giant mounted warriors bearing down on them from a totally unexpected quarter. Their murderous intent was obvious.

Bran mustered his own horsemen around him, convinced that an extra two hundred barbarians would have little effect, for Eoppa's fighting square was being driven steadily back and was on the verge of disintegration under the pressure exerted by the combined British and Pict foot soldiers. But the front rows of Eoppa's fighting square were unable to retreat, for the supply carts provided an unyielding bulwark at their backs. It was time now for Eoppa to unleash the remaining archers who had been waiting behind the wagons for a time when the battle had reached a critical point. The archers were ordered to fire indiscriminately towards the rear of the mad melee, even at the risk of killing or wounding some of their own men. And so, at point blank range, they relieved the Anglii warriors from impending defeat.

'For Arthur: For the Last Dragon!' Hundreds of Dene throats had begun to shout the battle cry.

At the same time, a glance to his rear let Bran see Arthur's cavalry charge approaching. He screamed obscenely in a high treble, as if his lifeblood was contained in that shrill exhalation. The British warriors around him stared at their lord and master with superstitious horror.

For Bran had seen and recognised the long-dead Arthur who was riding at the forefront of the charging cavalry. He had no need to hear the battle cry, for he remembered that hair, those shoulders and the set of the man's head. The true heir had come!

'It can't be! The bastard's dead!' Bran screamed his frustration out to the noon sun, which was awash with the beginnings of autumn cloud patterns. 'Artor is worm food! Not even Arthur can return from his grave!'

Were the names of father and son already one and the same within his age-soaked brain?

Arthur could see Bran's screaming mouth, but made no move to acknowledge the king's superstitious fears.

His cavalry charged directly at the British horsemen and he had no further time for thought or tactical considerations.

Arthur's cavalry charge hit the rear of the British lines like a thunderbolt. He had wondered if he had the strength of mind to raise his sword against his own countrymen, but when one angry man tried to gut Arthur's horse, he instantly became an avowed enemy and was unhesitatingly struck down.

Conscious of the infantry fighting in the press around him, Arthur dismounted and sent his horse running with a slap to its rump, then turned to face the press of warriors who were fighting so closely that they had difficulty lifting their arms. Unlike his father, who had always been comfortable when conducting a battle on horseback, Arthur had spent too many years balancing on heaving decks or standing toe to toe with implacable enemies in hand-to-hand combat. Once the effects of an initial charge had been absorbed, horses became a liability, easily gutted and just as likely to strike out with hooves and teeth at friends as at foes.

Once on foot, he set about the deadly business of killing. Bran was being forced to fight on two fronts now, so Arthur's eyes scanned the edges of the forest. The whole plan would be in peril if Ragnar failed to initiate his attack. Then Snorri and his warriors hit the rearguard with a savagery honed through generations of warfare. The added height and reach of the Dene warriors made their skills difficult to counter, and their ferocity terrified the British foot soldiers.

Where is he? Where is that damned rearguard? The voice pounded away in the back of Arthur's skull, leaving lances of pain in its wake. This battle was still evenly poised and, without Ragnar, the outcome was uncertain. Eoppa's men were nearly done and, as Arthur had advised, the Anglii king had been forced to bring the last of his troops guarding the flanks into the front line, where they could give new heart to exhausted men.

Bran rode through his own men with the manic energy of a younger man, although his eyes were growing increasingly wild as he sought out the tall figure of his nemesis. But, on a battlefield filled with very tall men, Arthur had concealed himself effectively so that he appeared to be just another barbarian among many. Bran could feel hope draining from his body; in his crazed state, he began to wonder if he had imagined that brief glimpse of a feared and loathed face. He shook his head with an old man's awkwardness.

'For Gilchrist!' Snorri's barbarians called at the top of their voices. 'For Gawayne!'

More cries rose up and Bran shivered as he imagined doom galloping towards him on a skeletal horse. He could almost see the ghostly rider that wore Gawayne's careless grin like a mask, but Bran's ambition still fought to sustain his aging body. Then as he gazed around the whole battlefield, the old king suddenly saw smoke rising from the margins of the forest behind him. He watched in horror as Ragnar led out the last contingent of two hundred and fifty Dene warriors.

* * *

The battle continued to rage around Arthur, while the tidal ebb and flow of death was as seductive and compelling as wicked, unholy lusts. Biting his lip, he managed to avoid the wild swing of one Otadini warrior that would have removed his head if he hadn't been totally alert.

'Flee, you young fool!' Arthur yelled across at his opponent. 'You can't win this contest because I'm the Last Dragon, King Artor's bastard son, and Fortuna is on my side. Uther Pendragon was my grandsire, and I'm not fated to be defeated by any Otadini.'

Even as he spoke so vaingloriously, Arthur regretted his words. The gaining of a throne required a strong stomach at times, so he dashed down the Otadini's sword until it embedded itself in the soft ground, still held by the shaking hands of the exhausted young warrior. The terrified youth looked dumbly at Arthur, for he supposed that Arthur would take his life. Instead, Arthur stamped on the blade and smashed it into two pieces with a well-timed blow.

'Go, boy! Leave! Run for your life! And tell your friends that you lived today because King Ida himself gave you leave to depart from the field of battle.' The sound of that strange name on his tongue made Arthur feel a little odd, but such was the bargain he had struck with Eoppa.

The young Otadini warrior took to his heels, so Arthur roared from deep inside his chest, a sound of such destructive force that several other warriors flinched backward from the pale glitter of his eyes. After that, it was almost as if the Otadini boy had initiated a general retreat, for several other warriors seized the opportunity to extricate themselves from the battle and move towards the rear. The Dene warriors howled with triumph and derision, and then redoubled their efforts. The ring that had originally been surrounded by Picts and Britons began to swell, constrict and then change shape, forcing Bran's infantry to fall back against their comrades who were tightly pressed behind them.

Once the retreat began, nothing could stop the panicking British tribes. Without a uniting leader of their own, they had no strong hand to hold them steady when the moments of testing came upon them. Bran had won the field on countless occasions in the past, but that was in the south, conflicts that were close to home. He was an outsider here, who hadn't shared the history of the north, or the suffering these people had endured at the hands of the all-conquering Saxons, Angles and Jutes. Although he shouted encouragement, only those men of the Ordovice and some of the bitter Picts were prepared to hold their ground when the pressure was applied. Like smoke, the disillusioned troops were soon swallowed by the forest.

Before the battle began, Arthur had given specific instructions to all his men, including Eoppa and the Anglii warriors, of the actions they should take if Bran's army showed any signs of disintegration.

'I've always believed that the ordinary farmer who is forced to fight will take to his heels if he sees defeat staring him in the face. Any man who flees should not be hunted down! There must be a place for people of all races in the society that we hope to create in the north; we must all become Britons if we hope to create a new and prosperous kingdom. Without putting yourself or the man beside you at risk, show a modicum of mercy towards our enemies. It's true that the man to whom we show mercy today might live to wield a sword against us tomorrow. But I believe that there is enough land for everyone. so I'm prepared to give succour to any warrior or farmer who lives within the borders that we carve out. I'm tired of fighting to avenge the old wrongs, and chasing repayments on debts that have been paid again and again in blood.'

'Your enemies will think you're weak,' Eoppa had stated with finality.

'What do we gain by killing everyone who runs? Sooner or later, the same men we defeat will be forced to trade in our towns and come to us to have their conflicts arbitrated. We can win enormous ground with all our people by being reasonable during the peace and strong when situations demand strength.'

Several of the jarls and thanes had nodded then, for they could see the advantages in what Arthur proposed. But peace had eluded Eoppa for most of his life, so he could scarcely imagine a world where men of different tribes and nations could live in peace together.

Eventually Arthur had wrung an unwilling agreement from his advisers. The wisdom of that decision would soon be tested, so Arthur prayed that he had been right in his assertions.

The Picts redoubled their efforts as the Britons began to disappear from the front ranks, for they were mad to be revenged for sins committed against them by earlier generations. In the confined space of this battleground where the Anglii defenders were pressed backwards against the barricades formed by the supply wagons, the blue-dyed warriors died in bloody droves. The earth had been churned into a grassless and bloody mud where the most nimble warriors were hard pressed to maintain their balance. Meanwhile, the piled bodies of the dead and wounded threatened to topple those few horses that were still alive, and spill their riders into the slurry.

Arthur saw the reality of the battlefield through a haze of blood. His sword had carved its way through so much human flesh that his skin and clothing felt saturated. Fine mists of that same blood had penetrated the protective coverings of his helmet, mailed shirt and greaves, while his boots squelched as he walked. Sickened by the stench and the stickiness that made his skin itch, Arthur disengaged his mind and climbed onto a section of one of the wagons where he could stand with Eoppa's bowmen and view what remained of the battlefield.

From atop his horse, Bran could see that the battle was effectively over. A quick calculation revealed that only two hundred or so of his force remained on their feet while the Dene and Angles were reaping lives with the grim heartlessness of butchers in an abattoir. The Picts alone were holding their positions to the very end, despite their losses, but Bran knew he had suffered a major defeat. His instinct for self-preservation convinced him that he must survive this conflict, so as soon as he saw a break in the press around him, he drove his injured horse into the gap and fought his way through to freedom, careless of any warriors who were trampled in his path, whether they were friend or foe.

'Bran's running!' Arthur screamed, but none of the combatants heard him above the din of battle. Impeded by his armour, Arthur tried to find an abandoned horse, cursing the fates that would leave Bran alive to be a perpetual thorn in his side until the day the old king died. Eventually, Arthur stumbled along on foot in a vain attempt to reach Bran's flagging horse before it escaped into the forest.

Bran must have angered the gods, or else Arthur was still their darling. Thorketil had seen the mounted figure cutting across the battlefield in a long diagonal that would bring him to the forest where he would be safe from Ragnar's forces. Without hesitation, he drew his powerful bow and brought down the already-wounded steed. Horse and rider fell in a tangle of limbs, so when Arthur reached the twisted figures, panting and near spent from his exertions, he found Bran trapped under the dying animal's weight.

Arthur's first task was to kill the suffering horse before its thrashing hooves caused more damage.

Then, exhausted, Arthur sank down on his haunches into the deep grass, taking care to stay beyond the reach of Bran's sword blade. When his breathing eased, he gazed directly at his kinsman and realised that Bran's internal organs had been crushed during the fall. The King of the Ordovice would never again plague Arthur's life.

'Our enmity has been such a waste, kinsman,' he said with real regret. 'You had the pleasure of knowing both my fathers, so there have been times when I would have liked to be your friend. More's the pity!'

Bran's hazel eyes suddenly snapped open.

'So I finally forced you to kneel before me . . . but it isn't the way I hoped it would be.' Bran coughed up some small gouts of thick blood which he managed to spit onto the grass, although even these insignificant movements caused him great pain. The dying man's lips were white and bleeding where he had bitten them; it was plain he had only moments to live.

'Why was it necessary for us to come to war, Bran? All we've achieved by your conflicts is to give more and more land to the invaders. You've proved to be more deadly to the British cause than Modred, the Matricide.'

Bran tried to laugh, but any sound came out as a gurgle.

'You don't know what it was like to always be overlooked . . . during my youth. You never saw him! Gods, but Artor could blot out the sun! I grew up in his shadow, but I grew smaller and weaker because of him.' Bran coughed again, but the action caused so much pain he was unable to clear his filling lungs. 'I wanted him to notice me . . . and to love me, but he never would . . . although I spent my entire youth in his service. Then, when he died, I was passed over . . . for my own son.'

'I don't know how to answer you, Bran. I never knew Artor at all, yet you've always hated me because I looked like him. He cost you far too much!'

Bran nodded his agreement, almost sane in the extremity of his dying agony.

'It hurts . . . just to look at you,' he whispered. 'He cost me . . . too much.'

'I forgive you for any sins that have been committed in order to cause me harm, Bran. You can go to the shades in peace, at least from this quarter. I will ensure that your ashes are returned to Ector with your honour intact, for you are the last but one in a great bloodline.'

'What of . . . of . . . you?' The king's eyes were dimming, even as he struggled to stay conscious.

'Me? I will no longer exist, for I will be known forever as King Ida of Bernicia, the northern land that lies beyond the Wall. History will judge me by the name of a stranger, so it could be argued that you've finally become the victor in our conflict.'

But Bran had already fallen into the coma that comes before death, so he never heard Arthur's lament. His face was a death's-head and Arthur felt a desire to weep come sweeping over him. This old man, who had caused so much death and destruction, was simply pathetic.

'Fly high, Bran. But if you don't reach the abode of heroes, then your grandfather might speak for you at the foot of heaven. Your life has already been a kind of hell, but I'll not judge you. I haven't earned the right.'

Behind him, Arthur could hear the Dene warriors killing the last of those Picts who refused to yield, but he lacked the heart to participate in the slaughter. The grass was very peaceful and to sit in the warm sun with Bran seemed to be a fitting task for a family member. Eventually, the old man's chest ceased to move. A bee came along to explore a late patch of clover and Arthur saw a small black and white butterfly flitting through another stand of gorse bushes. Nature, as always, was the winner on this particular day.

Many men would be burned after this day, and their ashes would be blown away in the sea breeze. But for Arthur, the cries of gulls would speak of the far shores that he would never see again.

He would have sat in his filthy armour beside his kinsman until the night came, but Gareth finally arrived, woke his master from his strange trance and led him back to his duties.

EPILOGUE

THE FIRST WINTERS

Arthur fulfilled his promise to Bran and had him cremated separately from the men under his command. His remains were placed in an urn worthy of the grandson of a great king and Arthur sent the urn, Bran's armour and his personal possessions back to King Ector in the safe hands of Germanus. Wisely, Ector chose not to ask who Ida was, and how he knew so much about Bran of the Ordovice.

Eoppa and Arthur returned to Segedunum, wagons groaning with plunder. The gates to the north of the fortress were forced open and Arthur knew that no one remained who could stop the inexorable influx of Angle and Dene settlers. Arthur saw the pointlessness of cowering within Segedunum when the whole north offered thousands of sites where he could build a fortress of his own, so he made regular forays into the countryside in company with the settlers who were pouring into this deserted and waiting land.

Eventually, he found a suitable site late in the cruelty of winter when, half-blinded by a snowstorm, he took shelter in a ruined cottage overlooking the sea on a high rocky headland. Protected on three sides by the terrain, it offered all he could desire. And so construction began on the fortress that would become Bamburgh Castle. Here in the north, he would build his court in stone and timber that would last down the centuries.

The fortress rose and rose as his artisans and builders strained at their task until, eventually, he came to its walls with his women, his sons and his bodyguard. Here, the Dene host could settle around him and force the earth to bear.

Yet, on some of the brightest days when the winds were fair and the gulls cried with particular urgency, Bearnoch would find him on his own battlements as he stared seawards with eyes that were wet with loss.

'Come inside, beloved,' she would beg him, seeing the dark mood had come upon him. Sometimes, he would let her distract him with talk of his children or the threshing, and sometimes he was beyond her reach – or her love.

Then she would send for Sigrid.

Sigrid understood the loss of Maeve, of Stormbringer and the simple life he had enjoyed as a Dene mercenary. She, too, heard the cry of a sea that was lonely for a lost lover, but when he spoke of the green she-dragon who was calling him to join her in the depths, Sigrid wrapped her long legs around him and trapped him anew in the pale nets of her hair.

Yet Arthur was sure that somewhere, beyond time and space, the she-dragon keened on her couch of bones, while she counted her treasures and hungered for his presence. The sea and the gulls were her voice and he remembered her predictions. He had become the King of Winter, but he was not entirely lost.

His two women kept him sane in their separate ways, as the sea sang to him from his lonely battlements and he waited until the purpose of all suffering was finally revealed to him.

He would wait for a very long time.

AUTHOR'S NOTES

The last two books of the *Twilight of the Celts* trilogy mark a major departure for me from the accepted stories that make up the Arthuriad. My chief concern over the nine books was to make sense of the chaos of this period and demonstrate how inter-locked and interrelated the various races were that would eventually call Great Britain home.

The culture of the Dene warriors was barbaric in many ways, but they were far more cultured than popular opinion believes. Hagar the Horrible has much to answer for, including a helmet with horns that the Dene never wore. Lack of land was always the chief problem for the Danish tribes, as it was for the Angles, Saxons and Jutes. Jutland and its associated islands, including Skania, which was Danish well into the modern era, consisted of so little arable land that expansion was constantly necessary to keep the growing population fed, housed and clothed. Yet only limited numbers of Danes came to Britain until the Viking era, which was several hundred years after my tale, despite the difficulties they experienced during the middle of the sixth century.

What, then, caused the Dene tribe to renounce expansion in the sixth century? The answer seemed very simple to me, as I read between the lines of the few details of this period that we actually know. Justinian's Disease would, and did, kill vast numbers of people in Europe, just as the Black Death would do in medieval times. So many people died during the passage of these contagions that pressures on land usage were significantly lessened for several generations. Men and women do not leave their homes and embark on a migration to other strange lands, such as Newfoundland and Greenland, without a good reason.

Dene interest in the British Isles was cursory until later years, but it did exist in the sixth century. The Dene and the Norwegians were superb sailors and historians have postulated that they developed practical navigational instruments that allowed them to travel over large tracts of water without losing their way. However, such devices are problematic. One detail is certain: the Dene sailors travelled beyond the sight of land, and they were travelling over vast expanses of ocean during the time frame of my story. Settlements in the far north of Britain were feasible, especially around the time when the effects of Justinian's Disease emptied large sections of the land.

Like all historical matters that occurred during these centuries of turmoil and violence, my proposition for the halt in Dene expansion could easily be incorrect, but one educated guess is as good as another.

I have tried to demonstrate the events occurring throughout Britannia and Europe that led to the demise of the British Celts and forced them to drift into the south-west of their lands. Again, some historians have spoken of the possibility that the Britons of the west suffered more from Justinian's Disease than the pagans who were domiciled along the east coast. This theory supposes that the Celts traded widely with the Mediterranean lands and other trading nations in southern Europe. The disease would, therefore, have caused greater devastation in the west than among the more insular Saxons, et al., who tended to trade only with the Franks and Saxons of western Europe.

Ida and Eoppa were real people, as are most of the noble characters that inhabit the pages. Hrolf Kraki is lauded in one of the Dene sagas where his propensity towards theft is told in depth, much as I described it. His cousin, Frodhi, also lived and ruled briefly, although details of his death are sketchy and would require validation if used in any historical tome. I enjoyed giving him a particularly gruesome death. Incidentally, I discovered that the venerable Tolkien derived the names of many of his characters (Frodhi, Frodo, etcetera) from the lists of ancient kings who were prominent in Dene history.

The status of women in Dene society was higher than in most other European countries, including Britannia. Women managed the estates and ensured they were running smoothly during those times when the men were at war or a'rovering. Therefore, they were accorded a much higher position in society than in other countries. For example, girls had their own names and a surname (e.g. Frith Eriksdottar), although it is notable that spellings of names differed according to the source material. A woman might achieve fame as the daughter of a man, but at least she had a name in her own right, a rarity in many European societies. As a point of interest, the remains of one ancient ship found buried in Norway is actually the grave of a woman.

Slavery was also a feature of Dene society, although it was not as brutal as in other parts of Europe. As the average Dene was both a farmer and a sailor/warrior, his lands always needed workers, positions that were filled by slaves taken in battles.

These men and women could be set free and absorbed into Dene society.

I have tried to include many of the interesting details that we now know about Dene society, although more and more information is slowly being learned about this tribe and its unusual customs. Any errors that have been made through the scarcity of research material are my own fault entirely and I apologise in advance for those or for any omissions. However, I hope you come to share my admiration for a very unusual people who had a huge effect on Europe and Britain during the seventh, eighth and ninth centuries.

As for my Arthur, I haven't attempted to make him anything like King Artor, his father. Arthur's childhood was quite different from that of his sire and his needs and desires were quite separate as well.

To accept a name change from Arthur to Ida would be unthinkable for my version of the High King, King Artor, but his son used the losses inflicted on King Eoppa to power his ambitions and secure the future of his followers who came to Britain from the Dene Mark. It is worthy of note that it was quite possible for a charismatic leader to acquire a large group of followers and warriors for whom he would become responsible. In their search for new lands, these followers would go to places selected by their leader, including distant countries. This can be seen in the migrations of Saxons, Jutes and Angles during the fifth and subsequent centuries. Mention is made of Scandinavian migration among the Rus in Russia and other places along the trade routes through to Constantinople.

Among other migrations, the Dene would colonise Normandy (North-man-land), Iceland, Greenland, Newfoundland, Dublin and the Scottish islands, to name a few. Even present-day York

(Jorvik) still bears the marks left by Viking migration. To forget the importance of the Norwegians and the Dene in the development of Britain is to deny one of the major influences on the development of British culture.

My Arthur is a man who does his best with what he has at hand. He lacks his birth-father's vision and his foster-father's strength of character, but he consistently does his best to be a decent man. I can imagine how he would have hated the weight of his responsibilities, but the world of the sixth century was a violent and cruel time in which to live. To survive, he was forced to make certain moral concessions which must have caused him pain.

I couldn't resist the impulse to give King Artor's bastard child a glorious future as King Ida of Bernicia, the kingdom he created by force of arms. He is reputed to have sired twelve sons and built the remarkable fortress called Bamburgh Castle. His grandson combined Bernicia and Deira to create the powerful kingdom of Northumbria which would exercise enormous power over Great Britain for hundreds of years.

So many powerful men would go on to claim Ida as an ancestor, and Ida's kingdom, which would always have a significant Scandinavian influence, would never be defeated by the native Britons. Ida would defeat them in battle, again and again, until his eventual death. As an interesting aside, the creation of Lindisfarne Island, the prominent religious centre, is credited by some sources to Ida, who is reputed to have established the island settlement.

And so Ida lives on.

I've finally finished what I initially set out to do. I wanted to put all the legends together to create a seamless pseudo-history on the Arthuriad that stretched from the birth of Myrddion Emrys (or Merlin) to the post-Arthurian period that tells us what happened to the Celts after the death of Arthur, the High King.

The ad hoc nature of the legends and the myths always irritated me because many of them were set in the wrong time periods and the antagonists such as the Angles, Saxons and Jutes never figured in the tales. I hope I've made sense of these anomalies, at the very least, even as I've had to meddle with fictional aspects of the legends at times.

It is worth mentioning that the Scots speak of their own versions of the Arthurian legends and refer to sites such as those discussed in my version of King Artor's bastard son in Bernicia. Many notable experts speak of possible confusions between the Dux Bellorum and a later prince, just like the earlier confusions that existed between Ambrosius and King Arthur in the south of Britannia. In part, my story addresses some of these conclusions.

I have tried to explain many of the inconsistencies within the legends. In doing so, I hope I've prompted you to think about an ugly time in British history which is largely ignored, yet it's one which served to shape the emerging character of the British Isles and its peoples.

With the destruction of the scrolls and those manuscripts that had been stored in churches and official buildings in the Celtic towns, there are only small fragments of the legends in existence in written form. In the end, we will never know for sure what happened during that wonderful period that existed fifteen centuries ago. The Saxons, et al., were the successful invaders who destroyed many of the histories and scrolls that rested in the churches and they replaced much of the data with their own version of the facts.

The victor always writes the histories, and that reality is a good enough reason for us to take many ancient facts with a pinch of salt. However, we do know that a Dux Bellorum lived, and this incredible man stopped the Saxon menace for some fifty years. And so the legends of King Arthur came into existence.

The High King is the best example of our need for a perfect role model so, if he was invented, he still represents a time when a Dux Bellorum lived who taught the British people how to respond to violent invasions, hopelessness and struggle. The legends of Arthur are now the Matter of Britain and such a great role model can never really die.

He has truly become the Once and Future King.

M. K. Hume

January 2015

GLOSSARY OF PLACE NAMES

Arden (Forest of Arden)	Warwickshire, England
Bramburgh	Din Guardi, Capital of ancient Northumbria, England
Brandenburg	Ancient town in Germany
Bremenium	Rochester, Northumbria, England
Caer Gai	Llanuwchllyn, Gwynedd, Wales
Calleva Atrebatum	Silchester, Hampshire, England
Calmar	Port in Smaland, Sweden
Cataractonium	Catterick, Yorkshire, England
Cimbric Peninsula	Jutland
Cymru	The Celtic name for Wales
Daneverke	Ancient earthworks/fortifications near Schleswig, Denmark
Dean (Forest of Dene)	Gloucestershire, England
Fulda	Ancient town in Germany
Gesoriacum	City in France
Gotland	Land of the Geat
Halland	Province in Sweden
Halle	Ancient town in Germany
Heorot	Hall of the Danish King
Hibernia	Ancient name for Ireland
The Holding	Stormbringer's farm on Ostoanmark
Limfjord	Fjord in Denmark
Litus Saxonicum	The Saxon Shore. Loosely defined as the English Channel

Lund	Ancient town in Sweden
Metz	Ancient town in France
Mirk Wood	Forest surrounding Lake Wener in Sweden
Molzen	Ancient town in Germany
Moridunum	Carmarthen, Wales
Noroway	Norway
Oland Island	Second largest island in Sweden
Opland	The western mountain regions of modern Norway
Ostoanmark	Modern Zealand
Reidgotaland	Part of Gotland
Reims	City in France
Rheged	Ancient kingdom in the northwest of England
Rhenus River	The Rhine River
Rugen Island	Island in Germany
Schwerin	Ancient town in Germany
Sjaelland Island	Island in Denmark
Skandia	A term used for all the nations of modern Scandinavia
Skania	Province in Sweden that was ruled by the Dene
Smaland	Province in Sweden
Sognefjord	Ancient town in Norway
Soissons	Ancient town in France
Speyer	Ancient town in Germany
Vagus River	The ancient name of river that leads to Lake Wener
Vaster Gotland	Part of Gotland
Verterae	Brough, Cumbria, England
Vinovia	Binchester, Durham, England
Wener (Lake)	Lake in Sweden

GLOSSARY OF
BRITISH TRIBAL NAMES

Atrebates
Brigante
Catuvellauni
Coritani
Cornovii
Deceangli
Demetae
Dumnonii
Dobunni
Iceni
Otadini
Ordovice
Selgovae
Silures
Trinovantes